Red Geraniums

Red Geraniums

For Virginia,
Sally Salisbury Stoddard

Sally Salisbury Stoddard

iUniverse, Inc.
Bloomington

Red Geraniums

Copyright © 2013 by Sally Salisbury Stoddard.

All rights reserved. No part of this book may be used or reproduced by any means, graphic, electronic, or mechanical, including photocopying, recording, taping or by any information storage retrieval system without the written permission of the publisher except in the case of brief quotations embodied in critical articles and reviews.

iUniverse books may be ordered through booksellers or by contacting:

iUniverse
1663 Liberty Drive
Bloomington, IN 47403
www.iuniverse.com
1-800-Authors (1-800-288-4677)

Because of the dynamic nature of the Internet, any web addresses or links contained in this book may have changed since publication and may no longer be valid. The views expressed in this work are solely those of the author and do not necessarily reflect the views of the publisher, and the publisher hereby disclaims any responsibility for them.

Any people depicted in stock imagery provided by Thinkstock are models, and such images are being used for illustrative purposes only.
Certain stock imagery © Thinkstock.

ISBN: 978-1-4759-7416-4 (sc)
ISBN: 978-1-4759-7417-1 (ebk)

Printed in the United States of America

iUniverse rev. date: 02/23/2013

I

Kate pulled the shears out of the pocket of her long apron and began clipping the overgrown grass around the simple, unadorned gravestones in the Gypsy Cemetery. She loved this tiny out-of-the-way place where she could get away from the clamor of the one-room school where she taught, and she could get away from her family's busy farm life which wasn't always pleasant for her.

Kate struggled now with the long prairie grass intermixed with foxtails in seed. She had promised herself she would trim the area, though she didn't like outdoor work as much as her mother and sisters did. She wanted it to look nice, but the tough stems defied her shears and her right hand soon bore a deep red dent around the thumb. Kneeling by the smallest of the graves, she felt as keenly about the death of this child as she would have if it were the final resting place of a child she'd never had.

It's odd, she thought, that we drive the Gypsies out of town as soon as we see their bow wagons heading our way, but when a Gypsy woman died, while they encamped near here some years ago, Mr. Gilbert readily accorded them this piece of land to bury their beloved. He even allowed them to mark off the area with a low wrought-iron fence. 'Consumption,' one of the local farmers opined, and folks shook their heads, dreading the scourge of tuberculosis.

They came back later to bury this child also and his father and later two more. Still, neighbors felt bad about the Gypsies' loss in spite of conventional wisdom of local folk that Gypsies would 'steal you blind' and even 'kidnap your children'.

Kate remembered one January day when three bow wagons pulled into her family's farmyard just at breakfast time. Kate had watched as the oldest Gypsy gent dropped down from a wagon seat and stood waiting until Pa went out to greet him. Pretty soon all of the families in the caravan hopped down and headed for the house. Pa invited them in. Ma drew in her breath, closed her eyes, and looked heavenward seeking divine intervention, but there being none, she bustled about the kitchen 'putting another bean in the pot' as the family saying went.

The Gypsies filed into the dining room, but refused to sit down. Instead they filled the plates they had brought by reaching across the shoulders of family members to dip into the platters of pancakes and homemade sausage. On a signal from the old man, they carried their plates out and disappeared into the gloom of the impending snow storm.

Obviously frightened, Ma upbraided Pa in front of the children after they left. He patted her on the shoulder and said, 'Now, Annie, no need to be upset. Nothing happened. Nothing happened. It's going to be mighty cold today and it's good we had something to give 'em to keep 'em warm.'

Indeed, nothing had happened, but Ma cried and sniffled, 'But it could have. It could have.'

Now, as she tidied up the Gypsy graves, Kate thought about how she missed Pa. He'd been gone seven years. Maybe missing him was why she'd never married, she mused. Sometimes at Sunday dinners with their frequent guests, she'd heard jokes about old maids when she went to the kitchen to fill the gravy bowl. At 30 she had resigned herself to such talk but had not given up hope of marrying. After all, her sister Lina hadn't married until she was 27.

Pa had often told her how pretty she was, but she hated her short, stubby nose, so unlike her mother's, a straight one with character. Even so, people remarked on how lovely Kate's softly feminine profile was, her upper lip slightly protruding over the lower above her daintily curved chin. She hated being short and 'ample' instead of slim like her mother and her mother's people. She took after her father's side. Her clear blue eyes, set above cheeks of palest pink, could pierce the mischief of any student and had melted the hearts of more than one young man, but none of them measured up to her Pa.

'There!' said Kate as she sighed and sat back on her heels to appreciate her handiwork. The graves now clearly stood out from the grass and weeds. The October breeze swirled golden elm leaves from the trees overhead and sprinkled them in her hair and into her lap.

She picked up a leaf and, holding it by its stem, she traced the serrations along its edge with her fingertip, but she wasn't thinking about the leaf.

She was wondering what it would be like living in town. She never had, but she knew she could not stay on the farm after her brother Angus' marriage to Lizzie Scott next spring. She was sure she and Lizzie would never get along. Lizzie was too imperious, and she herself was more than a little outspoken. It seemed like a good time to make a move—not just in her living quarters, but in her job as well.

'Hello, Miss MacLean. It's a nice day, isn't it?'

Kate was startled by the sound of a pony and rider. She shaded her eyes and looked toward the late afternoon sun to see Lizzie's nephew, George Albert, stopped on the road, his pony shivering to get moving.

'Why, yes it is, George Albert. I'm just doing a little trimming here in the cemetery. Winter will be along.'

'Well, I'll see you in school on Monday. Good day!'

Imp that he was in school, ten-year-old George Albert certainly comported himself well enough today. She suspected that he was the one who had written 'Miss MacLean loves Benny Barlowe' in large letters on the blackboard one day when she went out to fetch more cobs for the fire. Benny had, in fact, asked her out several times and she went with him, but she certainly didn't love him. Just to be sure, she'd made it clear that they could be no more than friends, in spite of the fact she'd let him kiss her. In any case, it was none of George Albert's business who she loved or didn't love.

Still, she knew that by Monday her place of solitude here in the cemetery would be known to all her schoolchildren. George Albert would say, 'I saw her down on her knees trimming the grass in the Gypsy Cemetery with her apron on!' No matter. She would not have to endure any more pranks from him or any of the other children once she left that schoolhouse behind her, come the new year.

For 10 years now, Kate had walked the quarter mile along the fence lines bordering the farm on the north or cut across the corn fields to the little schoolhouse to teach the children from the neighboring Long's Creek farms. Sometimes, if the weather looked mighty bad, she'd brave the ride on the back of the gray mare, but it wasn't easy to hitch her short, stout body onto the crusty old saddle. In any case, she never quite trusted any horse after the time her sister Augusta's pony, Rollie, had thrown her off. She wasn't hurt much, but very frightened.

Teaching ten or twelve children of various ages in one room was not easy, but neither was it hard work. Kate believed in strict discipline which did not endear her to her children, but they responded by obeying—most of the time. When she found the message on the blackboard, her face and demeanor caught fire as did the cobs she flung into the round stove that heated the center of the schoolroom. Hands impressed into her ample hips, she had turned to the class all of whom were suddenly very studious. She strode to the blackboard and erased the childish printing without saying a word.

Kate had never wanted to teach but there was little else a young woman was considered capable of doing, so she took the Normal course in the year beyond high school. 'My,' everyone said, 'weren't you fortunate to find an opening in the Long's Creek school so you can live with your family?' She, of course, agreed with them. If she had been forced to board around in the homes of her schoolchildren, as some teachers had to, she didn't know whether she could bear teaching at all. This way she didn't have to abide evenings with one or more of her school-children and their families.

Secretly, Kate had thought when she started teaching that she would marry soon and be a farmer's wife like all the women in her family. When she was seeing Benny Barlowe, the thought crossed her mind that maybe she should just settle for him, but she couldn't. She just couldn't. The last two years, though, she had begun to wonder if the coming years would find her still stoking the fire of the little schoolhouse every winter morning and banking it at night. She resigned herself to live life as it came rather than as she had dreamed it would be.

Then, one Sunday when she was visiting with Mrs. Shortt after church, she learned that Mr. Shortt, the studio photographer in town, was having trouble selling his business. After the dinner dishes were washed and put away that day, she went to her room to think about what Mrs. Shortt had said. Her mind was in a turmoil. Could she possibly become a studio photographer? The prospect of it both frightened and challenged her. What would it be like being a business woman?

The next few days she mulled the prospect over and over in her mind as she went about her daily routine at home and at school. The more she thought about it, the more she was determined to invest her eleven years of savings to buy Mr. Shortt's photography business. It seemed like a good time to make a move.

'Oh, my!' she exclaimed out loud when she realized the sun was dropping rapidly. She would have to hurry across the Gilberts' fields to help Ma fix the supper. She rose and smoothed out her rumpled lavender print dress. She sniffed the smell of fall in the wind and thought how frumpy she must have appeared to George Albert. She prided herself on the extra nice school dresses she sewed during the long evenings after the dishes were neatly stacked in the wall cupboards between the kitchen and dining room. Now the stubble in the cornfields caught on her cotton stockings, but it would take too long to go around by the road so she pressed on, thinking how she would miss this walk to her sanctuary in the Cemetery once she moved into town.

'Where have you been, Katie Jane?' her mother demanded as she opened the door to the screened-in porch.

'Why, just out for a walk,' Kate hedged. 'What do you want me to do for supper?' She hoped to distract her mother from further prying. Much as she disliked her mother's sternness, she found herself copying it more and more in handling her schoolchildren. 'Shall I put a clean table cloth on?'

'Yes, take that blue sprigged one. And put on clean newspaper mats, too.'

How Kate hated those newspaper mats. Her mother said when the children were young that those mats were sensible because they saved washing and ironing the table cloth so often, but her mother still insisted on using them even though Kate's younger brothers were fully grown. Kate grumbled to herself about the many hours spent cutting them to have fancy edges—as if they were fine linen. Kate swore she would dispense with newspaper mats when she moved into the tiny apartment behind the upstairs photography studio, and she would never make her future children use them.

Now she lifted the four corners of the table cloth to gather the crumbs and stopped midaction, her mind suddenly turning to her future. Children? What she needed to know now was how to become a photographer! The prospect was daunting. She assumed that Mr. Shortt must have always known how to take pictures and print them. He was, to her, the ultimate in professional photographers, the wizard who produced wonderfully fine pictures of their neighbors and friends with seemingly no effort at all.

'Kate! Have you got that table set yet?'

'Ma! I'm not a child,' she said scooping up the cloth to run out to the screened porch. With a one-handed swoosh, she emptied the crumbs on the ground outside the door and dropped the cloth into the laundry basket on the back porch.

* * *

As the days became shorter, Kate continued her daily teaching chores but she often let her mind wander, even in the middle of an arithmetic lesson for the second-graders. She thought about what it would be like leaving these children, but she also thought about what it would be like leaving the farm—the home where she had grown up. There had always been people around. They could sometimes be irksome, but they could also be very pleasant and fun.

She wondered what living alone in town was going to be like, where she would have no one to bother her, but also no one to share the day's happenings with. Maybe she should have tried to find some place to board, but no! She wanted to try living in her own place.

She liked to think her family would miss her—as she would miss them. They did say they didn't know what they'd do without her. Of course, they also were apprehensive about her ability to succeed. Angus chided her, 'What would Pa say if he were alive? I'm not sure he'd approve.' That didn't bother Kate because she was sure her father would approve and wouldn't hesitate to say so.

Her mother fussed that Kate didn't know how big and bad the world really was, that she was too naïve, and that she would let people take advantage of her. 'Yes, Mother, I know I'll have to be careful, but I need the chance to try.' Kate knew in her heart that she was going ahead with the venture no matter what her family said.

Her mother, always needing to have the last word, said, 'Well, you know Angus is getting married, and he and Lizzie may fill all the bedrooms so there may not be any place to come home to if it doesn't work out!' Kate smiled at the image, but knew the truth of it as well. She wondered if her mother secretly envied her this chance 'to be somebody'.

Each Saturday now, she drove to town to learn the photography business from Mr. Shortt. She felt a sense of awe each time she dipped the gelatin-silver-coated glass plates into the developer and watched the negative image forming! Transferring the image to paper was equally amazing. She wondered if she would ever be able to take it for granted.

Mr. Shortt taught her how she could add shading or soften the edges by using a cardboard. He even showed her how, with a tiny brush and a bottle of ink, she could give womenfolk long lashes and even 'correct' eyes that appeared to be two different sizes. She realized it was a real art and it would take her some time to become as proficient as Mr. Shortt. By early December, Kate was becoming quite comfortable with the technical aspects of producing saleable photographs.

Posing people for those photographs in the studio was another matter. As she watched Mr. Shortt work with wriggling children, she realized she would not be as far removed from the classroom as she had hoped. 'How did you manage to get Josiah Bauer to sit still so long?' she asked.

'Well, I just pretended I was his grandpa,' he laughed. Indeed, he had the manner of an indulgent and loving grandfather. He smiled and cajoled and promised a maple sugar candy at the end of the session. Somehow he remained infinitely patient when Benny Barlowe's little nephew ruined one take making figure-eights with his mouth by sucking in his cheeks. In any case, she knew she would have to copy many of his techniques for handling people because she wanted, more than anything else right now, to show her family that she could succeed.

One late afternoon in December, Kate sat in the seldom-used parlor at the skirted table as the wintry winds whistled around the unprotected windows of the farmhouse. She clamped her short, plump fingers on the corner of a sheaf of papers, being careful not to cover the important looking writing on the top page of the documents.

Through tiny, wire-rimmed glasses perched tentatively on her nose, she squinted at the lawyer-looking script with its *'whereas-es'* and *'therefores'* and *'aforesaids'* which she decided would be confusing to anyone with less than a law degree. Still, she was willing to struggle with these official papers because, once signed, they would dictate the direction of her life for the foreseeable future. With them, she would become a photographer instead of a teacher.

'Kate! Kate, where are you?'

Kate recognized her future sister-in-law's voice coming from beyond the closed door to the parlor. She hoped Lizzie, who was visiting for the day, would give up whatever mission she had in mind for Kate. Their relationship had been relaxed and girl-friendly until her brother Angus decided to marry her. *Maybe I'm just jealous of Lizzie's closeness to Angus,* she thought.

After her younger brothers, Lynus and Jessie, decided to sell their shares in the farm and move to Saskatchewan where Uncle Martin lived, Angus, probably at Lizzie's urging, asked if Kate would sell him her share as well so that he could have clear title to the land. She consented after deciding to leave the farm.

It was not that she wanted to farm anyway. In fact, even now she had little to do with the actual farm operations, feeding the pigs, plowing fields, and the like. Nevertheless, this farm had been the only home she'd had. She knew she was unsuited for farm work, but she felt she was equally unsuited to her life as a teacher in a one-room school. Selling her share in the farm would bring her a small income until it was paid off. These documents she was now perusing would free her from both, but they frightened her, too.

She heard Lizzie call her name again, but she didn't answer. She just smiled and went on with her task of sorting farm papers and photography studio papers, signing and dating them as needed. She slipped them into an envelope to await the final transactions.

It had not been easy to come to this stage in the negotiations. After she heard about the availability of the studio, she went to town without telling her family of her interest. She knew they would have immediately raised objections. On visiting with Mr. Shortt and arriving at the terms of the transaction, she had decided on her own that she wanted to make the change.

In fact, she left the studio that day and immediately walked across the street to the bank to talk to Mr. Thomas, the bank president, about finances. 'Well, Miss Kate,' he said, 'you've managed your money very well. I wish all our young people were as smart about money as you are. I think you'll do very well in the photography studio in spite of what some people may say about a woman doing that work. I've got to tell you, though, that it won't be easy being an attractive young woman doing business with men.'

Kate thanked him for his confidence. 'I'll do everything I can to make my family and the town of Tingle Creek proud of me,' she said as she solemnly shook his hand. She knew her mother and Angus would not have approved her making this tentative overture but she was firm in her resolve to follow through on her plan.

The day before Christmas, Kate drove the buggy into town to Mr. Shortt's studio at Third and Main Streets. She reminded herself that from that day forward she must quit calling it that. It would become the MacLean Studio. She smiled imagining how her sign would look.

When she arrived, Mr. Cameron, a friend of her family's, was there to pay for his photographs which Mr. Shortt had wrapped ready for tomorrow's festivities. 'Well, Katie Jane,' he said, adopting her father's manner of speaking to her, 'I'll be bringing the new baby for a photo when he gets to be big enough.'

Kate smiled. She liked Mrs. Cameron a lot and with the promise of their continued business, she felt buoyed at her new prospect. After Mr. Cameron left the studio, Kate sat down across the table from Mr. Shortt and signed the final papers, making the studio hers. Then Mr. Shortt stood up with a smile on his face and reached into his vest pocket. He pulled out the key to the studio and ceremoniously handed it to her. They shook hands solemnly.

'Kate, the place is yours now. I'm sure you'll do fine. Don't forget! You can't give away your work—no matter how well you know the customers. It's a business deal.' Perhaps he sensed that Kate, beneath her stern exterior was a bit soft, after all, or maybe he just thought women weren't tough enough to be business people. In any case, Kate thanked him for his kindness and his expertise.

'What will you and Mrs. Shortt do now?'

'Well, Mrs. Shortt has family in Kentucky and she's a hankering to see them so we'll be going south, but not until after the first of the year. I wish you the best of luck—ah! but you won't need that. You'll be just fine. Good-bye—and Merry Christmas!'

'Good-bye, and Merry Christmas to you and Mrs. Shortt.' Kate heard him clomp down the painted wood steps to the street. She looked around. She was all alone.

She walked slowly across the studio, edging around the elaborate, but somewhat shabby, stage furniture every photographer kept to make customers' portraits as fanciful as possible. Next week, when Angus and Lizzie's brothers moved her furniture in, she would rearrange this room to make more space. She stopped at the camera on its ungainly tripod and, tipping her head to the side, she said out loud, 'We're going to be good friends, you and I!' Then she smiled, wishing the first customer would come through the door just now. She was ready. Tomorrow would be Christmas, but Kate, buoyed by the successful transaction, just knew that Christmas had already arrived.

* * *

Christmas morning Kate was up early to help with breakfast as usual. She knew there would be no special mention made of the importance of the day, but they could at least expect pancakes with maple syrup tapped from their trees in the grove.

When she was a small child, Christmas always had a special place in the year's calendar, but not now. In those early days her father would greet her on Christmas morning at the foot of the stairs with a hearty 'Oh, ho, ho! My darling Katie Jane!' and he would sing as he gathered her up in his arms and danced to her place at the breakfast table. Dressed in her Sunday best, she would laugh gleefully. She realized now that she had looked forward to this special attention as much as to the shiny bright orange that sat proudly in the center of her plate—and the absence of the newspaper mats for just this one day a year.

Beside her plate, there had always been a package with a practical gift sewn by her mother or her big sister Lina—perhaps an apron or an embroidered handkerchief. If it had been a good year on the farm, she might find another package by her plate as well, tied with a red ribbon. One year there was a doll with a China face and hands and cloth body. She was wearing the most beautiful of lacy dresses tied at the waist with a pink ribbon. She named her Martha after a little girl she read about in a book. Once a package came all the way from her grandmother in Wisconsin. In it were handknitted mittens for each of the children. 'Ma,' Kate declared. 'How did she know my size? And how did she know my her favorite color is purple?' Her mother just smiled.

The rest of the day the big, wide doors to the parlor were thrown open and a fire lit in the hard coal stove in that room. She loved to sit in front of the isinglass panels in the latticed door to watch the flames shoot up toward the dome on top, its chrome top-knot glistening in the fire light.

After the dishes were done, the family gathered to play games. They invented most of them. Today, of course, there were no small children to laugh with delight at special surprises, but it would have made no difference because many years ago Kate's sister Ann Marie had died on Christmas Day when she was just 16.

Her death had been hard for eleven-year-old Kate to understand. When Ann Marie fell sick, Kate did her best to cheer her up. She regularly visited her sick room to tell her about the happenings on the farm. 'Guess what, Ann Marie,' she'd say, 'Pa bought some fancy chickens. They've even got pants on them. Well, you know, not really pants but fuzzy feathers on their legs.' Ann Marie had a faint smile for her little sister.

'What about Rollie?' Ann Marie whispered when she could gather the strength, her lips too dry to speak properly. Kate would find the balm and gently touch it to her lips.

'Oh, Rollie misses you a lot. You're his favorite, for sure. He doesn't like to have anyone but you ride on him. I tried to ride him once, but I guess he just wants you.' Kate usually chattered on and on, hoping something she said would make Ann Marie want to get well. Kate thought she could if she really wanted to, but none of her efforts prevented Ann Marie from slipping away in the early morning hours of Christmas Day. Kate cried for most of the day, but gradually came to accept that Ann Marie was gone, simply gone.

Her mother did not—indeed, could not—cry, and she never forgave God. 'How can anyone believe in a god who would take away a child on the day of Jesus' birth?' she said. After that day, she refused to acknowledge the existence of God and would not allow any of the traditional Christmas celebrations in her home. About that time she joined the Universalist group where she could believe what she needed to.

'Now, Annie' her father had pleaded, 'there's no use punishing the little ones because we can't have Ann Marie with us.' But Kate's mother could not, would not, see things otherwise.

Today was no different than most of the Christmases in recent years, except that Angus was spending the day with Lizzie's family, a mile west and a mile and a half south. Kate rather envied him. The neighbors all talked about what a jolly family the Scotts were with such a robust sense of humor. If that were so, Kate wondered why Lizzie was so bereft of one. In any case, with or without gifts, Christmas at the Scotts would be celebrated with much joy and laughter.

As she cleared the dinner dishes, Kate speculated about how Angus and Lizzie would celebrate Christmas next year, after their marriage. After all, they would be living in this very house. Would her mother allow them even the smallest sweet-smelling cedar tree for Christmas? She smiled to think that next year she, at least, would be able to observe Christmas as she wanted to in her own apartment.

'Don't you want to play pinochle, Kate?' her brother Lynus begged as she hung up her dish towel. 'It's lots more fun if more people play.'

Kate knew that it would be Lynus and Jessie's last Christmas at home before they moved to Saskatchewan, but she declined. 'No, thanks. I've got lots to do before I move into town tomorrow.'

'Oh, but there's plenty of time, and remember what fun we always have? You don't have that much to move. Your organ's too big to take. Anyway, you can always come out here to play the organ. Maybe I'll learn to play it. Oh, that's right—I'll be gone.' He and Jessie laughed at his joke even if Kate and her mother didn't.

She knew she could always go to the farm to play the organ, but as a practical matter she knew she probably wouldn't because it would mean hiring a buggy in town and going the five miles south of town. She would miss the organ. Playing music for herself after days in the schoolroom had made her happy.

Lynus went on. 'I'll bet you'll be mighty tired of city life before a month's up and you'll wish you were back home playing that organ. Come on now. I'll deal you a hand.'

Kate, her mind concentrated as it was on settling her new apartment, was not even tempted. 'No. No, thanks. I will be upstairs packing my clothes. I want to be well organized so I don't forget anything.'

'Well, I approve of that,' her mother said without breaking the rhythm of her knitting. She was noted for knitting beautiful lace on the smallest of needles. The lace pillow case edging she was working on was so fine that being distracted might have caused her to drop a stitch. She sat by the west window to work. Even so she had to hold the needles at arms' length to focus, disdaining the magnifying glasses her children had bought her.

'Ma's arms didn't grow long enough,' Kate's brothers had laughed, but her mother at 67 saw no humor in growing old.

Kate opened the stair door and carefully closed it so as not to compromise the warm air in the dining room. She went up seven steps and turned at the landing to glance out the window at the wintry landscape enveloping the farm. A buggy clopped into view from the north. She wished it were Angus coming back from Lizzie's folks' place, but as it came closer, she saw that it was Doc Longstreet's buggy. He must have been over at the Gilberts. Old Mr. Gilbert wasn't expected to see the new year in. She went up the last six steps.

It occurred to her that she would miss the stairs and the window at the landing when she lived in town. There, the stairs to the studio rose straight up from the street level without any pause, and they were closed in with no window to see out. Yes, she would miss this house and the family and the Good Tidings church, but what an adventure she was going to have.

There had been long discussions about what Kate would want and need and what she would have to leave behind. No one questioned her taking her dresser, but the platform rocker her grandmother had left to her was mentioned as being too much. Just a week before, the topic came up again. 'I don't care if the apartment is small—I intend to take my platform rocker,' Kate said flatly.

'Kate. Kate,' her mother countered. 'Why can't you see you don't have room for it. You are so stubborn. I don't know how you came by the mulishness. It must have been from your father's side. Certainly my side was never perverse.'

'Ma, it's my chair and my apartment, and if I want to take it, I will. You've got plenty of furniture in the parlor already. See, you could just move this table over this way a bit and it would fill in the place where the chair sits. Why do you insist on making me look mean-spirited for wanting what is mine?' Kate objected. Still, for all her intensity, she didn't want to push her mother too far.

Angus had sat listening to the rightness of both their arguments until he finally spoke.

He loved both these women who had shaped him in so many ways. Since Lizzie came into his life, he had become impatient with Kate's struggle for independence from her mother and with their mother's struggle to hold on to her.

'All right! All right! Wait a minute,' he demanded. The two women paused. Her mother had come to lean heavily on Angus after their father died. Kate and Angus had been best friends growing up, the other brothers and sisters being too old or too young. After their father's death and their purchase of this place, Kate also saw Angus in a different light as he assumed the position as head of the family and manager of the farm. Being unmarried, she had become more dependent on him as a companion and escort at community events. She also deferred to his greater competence in money matters and usually consulted him about her financial affairs.

His commanding manner had startled both women, though privately they agreed with his right to assume it. 'Look, Ma,' Angus continued calmly. 'Kate has to have something she treasures with her. She can't take her organ so she needs her chair. She's going to miss us a lot as it is.'

'Oh, she'll be home every Sunday. She can sit in it then.'

'Not if the weather's bad, she won't. Besides, Lizzie has a nice chair her mother is going to give her and she has to have a place to put it. This chair goes with Kate. Where she puts it is up to her. That's final.'

Kate opened her mouth to speak, but refrained. Her mother's tight-lipped frown indicated unhappy capitulation, but she didn't question Angus' judgment.

* * *

For a year now, The MacLean Studio sign had hung at the corner of Third and Main Streets, placed so that passersby from either direction could read it easily. Kate had invested enough to have Old English lettering done in black, edged with gold on a white background. Standing on the corner admiring it as the sign painters were screwing in the brackets on a cold day in January, she smiled with satisfaction.

Mr. Sedlow, whose meat market was below the studio, had come out wiping his hands on his apron. 'That looks mighty professional, if you ask me,' he said. Kate beamed.

'Thanks, Mr. Sedlow, I value your opinion. I guess you don't have to hang a shingle—everybody knows where your shop is!' she said.

'Well, as I said when you moved in, if there's ever anything I can do for you, you just let me know, Miss Kate. I'll do what I can to help you. Not many women in business around here. I spose there are in Omaha and places like that,' he added.

'I know that's true, but that makes me all the more determined to make a go of it,' said Kate. 'But now I must get to work! Good day!'

The first few months had been very busy, trying to organize her new life while seeing to her customers who were few at first but were now coming in increasing numbers. There was much for her to learn, of course, but she'd made a good start. She liked working with folks from the area, some she'd known all her life but some new ones, too, as they arrived for a sitting.

They came up the stairs dressed in their finest, anxious to impress succeeding generations with their gentility, their special relationships, their importance in the ongoing life of the family and the community. Each session was a ritual sitting. Kate understood the gravity of the event which she, the photographer, was orchestrating.

She greeted each person and family at the door. 'How do you do, Mr. Stone? Mrs. Stone?' she asked. 'And what are the names of these fine looking children?' she would ask. 'Do come in.'

She hardly recognized some of the folks. She had never seen most of the men in anything but very worn blue denim overalls, the uniform of their trades, but now they arrived at the studio in suits that emerged from trunks only for weddings, funerals, and photographs. They smelled of mothballs. Sometimes the buttonholes were stretched across maturing midriffs that defied the confines of the suit measured when the wearer was young. Actually, the discomfort these men felt made it easier for them to sit still because any movement in stiff collars and tight suits was uncomfortable.

The women wore silk taffeta dresses smelling of cedar chips. The tight bodices of the dresses stretched across bosoms that had nourished several children. The women fussed at their hair in the little mirror on the dressing table and adjusted the angle of their beribboned hats to flatter their plump cheeks. Kate reassured them by saying, 'Oh, my, Mrs. Stone, you look very fine just as you are.'

The children, too, were dressed in their Sunday finest. Little girls, with hair teased into long ringlets and tied with grosgrain ribbons, wore long brown cotton stockings, invariably wrinkled at the knees and ankles, beneath their ruffled and starched dresses. Little boys came in grandma-sewn sailor suits, their hair slicked down with pomade. Most of them, unaccustomed to wearing shoes in the summer, looked awkward in high-top Sunday shoes waxed and polished until they reflected the light. Their mothers, wanting to ensure that their angelic children were filmed accurately, combed and re-combed the children's hair until the last possible minute. Babies and toddlers—boys and girls alike—wore christening dresses or, as they learned to walk, dresses below their knees. Kate was amused that all this fuss was made so she could do her job to their liking.

Kate found that her customers and occasional visitors stimulated her thinking, and she was intrigued with her new world. It's true their conversations were mostly limited to the weather and whether the corn was 'going to come in good' this year, but it felt right to have the world outside brought in even for this short time because, in between sittings, it often seemed lonely in her little apartment.

When she felt she had time, she attended the Methodist Episcopal Church on Sunday mornings and sometimes the Ladies' Aid meetings midweek. She met several new people there, like Jean Burchett who was the only other single lady. Jean seemed genuinely friendly to her, but aside from seeing her at the church, she didn't see her often because Jean lived with her parents on a farm. Once Jean stopped in at the studio to visit. Kate was surprised when she answered a tentative knock on the door and there stood Jean. 'Come in, come in,' Kate urged and indicated she should come into her apartment instead of the studio. 'I'll heat up the tea water. I was just about to have some myself.'

'Oh, but I don't want to interrupt your work,' Jean apologized. 'I mean, I was just passing by and—well, I've been curious to talk to you about your job, so I just told myself to go ahead, but I know that's very impolite without asking you first, and if I'm bothering you why just say so and I'll be on my way.'

Kate said, 'Of course it's no bother. I need to leave my work once in awhile to collect my wits about me again. There's so much to learn on this job. Would you like some oatmeal cookies? I made them yesterday.' In fact, it had felt good to Kate to take on this very ordinary housewifely task as a diversion. Jean readily accepted and they drank their tea and shared family backgrounds and town gossip—though the latter was mostly Jean's contribution.

When Jean got up to leave, she promised not to drop in very often, and Kate believed her, reassuring her it was all right unless she had a sitting or a rush order to finish. Jean brushed the crumbs from her skirt and smiled tentatively and then rushed out the door almost forgetting to say 'goodbye.'

Kate went to the studio and watched Jean getting into her buggy. In fact, from her studio, Kate could look out the window almost any time of day and see people passing by on the board walk below. She speculated as to where they were going, and sometimes she guessed right—at least according to Jean Burchett's accounts of the activities in the community.

While she missed being out in the country, from here she could at least see the tops of trees beyond the buildings across the street and in the town square just to the west. Sometimes she took a short walk to the town square, where the trees were tall and the flower beds beautifully groomed. It seemed to satisfy her longing for the countryside. All in all, she was happy that she had made the move to town.

Red Geraniums

After one of Jean's visits, while she mixed chemicals to process a set of negative plates, Kate became absorbed in thinking about this enterprise she'd undertaken. She began to think of herself as a recorder of history. After all, once the print dried and was mounted, someone many generations later might hold that photo and say, 'That was my mother's wedding picture,' or 'Wasn't my grandfather a handsome man! I do think my brother Walter takes after him!' or 'My those brass buttons make him look important!'

If she gave little David a book to hold, people forever after might think of him as a bookish lad. If she suggested Mr. Thorson stand behind his sitting wife, Kate knew he would always be judged as being the taller of the two, whether he was or not. If she suggested using the red velvet arm chair instead of the wicker chair, viewers might think the subject was more sophisticated.

These were serious decisions to her. She could not explain them to her clients. They would have thought her pretentious. Of course, she had to satisfy her customers, but beyond that she could make choices that satisfied her own sense of propriety and her sense of the artistic. Whatever she chose to include must capture the photographic imagination, the magical qualities that belonged to photography.

Kate sometimes compared her work to portrait paintings which preceded photography as a recorder of history. She knew, though, that a painting might or might not represent a person very well. It would depend on the skill of the artist, but she also knew that while photographic portraits were, in a sense, exact copies of a subject, they too could be distorted by the photographer's manipulations and by the quality of the materials used. She realized that she, like the portraitist, was in a sense 'inventing the truth'—but apparently her clients liked what she did because they came back and sent their friends.

She wanted to discuss all these notions with someone who would understand, but there was no one in Tingle Creek to share her thoughts with. Once when she visited Mr. Thomlinson in his studio in Almora, she tried to talk to him about such things, but he merely looked puzzled and politely changed the subject. Kate wondered if anyone saw photography in the same way she did. Did anyone else think about how the picture would look on a parlor wall or on top of the piano? Ah, well. She'd just have to get on with her work in her own way, using her own sensibility as a guide.

The very nature of her work, being so esoteric in most people's minds, kept her cut off from friends and neighbors in some ways. Before moving, Kate had always enjoyed going into town on Saturday nights when the farmers brought their families to Tingle Creek. It was a time to shop and socialize on the street corners and to hear the high school band play in the town square in the summer.

Kate couldn't do that now. She needed to keep the studio open on Saturday night for farmers' convenience. She tried to explain that to Lizzie one time when she complained that she never got to visit with Kate anymore. 'Well, Lizzie,' she'd said, 'I know business hasn't been very brisk those nights, but it's enough to keep me in the studio. I do hope you'll come by though when you come to town.' Lizzie said she'd see if she had time.

Then there was the problem of being older and a single woman. For church events and school programs, a single woman was an anathema. When she was living on the farm, she could join in family social occasions at home or go out with the family to visit neighbors or attend programs and be perfectly acceptable and accepted. Now, she didn't feel right about going alone.

When she was living with the family, there were lively conversations at home in the evenings at the supper table and before bedtime. With a twinge of sadness, she had to admit she missed her father. He would have reassured her about her decisions and about the possibility of marrying and starting her own family. It would not have changed the fact that she didn't have a special beau—a man who loved her as much as her father had. Sometimes at the end of a day in the studio, Kate lamented, 'Pa, where are you now when I need you so much?'

Besides missing her father, though, she allowed that she missed her mother, too. Her mother read a lot and liked to talk to Kate and Angus about things like the entries in *The American Encyclopedia, the Biography of Eminent Men of Europe and America, and the Lives of Distinguished Travelers*, by Thomas H. Prescott, A. M., which Uncle Rufus had sent. It was a beautiful book, illustrated with over 100 engravings in an elegant binding. There was so much to learn from this book, and now Kate wished she had the book and could talk to her mother about it. Kate even mentioned to her mother that she would eventually like to have the book. Her mother had allowed that that might be possible.

Red Geraniums

* * *

One Saturday night Angus came into town as usual. His family had expanded with the addition of John, named after his grandfather, and a year later, Robin, who was called Robbie. Kate loved to see the boys. She could hear Angus talking to the boys as they came up the stairs to the studio. Without knocking, they burst in the door, three-year-old John came rushing to hug 'Aunt Katie'. Kate loved these two bright-eyed little boys and she was always glad to spend time with them. Without Lizzie, the conversation was different, more relaxed.

'Kate, you haven't been to the farm since—well, I think it's since Robbie's birthday. That's three months ago! Why don't you just come home with us tonight and stay til tomorrow? It would be fun for all of us.' Kate wasn't so sure Lizzie would think it was fun, but she agreed to come in the morning. It seemed like the right thing to do.

Promptly the next morning, Kate went to the livery stable. By skipping church in town, she could arrive at the farm early enough to put pies in the oven before the family left for the Good Tidings Church. It was her father's family's church although her mother never went any more and chided the rest of the family about the foolishness of worshipping the Trinity. 'If you must worship, one god is all you need in this life,' she admonished them, 'but find one who won't punish you by taking away one of your children.' Kate thought about this as she walked east on Main Street.

Harold Jones, the owner of the livery stable, smiled brightly as Kate walked in, but she was all business. 'I'd like the small buggy, Harold.' Harold tipped his sweat-rimmed hat and asked her if he could take her for a ride on that crisp November day. She looked at him, as she always did, as if he were a child, though he was only five years younger than she. 'No thank you,' she replied crisply.

'All right, Miss Katie Jane.' He went to hitch up Billie Jean, the gray mare, to the highly polished but shabby buggy with its slightly threadbare seats. 'You don't need to pay me this time. It's my little gift to you.'

'How absurd! Of course, I'll pay you, just as I always do.'

'Well, be careful. Billie Jean's a little skittish just now. Here, let me help you in.' Kate frowned but took his hand and hoisted her plump little body onto the seat. Harold Jones hardly had time to step back before Kate slapped the reins across Billie Jean's rump and the buggy wheeled out of the barn and onto Main Street, leaving the smell of hay and horses behind.

She looked back briefly to see Harold with one hand clasped onto his hat and the other raised as if to add a note of caution or, maybe, just to wave goodbye. 'Hmmph,' she thought, 'that young man will be a good catch for some young woman—him owning his own business and all—but not me.' With that she settled down to enjoy the challenge of the rutted road as it went west and then south toward the home place. The smell of the countryside was different, and she smiled thinking it smelled like 'home'. Immediately she realized it was no longer her home.

Angus met her at the boardwalk leading to the north door of the house, the one which everyone always used even though it wasn't the 'front' door. He helped her down. 'I do believe, Katie, that you're losing weight. Are you eating enough there all by yourself?'

'Of course, I am,' she said and, smoothing her long coat, she walked up the walk. It was good to have these boards that Angus carefully nailed to stringers so that water would drain through and keep the way to the house passable in every kind of weather.

She remembered the first time she went to the farm after Angus and Lizzie were married. She had wondered if she should knock, but it had been her home for so many years, it didn't feel right, so she just called out, 'Good morning,' as she opened the door to the screened back porch and then the kitchen door. It felt good to be home again. The house smelled right with just the right blend of freshly baked bread and roasting meat.

Kate could hear her mother and Lizzie talking in the dining room as she shed her coat and hung it on one of the wooden pegs by the porch door, taking her farm apron off its peg at the same time. Her mother came into the kitchen with a half-smile on her face. 'Oh, so you've come.' Lizzie appeared behind her, wiping her hands on her apron. Even with an apron generously gathered at the waist, the swelling of Lizzie's belly was apparent.

'Yes, I thought I could help with the pies before church.'

'All right. I've got the crust made. You can roll it out. Now remember to even it out to the edges. You were never very good at that.' Kate wanted to say that never seemed to deter buyers of her pies at church bazaars, but she held her tongue. She was resigned to the fact that her mother never allowed for the possibility that she had changed in any way.

She took the heavy, maple rolling pin in her right hand as she deftly floured the marble slab on the wooden counter top with the other. She was determined not to spoil her enjoyment of the day at home. The dough was softer than she herself made so she sprinkled some flour over it and the rolling pin to keep them from sticking. 'You don't need that much flour,' Lizzie observed. Kate glanced up briefly but kept on rolling. The dough caught on the rolling pin and pulled at other parts of the crust as she worked.

'Well, maybe you should do the pie crust,' Kate said. She wanted to like Lizzie, but she felt her face flush with irritation.

'Oh, no, no. You're doing just fine.'

Unconsciously, Kate found herself checking the depth of the crust from the edge to the center to see if her mother would be pleased with her results, assuming she would not, no matter what. She lightly rolled the edge of the upper right quadrant a little more and then stooped to find a pie tin in the lower cupboard. 'It's already on the counter. Here—' said Lizzie.

'Oh, thank you,' Kate said flatly. She wondered why Lizzie always seemed to have time to oversee her work instead of seeing to the table-setting or stirring the gravy. Frowning, Kate lightly dusted half the crust with flour, gently folded it over, and lifted it into the pan, carefully centering it while pushing out the air bubbles underneath.

When a crack appeared on the edge. She moistened her fingertips and gently sealed it over. 'If you use that much flour, it's bound to happen,' Lizzie said over her shoulder as she turned the roast in its cast iron Dutch oven. Kate said nothing but went on smoothing the crust until it exactly fit the bottom of the pan. She took a table knife and gently trimmed the edges, eyeing her work with satisfaction.

'Are the apples ready?'

Her mother, who had been peeling and coring and cutting them up, said, 'No, of course not. I need some help.'

Lizzie quickly put the lid on the roaster and stepped across the kitchen. 'I'll help you, Mother,' she said before Kate could pick up a paring knife. Kate had sensed before that Lizzie and her mother had worked out an odd sort of symbiotic relationship, with Lizzie buttering her up when it suited her and her mother using Lizzie's compliance as a further indictment of her youngest daughter's inadequacies.

Kate turned to the task of rolling the top crust. She unobtrusively shoved the marble slab farther away from the line of sight of the other two women and turned her body ever so slightly so as to obstruct their view of her work. Assured of some privacy, she rolled the dough even more carefully than before. She eyed its depth and rolled it to perfection all the way around. Then she dusted one half with flour and folded it into a semicircle. Again she dusted half of the semicircle and folded it into a quarter circle.

Cocking her head one way, then the other, Kate took a knife and carved a leaf design in the dough that went through all four layers. She added triangular slits along the folded edges. Lost in perfecting her design, she was startled to hear her mother and Lizzie laughing. She frowned. It was a rare occasion when her mother laughed out loud and she wished she could have shared it. 'What's so funny?'

'Why, look at this apple!' Lizzie held up a deeply dented, wizened little fruit that looked like a hundred-year-old man. Kate smiled. Maybe the day would go well after all, she thought.

'I'm ready for the apples!'

'All right, here they go.' Lizzie dumped them into the crust.

'Don't you think that's too many?' Kate asked.

'Of course not,' Lizzie snapped. 'They'll be just fine.' Kate started to remove a handful of the apple pieces. 'I said they'll be just fine,' Lizzie repeated.

Had her mother been of a different temperament, she might have stepped in to work out a compromise, but instead, her mother snapped, 'Kate, do what your sister says.'

Kate's face turned red, the crimson brought on by August winds. 'Sister! Sister?' Kate was incredulous. 'Mother! She's not my sister!' With that, she untied and flung her apron across the three-legged kitchen stool as she stomped across the room. She grabbed her coat and hat and pulled open the door to the porch as if a strong north wind had blown it out of her control and ran down the boardwalk.

Angus met her at the foot of the walk. 'What—?'

'Ask them in there,' she flung back at him and ran to the buggy which he had kept hitched up ready to go to church. She stepped up into the buggy as if she were six feet tall instead of five and slapped the reins, clucking to Billie Jean. Angus, amazed, watched his sister tear out of the driveway.

On the way back to town, Kate's breathing returned to normal as her face cooled in the chill wind. The gentle slap, slap of Billie Jean's hooves was calming. Perhaps she'd been too hasty. But no! She didn't feel part of the family anymore. Whatever tenuous relationship she had with her mother seemed to have been transferred to Lizzie. Was she, perhaps, a bit jealous of Lizzie? Abruptly she turned Billie Jean toward the Gypsy Cemetery. She needed time to think.

* * *

Over the months after the pie incident, Kate managed to mend fences with her mother and Lizzie with Angus' help. Being with the family for an occasional Sunday dinner was too important to stay angry. Besides, she thought it was important for her to get to know the boys and and them to learn to love their Aunt Katie.

In town, life went on apace. One day Kate stopped at the Post Office across from Halley's Department Store to mail an order for supplies. Chancy McDonnell was ahead of her in line at the window. 'Say, Ray,' he said to Raymond Spencer, the Post Master, 'didja hear the latest? Mr. Thomas down at the bank's puttin' in a tellyphone.'

'That right? Well, Bill Sedlow over't the meat market's puttin' one in, too!' Mr. Spencer shook his head. 'Gosh, what won't they think of next!'

'I even talked on it,' Chancy McDonnell bragged, 'and I heard Jean Burchett's voice clear's a bell. Ya know they put the telephone office up above the bank and hired her for the job of Operator. She lives there, too—across the hall from the Halleys. Anyway, Jean answers real nice, "Number, please," and then you have to tell her. Course, I didn't know no numbers to call.'

'Well, I don't know if the guv'mnt'll ever get around to putting one in here. Here's your stamps, Chancy. Stop in again sometime when you ain't got nothing to do.' Mr. Spencer laughed, and Chancy McDonnell slapped his hand on the counter and roared as he paid his money and left the window.

Kate wasn't surprised about the bank wanting a telephone, but it surprised her that Bill Sedlow at the meat market would think it was worth the money. Nevertheless, for the next several Saturday nights when farm families came to town to shop and gossip, folks would flock to the meat market to take a closer look at this marvel.

Each man—it seemed to be only the men—stepped forward to try out the new contraption, with Bill Sedlow prompting them, in between filling pork chop orders. They cranked the handle and held the receiver to their ear with tentative hands. 'Sort of like an ear trumpet,' remarked Solomon Wingert.

A smile worthy of a true miracle spread across each sunburnt face as they listened. Bill Sedlow said, 'Didja hear Jean Burchett, the operator?'

The caller turned to Bill. 'Yah,' he said, 'but she asked me what number I wanted and I don't know no numbers.' Everyone laughed. Often the caller would speak into the mouthpiece then and apologize for bothering Jean Burchett. Jethro Beggott, though, was half-drunk, and wheezed loudly into the mouthpiece. 'I just wanted to hear your sweet voice again, Miss Jean!' Spying Kate standing a few feet behind him, he said loudly, 'Here, Miss Kate, why don't you try it?' Kate, embarrassed by the attention, hastily left the shop.

Twice Kate had received a letter and a visit from a representative of the Independent Telephone Company extolling the wonders of the instrument and touting the increased business it would create for her. A Mr. Williams from Fremont showed her some pictures and read her a description of the phone he thought she ought to have. 'Why, Miss MacLean, your business will pick up to where you may even have to hire a helper if you put in this Bell telephone. I'd practically guarantee it—but of course, the company won't let me.'

She scoffed at the idea. Even though she had been surprised and pleased that her business sense was more astute than she anticipated, she found it was easy to say, 'No.' Having the courage of her convictions was one thing she learned well from her mother. 'I'll wait until they get the kinks out of it,' she told the salesman as she showed him to the door.

One evening on her day off, Jean Burchett came to call. She tried to talk Kate into installing a telephone. (Jean Burchett always called it properly 'a telephone', not just 'a phone'.) Kate's resolve remained strong. 'I don't need a phone. Who would I call? My customers are mostly farmers—like your folks. They're still struggling from the Depression of '93—well I don't mean your folks are—but you know there's no money to spend on frivolities.' Jean shrugged.

As Kate saw it, her modest income didn't allow it, but she didn't want to discuss her finances with Jean, who, in the short time she'd been on the job as operator, had become the town gossip, what with all she overheard.

Red Geraniums

'Besides,' Kate said, 'if I need to call someone, Bill Sedlow says I can use the meat market phone anytime, but I don't expect I'll need to.'

'Oh, I know,' Jean conceded. 'Stu Jackson down at Jackson's Tap said most folks aren't going to get one—and I wouldn't either if I had to pay for it. But Stu says these young fellows in high school think their lives won't be complete without one. He ought to know. His own son is one of them. Stu said he asked some of them who they'd call and they didn't know, but they were sure that someday they'd really need to call someone.' Jean went on, 'Young people today are getting lazy, don't you think so? Even so, Stu says the Lincoln Journal is predicting there'll be a phone in every home before long. Well, it's good for my business anyway!' Jean paused. 'I'd best be going. I have to be on duty early tomorrow. Thanks for the tea and cookies. I've got to get that recipe someday.' Kate saw her to the door.

On Wednesday following her visit with Jean, Angus stopped by the studio as he often did when he brought cream and eggs to town. 'Well, Kate, you won't have to wait on someone coming into town to get our news from now on!' He grinned broadly and his ever-present dimples deepened more than Kate had remembered. She studied his face a minute, not thinking about what he had said.

'You know, you look more and more like father,' she exclaimed.

'I suppose that's not too surprising. Aren't you curious about what I just said?'

'Oh, yes. Yes, I am. I assume that means you've put in a phone.' Kate was surprised that her mother would allow a phone, but she figured that Lizzie and her sister Mary had talked Angus into subscribing because Jean Burchett said Mary and her husband Joe had one now.

'Not yet. Tomorrow.'

'You must be feeling really flush after you sold that last batch of hogs! Where are you going to put it?' She suspected that Angus and Lizzie couldn't afford a phone any better than she could, but it would be nice to be able to call them in an emergency (if it happened during Mr. Sedlow's store hours so she could use his phone).

'Oh, we already have the box in the house. I guess you haven't been out for awhile. It's on the dining room wall right beside the kitchen door. We've just been waiting for the wires to be strung this far south. Why don't you come out and try it? You could call Jean Burchett. Why not come in time for dinner tomorrow? You don't need to bring anything.'

Kate said, 'All right. I will. Thanks.' She usually didn't have time midday, but it just so happened that she had nothing scheduled.

As Kate drove Billie Jean south toward the farm, she couldn't help noticing the periodic telephone poles along the highway. Some time ago, the newspaper said they had been hoisted into place with the help of a team of draft horses, soon after phones had been installed in town. The paper said it would take another five months before the wires were strung—and here they were now.

Angus came to meet Kate as soon as she drove in. He helped her down from the buggy and they stood by the lilac bushes watching the telephone company workers. She felt a certain excitement as the workmen unreeled the wires from the pole by the road to the insulated peg on the side of the house above the screened-in porch.

Kate and Angus went inside with the lineman. 'Pardon me, ma'am,' the workman said to Lizzie, who was standing by the phone. She moved away as he opened the box and threaded a few wires and anchored them tightly. In a few minutes, he closed the case and cranked the handle on the phone. 'Jean, this is Jim out at Angus' place. Just wanted to make sure the line's working.' He hung up and stood by the phone apparently waiting for something. There came a *brrring brrring ding* in the room, two longs and a short. 'That'll be your ring,' he said. Lizzie stood by with Robbie in her arms. Her plump cheeks reddened as they always did with excitement.

'May I try it?'

'Of course. Do you know how?'

'Oh, yes! My sister has a phone, you know.' She handed Robbie to Kate, cranked the handle and waited. They could faintly hear Jean Burchett's voice as Lizzie held the receiver away from her ear, 'Number, please?'

Lizzie seemed impatient. 'I want Mary, of course. I don't know her number. Don't you know her number?'

Lizzie repeated, 'She says the number's 5-3.' Kate couldn't help marveling that Jean could plug Lizzie into Mary's line so quickly, but there were so few telephone numbers Jean must have memorized each one as quickly as it was added to the system.

'Hello? Hello, Mary?' Lizzie smiled. They chatted for at least three minutes. 'I declare!' said Lizzie. 'It's amazing—just like we were talking in the same house.' Kate noted though that they apparently had to talk much louder than they would have if they'd been in the same house.

'Don't you want to try it? Or better yet, why don't you get a phone and then we can talk,' Lizzie offered.

Kate's mother broke in abruptly. 'It's time we sat down to dinner. Come. Come. You can talk on the phone later.' Kate left soon after they ate, thanking Lizzie for the dinner and saying she had to get back to work. Her mother and Lizzie nodded.

Angus followed her. 'Kate? Come again. We don't see enough of you,' he said as she opened the screen door for her.

'Thanks, Angus,' she said as he helped her into the buggy. 'I'll be around again sometime soon.'

* * *

Several months later, on a Thursday afternoon just as Kate was smoothing Mrs. Thomas' hair for her portrait in the red velvet chair, there was a knock at the door. Kate excused herself to Mrs. Thomas. When she opened the door, Bill Sedlow stood on the landing wiping his hands on his blood-stained apron. She was surprised because he seldom came upstairs. She smiled. 'Hello, Mr. Sedlow.'

'There's a phone call for you, Miss Kate.'

'For me? Why . . . I . . . Will you excuse me, Mrs. Thomas? I'm so sorry. Do you mind? Do make yourself comfortable. Perhaps you'd like to read one of my photographic magazines.'

'No, no. I don't mind.' Being a banker's wife, Mrs. Thomas would know the importance of a phone call. It was not to be taken lightly.

Kate followed Bill Sedlow down the outside staircase. The welcome warmth of the March day rose from the street below as they neared the bottom of the stairs. Kate took a deep breath of the fresh air smelling of damp earth. 'I do believe it's going to be spring soon, Mr. Sedlow.' Her easy manner belied her worry about using the phone. It would be her first phone call.

'I hope so. Winter's been a bad one. Yup.' He opened the tall front door with its engraved glass panel and indicated she should enter first.

They skirted around the counter to the wall behind the large butcher block table. Bill Sedlow pointed to the cone-shaped earpiece attached to a cloth-covered cord from the oaken box on the wall as if he thought Kate had never seen anyone use a telephone before. 'You talk in there,' he said, and then added, 'Oh! I guess I ought to angle that mouthpiece down a bit for you.' She took the receiver in her left hand as she had watched others do and held it to her ear, looking up into the mouthpiece as if she might see the speaker. She said nothing.

'You need to say Hello,' Mr. Sedlow whispered.

She glanced at him and then, in a soft and hesitant voice, said, 'Hello. This is Kate MacLean.' She thought she heard Lizzie's voice coming from far, far away. Kate fairly shouted into the mouthpiece. 'You'll have to speak up, Lizzie. I can't hear you.' This time Lizzie's voice crackled in the ear piece. Kate turned to Bill Sedlow, handing him the receiver. 'This thing isn't working.' The look on her face was relieved and triumphant.

'Here. Let me try.' His deep bass voice, which filled the choir loft of the Methodist Episcopal Church on Sunday mornings, now filled the high-ceilinged shop as he spoke. 'We can't hear you. You'll have to talk louder,' he roared and handed the receiver back to Kate.

'Hello, this is Kate.' The line crackled and then she heard Angus' voice come through distinctly.

'Katie?' Angus hadn't called her that for a good number of years now.

'Yes?'

'Katie . . . ?'

Kate was becoming impatient. 'Yes. Speak up, Angus!'

'Katie . . . Kate, our mother died this morning.'

Kate backed away from the phone as if she had been struck with a buggy whip. She reached for the meat counter to steady herself. The receiver slipped from her hand and swung on its cord striking the wall and bouncing forward and then back to strike the wall again before quieting with a shiver the length of its cord.

'Kate!' Mr. Sedlow's concern apparently overcame his propriety in calling her by her given name. 'Miss Katie, I mean. Are you all right?' He reached for the stool where he sat to grind the sausage he was so well-known for. It was almost too high for her to sit on, short as she was, but she leaned against it oblivious to the possibility that it might have been smeared with meat fat over time.

Bill Sedlow looked worried. 'Ma'am? Can I do anything for you?' She stared at the crudely lettered Sedlow Meat Market sign across the big front window, but she could not have said whether the lettering was backward or forward; it simply gave her a safe haven for her thoughts at that moment.

Mr. Sedlow picked up the dangling receiver and spoke into the phone. 'Hello? Hello?'

Loud enough for Kate to hear, Jean Burchett's voice came on, saying, 'I'm sorry, Mr. Sedlow, your party hung up.'

He replaced the receiver and took off his apron, keeping an eye on Kate all the while. Gently he touched her on the shoulder. 'Miss Kate? Miss Kate, can I help you back upstairs? I hope it isn't bad news. I'm afraid I'm not very good with things like that.'

Kate's eyes searched the scrubbed pine boards of the floor in front of her. Then she looked up at him, the tears on her cheeks glistening faintly in the light from the north windows. She sniffed and swallowed and reached into her pocket for her embroidered handkerchief, one of the many her mother had made and given her over the years. She studied its crocheted edging and the nosegay of violets, and then the tears poured out in earnest. She wiped her eyes and her nose. She was glad Mr. Sedlow was there, but he would never understand the mixture of feelings that filled her soul at that moment. Nor, in fact, could she. 'Thank you. It won't be necessary.' Kate knew she should have told him about her mother—Jean would spread the word all over town in a short time anyway—but she couldn't talk about it just then. She stood up to leave.

'I'll come with you—to make sure you're all right.' They stepped out from behind the counter just as the door opened and Mrs. Glaser entered, holding her shopping list in her gloved hand. Bill Sedlow turned to her. 'I'm sorry, ma'am. I'll just be gone a minute.'

Upstairs Mr. Sedlow excused himself and Kate turned to Mrs. Thomas. She said nothing about the phone call to Mrs. Thomas, but her usual bright disposition had given way to an unusual solemnity. Mrs. Thomas cocked her head on one side but did not ask. She spoke quietly and carefully in the manner that befitted a banker's wife. 'Miss MacLean, I hope it isn't bad news.' Kate murmured a vague reply as she stepped behind the camera, draping the black cloth over her head and the camera. She was glad for the cloth to mask the rising tide of her inexplicable reaction of loneliness and despair. It took her a rather long time to adjust the camera lens, but she was surprised how good it felt to have something to do.

'Would you look straight at me now, please?' she said flatly. Then lightening a bit she added, 'Let's see. If you would tip your head down a bit so I can see your eyes more clearly—That's it. Yes. Thank you.' She was skilled enough now that the process was almost automatic. 'Now please hold very still.' The shutter release clicked faintly. 'Thank you. That's all I need. The proofs will be ready for you a week from today—if you could drop in about 4 o'clock?'

'Of course. Miss MacLean, you are so clever with the camera. Your pictures are very lifelike, very special. That's why I came to you instead of going to Mr. Thomlinson in Almora like some folks do. I'll be anxious to see the proofs. It's just like my children waiting for Christmas! In fact, I want to give some pictures to my children so they won't forget what their mother looks like after I'm gone.' It occurred to Kate that she was glad she had taken that last picture of her mother wearing the black silk taffeta dress with the pleated ruching at the neck and wrists.

Mrs. Thomas now smiled warmly, and Kate nodded and found some words of appreciation. Mrs. Thomas patted Kate's arm as if they shared a secret which was safe with her and said, 'A good day to you,' as she went out. Kate closed the door behind her and, curiously, locked it.

She stood with her shoulder against the door, feeling disconsolate. Perhaps if she sat down for a minute before working on Mrs. Thomas' plates, she could understand why she was feeling as she did. She walked to the red velvet chair and collapsed into its plush comfort. Her whole body trembled with unease. A cavernous sense of aloneness enveloped her, and her body seemed to pull in different directions causing her thoughts to be a mass of frazzled ends, tangled and unfocused. She shivered and drew her feet into the encompassing arms of the chair against the perceived chill. She hugged her knees, resting her head on them.

Thoughts raced through her mind. Had she heard Angus correctly? Was her mother really dead? Really dead? The whole idea that it might be so was greatly discomfiting. Was remembering her mother's black taffeta dress somehow self-fulfilling? Fragments of images captured her consciousness for fleeting seconds and then vanished.

She frowned deeply. She was not used to death although she'd certainly experienced her share of it. She supposed no one ever got used to it. But her mother—could her mother really be dead? There was so much unfinished business. She licked her lips and felt her eyeballs burn. So much unfinished business. At last she sat quietly until dusk overcame sunset. Even the creeping cold of the untended stove did not stir her.

She was jarred conscious by a vehement pounding, as a fist hitting wood. In the darkened room, she sprang from her chair, disoriented. The pounding stopped but the act of recovering her balance helped her place herself in the here-and-now. Then the pounding began again and intensified. 'Just a minute,' she called out. She stroked her cheeks and brushed the hair back from her face and smoothed the rumpled woolen skirt that had caught in tight folds around her when she slumped into the chair. 'I'm coming. I'll be right there,' she said.

Angus all but fell in the room when she turned the key and opened the door. She stepped back. 'Kate!' Kate could barely see his face in the faint glow from the street light, but his voice was angry. 'Kate! What have you been doing? You have no light on, and you didn't answer your door. I went down and Bill Sedlow was just leaving for the day. He said he hadn't heard you leave so I came back upstairs. Why was your door locked? Are you all right?' he demanded as he turned on the light.

Am I all right? she wondered to herself. Slowly, the memory of his earlier phone call crept into her consciousness. Tears reappeared. 'Yes, of course, I'm all right.' She gave no hint of emotion.

Angus, in a voice that was both gentle and plaintive, repeated his telephone message. 'Kate, our mother died.' With those words echoing in her head, her mother's death became real and flooded her with guilt and regret and longing and sorrow and even love—emotions she would have to sort out when she had time to focus, to adjust the lens of life to bring the fuzzy edges of a human relationship into clear sharp understanding.

Now she saw that her brother looked drained and anguished. He and their mother had always been close, and he sometimes asked Kate why she and her mother had such difficulty getting along.

'Oh, Angus, I'm so sorry,' Kate said softly. 'Here. I'll put on a pot of tea and you can tell me what happened.'

'No!' Angus' voice was gruff and commanding. 'Pack your valise. You're coming home with me. The funeral will be day after tomorrow and there are things to be done.'

* * *

Kate did not argue with Angus. In her tiny bedroom, she stooped to reach her valise from under the white-painted iron bedstead, brushing the quilt her mother and she had made for her hope chest. It stirred old memories of them working together by the evening lamp-light while Lynus and Angus played cribbage or pored over the Sears Roebuck catalog to find a part they needed for some piece of equipment.

Kate and her mother seldom talked as they sewed, but her mother stitched with great earnestness. Kate sensed that her mother felt she must hurry lest Kate not be 'ready for the marriage bed' when a suitable man came along. Actually Kate had begun to wonder if there was a man alive who could be certified 'suitable' by this judgmental woman. After Kate had seen a young man several times, her mother would find something to criticize about him. He wasn't smart enough for Kate, or his chin was too weak, or he didn't make enough to support a wife and children, and so on.

By the time Kate moved to town at age thirty, the quilt had lain in her cedar hope chest for ten years. That had been plenty long enough, Kate thought, when she spread it across her bed for the first time. 'Why, Kate,' her mother had said on her first and only visit to the little upstairs apartment, 'you should be saving that quilt for your marriage. That's what I made it for.'

'Well, Mother,' Kate said quietly, 'the fact is I'm not married and I see no reason to let it rot waiting for such a time.' Kate was tempted to gather the quilt up from the bed then and there and grandly offer it to her mother without even folding it, but she couldn't. She loved the Attic Windows pattern she had picked out and the chintz with its soft pink and lavender flowers she had so carefully chosen to 'see through the windows'. It would have broken her heart if her mother had accepted the offer, and she would not risk it.

She held her tongue and, instead, diverted her mother's attention to the lacy newspaper edgings she had cut for her cupboard shelves. 'See, Mother. I've made pretty edgings just like yours. Well, not just like yours. I'm not as good with the scissors as you are.' The subject of the quilt was dropped. Recalling the incident now caused Kate's heart to flutter briefly and she breathed deeply until her body relaxed again.

Out in the wintry dusk, Angus tucked the horse-hair robe around Kate's knees and clucked to the horse. He started to tell Kate about their mother's death, but he faltered and his voice drifted off. In the dim light of the street lamps, Kate looked straight ahead, not encouraging him to talk. She was not ready to listen as the light of the last street lamp faded into the growing dark of the open road.

The sound of the horse's hooves on the freezing crust of the March slush was muted with a sibilance that was peculiar to that ground condition. It was a kind of 'closhhh, closhhh, closhhh,' Kate thought, a counterpart

Red Geraniums

to the steady swoosh of the buggy wheels cutting a swath through the icy muck. These sounds slashed the silence as keenly as a knife and the blackness of the night closed round them. Hunched against the cold, they rode the rest of the way without speaking.

Kate had little to say to Lizzie at supper that evening though Lizzie prattled on and on about the arrangements for the funeral. She said, 'My, how alive Mother MacLean looks now that the undertaker has finished his work.' Angus quietly hushed her. She reddened and fell silent.

After supper, Kate made no move to help Lizzie clean up in the kitchen but sat listlessly at the table. Finally, she roused herself. 'Angus, may I have a lamp? I want to say goodbye to Mother.'

'There's a lamp already lit in there. Here, I'll open the doors for you.' He slid the north door of the parlor into its pocket in the wall and started to open the south half as well.

'This one will be enough, Angus.' She slipped through. He started to say something, but she raised her chin, closing her eyes. He quietly slid the door behind her.

Kate turned up the parlor lamp. She particularly disliked this lamp with its pink glass chimney edged with its frilly glass scallops and and gaudy painted roses. The pierced brass base sat on what she called 'golden gewgaw legs'. Ah yes, she thought, the requisite gold painted pretense. Nevertheless, she welcomed the bright glow of the burning wick which seemed to take the chill off the unheated room.

In the center of the room, stood a rather small rectangular box draped with green baize, hardly bigger than the cob box in the kitchen, Kate thought. When she lifted the lamp from the corner table, she could see her mother's face and folded hands, translucent ivory in the soft light with dulled highlights defining the black silk taffeta dress.

She had expected to see a tranquility about her mother in death that was seldom evident in life, but in that light, at least, her corpse was unyielding, angular, and deeply shadowed. Her nose, so long and straight in life seemed even more so in death. The eyelids, closed over her liquid blue eyes (so like Kate's own), appeared to quiver in the lamplight. She'd heard it said that undertakers sewed the jaws and lips shut so they wouldn't draw back from the teeth, and she supposed Mr. Wilson had done so that morning when he came to prepare her mother's body, but she could see no stitches, just an odd dimple in her chin that had not been there in life.

Kate returned the lamp to the corner table and sat on the edge of the oak rocker, leaning forward with a frown on her face as if an angel might appear to chastise her for her reaction to her mother's death. The events of the day leading up to Angus' arrival at the studio were very vivid now, and she shuddered, remembering her sense of disorientation.

Out of her ponderings, the image of her father's dead body took form, and she wondered if her mother's death had been easy like her father's. She remembered seeing Lynus and Angus bringing their father from the cornfield where the heart attack had felled him. She remembered the shock of realization that he was dead when they laid him under the oak tree west of the house. Now she wept quiet tears, drawing her hankie with tatted lace edging from her dress pocket.

At the time of her father's death, Kate's agony had been only partly assuaged by helping her mother conduct the necessary preparations for the funeral. She and her mother had bathed his body, covered it with a clean, carefully pressed cotton sheet, and waited for Mr. Casey, the undertaker, to arrive. It was the first time she had seen a grown man's naked body and, old as he was, it nevertheless shocked her. She had hid her embarrassment as best she could and worked vigorously to remove the smell of death that had already begun.

Her mother never questioned the appropriateness of her participation. Indeed, she had said on more than one occasion, 'It is an honor to lay out the body of a loved one.' Kate wanted to believe it was so, but she really wanted to remember her father as she had known him.

Thinking about this strange male organ had made her realize that in its functioning years, it was partly responsible for the fact that she existed, but she did not want to think about him in the role of procreator. She wanted to remember him cheerfully going about his daily duties, joking with the children, singing hymns while her mother played the organ. This was the father she wanted to honor, not the one lying naked on the cool white sheet.

Sitting here by her mother's coffin, she felt a bit weak, too, but for a different reason. She wished her mother had not given orders that there was to be no fancy casket and no church service.

For her mother, it was a principled decision. 'It's sheer foolishness,' she used to say, 'to fill a body with preservative and bury it in a fancy box. The bodies of dead humans are no more sacred than the bodies of dead animals and they're picked clean to feed scavengers. That's nature's way.

Those Zoroastrians do it right. They put their folks' bodies in a tower for the vultures to pick clean. Even cremation would be better than burying a lot of fanciness to impress neighbors who forget you once you're gone anyway. If I must be embalmed, at least I can be buried in a plain pine box and I expect you to see to it.'

In a way, Kate could see that this attitude made intellectual sense. Like her mother, she didn't care what the neighbors thought, but guilt ruled her emotions now. She felt guilty about their strained—in some ways, estranged—relationship, and with her mother now lying in this plain pine box, she had no chance to make amends. She wished she had tried earlier. Well, she had in a way, and so had her mother, but never at the same time, it seemed. She would have to relieve her guilt by making sure her mother was honored for all the things she did right.

The night wore on and still Kate sat with her mother, as if closeness in death could narrow the unbridgeable chasm in life. At last she dimmed the light and climbed the familiar stairs, not to her old room—that was now the boys' room—but to Lynus' old room.

* * *

Midafternoon the next day, Mr. Casey along with Lizzie's brother-in-law, Joe, their neighbor, Harold Barlowe, and Bill Sedlow carried the closed casket out to the front yard and set it on a pair of wooden crates draped with horsehair blankets. A small group of neighbors and Lizzie's people from Union Township stood here and there on the half-frozen ground, avoiding the shade of the trees where snow still clung to the brown grass. The March sun shone through the haze, but the wind from the north was chill and the little congregation pulled their shawls and fur caps closer about them.

At a nod from Angus, Mrs. Lucretia Small, the Universalist minister from Almora, began to sing 'Blest Be the Tie That Binds.' The women and children joined in, slowing the tempo with wavering voices; most of the men merely mouthed the words, but Mr. Sedlow's voice anchored the melody.

Kate had always liked Mrs. Small though she had never attended any of the Universalist services in the Almora Opera House. Her mother rarely attended the services, but she gave generously to support the tiny, growing church, and Mrs. Small visited her mother when she was traveling through the area.

Kate knew her mother rejected the notion of the Trinity, and she thought she herself did, but she wasn't quite sure. In any case, the Universalists seemed to be the only church that welcomed women preachers. Kate approved of that, but then again she wasn't quite sure it was appropriate for women to represent God. Becoming a professional woman herself, Kate had come to appreciate the trials Mrs. Small had to face every day in establishing her credibility as a 'person of the cloth', but Kate never expressed this to her.

When Kate's mother turned sixty-five, she had called on Mrs. Small to make perfectly clear what funeral rites would be acceptable to her when the time came. She insisted that Angus and Kate go with her to attest to relatives and neighbors later that she had been sound of mind and body when she set forth her last wishes.

'Now, Mrs. Small,' Kate's mother had said, 'we all know that people who haven't much else to do will spend valuable time gossiping about neighbors, asserting that they know best what others *should* do, and bemoaning what folks *really* do. I will not have such gossip about what I believe is my right to determine the nature of what will be said over my dead body.' Tiny Mrs. Small, rocking back and forth as Mrs. MacLean talked, nodded her approval. Kate's mother went on. 'I want to make it clear that a hymn, a brief prayer and a few words about my beliefs in Universalism are sufficient to lay me to rest from the labors of this earth.'

Mrs. Small leaned forward as Kate's mother finished speaking. 'You are quite right that you should have the say about your interment. It has been your spiritual journey up to now and it should be yours even at the end of your blessed life. It is important to be realistic and plan ahead.'

Angus squirmed on the horsehair settee and spoke with urgency. 'Now, Mother, you know Lizzie's people are all good Methodists. They're going to think this is quite peculiar. Not to mention other neighbors. After all, you're not going to die for some time yet and you may want to change your mind.'

'I will not.' Her pronouncement had a note of principled defiance and finality. 'Folks ought to think ahead. Maybe they'll learn something from a service that doesn't dillydally around about a life well lived and all that nonsense. Most of our lives are strictly ordinary, and if the truth be told at funerals, funerals would be a lot shorter. That would certainly be refreshing. If there is a God, he'll approve.' Then she added, 'And I don't want my face showing during the funeral. You nail that lid on the coffin before you bring the box outside.'

'Outside! But Mother, what if it's in the middle of winter?'

'All the better. The funeral will have to be brief then, won't it? Yes, I want my funeral on the front lawn, you hear?' Kate said nothing, but pondered on her mother's convictions.

In the end, Angus acceded to their mother's wishes as she knew he would, and the funeral was over before the congregants had to stamp their feet to keep warm. Immediately after the closing prayer, the pall-bearers loaded the coffin onto the wagon waiting discreetly behind the lilac bushes by the driveway, and the four of them drove off toward town where the body would be kept in the ice house until the ground thawed enough to dig a grave.

Kate, standing apart from the rest during the ceremony, remained fixed in place as the wagon disappeared from sight and the group moved into the house to get warm. The delicate pink of her cheeks was blotched from holding back tears, tears she little welcomed or understood. Her mother, after all, was old. She had to die sometime. She had said so herself. Kate knew she would miss much about her, even her sharp tongue, but more importantly, she would miss the spirited talks they'd had about history and important people which she hadn't appreciated at the time.

With her mother her father and Ann Marie all gone, her older sister Lina and Jessie and Lynus in Saskatchewan, Kate wondered if she was now the family matriarch. She was the oldest living woman in the MacLean family, but as the thought occurred to her—and the corner of her mouth twitched ever so slightly—she guessed she couldn't be, having never had children. Her mother would have loved debating this semantic point. On that note, Kate's unspoken grief eased, and she went into the house to visit with family and neighbors over a cup of coffee and the roast beef sandwiches she and Lizzie had made from the bread fresh-baked that morning.

II

Life became mostly routine again after her mother's funeral, but not quite. Kate's memory of her loss—and it began to feel more and more like a loss—haunted her at odd moments. Today as she shivered, hurrying back to the studio after depositing money at the State Bank, she thought how her mother would have admonished her to wear her heavy winter coat for another week at least. It was early May, but winter hung on and the early trees reluctantly bloomed briefly the week just before a terrific windstorm. Even now as she glanced across at the park, the remaining vulnerable blossoms formed a snow-swirl around the bandstand and the benches. Her light wool spring coat, which matched the bright clear sky, now felt like so much cheese cloth in the biting wind.

On returning to the studio, Kate closed the door behind her, glad to be out of the wind. She shivered briefly then traded the coat for a woolen sweater Lizzy had knit for her birthday the year before. Kate stoked the kitchen range and set a pan of leftover soup to heat for lunch. In spite of the brightness of the day outside, she felt dispirited. Life had become almost too routine.

She had no appointments, and the quiet felt good. On the other hand, she loved the sound of the many booted feet that tromped up the stairs, all coming for the happy-family pictures she produced. She envisioned herself as weaving legends about people's lives for generations to come, but today, it seemed, no amount of pink and white blossoms the wind pasted on her north windows could lift her spirits.

She opened the kitchen cupboard to choose a soup plate from her mother's set with its sepia-colored transfer prints of flowers. She held it above the soup kettle and ladled the steaming chicken and carrots and potatoes into it using her metal one-cup measure with its bent handle. She placed the steaming dish on the little table and reached into the silverware drawer for a soup spoon. She wasn't very hungry but she thought maybe she'd feel better if she ate something warm. She reached for her book, but she didn't feel like reading just then.

She fell into thought as she sipped the steaming brew. Since her mother's death, Kate had felt even less like going to the farm on Sundays. Oh, she had helped out in the kitchen when baby Netta was born, but it was only a peripherally happy occasion for her. Of course, she was always glad to see Angus when he stopped in. They always carried on a spirited conversation over the cups of tea she brewed for him. Lizzie seemed somewhat at a loss as to know what to say to her. Kate wondered if Lizzie might be a bit jealous of her life as a business woman. Still, these days Kate sensed Lizzie wanted to be friends but maybe didn't know how.

Angus still persisted in inviting her to the farm and told her he'd come to get her. Kate would remind him that she was going to church in town now. 'It takes too much of your time to drive back and forth extra to get me,' she said. 'Besides, I need to work on my business papers. I don't have time while I'm working with customers during the week.'

'Even on Sundays?'

'Why, yes, of course.'

'But Katie, don't you get lonely? Don't you want to see you Netta and the boys? They're growing fast and you're missing that,' Angus said one day when he and the boys were in town. Robbie tried to squirm off his father's lap and squealed as Angus tickled his ribs.

Kate wished she could relax and just enjoy little children, but she couldn't. This was surprising for a former school teacher, but she hadn't become a school teacher because she loved little children. Kate had had no trouble in the schoolroom. The little ones responded to her sternness with quiescent obedience, and she found she quite enjoyed the older ones because she could relate to them on an intellectual level that appealed to her.

Her reluctance to play with little children didn't affect her enjoyment of taking pictures of them though. Once behind the camera she could give orders and do little tricks to hold their attention, but small children on her own lap were another matter. In spite of this, she still had a longing to have a child of her own. She just assumed that she would naturally be a good mother to her baby when she had one. After all, there hadn't been anything about Lizzie that would have indicated she would be a good mother, but Kate knew that she was.

Spending a day at the farm with the family was usually fun and rewarding, she had to admit, but Kate's commitment to 'think about it' was the only promise she would make to Angus. When Sundays arrived, she creatively rationalized her staying in town.

Kate really did like her work. It didn't seem like a chore to take pictures and print them.

She set aside her vague sense of loneliness when she was immersed in her studio work. Living in town essentially freed her from family obligations, and her ambitions for her business expanded. She had ordered extra photographic supplies and spruced up the studio. She bought a new table for a prop with turned spindle legs and a marble top, and she mended the blinds so they pulled more easily and looked more presentable.

She was ready for more business and she set about increasing her customer base. She drove to Almora, the county seat, to place an ad in the weekly county paper. The ad, which would run each week for a month, cost the equivalent of a sitting—a hefty price, Kate thought, but sensing the ad would be good for her business, she spared no expense. It had to be done right.

In the center of the ad was an oval-framed picture she'd taken of John standing beside little Robbie, propped up in a child's wicker chair in his long christening dress. Decorative flowers and flourishes filled the corners of the ad on either side of the picture. Below, the width of two print columns, Old English lettering boldly proclaimed 'MacLean Studio'. Beneath was a motto Kate had thought of one morning as she read a book her mother would never have approved of, a novel. The motto was: 'Where both saints and sinners look good.' She smiled because she knew her father would have enjoyed the humor and her mother would have at least enjoyed the play on words, but she wasn't sure about Angus and Lizzie and did not consult them. Below she added the particulars: Third and Main Streets, Tingle Creek, Phone 123. Call for an appointment.

The telephone number in the ad was most astonishing to Angus and Lizzie and folks in town who knew her. At first the idea of installing a telephone hadn't felt right to Kate. She had talked for over a year now about how silly it would be to capitulate to this popular, but—as she saw it—unnecessary fad. Nevertheless, as Kate could hear the phone in the meat market below ringing more often, she could only surmise that Bill Sedlow's phone must be adding to his business. Once she had drawn this inference, she determined that it was a necessary business expense

Red Geraniums

and never looked back to her days of gibing those too weak to resist the novelty.

Mr. Marshall, the telephone company representative, came for her to sign the agreement. 'Thank you, Miss MacLean! We have an agreement. Your number will be 83. I know you won't regret it.'

'8-3!' Kate remonstrated. 'It can't be. My number must easy to remember and the only suitable one is 1-2-3! The telephone is purely a business proposition and nothing more.' She was determined it would not be an instrument of gossip as she knew Lizzie's and Mary's were, even though she secretly enjoyed hearing gossip Jean Burchett passed along. 'I won't sign without your guaranteeing me that number!'

Mr. Marshall gently gave in.

Now she felt she was ready for the rest of her life as a studio photographer. She appreciated her earlier life on the farm, but town was where she wanted to be. She knew she already enjoyed a reputation as a competent businesswoman, but she had to be careful. She thought about all this as she dipped her spoon into the hot soup. She put a smile on her face and, as soon as her soup was finished, she started her work. Yes, life really was good.

* * *

Each day Kate roused early to cook her breakfast and air out the smell of fresh sausage frying before her first client arrived. She ritually cleaned up the studio in the evening so she could take time to read as she drank her morning tea. Kate spooned sugar into her cup first the way her mother had taught her, followed by milk which she poured from a small china pitcher. Finally she added the steaming hot tea which had been steeping in the pot. She never allowed herself to read 'more than two cups worth' so she would be in the studio promptly. Sitting in her rocker now, she picked up her book.

She depended on local sources for reading materials since the library in Almora was too far to go. When she moved to town, she inquired from the school superintendent, the doctor, and the banker about their books. Kate found that only Mr. Pedersen, the town lawyer, had an extensive library beyond his law books, so she considered herself fortunate to have become friendly with Mr. and Mrs. Pedersen at the Methodist Episcopal Church.

She was currently reading *'The English Gypsies and Their Language'* by Charles G. Leland which had been published a number of years earlier. She had found it on the Pedersens' shelf. It was fascinating, and she knew of no other books about Gypsies.

Absorbed as she was each morning, she often forgot about the time, hence the two-cup-rule. In spite of her other differences with her mother, she appreciated her mother's love of reading. Her own reading habit began early in her life and never waned. If her supply of reading matter dwindled, she simply re-read old material.

Many's the day she thanked her parents for subscribing to the *Youth's Companion* magazine for her tenth birthday present. Every evening, when farm chores were done, she was happy to read its wonderful stories to Lynus and Jessie. Angus would often sit at the side of the room pretending to play solitaire, but she knew he was listening, too.

Today as she drank her tea, she thought about the wall case for the *Youth's Companion* magazines that still hung in the dining room at the farm. Soon after she started receiving the magazine, she had found an advertisement for the dual-purpose case to hold the magazines, and she became hopeful, but not really hopeful, that she might one day own one. She knew that neither her mother nor her father were much given to adorning their lives with what they considered frivolity, so even a clever, utilitarian piece such as the *Youth's Companion* case was would likely be rejected.

Kate had learned not to ask or at least not to be too disappointed when her wishes weren't fulfilled. Nevertheless, she spoke to her father one morning as he was leaving the house to hitch up the team. 'Papa, just look at this! Could we get this case for our *Youth's Companion* magazines?' She jabbed her finger at the advertisement in the current magazine. 'Could we? Could we? Just see how beautiful it would look on our wall! It would keep all my magazines neat. And it's only a dollar and a quarter. I wouldn't ask for another thing!' Her father smiled and said nothing but tweaked her nose and went on to the barn. She had had no choice but to go about her chores and her schoolwork as if she had never seen the ad or shown it to her father.

Then one day Kate spied her father as he returned from delivering cream to the creamery in town. Kate and the boys accosted him as usual at the foot of the boardwalk. They always hoped for something special from town—a hoarhound stick or a dill pickle and even a lollipop. Today though he didn't say anything to the children's begging but lifted a thin cardboard carton about two feet long and eighteen inches wide out of the wagon.

'Papa, Papa,' they shouted, dancing around. He set the box down and solemnly reached his roughened hands into his coat pockets to show that he had no treats. He looked sad but picked up the box and marched up the boardwalk to the screened porch. The children slunk into the house after him, feeling somehow cheated. If he'd said he had no money for treats, they would have understood, but there was money for whatever was in the box so they were especially disappointed.

'Sprobably just somebody's long underwear,' Lynus pouted as they followed their father into the dining room and gathered round the table. The box was not unlike those sent from Sears Roebuck with dress material or a jacket for one of the boys. From his trousers pocket, their father ceremoniously drew out the large pocket knife that had been his pride and joy since the Christmas of his fifteenth year back in Wisconsin.

'Well, let's see what we have here!' he said, carefully slashing the bindings and pulling aside the excelsior packing. There before them lay the most beautiful painting of dazzling pink and purple and blue flowers arranged in a marblized vase of palest green set on a lace table cloth. The gilded plaster frame was sculpted into Rococco ripples of vines and berries.

'Oh!' Oh! Oh!' breathed an awestruck Kate. 'I've never seen anything so beautiful.' She glanced at her mother standing by the wall buffet. She saw a flicker of appreciation cross her mother's face, but her mother said nothing.

'Well! Let's see how this opens and then let's see how those *Youth's Companions* fit in here.' Her father found the catch on the top edge and deftly swung the frame open on its bottom hinge, a gold-colored chain keeping it from opening all the way. Kate picked up a handful of magazines from the side table and, as her father held up the picture case, she slipped them in.

'Oh. Isn't it remarkable? How could anyone think of anything so clever? Let's see how it looks like on the wall!' she cried delightedly, dancing up and down. 'Over here! Let's put it right here!' Her father winked at her and went to find his hammer and a nail.

Remembering this special gift, Kate mused now that she had not thought to ask for the *Youth's Companion* case when she moved into town.

Perhaps Angus' children would appreciate it as she had. Meanwhile, after she finished her second cup of tea, she turned her attention to the pile of well-worn copies of the *Youth's Companion* magazine she kept in the studio for children to read when they came in for a sitting. After they left, she always re-stacked the magazines, clucking to herself about the dog-eared corners. Once everything was neat and in place, she was ready for her first sitting of the day.

* * *

Since reading about Gypsies in Leland's book, they had been very much on Kate's mind even before Jean Burchett rang the general alarm on all the phones two hours ago to warn everyone that a Gypsy caravan was heading toward town. The Sheriff told Jean to advise everyone to lock their doors and to look sharp if the Gypsies came into their places of business.

Surreptitiously, Kate watched out the window as three colorful bow wagons slowly drove along Main Street and stopped in front of Halley's department store. How beautiful their horses are, she thought to herself. Then she saw women and children pour out from the back gates of the wagons and fan out along the shopping district, some going into Halley's, some into the hardware store, some into the drugstore. None went in the bank as far as she could see.

The women moved quickly, as if in a dance. In the midday sun, their skirts blazed with color, deep reds, bright greens and golden yellows with colorful embroidery and ribbon work and patchwork and some thing else. Tiny glints of light flashed as if tiny mirrors were embedded in the fabric, catching the sun. Kate wished she could capture this sight with her camera.

She thought about that morning on the farm when the band of Gypsies had arrived asking for food. The sun was not yet up that winter day so the dining room was cold and dark, and her impression of them was one of dark foreboding, huddled as they were in thick woolen coats and capes and heavy shawls. There was none of the sparkling movement she saw here on the street. Watching them now made her want to twirl with the same freedom they seemed to have.

She saw townspeople scurrying along, heads down, avoiding eye contact with the visitors, the townswomen clutching their purchases closer to their chests, the men automatically putting their hands into the pockets where they carried their money.

The Gypsy children, dressed in ragged clothes as drab as their mothers' skirts were colorful, fanned out to accost whatever person happened along. Kate watched a little wisp of a Gypsy girl stop old Mrs. Simpson. The child, her face screwed up in a pitiful pout barely visible in a tangle of dark curls, thrust her hand in Mrs. Simpson's face. Kate imagined how her voice must have whined for money.

Mrs. Simpson whirled around and tried to brush the child away as she bent her upper body in the direction of home a block away. She charged ahead but the child again stepped in front of her and Mrs. Simpson faltered, a little off balance. Finally she reached in her bag and dropped something into the child's hand, while clutching her bag closely. She again brushed the child away, almost spilling the coins from the girl's hand, and made her way past the band shelter in the square until she turned the corner north. It was obviously a gargantuan effort for the old woman. Kate could imagine that she opened the door of her house, carefully locked it, and fell exhausted on the couch.

Just then Kate heard footsteps bounding up the stairs, as if their owner was in a terrible hurry. There was an insistent rap on the door. Kate had not thought it necessary to lock the door to her studio because she thought she remembered that Gypsies do not believe in having their images recorded. Maybe it was Bill Sedlow being solicitous of her welfare. Again the sharp rapping. She went to the door and pulled it open.

There on the landing stood the handsomest man she ever remembered seeing. He towered well above her at what she guessed must be almost six feet tall. His lanky frame made him seem even taller. 'Good morning, Ma'am.' Kate was taken aback. Why, he was the man she had seen driving the lead Gypsy wagon! Had he come to rob her? She would not have been able to force the door closed if he resisted. Her eyelids fluttered as she tried to think of split-second options. She saw none.

At least he was a polite thief, if that was his intent, and civility counted in her family. Her father had invited a whole Gypsy family into the house and nothing untoward had happened. Maybe if she were equally hospitable, he would go away. 'Uh . . . Uh . . . May I help you?'

'I'd like to have my picture taken.' His voice was husky and strong.

'Oh, but—' She started to protest, but thought better of it. 'I—I—have another customer coming soon.' It was not an out-and-out lie; she didn't say that the customer would be coming immediately, but it made her uncomfortable to have to excuse her reluctance to deal with this man.

'Well, but it won't take long, will it? I don't have much time either. You see, my party will be going on west just as soon as we pick up some supplies.' His smile widened the handsome mustache he wore with such flair, and the gentle brown of his skin reminded her of the finest sepia-toned photographs she'd seen on exhibit in Des Moines on her only trip there. He seemed to assume that she would know who he meant by 'his party'.

'I could just sit on that throne—like a king, you know,' he said and pointed to the red velvet-covered chair. 'I *am* a king, after all.' His strong accent identified him as being from somewhere else, but she had had little contact with black-eyed, black-haired foreigners and she couldn't guess his origin.

'Well, but I couldn't have the pictures ready for you before you leave town,' she said and hoped this practical point would excuse her.

'That's no problem. I'll just pick them up on my way through town next time.'

'Next time—? And when would that be?'

'Oh, sometime in the next six or eight months—not very long. I'll be back before you know it.' His voice was pleasantly teasing, not unlike her father's. In fact, she thought, her father would have liked this man. He seemed downright mannerly for being so roughly dressed. And that face! What a challenge it would be to capture the essence of that face! But, of course, capturing the essence, the soul, of a person was the very reason some people avoided having a photograph made of their faces.

'I hardly know what to say. I mean, I do charge for taking pictures, you know.'

'That should be no problem. I'm sure that there is some work I can do for you in exchange for the photograph.'

Kate was skeptical. She frowned and the left corner of her mouth drew up momentarily.

'What kind of work could you do for me? I don't have a farm. I don't have a buggy. You know nothing about photography...'

'Do you have an old kettle that needs a hole fixed? Aha. I see you do. Would three holes pay for my picture? Or—make it as many holes and kettles as you want.' He smiled broadly and his dark eyes sparkled like starfire.

Kate could not think of a polite way to suggest he leave—and she didn't really want to. 'All right. Come. Let's move the chair in front of this fringed drape.' The activity felt good. She had begun to feel weak standing so long looking up at his face, or at least that's what she thought caused her unsteadiness.

The man sat with his knees to the right as she suggested, his face turned a bit away from the brightness coming from the tall windows. Mr. Short had taught her to turn the client's head so that the smaller eye—he said everyone has one eye smaller than the other—would be closer to the camera and hence look larger. Kate didn't want to search the man's face overmuch, but she could not see such an imperfection in this man. In fact, even his nose was tightly centered in his face and his ears were at the same height in relation to his eyes. Truly a remarkable face, full in the cheeks, strong in the jaw.

'May I ask your name? It's awkward trying to position you without addressing you by your proper name.'

'Just call me Gyorgy. And what may I call you?'

Kate ignored his question. 'But I must know your family name. Don't kings have family names? It would not be proper for me to address you by your given name.' Kate busied herself with the brass adjustment mechanisms on the camera, trying to fit him into the opening. Even upside down as he appeared on the viewing lens, he was a most extraordinary man.

'Call me Mr. Gyorgy, if that makes you feel better.'

She didn't know why he hedged about his family name, but she guessed it might cause some vexation in his life which apparently being photographed would not. 'All right, Mr. Gyorgy. I want you to put your right hand on your knee—just easily, you know. Yes. Now you put your left hand on the arm of the chair.'

'Does this pose make me look like a king? You know I told you I am a king so I think I should look like one, don't you?'

She wasn't sure if he was teasing or serious. 'What do you mean you're a king? We don't have any kings in America. This is a democracy, after all.' The idea irked her, but the words were her mother's and she was surprised to realize they came from her own mouth. Nevertheless, his 'kingship' intrigued her. She had read in Mr. Pedersen's National Geographics about how kings lived and that life did sound rather romantic.

'Oh, we Roma have kings. I know, you call us Gypsies but we're really Roma. Actually, having kings is just a way of talking about our leaders. And yes, I am the leader of this *kumpania*. That's like a group of families.'

'Are you going to have pictures taken of your wife and children, too?' Kate ducked under the black cloth as her voice rose a little too shrilly at the end of the question. She really didn't want to hear the answer, but still she needed to.

'I'm not married yet. I'm still looking for a wife. Do you know any single women as beautiful as you that are needing a husband?'

Kate was glad for the cloth though it seemed awfully hot under it. 'All right, Mr. Gyorgy. I'm ready. I'll just put the glass plate in and you'll have to hold very, very still for a minute.' She slipped the darkslide away and counted and then returned the darkslide to cover the glass negative. 'I'll take two more.'

She went to the dark room and leaned on the cupboard shelf to steady herself. Maybe I'm coming down with something, she thought. Reaching the box of plates on the third shelf, she took one out and returned to the studio. 'Now, if you move the chair closer—Yes. Yes. That will be enough. Now look directly into the camera. I'll take one just of your head and shoulders, Mr. Gyorgy.'

Kate repeated the name in her mind over and over. The name had a softness to its masculinity and her tongue was becoming accustomed to the whirring of the second 'g'. Well, at least she thought it would be spelled with a 'g', but maybe it was a 'j'.

'Ah, that's fine. Now look right this way. No, perhaps you should look slightly toward my left shoulder and tip your head ever so little.'

'The better to see you,' he laughed and his grin showed in the frosted glass viewing lens. 'You are awfully small, you know.'

'If you smile, it will be harder to hold the full minute that it takes and the picture will be blurred.' Flustered, Kate was thankful for her experience so that most of her commands were instinctive and rote. This routine was the only thing that allowed her to keep her equilibrium with this exotic stranger. Even so, he was obviously enjoying whatever effect he was having on her.

'I'm ready now. You can't smile! Hold it just like that—perfectly still now.'

She finished the sitting, taking three poses in all in spite of her head feeling fuzzy. 'I'll have the pictures ready for you when you come back

Red Geraniums

to town.' The mention of such prosaic property brought her back to her usual business-like demeanor. She moved toward the door, indicating the session was over. 'I hope you have a good journey,' she said with her hand on the latch.

Gyorgy gravely nodded. 'I'll send one of the children to get the kettles. And I will be back.' He turned and disappeared down the stairs.

Kate sank into the red velvet chair as if to absorb the remainder of his body heat.

She sat with her eyes closed, her face bathed in the subtle light from the windows. Curly wisps of her hair were dampened with perspiration. Against the light diffused through her lids, she saw the image of Gyorgy's face, his dark eyes and the grin that made the ends of his mustache twitch. She shook her head and wet her lips, trying to disengage the image. Suddenly she hopped up, remembering the kettles to be mended. She was glad she would have an excuse to see Gyorgy again.

* * *

After Gyorgy left, Kate began her interrupted work in the studio. First though, she needed to get out the kettles for Gyorgy's repair work. Sure enough, a small knock came at the door and two little urchins stood there shyly. 'Oh, you came for the kettles, didn't you?' They nodded and she handed the pots to them. With a bright smile on their faces, they turned and trotted down the steps. She smiled, watching them. 'Can they be as bad as everyone says they are?' she wondered to herself.

She needed to get back to her work but she thought about Mr. Gyorgy as she readied the studio for tomorrow's sittings. He seemed different than she expected. Not only was he a handsome man, but a true gentleman as well. Still, she was somewhat apprehensive about what her customers might hear about her accommodating the Gypsy who came to her studio.

She went to the window, edging carefully behind the drape to peek out without being seen from below. Main Street was empty, no colorful Gypsy wagons, no Gyorgy. 'At least I have his picture!' she thought. 'Or, I will when it's developed.' She felt her face warming at the prospect of holding his image in her hands. She shook her head to rid it of thinking about this man she'd barely met and turned to go wash her face in cold water.

Just then there was a knock at the studio door. Could it be . . . ? She patted her hair with damp palms and smoothed her brown cotton paisley dress. As her hands outlined her rounding breasts and pulled the wrinkles from her shirtwaist, she wished, in passing, that the bustier she insisted on wearing to narrow her waist would not make her feel so breathless.

Straightening her shoulders, she opened the door tentatively. There stood Mr. Berringer, the photographic supplies salesman who came by once every six months or so. 'My, my, Miss MacLean, you look prettier than ever!'

Her smile faded and her eyes lost their sparkle. Quite aside from her disappointment, she was disgusted. How dare he, this homely, aging, married man see fit to comment on her looks even before saying 'Hello.' Angus and Lizzie would have said he was just trying to be polite, to compliment her, but she felt as sticky as she had after Benny kissed her.

Well-trained as she was to be at least civil, if not lady-like, she returned his greeting. 'Hello, Mr. Berringer. I had not expected you for several weeks yet.' The smell of his gentleman's perfume made her nose twitch.

'Yes, well, I was called home to Omaha and so I thought I'd stop in on my way back from Grand Island. It's always a pleasure to look on such a lovely creature as you!'

Kate's eyes narrowed and she pursed her mouth in an expression that in children often precedes a cutting taunt. She breathed deeply to control herself. 'Then I take it you have no new specials since the last time you came. You remember I told you I have to cut costs. It's not easy to make a living as a photographer when the price of supplies keeps rising.'

'No, of course not. But then, you shouldn't have to be doing this work. A beautiful woman like you will make someone a good wife.' Mr. Berringer's grin was repugnant. 'Why, just this last week I met a man down in Kansas City who would make a wonderful husband for you. He owns a grocery store, but poor man, his first wife died of consumption two years back, leaving him with two children, very clever children at that. When I go there next time I could tell him to write to you. Yes, I think I'll do just that. I'm a good matchmaker. I tell you I have an unerring instinct for finding the right mate for a friend. After all, I do consider you a friend, even if we have business dealings. I'd marry you myself, but the missus wouldn't understand.' He broke into coarse laughter. Kate stared grimly at him and her cheeks brightened to an agitated red.

She dismissed him curtly, opening the door as she spoke. 'I don't need anything now. Good day.' Mr. Berringer stepped back. His mustache twitched erratically. There was deep hurt and puzzlement in his green-gray eyes. His shoulders crumpled.

Kate saw a small frightened man, quite different from the man who knocked on her door only minutes before, but she knew his bombast would return. She knew he would not only enlarge on her discourtesy while he was drinking beer with the men at Jackson's Tap on his way out of town, he would take pains to make it appear that he had put her in her place. Calculating the possible damage to her business, she concluded he would only add to the town gossip but could not hurt her solid reputation as a business woman. At least, he apparently hadn't heard about Gyorgy yet. As he hesitated at the door, she could see that he struggled to regain his composure.

The sound of footsteps on the stairs caused both of them to turn. Jean Burchett burst into the hallway. 'Well, I'll just be going,' Mr. Berringer murmured as he picked up his case of samples and fled down the steps.

'Kate! What was that all about?' Jean panted.

'Oh, Jean, I'm so glad you arrived when you did,' Kate smiled.

'What's been happening up here today? The whole town is talking. They say you had a Gypsy chap up here for an hour. Are you all right? What was he up to? Did he rob you? Did he touch you? Did you check everything? What did he say? Was it that really handsome one the clerks in Halley's were talking about? And who was that man that just left?'

Kate worked hard to control her emotions. She realized it was the first of a number of conversations she would have to try to explain the events of the afternoon. 'Come, Jean, let's have a cup of tea.' The familiarity of the kitchen calmed her. 'Who's tending the switchboard? Don't you have to be on duty now?'

'Oh, Mrs. Halley said she'd help me out any time I needed to get away—like now.'

'Well, I don't know where to start,' Kate began hesitantly, measuring her words.

She was reminded of a recent conversation she'd had with Jean who said she'd overheard the Rondevall girls and their mother talking about Kate after the church service at the Tingle Creek Lutheran Church. The Rondevall twins had been Kate's students when they lived out in the country before their father died.

Jean had begun breathlessly. 'One of the twins said she didn't understand why you didn't stay teaching. She said you were her favorite. And then the other one said teaching is certainly a more honorable profession for a single lady than being a photographer.' Jean hardly paused. 'Their mother—well, she said that everybody thought you would marry Benny Barlowe and wasn't it a shame that he's going to marry that woman from over near Walker. Mrs. Rondevall said Benny's mother's just sick about it. She says Mrs. Barlowe really likes you a lot, but then—well, then she called you mule-headed.' Jean stuck her nose up in the air in imitation of Mrs. Rondevall. 'I don't think that's so at all and you are my best friend so I should know. Anyway, I didn't want to listen to any more of that kind of talk so I left.'

Kate did not yet trust Jean with her deepest feelings, but she longed to talk to someone about Gyorgy. She missed the easy companionship she had had with Margaret Gilbert during their growing up years, living across the road from each other. Margaret, like most of Kate's school friends, was married now and moved away. None of Kate's friends in town had become a confidant. Not even Angus now. She knew she'd be hearing from him, though, just as soon as he heard about Gyorgy's visit, if for nothing more than to make sure she was all right.

Jean brought her mind back to the moment. 'Kate! You must tell me! What was he like?' Jean begged.

'Well, really—' Kate began, 'there's nothing to tell. Mr. Gyorgy merely wanted his picture taken and I took it. He was never anything but a gentleman, far more of a gentleman than that salesman who just left, I can tell you.'

'Oh my, Kate. I wish I'd seen him. Do you think he really will come back? Will you call me so I can see him? Can you show me his picture?'

Kate stood up without answering. She suddenly felt very tired. 'I'll call you tomorrow. I must get some supper, and then I have work to do this evening. Thanks for coming by.'

After Jean left, Kate sat down to sort things out. She knew that in many ways she would never be the same after meeting Gyorgy. Life would probably be easier if she were married—if for no other reason than to stop the idle manipulation of her options by people whose business it wasn't. Most people would say women were better off marrying—somebody, anybody—than being single.

Red Geraniums

She knew very well why she wouldn't agree to marry Benny Barlowe. She wasn't attracted to him, except as a friend. He was no better than most of the eligible bachelors in the county who mainly wanted to talk about corn prices or who would win the week-end softball game. She'd tried to talk his way, and she tried to carry on discussions about philosophy and world events, but she hadn't succeeded with either. She guessed her mother had spoiled her for finding a suitable man among the available ones.

* * *

That day, the day the Gypsies came to town, sparked a feeling in Kate that she could not identify. It wasn't like a sudden happiness on hearing good news or a sudden bright idea for solving a problem. Outwardly nothing had changed. She was no lighter on her feet, no prettier or smarter, and certainly no richer. Certainly her newfound celebrity status brought on by Gyorgy's visit was not welcome. There seemed to be no reasonable explanation for her excitement.

The feeling faded over the next few days, but in the darkroom a week later, it grew stronger again as she finally watched Gyorgy's image appear, first in the negative on the glass plate, and then in the positive on the new Velox paper. She alternately admired Gyorgy for being such a handsome man and congratulated herself for being such a competent photographer.

Usually she was anxious to see how well she captured her subjects, but surprisingly, she hadn't rushed to finish Gyorgy's pictures. It was almost as if she had been afraid of seeing him—or at least his image—again.

Now, satisfied with her results, she set about washing the chemicals from her hands—those hands so unlike her mother's slim, tapered fingers and wrists. She was surprised how often she thought about her mother, and the echo of her mother's voice had not left Kate when the sod covered her grave. She heard her mother's admonitions as surely as if her mother had just got word of Gyorgy's visit to the studio. 'Whatever were you thinking!' her voice demanded. 'Ladies don't entertain such men even for a minute. Why didn't you lock your door like the Sheriff said you should? You know you can't trust those Gypsies. I'll bet everyone's talking about your foolishness.' Even Kate's excitement at seeing Gyorgy's image could not blot out her mother's disapproval.

Sally Salisbury Stoddard

'So he said he wanted his picture taken. Did he pay you anything in advance? How do you know he'll come back for that picture, let alone pay you if he does? Fix your kettles? Ha. We'll just see.' Kate paused at the wash basin as this imagined tirade from her mother resonated in her mind. She wanted to remind her mother that, after all, her father had invited Gypsies right into their house. But she could not. She hung her head as if her actions were something to be ashamed of and scrubbed harder at her fingernails with the lye soap she and Lizzie made the previous summer.

As her fingers reddened with rubbing, her heart stopped pounding and she looked up at the handsome portrait of Gyorgy hanging to dry. She couldn't help but smile as the professional photographer in her envisioned the picture mounted on a rectangle of gray photomount board bearing the name 'MacLean Studio, Tingle Creek, Nebraska,' imprinted in gold in the lower left-hand corner. Gyorgy's remarkable looks would have been hard for any photographer to spoil, but she cocked her head to one side, studied the picture, and tilted it back the other way, satisfied that she had captured a remarkable likeness of the real Gyorgy.

Her sense of the appropriate made her wish that he had been wearing a finely tailored suit and a fashionable shirt with a high collar instead of the frumpy woolen suit and coarse, collarless shirt he wore. Why, he would pass for the finest, most respected gentleman in any town if he dressed the way she thought he ought to be dressed, given the extravagance of his good looks. She blushed at the thought.

No matter what her mother might have said, Kate never questioned whether Gyorgy would be back. She was sure he would be, but in case she was wrong, she had his picture to remember him by—although she knew that, even without it, she could never forget him. As she left the studio, it occurred to her that she had no idea when Gypsy caravans might be expected to come through town, and she could not have said whether the same *kumpania* came each time so she couldn't guess when he might come again. She just knew she wanted to see him again though her desire made no sense.

Seeing his image appear in her dark room heightened a sense of urgency in Kate which had begun about the time of her mother's death. Her breakfast of Mr. Sedlow's fresh sausage with eggs seemed irrelevant. 'My goodness,' she thought, 'I'm 35 and my life is more than half over!' The thought of her mortality made her pause as she buttered her toast. With her knife poised in the air, she turned it as if to emphasize this point to an unseen interlocutor. 'My problem,' she went on, 'is that I really want to be like other women. I want to have a husband. I want to have children, but not with just any man. And no, Gyorgy can't be that man. He can't! But, still...'

She poured her first cup of tea and continued pondering her status. She couldn't have children without being married. Indeed, if she didn't have children soon, she wouldn't be able to have them at all. She sighed, knowing that women without children were often regarded as less than human. She'd even read that they were turned out of the community in some societies. Kate shuddered.

Kate and Jean had discussed the problem once, in a shallow way. It seemed too frightening for Jean to talk about. 'Well, once I brought this up with Angus and Lizzie,' Kate had said to Jean, 'and all they could think to say was I should have married Benny Barlowe. Good lord, Jean, if my status in life depended on that man, I'd choose to be an outcaste, thank you.'

'Oh, Kate, don't say that.'

'Don't say what? Don't say that I think Benny Barlowe was less than a good catch?'

'You know very well what I mean, Kate. Anyway, I'm not going to get married until I'm good and ready.' Kate had already heard Jean's tales of her boy friends. They were few and never stayed around long. Folks in town considered Jean to be rather homely with ears too big and chin too pointed, but Kate thought she would make some farmer a good wife, if only she wouldn't talk so much. Her man would probably choose to spend a lot of time in the barn. Nevertheless, Kate felt sorry for Jean because she had no ambition beyond marriage. True, Kate's life lacked definition, but she found great satisfaction in her work. She wondered if she would want to leave the studio even if she did marry.

She picked up Leland's book with a new sense of excitement. She had borrowed the book from the Pedersens long before Gyorgy came to the studio. She had always liked visiting with Mr. and Mrs. Pedersen. Their conversations ranged from the Spanish-American War to Theodore Roosevelt's naturalist interests to Carrie Nation's antics in Kansas. Now she wanted to talk about Gypsies and felt she couldn't bring up the topic even with the Pedersens. She had been fascinated to learn that Gypsies originated in India. That, she surmised, would account for Gyorgy's swarthiness and his sparkling dark eyes.

She emptied her tea cup, put the book down, rose slowly from the chair, pulled on the smock she wore in the studio, and carried her dishes to the enamel basin where she washed them. Then she walked across the hall to the studio.

In the dim light, she thought she saw something white under the door at the top of the stairs. She bent over and tugged at the corner of an envelope. Her name was on the outside. She slipped it into her smock pocket and opened the studio door. Closing it behind her, she moved across the room to the light of the window. Hastily, she tore open the white envelope. Inside was a sheet of paper with some poetry. She read down the page and, as she read, her face felt warm and she put her hand to her cheek. She quickly sat on the nearest chair.

Was this a joke? She hoped not because the poem was too nice, but who could or would have written such a verse? Oh, there were many poems in her grade school autograph book, some silly, some sentimental, some beautiful, but none directed specifically to her. Ah! Maybe, if she found her old autograph book, just maybe, she would recognize the poet's handwriting, but it was getting late. Sleuthing in the autograph book would have to wait until evening.

That night as soon as the pans were washed and put away, she went to her wardrobe and pulled a box off the shelf. All her precious mementoes were stored in a very pretty box someone had given her mother. Inside, she immediately found the autograph book. It had a rather plain cover compared to those of some of her friends, but still the forest green cover with the gold emblem of a quill pen and ink bottle was quite nice. She leafed through it, alternately smiling and laughing.

There was one verse that used to make her blush, but she'd now outgrown that. It was one Benny wrote in her book, as well as in some other girls'. She had been tempted to cut out that page but on the reverse side there was a nice poem from her friend Mildred Manton and she couldn't do it. Mildred's poem was cleverly couched to fit in with their school lessons and she wanted to preserve it.

> The verb 'I love', I learned at school.
> 'Thou lovest' follows next in rule;
> 'We love' let us say together, proving
> Thus we love each other.

Poor Mildred died in childbirth a couple of years back. No, she would not erase this token of her friendship. Benny's stupid poem would remain. At least she could now laugh at it.

> I love you sincerely, I love you almighty
> I wish my pyjamas were next to your nightie.
> Don't get excited and don't be misled
> I mean on the clothes line and not in bed!

She leafed on through the little book but did not find the tell-tale handwriting. She re-read the poem delivered under her door, checking the slant of the penmanship, the curls on the letters, and the little drawing of a spring violet in colored pencil. She wished that, in fact, the writer had meant it—and meant it just for her—but she had no hope that it was so. But why would someone write it?

She tucked the poem back in its envelope and put it in the box with the autograph book. Maybe the writer—if indeed it was a man—would identify himself someday. She hoped so and didn't hope so, since he didn't seem willing to come forth. She was about to close the box, but decided to reread the sweet poetry once more.

> Miss Kate, you are my love.
> Your eyes of blue are from above.
> The pink of your blush
> Can cause me to flush.
> I long to hold you tight
> And kiss your lips so right.
> Will you ever look at me?
> Alas, I'm afraid it shall never be.

Who would have slipped this sweet verse under her door without her hearing footsteps on the stairs? Would she ever know? She sighed, smoothed the letter, laid it on top of the autograph book, closed the box, and returned it to her cupboard.

* * *

Each work day, Kate arose, checked the studio, worked with clients or processed pictures in the darkroom, kept her account books at the secretary she'd recently purchased, cooked and ate her meals, and read whatever time she had left. There was little time for community activities, but she learned from her customers—and Jean—who was getting married, who was having a baby, who was running for school board, and other vital statistics of the town. Kate prided herself that she seldom asked questions. People just liked to talk and she provided a convenient ear much as Bart Biggs, the barber, did.

She seldom went to the farm on Sundays. Angus and Lizzie had their own lives so she didn't feel as close to them as she had earlier. Even so, she had developed a certain fondness for Lizzie. It was obvious that Angus loved Lizzie and the children so Kate was content. She did enjoy the boys and Netta when she went to the farm. They were bright and well-behaved, for the most part, and seemed to relish her attention. It gave her great pleasure to spend odd hours looking over the books at the drug store to find ones suitable for children.

It was an ordinary kind of life, she thought. At least, that is what Kate's life was like before Gyorgy came. Then one day at Halley's Department Store, she heard Mrs. Burt and Mrs. Griesen in the far aisle talking about her. Kate's cheeks reddened. The women evidently had not seen her in the corner, hidden by displays of enameled canning kettles and cast iron skillets. 'Well, that's right,' Mrs. Burt was saying. 'If Kate MacLean had just run down the stairs when that Gypsy chap came. . .' The snap of the pillow case she was examining muffled the rest of her remarks.

Mrs. Griesen's voice came through clearly as she faced in Kate's direction. 'If she'd just stayed in her teaching job at Long's Creek, none of this would have happened, or even could have happened. It's just not proper for a woman to be alone with a man in a compromising situation—even if nothing happens. It isn't even safe. She was just lucky—especially with a Gypsy. I always say there's a place for women in this world, and they ought to stay in it for their own good. Why in the world she thought she could run a photography studio like a man is beyond me. Uh, Mabel, what do you think of this embroidery pattern with the cute ducklings?'

The more Kate heard, the more she wished she were thin enough to slip out of the store without being seen. She knew that if she emerged, her fair skin flushed, they would know she had overheard their remarks about her. She didn't want to hear any more. She tried to concentrate on the wares before her, but their voices insisted their way into her consciousness.

Kate didn't know Mrs. Burt very well, but she had certainly been cordial when they met on social occasions. She knew Mrs. Burt had grown up on a farm, married a local farmer, and moved to town three years ago because of Mr. Burt's bad neuralgia. Kate was at least willing to believe she meant no harm by her judgment.

On the other hand, Kate hardly knew Mrs. Griesen at all. She lived on the north edge of town in a big house her husband had built for her twenty years ago. She was the envy of every woman in the area because of the house, but Jean Burchett said Mrs. Griesen had few friends. They were, after all, Catholic and seldom attended social functions in town because their children attended the Catholic school in St. Mary, seven miles north and a half mile west. It angered Kate that someone who knew her as little as this woman did would think she was more capable of making decisions for Kate's life than Kate was. She seethed, wondering what she would hear next.

'It's all right, but I think this basket of roses is prettier than those ducklings. Depends on whatcha want, I guess. If you made the roses red and pink, it would look quite beautiful. Well, as you were saying about a woman's place, though—y're right.' Mrs. Burt tried hard to emulate the speech of the educated church women she knew in town, but she couldn't carry it off consistently. 'I was always glad t'have a man in my life—'n' I got a good 'un. If Kate MacLean'd just a'married Benny Barlowe, all 'er problems would'a been solved. She wouldn'a had to teach school no more and certainly not been in a dangerous business. She'd a had Benny to pertect her.'

Mr. Halley, a tall, lean man in a proper suit with fashionable lapels and starched collar, could see over most of the merchandise displays and knew who was in his store from moment to moment—even Gypsies. He sidled up to the women and whispered, 'Ladies, please keep your voices down. Miss MacLean is buying a gem pan, and I wouldn't want her to hear you.'

The two women muffled a choking sound. Mrs. Burt looked at the floor. 'Oh, I'm so sorry, Mr. Halley,' breathed Mrs. Griesen at the reprimand. Both women abruptly dropped the pillow cases without refolding them. Shielding their faces with their gloved hands as best they could, they edged toward the door without saying another word and slipped out the door.

Mr. Halley walked stiffly over to where Kate stood. She pretended to study the pans carefully, head bent forward so that only the wisps of hair on the back of her neck greeted him. 'Now, Miss MacLean, you just don't worry about those two women. I, for one, believe you are a fine artist with the camera, finer than any man could be. Why, just the other day, Mrs. Halley was saying she's never seen such beautiful pictures as you take. You know that we're happy to have you in the business community, even if it is a bit unusual to have a woman doing this work.' His usual slow speech habit quickened to hide his embarrassment for her. 'Now, did you have in mind a gem pan for six muffins or twelve?'

'I just can't decide,' Kate said. 'I guess I'll have to come back some other day.' She turned to face him, her voice quieter than usual. 'Thank you. I must get back to my work. Good day.'

'Good day, Miss MacLean.'

Overhearing Mrs. Burt and Mrs. Griesen had shaken her confidence in herself more than a slacking off of her business might have done. Emerging onto the street, she deftly skirted the men sitting on the bench in front of the hardware store and, head down, walked west to the drug store and went in. She kept her eye out for other customers that might be in the store. 'May I help you, Miss MacLean?' Joe Jenkins called from behind the counter.

'No, no.' She searched for an excuse and her eye lit on the book and magazine counter. 'I just wondered what new books might have come in. You said there might be some coming.'

'Well, nothing came in the box we picked up at the depot yesterday. I've put all of those things away already. Sorry, Miss MacLean. Shall I let you know if they come in this afternoon?'

'Oh, that won't be necessary. I'll just drop by again, thank you.' Kate's breathing had almost returned to normal and she felt it was safe to return home.

* * *

Some weeks later, the phone rang early one morning before Kate was up and about. It was Jean Burchett, bursting with news. 'Kate!' she shouted into the phone. 'Guess what!' Jean's voice exploded with excitement. 'I've

Red Geraniums

just got to tell somebody! Someone left a foundling on the Simpsons' doorstep!' Certainly a foundling left on someone's doorstep was a rare occurrence, but such an event in a small town like Tingle Creek took on enormous proportions. Kate would have expected Jean's outburst, but Kate couldn't explain her own, unvoiced excitement at hearing the news.

As the story spilled out, Jean said she hadn't gone to bed yet when she had a call from Mr. Simpson to plug him in to the Sheriff. 'Get me Butch Jamieson, Miss Burchett! I've got a foundling here!' Jean said he sounded almost triumphant.

'"Right away, Mr. Simpson," I said. "Uh-oh. I see the lamp is out in their living room. They must've gone to bed, but don't hang up. I'll keep ringing. It might take Mr. Jamieson awhile to get to the phone,"' reported Jean, who reveled in her status as conveyor of town happenings. As Jean repeated this conversation with Mr. Simpson, she added, 'Sure enough, Kate, I listened in and Mr. Jamieson sounded real sleepy, but he told Mr. Simpson he'd be right there, and I saw him leave the house no more'n five minutes later. Mr. Simpson called Doc Longstreet, too, and he said he'd hightail it to the Simpsons as fast as he could.'

As Kate listened to Jean tell the improbable tale, she felt a strong urge to see this baby, to hold him, to rock him gently in her grandmother's sewing rocker. By nine in the morning, Kate was sure that the whole town knew about the baby boy found at the Simpsons.

By that evening, Kate had heard Mr. Simpson's story from Lizzie out in the country at ten o'clock and from Bill Sedlow downstairs in the meat market when she went to buy some neckbones for soup at eleven o'clock. Mrs. Pedersen dropped by the studio late in the afternoon. 'Oh, my, Kate, have you heard?'

'I assume you're talking about the foundling at the Simpsons, aren't you?' Kate said.

'Well, yes. I dropped by to see the baby just before noon. You really ought to go see the little one for yourself.' Mrs. Pedersen said that Mrs. Simpson was busy all day with the parade of curious townspeople, giving them coffee and her special doughnuts. 'You know, I can't help wondering why the Simpsons.' Kate, too, had wondered about that. The Simpsons were old—probably in their sixties, she thought.

Mrs. Pedersen went on, 'It wasn't that they wouldn't take good care of the little one. In fact, I asked if they intended to keep him. Mrs. Simpson just laughed and said probably not. She said Rev. and Mrs. Barton might be interested—not having kids of their own and all, but since nobody knows what kind of family he came from, they don't think it'd be a good idea to ask for him. I expect he's a little bastard child and you know how skittish folks are about them.

Kate was stunned. 'Oh, Mrs. Pedersen, how could anyone not want an innocent little baby? He couldn't help what his folks did. I wouldn't mind adopting the little fellow myself,' she blurted out and then wished she'd held her tongue.

'Well, but of course, you couldn't adopt him.' Mrs. Pedersen didn't need to add, 'because you're not married.' Kate was sure she would be considered unfit simply because there was no man in her household. Mrs. Pedersen went on hastily, 'I don't know. I think it would be hard to raise a child you didn't know anything about. Inheritance is pretty important, you know—especially if the child doesn't look like anyone in the family. And what if it was a Catholic child? No, in a case like this, you just don't know what you're getting. Well, I'd best get home to make supper. It's always good to see you, Kate.'

After Mrs. Pedersen left, Kate realized she wanted more than anything to see this baby—Catholic or not. Just imagine! An abandoned child. Who could just leave a child to strangers like that? As much as she wanted to see the foundling, Kate knew it would not be as easy as simply knocking on the Simpsons' door. She could adjust her own schedule in the morning, but a housewife would be busy renewing and refreshing the appearance of the house and its occupants, doing the laundry and beating the rugs and baking the bread. No self-respecting housewife would be ready for guests in the mornings.

Kate decided to call around three in the afternoon or early evening. It was several days though before she had enough time free for the visit. She called Jean Burchett each morning, 'Jean, have you heard anything new about the baby left at the Simpsons?'

'No, I haven't. I did stop by once, but I'm too busy to go very often. Um . . .' Jean hesitated, as if choosing her words carefully, and then went on. 'My, but he's a sweet baby. Seeing him makes me wish I were married so I could have a baby like him.' She sighed. 'I wonder if I ever will.'

'Oh, of course, you will. Jean, do you think maybe I should offer to take a picture of the baby? I thought maybe the Simpsons might like one to remember him by after he's adopted.'

'I don't know, Kate. Oops, I've got another call here. Bye.'

Kate went about her appointments and her darkroom work with a new sense of purpose. She treated her clients with added deference in case they might be influential in the child's fate. Looking through the lens of the camera, she said, 'Why, Mr. Frederickson, you look very distinguished today.' Mrs. Frederickson, supervising the sitting from a stool off to the side, beamed and said, 'Why thank you, Miss MacLean. He does, doesn't he?' Kate told Albert Payne, the local Justice of the Peace, that she wouldn't charge for his portrait—professional courtesy, she said.

Finally, on Thursday afternoon just at tea time, she was free. In fact, she hurried old Mr. and Mrs. Danner out the door a bit sooner than might have been considered proper, but she hoped her parting smile and wave would make up for her lapse of manners.

Once they started down the stairs, Kate went directly to her apartment. She needed to hurry if she were to arrive at the Simpsons early enough so that her visit would not disrupt Mrs. Simpson's preparations for supper. Passing the small square mirror that hung next to the east window in the kitchen, Kate was astonished to see how frazzled she looked. Working under the black cloth tousled her hair no matter how tightly she combed and pinned it. Certainly she must not arrive at the Simpsons looking disheveled, but readying herself for the visit would take longer than she planned. Her frown in the mirror plainly showed irritation at the delay.

She heard her mother's voice reminding her, 'Now, Katie Jane, I've said it more than once—patience is a virtue and we women have to learn that if we're to be happy in this life.' Well, Kate was tired of being patient. As her irritation rose, she realized that, first of all, she had better calm down. Five minutes. She would make herself sit down for five minutes.

She walked back to the studio and edged herself into the red velvet chair, Gyorgy's chair. Without moving it closer to the north windows, she could only see the top of the elaborate facade on the bank building catty corner across the street. She tried to concentrate first on its lettering

Farmers State Bank
1863

and then on the symmetrical fleur de lis reliefs painted in muted pastels on either side. Instead, her mind kept wandering to the baby left on the Simpsons' porch.

It's odd, she thought; no one has given him even a temporary name. Everyone she talked to just called him 'the baby'. She pondered the question of an appropriate name. If he were my baby... if he were my baby... Suddenly she spoke out loud with great surety, 'I'd call him Alec. I like that name,' and the sound of her voice startled her for an instant. 'It would be nice to call him Alec Angus,' she thought. Yes,' she decided, 'I'll name him Alec Angus. Why Alec could stay right here in the studio with me. He would provide a source of amusement for the children who come in.'

Just thinking about 'the baby' as Alec Angus made her jump up and rush to her bedroom where she poured some water into the white porcelain basin from the matching pitcher with the dogwood blossoms on it. She washed her face in the cool water and pulled out a tortoise shell comb to smooth the stray hairs, until she was satisfied that she was presentable. Finally, she felt calm enough to walk the three blocks to the Simpsons'. She closed the door behind her and, head up, descended the stairs to the board walk. A thin haze masked the midafternoon sun as she went west past Mr. Pedersen's law office before crossing the street to the square.

It never occurred to Kate that her interest in the child would seem odd to townspeople. After all, everyone she'd talked to had dropped by the Simpsons since that eventful evening. Oblivious to all but her compelling need to see the baby, her anticipation grew with every step. She struggled to keep her face impassive and her step unhurried. At last, she knocked on the Simpsons' door.

* * *

Mrs. Simpson answered the door with the baby in her arms, snugly wrapped so his head was partially hidden by the blanket. 'Why, Miss MacLean, how nice to see you! I 'spect you've heard about this little guy, haven't you? Well, come on in. We were just sittin' down to a cup a'tea, the mister and I. Do have a seat. Here, you take the baby and I'll put on a fresh pot of water.' She thrust the baby into Kate's arms even before she had a chance to deposit her handbag and sit down.

'Do sit down, Miss MacLean—right over there,' said Mr. Simpson, pointing to a heavy wooden rocker near the door to the hall. 'A baby gets kinda heavy to hold after you've stood up awhile. But then I guess you're young yet. Heh. Heh.' Then he added, as if to apologize, 'This here chair by the window is the missus'—so she can see folks coming and going to town.' Mr. Simpson puffed on his cigar and tested the outer limits of the platform rocker opposite Mrs. Simpson's where he, too, could look out, but apparently that wasn't worth mentioning.

'Why thank you, Mr. Simpson. I expect you're pretty tired after having a baby in the house all of a sudden. Are you enjoying him?'

'Well, I can't say I am and I can't say I'm not. The missus mostly sees to him. He's a bit too small to enjoy, I guess. Mostly acts like a baby.'

Gently touching the baby's face and his hair without awakening him, Kate ventured, 'Can you tell me just what happened, Mr. Simpson?'

'Well, sure, I was sittin' in the platform rocker readin' my Bible—like I do ever' night—' he said. 'Danged if I didn't hear this crying—a sort of whimper and then a loud bawling. The Missus had gone to bed an' I thought maybe our old tomcat had got himself a rabbit—you know how they can scream when they get caught. Anyway, when the crying didn't let up, I got up to see what was happening. I figured a rabbit would've been dead by then.

'The noise seemed to be coming from the front porch—you know, the enclosed one where you just came in. I opened the front door and just inside the porch door there was this laundry basket just a-jigglin'! I touched the basket and looked inside. The light wasn't ver' good but imagine my surprise to see a baby! Anyway, the crying stopped a bit. Maybe he was surprised at seeing me! That little feller looked up at me with the biggest, bluest eyes you ever seen—I could just barely see by the street light. We looked at each other for a minute, but then that little feller just started bellerin' again. Well, I hollered for the Missus to get up. I never was much good with these little guys myself.

'Mabel—she come running out. I 'spect she thought I was half kilt the way I yelled at her. "Well, I never—" she said when she saw what was in that basket. You know how she is with kids. She just picked up that little guy and patted him on the tummy and he shut up and I swear he smiled. Magic touch, I always said. Yup, my Mabel has a magic touch with kids. They love 'er.

'Well, she just went to her motherin' like there hadn't been no forty years in between. I carried the basket into the house while Mabel carried the baby on her shoulder, pattin' and talkin' all the time so the baby just fell asleep, tired out by then, I guess. I called Butch Jamieson and the Doc.

Then I got my lantern—the one I used in the barn when we lived on the farm—and I went searching the neighborhood for the baby's mother.'

Mr. Simpson blew his nose loudly into a red kerchief and went on. 'When the Sheriff come by, he said he was sure they'd find the mother all right—can't hardly hide being in a family-way, can you? Do you suppose the mother's someone we know? I don't know anybody's been expecting, do you? I mean anybody that couldn't or wouldn't keep a baby . . . It's a pity, but some girls get in that way, you know. Ought t'be ashamed a themselves. Don't you think so, Miss MacLean?'

The fact that Mr. Simpson would condemn the mother without knowing her—or anything about her—struck Kate as being somewhat unkind, but she said nothing.

'Anyway,' Mrs. Simpson came into the room and took up the story, 'anyway, she must've cared a lot. Do you know, she made a whole outfit for this baby! It was right there in the bottom of the basket.' Mrs. Simpson said she didn't even have to hunt up diapers. 'And there was this little sailor suit. It was so sweet. Such fine stitching. My, how could she give up such a precious bundle as this? And that little boy's so healthy! Not a puny little thing like you might expect.' Mrs. Simpson sighed. 'Well, I gave him some milk—the mother even left a baby bottle—and he just drank it right down. Doc Longstreet says he's never seen a healthier infant. My, my!'

Kate asked Mrs. Simpson if they planned to keep the baby since it seemed like the mother must have wanted them to have him. Mrs. Simpson said, 'Probably not. We don't have any blue eyes in our family. Guess he wouldn't match!' Then she just laughed and laughed and said, 'Sides, we're gettin' kinda old for this kind of thing—much as I love my grandchildren, it wouldn't be fair to a young 'un to have us all the time. Mrs. Barton said she and the Reverend might be interested—not having kids of their own and all, but since nobody knows what kind of family he come from, they don't think it'd be a good idea. Nope, don't know who'll get 'im. I expect he's a little bastard child and you know how skittish folks is about them.'

Kate was stunned. 'Oh, Mrs. Simpson, how could anyone not want a tiny baby?'

'Well, I don't know. I think it would be hard to raise a child you didn't know anything about. Inheritance is pretty important, you know—specially if the child don't look like anyone in the family. And what if it was a Catholic child? In a case like this, you just don't know what you're getting.'

'But, Mrs. Simpson, a baby is innocent of all that. He couldn't help what his folks did. And some legitimate kids turn out pretty terrible, after all. I, for one, wouldn't care. I wouldn't mind adopting the little fellow myself,' she blurted out and then wished she'd held her tongue.

'But, of course, you couldn't adopt him,' Mrs. Simpson declared, 'since you ain't married.' She went on hastily, 'Not that you wouldn't make a good mother. You certainly would! And when you get married you'll probably have a whole passel of 'em.' Kate's heart sank. Of course, she would be considered an unfit mother simply because there was no man in her household.

Kate pulled the blanket back so she could better see the baby's face and hair. She was surprised at his thick mop of black hair. His cheeks were perfectly sculpted, or so Kate thought as she stroked them. His tiny lashes lay upturned on his cheeks as he slept. It occurred to her that Mrs. Simpson's remark about his blue eyes didn't make sense since she'd heard that babies' eyes often changed color after the first few months.

Mrs. Simpson left to get tea for Kate. She set the cup on the table beside Kate's chair. 'My, ain't he a pretty baby, Miss MacLean? Looks like a Gypsy in the making!' She laughed, but suddenly stopped as she caught a look from Mr. Simpson. She hurried past her remark as if to erase it. 'I guess you haven't had much experience with babies yet—'cept Angus and Lizzie's children. My, such well behaved children. I seen 'em in church. Do you want me to take him? I can just put him in his basket over there. He mostly eats and sleeps.'

Kate demurred. 'No, thank you, Mrs. Simpson. I'm just admiring his handsome face.'

'He's a beautiful baby, ain't he? And so good. Here, have a cup of tea. Do you use milk and sugar? I'll just add some. And here, have some of my sugar cookies. My children and grandchildren always say I make the best. Now I'm getting older, I don't make 'em as often, but they still want me to make 'em ever' time they come home. Hope you like 'em. Oh, but it's not going to be easy to drink tea holding him. Here—let me take him.' Mrs. Simpson made a move toward Kate's chair.

'Oh, no, no. I can just put my saucer on the table. No, no, I like holding him. We're just starting to get acquainted, aren't we?' The baby looked up at her very solemnly as if he had understood what she said and was assessing her as a potential mother. Very quickly the look of contentment twisted into a whimper and his tiny face turned toward the fullness of her breast, his mouth imitating feeding movements. The strange feel of the tucked shirt made his whimper turn into a full-blown howl. His mouthing her blouse embarrassed Kate and she put him on her shoulder and patted his back, but he would not be comforted.

'Oh, Miss MacLean, it's time for him to eat. Just wait. I'll warm up a bottle. Why, you know, his mother even left a bottle in the basket with him—guess I said that before, didn't I? I 'spect you've heard the story, haven't you?' Mrs. Simpson hurried to the kitchen.

Kate spoke in a louder than normal voice so she could be heard in the kitchen above his cries. 'Why, yes, Mrs. Simpson, I have. Is there any news on finding the baby's mother?'

'No,' came a voice from the room beyond, and Mrs. Simpson appeared at the door. 'The sheriff says he can't figure it out and nobody else can either. If it was someone in the neighborhood here, we'd all know, don't ya think? Must've been someone from outside just passing through, but why at our house? Our house ain't so fancy as some. Here, let me take him, Miss MacLean. He gets kinda messy when he feeds sometimes.'

'Oh, no, no. I'd like to give him his bottle. You just sit down and rest now. I think you've had some very full days here, what with having a baby plopped down in your lap, so to speak. I've watched Lizzie often enough.' She and Mrs. Simpson both knew that could hardly be counted as a lesson since Lizzie didn't bottlefeed her children.

'All right, Miss MacLean, if you're sure it's all right . . .' Mrs. Simpson sat heavily on the cushions in the wooden rocker across from Mr. Simpson at the front window. She sighed deeply, looking exhausted. With a few pushes of her feet in her crocheted slippers, the rocking motion put her fast asleep. Kate glanced over to see that Mr. Simpson's head had long since lopped onto his right shoulder and the forward-back motion of his platform rocker had ceased.

The baby made slurping noises with his mouth as he gulped the milk from the bottle. Kate smiled. It was all too perfect. She was, for all practical purposes, alone with this baby who so captured her imagination and now her heart. The weight of his head felt good on the crook of her left arm and his warmth suffused her with a glow, not unlike that of a birth mother cradling her infant. Even his baby-sweet smell affected her like heady incense.

Red Geraniums

She rocked gently as he nursed, admiring his dark hair and his dainty eyebrows. He frowned ever so slightly and she smiled indulgently. He was hers—Alec Angus. She had someone to love, someone who needed her nurturing, someone to return her love. Their closeness completed the circle that defines womanhood.

She began to think about the little suit she would make for Alec to wear the first day of school. It would be navy blue, a practical color for a little boy with knickers and knee socks. She pictured him in the frosted glass of the camera, grinning upside down. But then she was overcome with sadness to think he would leave her for even a few hours a day. Her visualization went on, honed by her photographic imagination, and she brightened at the thought of meeting him at the schoolyard gate at the end of the day, scooping him up in her arms and kissing him—yes, kissing him in front of all the other children—and he would be so glad to see her he wouldn't mind.

Suddenly, the baby coughed and choked and a volley of partially digested milk soaked the crispness of her shirtwaist. She was immobilized, not knowing whether to take care of her own needs or the baby's first. Mrs. Simpson's feet slammed to the floor and she moved to make amends for Kate's predicament. 'Oh, I'm so sorry, Miss MacLean. I'm so sorry.' She grabbed the baby, bawling loudly. 'Here, Harold, you take the baby. I'll help Miss MacLean with her shirtwaist. Oh, my, my, that milk can stain.' She ran to the kitchen to get a wet cloth.

Kate protested, jolted by the threat of losing him. 'Oh, he's all right, Mrs. Simpson. I mean, I'm all right. I mean, we're just fine. I'll just . . . No, no, Mrs. Simpson, it's quite all right. It'll be all right. I hope the baby is all right. I hope I didn't do anything to the baby.' Her sense of shame at failing the baby, at failing such a simple, motherly task was so great she stood up abruptly, brushing Mrs. Simpson's damp cloth aside. 'I—I—he seemed to be drinking so well.'

'Oh, no, Miss MacLean, he's just fine. He's done that ever since he came. Lots of babies have colic and I 'spect one who's lost his mother has lots to be colicky about. Now you just never mind. I 'preciate you taking 'im off my hands a bit. Why, when you have your own, you'll just know about these things.'

Kate bent to retrieve her handbag. 'Oh, it's late. I really must let you get on with your supper. Thank you for letting me see the baby.' Embarrassed, disappointed, discouraged, and sad, Kate blinked quickly to hide her tears and tried to salvage what dignity she could. 'Good day, Mr. Simpson. Good day, Mrs. Simpson. Your children are right—your sugar cookies are the best,' she added as she walked across the room and kissed the baby on his soft spot. It was, she knew, a good-bye kiss. Clutching her handbag to her bosom to cover the milk stain, she edged her way out of the room as inconspicuously as possible and went out the front door.

* * *

That night was torture as Kate lived and relived the events at the Simpsons. She slept fitfully, knowing the next day would be very difficult. She had a full set of appointments and canceling them was out of the question. She felt humiliated that she didn't seem fit to be a mother. Nevertheless, holding little Alec Angus in her arms had made her want more than ever to have a child of her own.

As she ate her breakfast, she tried to reconstruct what happened the night before, to find something in it that was good, but she was alternately defensive and ashamed and aggrieved. She reminded herself that even the most experienced mother had been spit on by a baby. Why should anyone care? They probably didn't, she reasoned and told herself it was all in her mind. Finally, she dried her tears and set her jaw, determined to go about her life and business as usual.

No matter what, she knew she had been foolish to become emotionally attached to this child on whom she had no claim and for whom she had no responsibility. Still, she wanted a child; the baby wanted a mother. What could be more selfish than denying her her right to be a mother, to raise this child with love and discipline and good humor? She didn't care whether he was born of a Catholic mother, that his eyes might not match hers, that his own mother abandoned him. She was sure she could be a good mother, but she was equally sure she would never be given the chance as along as she remained single.

She wanted to talk to Angus about the doorstep baby, Angus who could always fix what was broken. And wasn't she broken now? But she couldn't admit her failure, even to him.

She had no choice but to go on about the business of being a photographer. After a full day with nothing untoward happening—not even a phone call from Jean, she readied herself for bed. Donning her nightgown, she slowly tied the narrow satin ribbon at the neck. She lay down on the goose feather mattress waiting for the breeze from the south window to swirl over her, tickling the high spots of her prone figure, before passing out the west window. The heat of the day had settled into the room like an unwelcome guest ignoring hints to leave, and it was some time before a succession of breezes allowed her body to cool and her mind to rest.

Arising at five, her nightgown clinging to her moist skin, Kate padded into the studio to sit for awhile in Gyorgy's chair. Perhaps he, too, had been an illusion like her hopes of motherhood. Gradually the sun lit the bank facade across the street. Out of her musing one of the Psalms came to her, 'Weeping endureth the night, but joy cometh on the morrow.' She wanted to believe it. She was ready for the joy. She hoped the church fathers did know something about wisdom after all.

Once fully awake, Kate hurried back to her bedroom and went directly to her wardrobe next to her bed. She wondered how Mr. and Mrs. Shortt had ever fit the possessions of two people into the cramped space. Inside the wardrobe hung Kate's shirtwaists of cotton and silk and the single taffeta shirtwaist that matched one of her three skirts. Here also hung two full-length dresses left from her teaching days, one a challis, the other a black silk shantung saved mostly for funerals.

On a shelf over the hanging rod was a hat box covered with pale pink wallpaper dusted with polka dots and red roses arrayed in diagonal rows. A wide satin ribbon of pale blue hugged the box with an enormous bow on the top. The hat box had been a gift from her Aunt Isabel. It held her three hats, two very simple black ones and a third that was frivolous made of a deep purple velvet with a rusching of purple lace net encircling the crown and an edging of bright pink satin encircling the brim. Over the right ear, was an enormous pink satin rose. Kate had bought the hat with the first money she earned in the studio, but she had only worn it once. Maybe she would wear it at her wedding, she thought ruefully.

Beside the hat box two flat paste-board boxes held her table linen and napkins and a lacy white apron made by her by Grandmother MacLean in Wisconsin. Kate loved it, but had no occasion to wear it. She sometimes took the box from the shelf just to feel the fineness of the hand-knitted lace that edged the hem and the pocket and sighed, thinking how lovely it would be to wear it to serve dinner guests without first having to cook the meal.

Sally Salisbury Stoddard

Now Kate chose a brown cotton tucked shirtwaist to wear with her tan skirt that day. And then, in afterthought, she lifted the flat boxes just enough to pull out a slim rectangular package wrapped in brown paper lying unobtrusively under their bulk. She handled the rough brown paper as if it were very fragile. Furtively she looked over her shoulder to make sure she was alone and even glanced out the west window across the roof of the adjoining building. Laying the packet on the bed, she carefully opened it. There before her lay Gyorgy's pictures.

It was perhaps a strange place to store them, she told herself again. She didn't know why she felt the need to separate Gyorgy's pictures from the pictures of farmers and babies and Rev. Barton that she usually kept in the cupboard in the studio. Somehow she didn't think Gyorgy would be quite comfortable in the company of those others. Here, she thought, he would be safe from prying eyes, though she had no reason to think anyone had or even could go through her file of finished pictures.

Looking at Gyorgy's pictures now, she tipped her head to one side and smiled. Just imagine what her family would say if they could see him now! She looked again at the three finished pictures, one a portrait, one seated and one standing. She noted the light sculpting the planes of Gyorgy's face, the nose arcing above a thick mustache, the deepset, dark eyes complemented by the coarse black eyebrows.

She remembered how his hands had touched hers as he left that day. They were strong hands, obviously having known hard work, but they were kind, too. She estimated that had been almost five months ago and caught her breath. That meant Gyorgy might come back most any day now.

She caught herself wanting to make him appear in the flesh at that very moment and her whole body reacted with a warm shiver, centering somewhere below the row of tiny buttons down the front of her shirtwaist. Suddenly she grabbed up the three pictures and re-wrapped them, carefully placing them in the paste-board boxes once again. She slammed the doors of the wardrobe and stood with her back to it as if Gyorgy might, in fact, emerge from its depths.

* * *

Kate's habit of reading while she ate her meals was one she never wanted to break. She was most appreciative of the Pedersen's generosity in loaning their books. Not only could they afford more expensive books than Kate could, but each time she returned one, she could count on being invited for a cup of coffee or tea so she could discuss the book with them.

There were few people in the area who read the kind of books the Pedersens bought and even fewer who brought the intelligence and interest to them that the Pedersens did, so she savored their insights. Occasionally, the Pedersen's invited Rev. and Mrs. Barton to come as well. These evenings usually promised to be longer because Rev. Barton did go on a bit once he got started with an idea.

One day the phone rang while Kate was eating her breakfast. She frowned. Any intrusion on her reading time meant less time with Leland's book about Gypsies. Just this morning she had read about similarities between the Gypsy culture and the Jewish culture. She had only heard and read about Jews but had never met one. She remembered her father said he had met a Jew once, back in Wisconsin. He said the man didn't look any different from the rest of the townspeople so he thought all those stereotypes about their looks were exaggerated. Kate forced herself to put the book down and went to the studio to answer the phone.

'Kate? This is Angus.'

'Oh, Angus!' Her annoyance temporarily forgotten, she spoke with a smile. 'It's good to hear from you.'

'How are you, Kate? We haven't seen you for awhile. Well, I guess we did wave across the aisle last Saturday in Halley's Store. We hardly had time to say hello because we were hurrying to get home before Lizzie got too tired.' Kate accepted Angus' excuse, but mainly because but she was genuinely glad to hear his voice.

'I'm fine. How're the boys and Netta? The boys looked as if they've grown a few inches.'

'They have. Yup. It's amazing how fast they grow. Look, Kate, can you possibly help Lizzie cook for the husking crew next week? She's really been sick this time, you know—been spending a lot of time lying on the couch in the dining room when she can.'

'Oh, I didn't know she's been sick. What from? Don't tell me she's pregnant again!'

Angus sounded flustered. 'Well, yes. I thought you knew. We're hoping for another girl this time—a sweet younger sister like you!'

'Ha! That's not what you used to say,' but she smiled. It had been a long time since he'd tweaked her nose—the closest the family ever came to kissing—and she rubbed her nose as if she could almost feel his touch. 'I guess I could help if I know ahead of time so I can arrange my appointments. Things are a little slack just now because of harvesting.'

'If it doesn't rain, the corn in the northeast 40 ought to be ready by—oh, maybe Friday of next week. We're husking at Howells' on Monday and Tuesday and Barlowe's on Wednesday and Thursday if all goes well. Ours should only take two days if the weather holds, but otherwise we may have to work over the weekend. Would that be all right?'

'I think I can work it out.'

'Good. I'm going to hire several extra hands so there'll maybe be six or seven for dinner. But since you've done it so many times, we're sure to get an extra good meal. Besides, you know all about the kitchen.'

'All right. All right. I said yes,' she growled, then continued in a lighter tone. 'Have Lizzie call me. Maybe I can make a couple of pies here ahead of time.'

'Gee, Kate, this means a lot to both of us. The boys have been over at Mary's a lot but she's expecting, too, and she'll be tired after cooking for huskers over there. Lizzie insisted that I not ask her to help. Things haven't been easy. In fact, it couldn't have happened at a worse time.'

'I'm sorry, Angus. Why didn't you call me sooner? Well, let me know about the pies.'

Kate hung up the phone. Lizzie expecting again? Just imagine. Another one and three children already! Wouldn't it be nice if they gave one of them to me, she thought, but immediately purged the idea from her mind. It would never happen, nor should it happen.

On the following Friday, a pre-dawn glow seemed to rise out of the dirt road extension of Main Street beyond the railroad tracks as it straight-arrowed its way east. Kate walked past the bank and Halley's department store on the way to the livery stable. She heard the sounds of nearby livestock greeting the early morning, but mostly she smelled the earthy smell that comes with livestock. She heard some banging at the lumber yard down by the railroad tracks, but saw no one. The first rays of sun arcing across the road silhouetted the cottonwoods on either side.

Remembering the early morning risings on the farm made her nostalgic. She thought the dawn was as fresh as the milk that filled the pail when she was milking. And there was the particular odor of warm milk fresh from the cow. Dawn in town simply can't match dawn on the farm, she thought. It really would be nice to live on a farm! So strong was the feeling that she would have sold her business and bought a farm had she not, just at that moment, entered the shed of the livery stable.

'Good morning, Harold!' Her voice smiled with the exuberance the sunrise had inspired in her.

'Good morning, Miss Katie!' Harold matched her enthusiasm. 'You must be getting an early start. Will you be taking a little drive this morning before work?'

She was rather more curt than she meant to be. 'I'll not be back until late afternoon, Harold.'

For the first time since she had left the farm, she felt a certain excitement holding Billie Jean's reins, going west out of town. As the sun began to warm her back, she was determined to arise early every day from then on, quite forgetting that her penchant for reading was what really kept her from enjoying the sunrise.

At the farm, the over-sized teakettle of water was boiling with abandon on the cookstove when she walked in. Lizzie was having one of her worst mornings with bouts of nausea keeping her close to the bed. She lay in bed heaving into the chamber pot from time to time. It seemed that this child was determined to be difficult from the beginning. 'Where's Angus?' Kate asked.

'Gone to the field,' Lizzie managed to whisper. 'He took Netta over to Mary's.' Lizzie was obviously miserable, but Kate just shook her head and kept her counsel.

Knowing all the kitchen duties required on threshing days, Kate rolled up the sleeves of her shirtwaist and donned an outsize apron. She went about straightening up the bedroom and emptying the chamber pot and then went to the kitchen to feed the boys who were getting big enough to help a little. She instinctively fell into the well-known farm routines as if there had been no intervening years of professional life in town.

'Anything you need, Lizzie?'

'Nooo,' came the soft answer.

'I'm going to start the chickens then.'

'Kate? Kate, thanks. Can you watch the boys, too? I told them they had to be good for you.'

Kate stopped on her way to the kitchen to pat them on the head as they played with some blocks in the dining room. She had come to love these little boys. She would check on them again in a few minutes. 'You be good and we'll have cookies and milk pretty soon.'

Stepping into the kitchen set in motion a chicken-routine that was so ingrained from her years on the farm that every move seemed foreordained. Even being a professional photographer could not dislodge it. She toted the whistling tea kettle outside where she poured the scalding water into a bucket.

On the ground lay the inert, headless bodies of three plump hens where Angus had left them. She gingerly grabbed the yellow, muddied feet of one of them. As many chickens as she'd cleaned, she could never feel comfortable handling the peculiar, rough bumps on their feet that resembled so many crudely-turned wooden beads strung on a claw.

Grasping the feet, she plunged each body into the cloud of steam. Immediately the distasteful odor of wet feathers assailed her memory, and her nose twitched in disdain. 'Why me?' she thought, but she knew she could not have turned down Angus' request for help.

She sloshed each one up and down again and again to wet the downy feathers underneath the unyielding outer ones. She tried to be philosophical. Her endeavors, after all, disagreeable as they were, would produce the most exquisite chicken and dumplings in the neighborhood—in all of Nebraska, Benny Barlowe had once said.

Still, she involuntarily wrinkled her nose and grimaced. Her mother had taught her how to pluck and dress a chicken, but not how to deal with the smell. You could hardly call it an 'odor', she thought. 'Odor!' she said out loud. It was too nice a word No. It was worse than an odor. Stink? She dare not say that aloud lest her mother frown at her using such a slangy word. Stench? Maybe, but after all, there were many stenches in life—the outhouse stench, the barn stench, the stench of wet diapers, the stench of wet wool. How could one differentiate? She screwed up her mouth into a loud, spoken, 'Pee-you'. It was a word she'd not tried since her mother washed her eight-year-old mouth out with soap for saying it. She realized how spoiled she had become in buying dressed chickens at Bill Sedlow's meat market.

Sitting on the end of a sawed-off log, Kate worked quickly, pulling off handfuls of wet feathers—systematically denuding the back, the breast, the thighs, and finally the wings where the feathers clung tightly—until the carcass was bare except for the skin and pinfeathers. Delicate feathers stuck to her apron and to the loose strands of her hair that curled in the steam and to her hands and arms, damp from perspiration.

She lay each carcass on the cool morning dampness of the grass, awaiting the singeing over a burning piece of newspaper that would loosen the pinfeathers—and create yet a different nose-wrinkling smell. One downy feather insisted on tickling her moist cheek. She twisted her mouth and blew at it to no avail. She brushed at it with the gathers at the top of her sleeve and finally dislodged it by wiping it with the hem of her apron.

Interrupted for the moment, she glanced down toward the barnyard. Henry James's wagon and Mr. Barlowe's were parked just beside barn. She smiled, thinking of the number of times she'd ridden in Mr. Barlowe's wagon when she was seeing Benny. Those had been happy days when the certainty of marrying seemed much more likely than it did now.

All but one of her childhood friends were married—yes, married and having children and plucking chickens. If she'd married Benny when he asked her to, life by now would have been—and would continue to be—one long parade of chickens to be scalded and plucked and dressed and fried or boiled or roasted.

Her imagination hung them on a clothesline like so many pairs of long underwear with the long skinny legs pinned to the line while the empty necks and gangly wings dangled helplessly in the breeze. She mentally plucked one from the line, but by the time it was ready for singeing, another hung in its place.

She sobered, thinking much of life was like that. Food was prepared, cooked and eaten, dishes washed, dried, and put away in time for another meal; clothes worn and washed and dried and sprinkled and ironed and worn and washed and dried and sprinkled and ironed ... 'Maybe that's all there is,' she whispered to herself, frightened that it might be true. 'Maybe that is the meaning of life. Maybe I should ask no more of it.' She frowned, gazing at her hands reddened by the heat of her task.

'No!' Her voice startled her and she jumped to her feet. 'No! I want more!' Her rounding jaw suddenly jutted like Angus' and her clear blue eyes glinted. 'No!' she said out loud in the direction of Mr. Barlowe's wagon. 'No!' she fairly shouted, 'I want more!' Fiercely, she picked up the chickens and was glad all over again that she hadn't married Benny.

* * *

The last of the plucking finished, Kate straightened her back and stretched. As she glanced toward the barn again, she noticed three strange horses tethered to the post by east barn door. They were large, beautifully marked horses, a special breed she was not familiar with, the kind one might expect to be show horses. They seemed to be too special to belong to the usual temporary hands folks usually hired, but there was no other explanation for them. She shrugged. She had no time to satisfy her curiosity now as she turned and opened the kitchen door.

Inside, Lizzie leaned unsteadily against the kitchen counter, peeling potatoes. 'Now, Lizzie, I told you I can do it. Just go lie down.' Kate took her by the arm and steered her to the front bedroom where she could hear what was going on.

'Look, Aunt Katie, I drew a pitcher,' said John as they passed the boys on their way through the dining room.

'Well, that's a nice one. What is it?' Kate asked absent-mindedly.

'Why, it's a tree. Cantcha tell?' Kate smiled, and hastened Lizzie to bed. She tucked a light blanket around her.

'Now you stay there.' She said. Lizzie murmured her thanks, obviously glad to be back in a prone position.

The rest of the morning Kate was a picture of efficiency—cooking, watching the boys, setting the table. The potatoes were just ready for mashing when she heard the men stomp onto the porch and splash in the wash basins. Whoever thought of making the wash-up area separate from the kitchen was a smart person, she thought, as she pounded the wooden masher up and down. She paid no attention as the men passed her on their way to the dining room. She poured a swirl of cream and a daub of home-churned butter into the potatoes and mashed until they were creamy smooth.

Between the kitchen and the dining room, the housebuilder had constructed dish cupboards that opened from either side with a pass-through to save steps carrying the food to the table. Kate set the basket of fresh, hot squash rolls there. She had often thought about the wisdom of this kitchen-dining arrangement. Truly it was convenient, and the polished oak was beautiful as well. How she would love to have just such a kitchen some day.

In the dining room, chairs scraped on the hardwood floors as the men pulled up to the table. 'There, Robbie, how's that?' Angus' voice rose over the general hum of the men settling into their chairs, and Kate knew Angus had seen to it that Robbie had been lifted into his high chair and the boys were ready to eat. One by one she saw the dishes disappear from the pass-through as someone placed them on the table. Only the potatoes were left. She quickly scooped them up from the kettle into a large bowl and marched into the dining room.

The men were hungry and hardly looked up as Kate entered so it didn't matter that her hair hung in loose, damp ringlets around her face, defying the order she entrusted to the side combs. Her sleeves were still rolled up from the chicken-plucking revealing pale pink forearms not unlike those of a Rubens subject which she learned about in one of the Pedersen's art books.

'You haven't lost your touch, Katie!' Angus smiled from the far end of the table. She blushed at having been noticed at all. Her generous apron, covering her rounding bosom and tied securely at her waist, bore signs of home-canned beets and brown flecks of spattered chicken gravy. It did not occur to her to remove it for huskers who always fell to eating the minute the green beans and platter of fried chicken and spiced apple pickles were on their way around the table.

She reached across the nearest man's shoulder to start the potatoes on their way around. As she leaned forward, she found herself looking into a pair of familiar dark eyes which smiled at her. Her jaw dropped and she stared rather longer than she should have. Gyorgy! She smiled faintly, but did not acknowledge their acquaintance. She was greatly relieved at a fortuitous call from Lizzie in the front bedroom at just that moment.

'My word, Kate,' Lizzie exclaimed, looking puzzled, 'your face is so flushed. Are you sure you're all right? I can come help.' She half lifted herself from the bed.

'Of course not, Lizzie. I'm just cooling off after working so long in the hot kitchen. You know how it is. Now, what do you want to eat? I'll bring you a tray just as soon as the men have gone back to the field.'

'Oh, maybe some mashed potatoes. How I'd like some of that pumpkin pie, but I know I couldn't hold it. Actually, I'm feeling some better, but then I generally do about noon. Are the boys behaving?'

'The boys are doing just fine and I'll see that they get down for a nap. You just stay down and I'll be back soon.'

Kate paused for a long minute on her way through the parlor, holding onto the oak rocker to compose herself before returning to the dining room. She glanced into the oak-framed mirror above the Victrola. Dismayed at her disheveled appearance, she removed the combs and recaptured the stray strands of hair. There was little to identify her as a professional woman.

Sally Salisbury Stoddard

She brushed at the smudges of flour on her left cheek. Looking down at her apron, she shook her head. There was nothing she could do about it now, she thought, as she unrolled her sleeves and buttoned them at the cuff before she re-entered the dining room. She approached the table with rather more grace than was her style and removed the potato bowl and chicken platter for refilling, being careful to skirt Gorgy's chair. Still, she felt his eyes following her every movement, and she hoped Angus wouldn't notice.

She set the refilled dishes on the pass-through counter and turned to cut the pies. Of all her food accomplishments she was most proud of, her pies were the only one that her mother had freely acknowledged. Indeed, folks begged for her pumpkin pie recipe many times but she kept it a closely-guarded secret. Not for all the world would she reveal that it was a half cup of apple butter which added the surprising smoothness and flavor.

From the dining room, she heard the level of conversational bantering rise as the men ended the main part of the meal. She quickly put generous wedges of pie on dessert plates, remembering to cut smaller pieces for the boys. She placed them on the pass-through counter and saw them rapidly disappear into the other room. She turned to begin the clean-up process.

As she stored leftover food and scraped cooking pots, Kate's mind could not dislodge the memory of Gyorgy's eyes, warm and mysterious, and strangely inviting. She longed for an excuse to return to the dining room, to speak to him and him only, but her reverie was broken by the scrape of chairs on the wood flooring.

'Thanks very much, Kate. You sure haven't lost your touch in the kitchen,' shouted one man from the kitchen door.

'Kate, you promised a long time ago, you'd give the missus that pie recipe,' said another. Kate hardly turned around to acknowledge the various forms of their appreciation, but was glad for them nonetheless. Finally the thud of heavy boots and the boom of the farmers' voices faded away. As she turned toward the dining room door, she was surprised by Gyorgy's sonorous voice.

'Oh, Miss MacLean, I found these young gentlemen looking rather sleepy and they said you were responsible for them.' He laughed and his mustache danced a jig of delight as he handed her one boy for each hand. 'To be honest,' he went on, 'I stayed behind to beg you for your pumpkin pie recipe. It's the best anywhere—and believe me, I've been many places.'

Kate's mouth opened and shut twice before she could stammer a 'Thank you. And thanks for bringing the boys.' She looked down at them to avoid the frankness of his smile and ignored the question about the recipe.

'I'll stop by for my pictures when I have a day free. I need to work whenever I can since jobs aren't easy to come by these days.'

'I understand. You know my studio hours.' Kate's tone was very business-like as she stooped to pick up Robbie.

'Well, I must get back to the field. Thanks again.'

Kate left the dishes on the table to put the boys down for their nap, patting their cheeks and smoothing their ruffled hair with unusual tenderness. The boys quieted quickly. Then she went outside and cut three of the red chrysanthemums blooming in the shelter of the west porch. She laid them on the tray beside a plate of buttered fresh bread and mashed potatoes and green beans and took them to Lizzie. Lizzie smiled but didn't mention the extra attention.

Back in the kitchen, Kate worked at the clean-up until the boys' supper time. She heard the sound of horse's hooves and the rumble of wagons as the men departed for home. She lit a lamp in the dining room in preparation for the evening. Tomorrow she would begin the routine again, but how different it would be knowing she would see Gyorgy again, even if briefly and from afar—close enough to touch his hand, but worlds apart.

Angus came into the kitchen as she untied and removed her apron, stuffing it into her coat pocket to add to the week's laundry. 'Kate! Aren't you going to stay over? Why, we just assumed you would. If you leave now, you'll no more than get home and it'll be time to be up and driving out here again.'

'No, Angus. I told Harold I'd have the buggy back. Besides I have some business to see to tonight. I left supper for you and Lizzie on the range. Bring up three jars of that canned beef tonight and some carrots from the root cellar, will you? I'll get the rest when I get here in the morning.'

'Now, Kate—you sure? We can call Harold . . .' But Kate was already out the door.

Driving west to the highway, Kate gloried in the brilliance of the October sunset—oranges and yellows blending into halos of pink and green and blue, filling the expanse of sky above the flatness of the Nebraska prairie. It was a fitting end to the day which began with such a wondrous sunrise.

A sense of destiny struck a spiritual chord in her, a kind of epiphany, she thought. She stopped Billie Jean where the driveway met the highway and sat transfixed, her heart beating rapidly. After an indeterminate time, she shook herself and directed the horse north toward Tingle Creek.

Suddenly, at the half mile corner, she impulsively clucked to Billie Jean, and they turned smoothly, angling west and north until they reached the Gypsy cemetery on the west edge of Mr. Gilbert's land. She pulled the buggy off the road into the shadows of the overhanging elms and burr oaks that surrounded the little plot. She climbed down and walked to the square outlined by the iron fence. In the dimming light, she sank down beside the fence, realizing she had not been back to the cemetery since she moved to town, that is, 'before Gyorgy'. No question that seeing him again brought her here now, but no matter, she told herself—it was the place she loved, not Gyorgy.

* * *

Kate shivered as the chill October breeze touched her warm face. She drew her heavy shawl close around her, hugging it to her body. Inside, Kate felt quite warm. Perhaps this inner warmth was left from the hot work in the kitchen, or perhaps it was generated by the furiousness of her heart beat. Perhaps it was just heart palpitations that her mother warned her about. Still, the rapidity of her heart beat worried her. She felt her cheeks. Their normal warmth felt good to her bare hands and reassured her that she was all right. Probably she was worrying for nothing.

At peace with her body once again, her mind called her attention to the still distant, but approaching, sound of horse's hooves. She cocked her head toward the source, the seldom used east-west road a quarter of a mile south of the cemetery. Her eyes, now accustomed to the deepening dusk, searched the surrounding landscape to determine if someone might see her from the road. Well, of course, she couldn't hide the horse and buggy!

The clomp of the hooves turned toward the cemetery. For a sickening moment, it occurred to her that she might not be safe in this familiar setting. She mentally checked the woods and plum thickets behind her as they sprawled along the creek between the cemetery and the Gilbert place. Even the closest neighbor a half mile away could not hear her scream, if it came to that. Billie Jean pawed the ground ever so lightly, but Kate dared

Red Geraniums

not shush her. The fear of unknown possibilities suddenly choked her so she hardly breathed.

The tempo of the horse's hooves slowed as they came near. She sensed that the horseman stopped at the entrance, blocking any hope of exit in the buggy. Peering through the wrought iron vines that decorated the fence, Kate could see a man silhouetted against the last glow of the October sunset. She could do nothing now but wait and hope.

The saddle creaked as the rider shifted position. 'Miss MacLean! May I come?' Gyorgy's soft European accent in the quiet of the October evening flooded her memory with their meeting at the beginning of summer.

Kate remembered the bright and sunny day the Gypsies had come to town. She remembered delighting in the brilliance of the women's skirts so like prairie flowers blowing in the wind. From that day, the summer had been different for Kate, a strange mixture of joy and sadness. The gossip of townspeople, the unspoken but obvious disapproval of Angus and Lizzie, and the endless questioning about Gyorgy's sitting had distressed her more than she would admit, even to herself.

On the other hand, the muggy days of July had seemed less odious because there were the photographs of Gyorgy. Without doubt they were among the best she had ever taken, and her heart danced at the thought of being so close to his person for that one hour. There was, of course, the promise that he would return, but he hadn't. Most of the time she dismissed her feelings as school-girl foolishness until she saw him today at Angus' dining room table.

Now he sat astride his remarkable horse asking to talk to her again—the joy of summer remembrance incarnate. Kate rose slowly, but said nothing. 'May I come? I'd like to talk to you, Miss Katie. May I call you Miss Katie? I heard your brother call you that and so I think of you that way.'

Kate took a few steps toward Billie Jean. 'I must be getting back to town. I told the livery stable I'd have the buggy back by now.' She hoped the dusk and her voice control would not betray her mixture of fear and attraction.

'No! No, please. Please don't go. Stay a few minutes—a few minutes only.' Kate hesitated. Instinctively she sensed that she should be wary. But, she was in a position that she had no choice.

Gyorgy dismounted without waiting for her permission and slowly walked his horse toward her, dropping the reins when he came within a few feet. 'I won't harm you, Miss Katie. I could never hurt you. Please stay a few minutes and talk.' He reached out and took her hand, talking softly as he helped her to sit down again by the fence. 'Your hands are cold. Here, let me warm them.' She looked down at their clasped hands, partly as an excuse not to look him in the eye. His were rough and dark but well-shaped, contrasting with hers, so pudgy and ghostly white in the faint light. She did not want to pull away even though caution warned her otherwise.

'When I stopped in your studio last summer, I only wanted my picture taken. When I left, I wanted to see you again. You were so pretty, so lively, so capable, so professional. I'd never met a woman like you. You made me want to stay, and I wanted to return earlier, but times are hard and we have to find work wherever we can. I have a responsibility to take care of my people. We'll be moving on again soon after harvest, probably heading south for the winter where it's warmer at least.'

Whether Gyorgy's assessment was flattery or not, Kate's fear softened. She hazarded a look at him. 'Why do you keep moving? Why don't you settle down in one place—work to buy some land?' Kate was more than curious; she was genuinely interested in these mysterious strangers.

'It's not our custom. We work very hard, but we don't like working for other people. We would have to work for someone a long, long time to be able to buy land. People don't understand us very well, and . . .' He shrugged. 'I can't ask you to understand, either, but I wish you could.' There was a sibilance in his speech and a soft blurring of 'd's' and 'th's' whose origin she could not identify. 'Miss Katie, when I saw you again today—I knew that all those qualities I admire in you really belong to you, not just to the woman who takes pictures. In a way, you know, you're as fiercely independent as we are, or as we try to be.' This image of herself was new to Kate.

'Why did you accept my brother's job?'

'To be honest, I knew Mr. MacLean was your brother, but I had no reason to believe I would have the good fortune to see you.'

'No, I guess you wouldn't have known that, would you? You surprised me.'

'Were you glad to see me?' he teased.

'I . . . I didn't know what to think. After all, you didn't come back for your pictures even though you were working in the area. They're very good pictures, by the way.' Her chin jutted just a bit in defiant pride. She looked directly at him and smiled. He laughed.

Red Geraniums

'Why did you come here tonight? Some of my people are buried here, you know.'

'Yes, I know. I don't know why I came tonight except it's one of the quietest spots around here. I used to come here often to be alone when I lived at home on the farm and my mother was still alive. It is always quiet and pretty. During the summer the beds of red geraniums are like jewels floating on a sea of green fields. I don't know who plants them every year, and I'm always worried they might not come back the next year. I guess I'd have to plant them myself if no one else did. I'm sorry to see the frost has already finished them for this year.'

'Did you know that we believe that red is the appropriate color when people die?'

'I really must be going,' she said but did not attempt to get up.

'I've kept you too long. Please, when will I see you again?'

'Why, tomorrow at Angus', I expect.'

'No, I mean really see you—to talk to you like this? Can I meet you here tomorrow after work? I'll wait a decent amount of time after you leave, like I did tonight so no one will know. Or I could come first . . .'

'I don't know.' She rose, refusing his offer of help. 'I'm sorry. I just don't know.'

Gyorgy looked downcast. 'I know people in town were talking about my coming to your studio for a portrait. Lots of people believe gypsies don't like their pictures taken, but some of us do. It's just that we want to decide when to have our pictures taken. I don't want to disturb you. I promise to be careful.'

'You know about all that talk?' Kate was incredulous. 'How did you know?'

'We Gypsies know everything,' he said and laughed. 'You must have your fortune told by one of our women sometime!'

'Oh, no! I could never do that.' Kate looked horrified and shook her head. A fleeting thought of what her mother would say came to her mind.

'Here, I'll help you into the buggy, and then I'll ride a ways behind until we get to the highway—to be sure you're all right.'

'Thank you.' Kate flicked the rein across Billie Jean's rump, and they turned onto the road going north. The ride back to Tingle Creek helped Kate clarify her attraction to Gyorgy. He certainly had the characteristics of a good leader and he knew how to get things done, but she gasped to realize that she didn't even know if he could read! 'But my!' she smiled. 'He is most attractive!' Still, she knew her attraction to his physical being, his handsomeness, and his brawn could be no more than a passing fancy. Sorting things out in her head, she knew that logically that wasn't enough—but maybe it was!

III

The next day, she was able to talk more easily with the harvest crew and even to smile tentatively at Gyorgy. She let Angus persuade her to stay over and go to church with him and the boys, so there was no question of meeting Gyorgy in the cemetery again, though down deep she wished she it could be so. She went about finishing up the kitchen chores after feeding the husking crew and persuaded herself she was doing it for Lizzie.

Several days later, Kate stepped into the drugstore. 'Morning, Miss MacLean.' Calvin Trueblood's voice startled her. She hadn't seen Calvin behind the counter.

'Oh! Why, hello, Calvin. How is your new job?'

'It's fine, thank you. I like it. I'm learning a lot about business. Since I'm not going to college, I'm glad I can work here for Mr. Jenkins. A drugstore's not a bad place to be, you know.'

'What do you mean—not going to college? Why, Calvin, what can you be thinking of? Of course you're going to college. You've never talked about anything else and you're one of my best students ever!'

'To be honest, Miss MacLean, my parents just don't have enough money to support me, and I really need to help them out. Maybe after a few years I could save up enough to go, but—well, I don't care. After all, most people don't go to college. Anyway if I go, it'll be a long time before I can get married and have children.' Calvin blushed as he spoke.

Kate knew that Calvin wanted to study veterinary medicine, but she didn't want to make him feel worse if he really couldn't go. 'Of course, Calvin. I'm sure Mr. Jenkins is glad to have you here. He needs a smart young man like you who works hard.'

Calvin frowned at the compliment. 'Can I get anything for you, Miss MacLean?'

'I need some acetic acid. My supply is lower than I thought.'

'I guess you're the only customer that ever needs it.'

Kate laughed. 'Yes, I guess only a photographer would. Just put it on my bill.'

What a shame it is, Kate thought, that Calvin has to pretend he could be happy working in the drug store. Although she hadn't always liked the life of a school teacher, she had always taken special pride in students with great promise, and she never failed to write a letter of congratulations on learning of their special achievements. Maybe if she could help Calvin's parents see the long term advantages for him, they would realize the importance of working out a financial plan with the state college. She made up her mind to talk to them.

Back in her studio, she looked at her schedule. It would be much easier if Calvin's parents had a telephone so she wouldn't have to walk all that way only to find they weren't home. She clucked at the irony of her dependence on the telephone that she herself used to consider a foolish luxury. She decided to go to the Truebloods right after dinner on a weekday when she thought they would be in the house resting.

On the chosen day, Kate locked the studio door and walked east on Main Street. It would be a fair hike to their place at the northeast corner of town. Her short legs managed a sprightly step that gave the impression that she was always in a hurry, no matter what her errand. As she walked, her thoughts turned to the task at hand.

She had had only brief conversations with Calvin's parents at school programs and commencement. Mr. Trueblood had said no more than 'How do' and seemed a bit shy. People in town generally thought of them as quiet, responsible, God-fearing, and aloof. Kate knew they were the only Quakers in the area. Kate had never seen Mrs. Trueblood without her plain dark blue bonnet and simple dark blue dress without even a white collar. She wondered if that had something to do with their religion. Now she fervently wished she had read up on the Quakers in the Pedersens' encyclopedias.

At the corner of East Third and Judson, Kate stopped. She hadn't walked this far for a long time, and she thought she ought not arrive at the Truebloods too breathless and perspiry. She stood by the corner post of the Leonards' picket fence and reached into the small beaded handbag hanging from her wrist. Covered with jet black glass beads, the fringes and loops sparkled blue and pink and black in the October sun. She drew out one of her mother's embroidered hankies to pat the moisture on her forehead.

As she dabbed at her face, she saw Mrs. Leonard gently pull the lace curtain aside in an upper window. Feeling that she needed a better reason to be standing there than just catching her breath, Kate feigned a studied look at the maple branch hanging above her head. She frowned. There were no red, yellow or orange leaves to admire. The leaves had simply turned brown.

A sideways glance told her the lace curtain had not dropped back into place so Kate decided to tease Mrs. Leonard. Holding her hat with her right hand, her beaded bag dangling from her elbow, she lifted her gaze from the leaves and stared at the sky over the Leonards' house where Mrs. Leonard couldn't possibly see what she might be looking at. She chuckled lightly, but decidedly, at herself and Mrs. Leonard. Then she moved on.

This far north, there were only two houses on the east side of East Third Street, and in the next block a grove of trees almost blocked the view of the only house. Kate knew the banker had lived there before he built the large brick house across from the Methodist Episcopal Church. She had never walked this far north on East Third Street before, but she and Benny had driven by this place once when she was seeing him. Beyond this block, the quality of the road quickly deteriorated and she had a sense of being in the country, not in town. Her mental map of the area told her she had arrived at the Truebloods.

* * *

Kate turned in at the drive whose ruts were filled with cinders. Along the north side was a row of lilac bushes, like those her mother had planted on the farm. The leaves were brown now, but they conjured up the remembrance of the fragrance that had lulled her to sleep on spring nights.

Their presence seemed to predict that she would like Mrs. Trueblood, but still she felt uneasy about her mission. Just in front of the lilac bushes, lavendar chrysanthemums bloomed their last in great profusion. Mrs. Trueblood must have covered them each night to ward off the frost.

Kate turned her attention to the house and walked slowly toward it. Its lapped siding was weathered but the green trim around the windows boldly affirmed the good intentions of someone who must have been called away by more important things to do. She surveyed the porch stretching across the front of the house. It was bare except for a straight chair with a spindle missing in its back.

Through the screen door, she could see the front door with its oval window. Back home on the farm, visiting neighbors always went to the side door, but not knowing the Truebloods well, she mounted the single step to the well-worn floor of the porch.

Knocking tentatively at the edge of the screen door, she pulled her hand back quickly and stood off to the side, feeling it would be too forward of her to stand squarely in front of the door. To her right a few limp floribunda roses still clung to the vines on a crude slat trellis. As the deadness of the roses registered in her mind, it felt like much more than the minute or two it had been since she knocked. She fretted about how long she should wait before turning to leave.

A woman's voice suddenly broke into her thoughts. 'Why, hello, Miss MacLean. Have you walked all this way? Please, you must come in. You must be tired.' Mrs. Trueblood held the screen open wide. Kate murmured a thank you and thought how pleasant Mrs. Trueblood's voice was. But 'pleasant' seemed inadequate. Gentle? Yes, it was gentle, but not weak. And there was something more. Inviting, perhaps? Embracing? These words came closer to describing its unusual quality. She would think about it later.

Kate stepped into the small, cool parlor. The walls painted light cream seemed barren, with no wallpaper and no pictures or calendars like most people had. The upper reaches of the walls had yellowed, marked with the residue from a heating stove that had a prominent place in the room. Two square, solid oak arm chairs sat on either side of a square, spindle-legged table on which was a large kerosene lamp and a thick Bible.

'Do sit down, Miss MacLean. This sewing rocker of my grandmother's should just about fit you. She was petite, like you.' Kate hadn't noticed Mrs. Trueblood slip into the room off to the right to bring out a well-polished ashwood sewing rocker with a caned seat and back. She placed it near the front door. 'I hope the breeze coming in the door won't be too much for you.'

Kate was surprised and pleased to be called petite. Everyone else just called her short. Petite sounded much nicer. She smiled. 'No. No, the fall air feels good. Thank you. You're very kind to accommodate my short legs. Sometimes my feet don't reach the floor when I sit down.'

Mrs. Trueblood sat in one of the square oak chairs but said nothing. She looked at ease but seemed to have no need to carry the conversation further. Kate was accustomed to the hostess taking the initiative to open the conversation. Waiting, she rocked a little and looked about as best she could without seeming to pry. Opposite the front door, a wide opening led into the kitchen where she could see a heavy oak table, surrounded by five chairs matching the one on the front porch. A window on the east interrupted the cupboards lining the walls. Kate could see the newspapers lining the shelves with a plain, straight edge, not cut in a lacy pattern like her own.

Finally Kate, uncomfortable with so much silence, decided she'd better get on with her mission. 'I expect, Mrs. Trueblood, you're wondering why I've come.'

'I should be very glad if you've come for no other purpose than a social call.' Mrs. Trueblood appeared to relax. Perhaps she was unaccustomed to visitors. Kate seemed to recall someone saying that Quakers did not much believe in frivolities—that they mostly worked or read the Scriptures.

'Well, I do have a purpose, but first, may I ask you about your lilac hedge? The bushes look so full, they must have been beautiful in the spring.'

'Do you like lilacs, too?' Mrs. Trueblood looked up eagerly. 'Yes, they were lovely. There's a story behind them, you know.' She paused and looked down at her hands twisting the coarse blue fabric of her apron. 'Perhaps I shouldn't bother you with it, but you see, I was raised by my grandmother in Liberty. Have you heard of it? My grandmother was a fine woman—stern, but very good-hearted, and a staunch Methodist who never played cards or danced or drank any liquor. When my husband and I were courting, she disapproved, not because Mr. Trueblood was not a good man, you understand, but she was afraid that he, being Quaker, was so rigid in his strictures about simple living and his views of the world that he would find me wanting. She always said I was such a free spirit that any man would find it hard to put up with me or keep up with me.

'Anyway, before our engagement was resolved, my grandmother died quite suddenly, and I was left alone. My uncle, my mother's brother, said I could not stay alone, that I must either marry someone—he didn't know about Mr. Trueblood—or move in with his family. I'm sure he thought I would do the latter, but Mr. Trueblood persuaded me to marry him. I would have waited longer if my grandmother hadn't died, but I knew even then that that was what I wanted to do. My uncle sold my grandmother's house and all those beloved furnishings that he didn't want for himself. The only things he allowed me to take were the lilac bushes.' Her smile was sad and content all at once. 'Mr. Trueblood understood their importance to me, and they have moved wherever we've moved.'

Kate was genuinely touched, and she felt Mrs. Trueblood's trusting her with her story was a sign that she and Mrs. Trueblood could be friends. 'Imagine that! Inheriting lilac bushes. They are truly a precious inheritance, an inheritance that grows in a special way. That's a wonderful story!'

Just then there was a knock at the back door off the kitchen. Mrs. Trueblood excused herself and walked to the door. She opened it and Kate could hear a man's voice which sounded very familiar. She heard Mrs. Trueblood invite him in. 'Miss MacLean and I were just discussing lilacs. Miss MacLean, this is Gyorgy.'

'Why, we've already met.' Gyorgy looked intently at Kate. 'In fact, several months ago, Miss MacLean was kind enough to take my picture without an appointment.' He smiled.

Flustered, Kate felt a great urgency at that very moment to know when he would come to pick up the pictures. 'Will you be stopping by tomorrow to see the finished pictures? I think you'll find them quite satisfactory.'

'Not this time. Winter's coming and we've got too much work to do. Long as harvesting jobs hold out, we've got to keep moving. Next spring for sure.' Both spoke as if Mrs. Trueblood were not in the room and neither looked at her. She pulled a hankie from her pocket and coughed slightly. Gyorgy turned to her. 'Actually, Mrs. Trueblood, I came to say goodbye. We have to leave just now.'

'Just now?' Mrs. Trueblood's face showed astonishment.

'Yes, I just learned there's a husking job near Nebraska City and we have to hurry.'

Kate watched Gyorgy fingering his woolen cap. His fingers seemed to move around the edge as if trying to divine some message in the knobby configuration of the rough woolen threads.

'The wagons are packed and the family is waiting for me. As usual it's been real nice to stay under the willows by the creek. Nobody's bothered us and we could let the children roam without worrying that someone would carry them off. We will always remember your kindness.'

'You know that you are always welcome. It is our privilege to give your family shelter.' She turned to the kitchen counter where fresh baked

Red Geraniums

loaves of bread were cooling. 'Here. These'll give you a lunch along the way. And here are three little loaves. I 'spect the children will like them.' Mrs. Trueblood wrapped the bread in a newspaper as she talked and handed the parcel to Gyorgy who smiled his thanks.

'Good day, Miss MacLean,' he said and went out the back door.

Kate was clearly puzzled. The turmoil inside her head confused her. How indeed did Gyorgy come to know the Truebloods? How could the Truebloods have been so openly hospitable to a people that most folks considered to be pariahs at best? How could they have camped so close to town, and obviously more than once, without Jean's grapevine passing the word along? What was even more puzzling was her own attraction to this man. Did he weave some magic spell that caught her in its web?

Suddenly she was aware that Mrs. Trueblood had said something to her about coffee. 'Oh, no. No, thanks.' Kate shook her head to recall why she had come.

'I believe you had something you wanted to talk to me about.'

'Yes. Yes, of course.' Her head slowly clearing, Kate explained her mission as persuasively as possible. 'I do think,' she concluded, 'that the college will give Calvin a scholarship and with parttime work, he would be able to manage financially.' She leaned forward. 'I'm convinced, Mrs. Trueblood, that Calvin will do well in college, and after a few years of study, he will be one of the upstanding citizens of whatever community he chooses to serve. He is a real tribute to your excellent training. A fine young man, indeed!'

Mrs. Trueblood listened quietly while Kate talked and then hesitated before she spoke. Finally she nodded and smiled. 'We will certainly consider what you've said, Miss MacLean. I appreciate your confidence in Calvin.'

Kate gathered her skirts, ready to leave. 'I've enjoyed visiting you in your home, Mrs. Trueblood. I miss being in the country. It's been awhile now since I left the farm and living in the studio apartment just doesn't compare to the openness and freshness of the countryside. Thank you for your time. Please give my greetings to Mr. Trueblood.'

'I will, thank you. Please do come again. I believe we have more common interests than just Calvin!' Mrs. Trueblood smiled a bit mischievously as she opened the door for Kate.

'Well, then, goodbye.' Kate waved as she walked past the lilacs and once again as she started south down the road as the sun was lowering in the west. She remembered little of the walk home, so absorbed was her mind with the revelations of the afternoon.

* * *

Back in her apartment, Kate was exhilarated but tired from her long walk. In fact, the trip home seemed much shorter than going, probably because her mind was trying find a clue to her interest in Gyorgy. She recognized the giddy schoolgirl's attraction to a physically handsome man and a sober fascination with his exoticness. Finally, she had to acknowledge her great need to love and be loved by someone, but not just anyone.

She knew that Gyorgy as that needed companion was an impossible dream. She basically knew very little about Gypsies but realized she could not be one. She couldn't speak his language and didn't understand Gypsy customs. He, of course, could never abandon his duties as king of the clan. Her world would be limited to Gyorgy. This was all silly, of course. He wasn't in love with her and she wasn't in love with him, but she had to admit that he was very attractive. Of course, she chided herself, it could not and would not be, but still, Gyorgy's relationship to the Truebloods was most curious.

At home, she hung up her hat and shawl. Turning to her icebox, she realized she would not need to buy ice much longer as the weather was becoming decidedly cooler. As she looked into various food containers, she couldn't get interested in food. Life itself was much more interesting. Had she convinced Mrs. Trueblood that Calvin needed to go to college? Should she visit her again to bolster her first arguments? It would give her a further excuse to talk more with Bethany. Oh, my. When had she begun to think of Mrs. Trueblood by her first name? She must be careful not to slip up the next time they met.

She suddenly thought about the parting of Mrs. Leonard's curtains and took an impish delight in imagining the woman's curiosity at seeing Kate walking in the neighborhood. Probably tomorrow she would hear about it from Jean Burchett. She put together a simple supper including her homemade applesauce. That reminded her that Lizzie might need help canning apples this fall. She would call her in the morning.

She felt guilty about taking the whole afternoon off but decided she would read the most recent issue of *Wilson's Photographic* while she ate

Red Geraniums

and then work right after supper. She buttered another slice of bread and spread it with butter and some peach jam Lizzie had made.

One of the pictures in *Wilson's* caught her eye. It showed a child posed beside a homemade, gaily decorated wooden wagon. It was a delightful prop for a little boy, she thought. If only she could see it in color. As she carried her dishes to the enamel basin, she thought about the little wagon Uncle Campbell had made for Lynus and Jessie. What fun they'd had with it. She wondered if that old wagon was still in the barn at Angus'. She'd have to ask.

Once in her studio, Kate found it quite easy to work with a passion. Her love of photography had grown so much that making pictures became all-absorbing once she set out the necessary equipment and pumped several buckets of water.

When she bought the business, Kate thought of it as a job; now she thought of it as an art. She saw it as more than simply seeing her clients through the lens and pressing the shutter. She looked carefully at 'framing'. It was important to decide what would be inside the frame of the finished picture and what would not. She knew that what she excluded was important, too.

To her, the framing expressed the relationship between the photograph and the world beyond. It enclosed a photographic reality that allowed plain subjects to look important, naughty children to appear well-behaved without losing the sparkle in their eyes, and handsome men to exhibit flaws for all posterity to see. Within the photograph, Kate thought, every detail must either enhance the finished product or be eliminated, if possible. Would it be better if she were a little closer to better capture the grace of little Maude Thorson's hands? Did Judge James' shoes appear to push against the frame? Should she ask a subject to comb his hair?

These were serious considerations to her. She couldn't very well explain them to her clients, lest they misunderstand her motives. She had to make judgments that would satisfy them, of course, but beyond that, she could use these choices to make photographs that she thought proper and artistically effective. But was she, also, distorting reality if she framed a picture one way or another?

She often wondered how the first people to see photographic images must have reacted. In fact, people like herself must have been amazed, thinking it was magic. But what about a Hottentot or some tribal person from Borneo or Timbuktu? Would he recognize himself? For them, the images of everyday objects, or people they knew would surely strike them as nothing short of miraculous and mysterious.

Kate thought about all these things as she cleaned and straightened up the studio and worked in her dark room. Her friends who had never taken a picture could never understand them as she did. Even among professionals, she had found no kindred spirits. Mr. Shortt never said anything about photography being anything but a mechanical process—position the subject, look through the lens, press the shutter, develop and print the picture. She tried to talk about this with Mr. Thomlinson in his studio in Almora but he didn't seem to understand what she was saying. At least the photographers in *Wilson's Photographic* saw their medium as art!

Kate even thought about how each picture would look on the parlor wall in the subject's home. Hmm. Where would Gyorgy's photo hang? She smiled. Where, indeed, was there a wall to hang a picture of him in a bow wagon?

* * *

Kate's life settled down to what she described to Mrs. Pedersen as hum-drum when they met at the drug store one day in November. 'You surprise me!' Mrs. Pedersen said. 'Why, I think it would be quite exciting to have a position as a photographer! You've already told me how it pleases you when pictures turn out well. My goodness! Each one must be a challenge. Of course, I wouldn't give up being a mother for anything. Heaven knows there's a great deal of tedious work I have to do for my family. Even with my hired girl, I have to watch over her to make sure she gets in the corners when she dusts and that she irons Mr. Pedersen's collars without wrinkles. Still, I sometimes envy you having such an interesting position.'

Kate laughed, 'Oh Mrs. Pedersen, my working with prints I suppose is no different than trying to get the shirt collars right! There is still a lot of routine involved—just like in house-keeping or any job. Do come by sometime when I'm working in the dark room. I think you'd find it interesting. So, yes, I guess you're right—it really is interesting. Well, I must be going. Have a pleasant day.' Kate hurried off.

Later Kate was puzzled, remembering the conversation. Did she really have 'a position' or was it just 'a job'? She didn't know whether she had managed to convince her friend that even photography wasn't always exciting. In fact, posing squiggly little children or reluctant farmers could be downright difficult, and it was just plain discouraging when a glass negative broke or when a subject moved and blurred the picture.

Much of the time, though, it was a job—as routine as any other. Sittings came and went. The children she had photographed in their lacy white christening dresses were now toddlers—the boys in their first knee-length knickers and sailor suits and the girls in full petticoats and long, brown stockings and perky hair bows. The sensitive portraits she orchestrated depicted very well the subjects' timidity or playfulness, but it wasn't easy to make them sit or stand very, very still for the long exposure.

All week long Kate labored in her studio, and on Saturdays, she took care of her laundry and bread-baking and mending. The Saturday after her encounter with Mrs. Pedersen, she mixed and kneaded the loaves of bread that would last her until next Saturday. The feel of the yeast and flour mixture always filled her with nostalgia for her childhood when life seemed really simple. The slightly acid, floury smell seemed to contain the essence of what was important in life. No wonder Jesus and the disciples broke bread together at the Last Supper.

Baking bread was one thing she and her mother had done together three or four mornings a week without an undue clash of wills. Whether the children were in school or at home, her mother rolled out one hunk of the bread dough into a large rectangle for cinnamon rolls, glistening, buttery, brown cinnamon swirls to be popped into the oven just before school was out. The smell of freshly baked rolls heralded the children's return from school at four o'clock.

Kate sighed now as she punched down the dough. She could not eat a pan of cinnamon rolls by herself and doughnuts were too much trouble even if Mr. Sedlow did have good lard to sell. Her bread baking now was done as simply as possible.

One Saturday, Kate wasn't surprised to hear heavy clomping on the stairs. Probably Angus came to town on a quick errand, still wearing his work boots. Funny, she thought, how she could identify every sound in the building. It was a kind of protection, perhaps, alerting her to any noise out of the ordinary. The footsteps reached the landing, and there was a sudden silence followed by a gentle knock at the door—much gentler than Angus' knock would be. She dusted her hands on her apron as she pulled it off and patted the straying hair around her face.

She went to the door forgetting her still-rolled up sleeves. There stood Calvin Trueblood. 'Good morning, Miss MacLean. I'm sorry to bother you so early. I had to come now because Mr. Jenkins expects me to be at work at 9:30 and I like to be prompt.'

'Well, Calvin, it's not too early. Please, come in and sit down. Here I'll just get this book off the chair. Will you have a cup of tea?'

'Oh, no, Ma'am, no tea. No thanks. I won't stay but a minute. I've come to bring you a message from my parents. They would like you to come for dinner tomorrow, after church of course. I guess you know we have church in our house since there's no Quaker meetinghouse hereabouts. You'd be welcome to come to the service if you'd like though. We have visitors sometimes. We meet at nine o'clock.' Calvin paused, frowning at his shoes. 'Taint like other churches, I guess, 'cause we don't talk much and don't sing, but we pray to the same God as everybody else.'

'Why, thank you, Calvin. I'd like that—coming to dinner, I mean.' Kate wasn't sure an immediate answer about church was necessary. 'If I don't come for church, what time should I come for dinner? The Methodists are usually out about 12:30.'

'I guess about 1, maybe 1:30. We're not very formal about dinner time. I'll come for you in the wagon. My mother says it's too cold for you to walk.'

'You needn't bother, Calvin. Harold Jones at the livery stable will have a buggy available, I'm sure.'

'No, Miss MacLean. My pa said 'specially that I am to fetch you.'

'All right. I'll look forward to seeing you and your family tomorrow. Now don't be late to work.'

* * *

The next day a bright wintry sun hung low in the sky as Calvin helped Kate down from the wagon on returning from the Sunday afternoon visit. He smiled shyly. 'Thanks for speaking to my folks about my going to college. They would never have agreed if it hadn't been for you.'

'I couldn't have helped, Calvin, if we weren't all convinced that going to college will be the best for you. Now then, I expect you've got chores to do. Thank you for coming to fetch me and bringing me home.' Kate took his outstretched hand as he helped her onto the sidewalk, and she waved vaguely as she lifted her skirt to climb the steps to the studio.

Once inside, she hung her coat on the hook and deposited her hat on the shelf above. She lifted the tea kettle to check the water level and set it back on the range. Then she opened the door of the firebox and carefully selected a chunk of wood from one of the trees that had fallen in Angus' pasture the year before. She laid it carefully on the glowing coals and stoked it a bit before closing the door. The effort warmed her hands and her face glowed with the heat of the range. She sat in her grandmother's rocker, oddly content, rocking and reviewing every detail of the day.

It began as they sat around the Truebloods' table holding hands. All bowed their heads and Kate followed suit. There was no spoken prayer but Mr. Trueblood declared a loud 'Amen' after a time and all looked up and smiled. The conversation started off with the usual talk about the weather and the crops—farm-town talk known to women as well as men. Kate mostly listened as the food was passed.

'Now, Abraham, enough about corn and oats. I want to talk about Calvin's schooling.' Mr. Trueblood blinked and smiled at his wife.

'Of course. Enough of farming!' he said bemused. 'Miss MacLean, we are most grateful to you for helping us to see what is important for Calvin. We carefully considered your plea, and I admit I was highly skeptical that we could find a way to send Calvin to college. Nonetheless I wrote to the college in Lincoln as you suggested. We received a prompt reply which was most gratifying. The head of Animal Husbandry wrote that, what with Calvin's high marks, they could give him a scholarship, and if he works at the school farm, he should be able to afford college. We'll have extra work to do here to make up for all Calvin does for us, but Benjamin and Naomi are big enough now, so we'll get along.'

Calvin started to protest that he could stay, but his mother broke in gently. 'No, Calvin, you're going.'

Kate noted that Benjamin grimaced when his father mentioned extra work, but he didn't say anything out loud. In fact, Kate found it quite remarkable that the children were, indeed, seen but not heard, quite unlike the home she grew up in where the children were encouraged to enter into discussions of politics and local affairs, but they could be a bit rowdy, too. Reflecting on the discussion at the Truebloods as she rocked, Kate smiled. Her October visit had been fruitful for Calvin, after all.

Her mind then strayed to the conversation about the Gypsies camping in the Truebloods' back grove. How the subject had come up, Kate couldn't recall, but given the chance, she tested the waters with a tentative question.

'Did I understand correctly that Gypsies have camped on your land on several occasions?'

'Why, yes,' Bethany Trueblood began. 'They camped here first without our knowing it, but when we went to investigate, we found this family to be very needy. We shared food with them and came to know them as people. The Lord calls on us to help our fellow human beings when we can, so we have welcomed the opportunity to give them a place to stay when they come through.' She shook her head solemnly. 'Certainly Gyspies have been treated badly. They're abused by many people. These folks never stay long and they always clean up their camp site. We've found no fault with them, and we couldn't ask for better neighbors.'

Kate didn't know what to say. She had heard many folks reviling Gypsies and spreading every manner of frightening gossip about them. She had listened and never taken a stand against those who did. Could she be as outspoken as the Truebloods in defending the Gypsies? Her positive contacts with Gyorgy made him seem somehow to be 'other'. He couldn't really be one of those that folk around Tingle Creek made fun of—and yet feared, could he? After all, Angus had hired him to work during harvest.

The confusion of her thinking was disconcerting. Still, she wanted to know more about Gyorgy. 'Of course, I've not had much contact with Gypsies, but I'm curious about their leader whose photograph I took. He said he was their king, and he told me he wasn't married, but I'd read that Gypsies marry young.'

'Oh, Gyorgy?' Mr. Trueblood smiled—and his blue-gray eyes sparkled under his bushy, graying brows and deep dimples that re-shaped his reddish beard. It was the first time Kate had seen him really smile. 'I expect every mother of a Gypsy girl old enough to marry would like to catch him for her daughter! I don't know why he hasn't married. He does seem to take his responsibilities for the clan very seriously. Maybe there is a girl waiting for him at the next stop. Who knows?' Mr. Trueblood's teasing manner had the effect of transforming him into a charming elf. Kate could see why Bethany Trueblood would leave her family and church for such a man.

Mrs. Trueblood smiled at her husband. Then she sobered and shushed the children. 'Now, Abraham, you make him sound irresponsible and that's not fair. Gyorgy said that clan leaders always marry within the clan. Otherwise he would be ostracized, and he takes his position too seriously to risk that, I'm sure.'

She went on to change the subject. 'Kate, I mean Miss MacLean—'

'Oh, but do call me Kate,' she said. 'I'd like it if you did.'

'And you must call me Bethany!' Both women smiled. Bethany continued, 'You must tell us about your photography business. How did you become interested in it?' Bethany Trueblood's change of subject was as sharp a break as a new chapter in a book, and Kate was very grateful to her.

Kate spent some time describing the process of taking and printing pictures, keeping it simple. The children broke in with many questions, and Kate's schoolteacher background helped her to answer them in words they could understand.

Looking back now over the last few hours, Kate felt closer to Bethany Trueblood because they could now use first names with each other, and she rejoiced at the prospect of a close and continuing friendship. The Truebloods' ties with the Gypsy clan would have to be accepted for what they were—a good family helping others. The hiss of the tea kettle made her jump. She rose to her feet to pour herself a cup of tea.

* * *

When she woke up on a cold Saturday morning in late March, Kate pushed the hope chest quilt away from her chin and sat up in bed, frowning and fingering the blocks that were put together for her marriage. 'I don't care!' she said out loud. 'It's better to put the quilt to good use!' She had been angry with her mother when she decided to use it rather than continue to store it. Now she wondered if that decision had been an omen, or just a symbol of her resignation to being single?

At breakfast, Kate sat fingering her cereal spoon, her book open, her mind distracted. Her life had not worked out as she had assumed it would. She might as well give up the idea of marrying and having children of her own. She took a sip of strong tea. In the bottom of the cup, a stray tea leaf swam lazily with the gentle tide caused by her stirring hand. She knew about Gypsy fortune-tellers reading tea leaves. Maybe she should consult one. 'What am I going to do?' she asked the leaf. The question had hung about for days now like the cowl of a monkshood.

As she lifted a spoonful of oatmeal, her hand stopped, midair. What choices did she have? There were few. She had given some thought to going to Kansas where Lina and her husband lived. After fifteen years of marriage, they had no children, and Kate wondered if Lina felt sad about that. She lowered her spoon to the dish. Tears formed. She brushed at them and swallowed. Just then the telephone rang. Engrossed in her misery as she was, the insistent rings sounded like distant church bells on a frosty morning. She blinked but her body didn't even twitch. The ringing continued. Finally, she went to the studio to answer it.

'Kate? This is Angus. Can you come right away? Now? Lizzie's going to have the baby and we could use your help.' Angus' voice was frantic. Kate said nothing. 'You said a long time ago you'd be willing to help. Remember?'

There was another long pause. Kate shook herself. 'Yes. All right, Angus. I'll get over to the livery stable as soon as I can.' Her voice sounded far off.

'Are you all right, Katie?'

'Yes. Yes. Just half asleep, I guess. I'll hurry.'

She stared at her partly-eaten cereal. She couldn't bring herself to eat it, but she couldn't throw it away either, trained as she was to clean her plate. Finally she dumped it in the covered bucket under the sink for Mr. Sedlow's pigs. Quickly she cleaned up the dishes so the mice that sometimes nosed about her apartment would not find anything to eat. Strong as she thought herself to be, she had never conquered her abhorrence of the furry little creatures. She thought they were cute in a cage when students brought them to school for a science lesson, but on the loose in her house she could not abide them. She banked the stove so it would retain its warmth throughout the day while she would be gone.

In the bedroom, she changed to a simple blue cotton shirtwaist and wool skirt with several petticoats to keep her warm during the long drive through the countryside. There was no telling what she might be called on to do at the farm, but down deep she hoped Lizzie's sister, Mary, would be there to help with the delivery. Kate had never been present at a birthing and knew only what women said about it. The whole idea, from what she'd heard, sounded totally disagreeable, except that everyone seemed to forget the unpleasantness as soon as the baby appeared.

She slipped on her heavy woolen coat turning up the fur collar against the cold and pulled her dark felt hat over the ringlets that framed her face. She sat on the kitchen chair to pull her galoshes on. It would be cold driving through the partially melted snow to reach the farm.

Harold at the livery stable was very solicitous of her well-being. Once she was in the buggy, he tucked a horsehair blanket around her knees and feet. It smelled of the livery stable. 'Will you be warm enough, Miss Katie? I could get another blanket to put around your shoulders.'

'I'll quite all right. Thank you, Harold.'

He still held Billie Jean's reins. 'Billie Jean's good on slushy roads, but you want to be careful when you return this evening. It'll be frosty.' He averted his glance. 'Uh . . . Miss Katie, we could drive over to Benton for the dance Friday night if you'd like. I know you're a mighty fine dancer. Several people have said so.'

Kate was taken aback. It had been a long time since Harold had asked her out. She had always declined. Amused now at his persistence, she hesitated. Harold looked up hopefully. 'I'll let you know when I come back.'

Things went well at the farm. Mary was taking care of Lizzie, and Kate cooked and entertained the boys. Angus came into the dining room to announce, 'It's a girl!' Kate had heard a cry from the baby a few moments earlier and smiled. Angus invited the boys and Kate to come see the baby. 'Would you like to hold her?' Lizzie asked generously.

Kate stuttered, 'Oh, I'm not very good with babies,' but Angus put the baby in her arms anyway. It was a lovely feeling, she thought, holding this tiny creature whose little hands and eyes were tightly closed while her mouth with its perfect lips opened and closed. 'Oh, my goodness!' she declared. 'She's just perfect!' Angus and Lizzie beamed. Kate handed her back to her mother. 'What are you going to name her?'

Angus looked at Lizzie with a quizzical smile. 'Well, have you decided on a name?' Lizzie shook her head. She looked tired but said, 'How about calling her "Jenny"?'

'What a beautiful name!' said Kate, and a broad grin spread across Angus' face.

'Of course, why didn't I think of that?' he said as he alternated between caressing Lizzie's face and Jenny's.

When Kate went to finish the kitchen work, her mind strayed to thoughts of birthing a child of her own. She continued her thinking all the way back to town. Back at the livery stable, she turned the reins over to Harold and smiled at him. 'Harold, I do believe I would like to go to the dance with you.' Harold beamed and insisted on walking her to her apartment.

* * *

The phone's ringing clanged in Kate's head as she quickly pulled her woolen robe over her flannel gown and shoved her feet into her knitted slippers. Its insistent ring at such a late hour on a Saturday evening must mean something dreadful happened to Angus or Lizzie or the children. A tumble of dire thoughts filled her head as she hurried to the phone.

She was overwhelmed with relief that is was just Jean calling, but she was disgusted, too, at the intrusion. Jean Burchett knew very well when it was convenient to call and when it was not. Actually they had not been together for some time now. Since Kate and Bethany Trueblood had become friends, Kate could not easily ignore the shallowness of her relationship to Jean Burchett, and she supposed Jean sensed that.

Now here she was calling after Kate had banked the fire for the night. Kate had often dreamed of living in a warm place which didn't depend on her manual labor. Maybe she could find a man willing to stoke the fire, but most husbands she knew went down to the barn in the morning without ever touching the wood pile in the box behind the stove. It was a woman's job to keep it going. She smiled briefly remembering her evening with Harold. She wondered whether he could be trained to stoke the fire in the morning and bank it in the evening.

'Kate! What's this I hear about you going out with Harold Jones?' Jean's voice was shrill. 'I thought you said you were never going to go out with him, no matter what. You said his hair was too long and he was too short, and I remember distinctly that you didn't like his chin—you said it was too weak. You said you couldn't get serious about a man with a chin like that! Besides he's younger than you. And now it's all over town how you and he went to the dance over at Burton and he kissed you right there on the dance floor. Oh, how could you, Kate? You knew the whole town would be talking. Well, I can tell you, I'm mighty surprised at you. I'm not sure I should be your best friend if you're going to carry on like that.'

Breathless, Jean finally fell silent. Kate was too dumbfounded to speak, and she didn't know how to handle Jean's obvious fabrications. It was true that she had finally given in to Harold's frequent importuning for a dance partly out of sheer loneliness, but partly because there didn't seem to be anyone else. But kiss Harold? Never. In the first place, he would have been too shy to ask and would certainly never have kissed her without asking. In any case, she didn't like him well enough to comply even if he had asked.

Finally, Kate spoke quietly into the phone. 'How many years have you known me, Jean Burchett? Have I ever given you reason in all that time to think that I was and am a loose woman? Why would you believe town gossip? Who did you get it from—those drunks down at Jackson's Tap? You know better! You know people will believe the worst. I'm surprised at you and I'm not sure I can be a good friend to someone who would believe such trash about me.' There was silence on the other end of the line. Kate squared her shoulders and lifted her chin. 'And now I have better things to do than listen to such nonsense. Good-bye.'

Kate's sat seething by the telephone. Her eyes burned with anger and fear of the possible consequences of such a vicious rumor—fear of Harold's reaction to it, fear for her reputation. Kate had enjoyed dancing with Harold. His command of their movements surprised her, and he was surprisingly light on his feet, apologizing profusely when he misstepped. They laughed it off. Even driving to and from Burton was pleasant. She had not felt so light-hearted and so comfortable with a man in a long time. She had thought she might accept a second invitation from him, one she felt quite sure would be forthcoming, or at least she began to hope it would.

The enjoyment of the evening was serendipitous. All the years she'd known Harold, her impression of him had been quite different. He seemed to exude the smell of the livery stable and his broad and stubbly hands seemed to be covered with the same leather as the harnesses he oiled so carefully to preserve their pliability.

As they rode along the rutted highway to the dance hall, she studied his face and was shocked to realize the he'd never seemed to have a face before. His thick, sandy mustache—so different in color from his dark brown hair—had been neatly trimmed for the occasion and his chin seemed more confident than she remembered it. Beneath his bushy eyebrows, gentle blue eyes returned her frank appraisal, as if he understood why she needed to reevaluate him. She didn't know how she could have missed all this before.

Harold didn't talk much during the evening, but when he did, he chatted easily about the effects of the weather on his business and asked her about hers. His voice was gentle, and Kate remembered hearing that soothing voice talking to the horses at the stable. He laughed heartily relating a story about Mr. Simpson returning to town quite drunk one night and insisting on his horse's driving up the steps to the bandstand in the park. 'You should have seen it! The horse balked and the buggy tipped, dumping Mr. Simpson onto the snow.' They both laughed.

Kate's happy memory of their evening together faded as the thought of Jean Burchett's phone call intruded. Kate knew no one could have seen her kiss Harold Jones because the fact was, she hadn't. The meanness of the gossip finally caused hot tears to flow. It's too late, she thought. Harold would never dare ask her out again, and if he did, she wouldn't dare accept. For the men at Jackson's tap, it was an idle amusement; for her, it was an invasion of her selfhood and her integrity in the community.

The next few days she vowed to distance herself from such nonsense by burying herself in her work. She would send for more photography magazines. She'd never taken time to read them very thoroughly before, but now that it looked as if her photography would be her life, she felt a certain urgency to learn all she could about the trade. It was not that she didn't like her work, but like most young women, she had always planned on marrying and raising a family. This expectation now seemed increasingly remote. She felt ashamed—afraid that somehow something she had done had caused the rumors to start though night after night as she lay awake trying to fathom it all, she could not find herself at fault.

She lingered over her evening cup of tea poring over the latest camera and darkroom techniques and materials. Sometimes she thought she should have taken the chemistry course in high school as Angus had urged her to do, but which her mother thought was irrelevant to a woman's life.

Nevertheless, the new techniques and effects she was reading about were fascinating. For one thing, she had never tried tinting her photographs, but in big cities, she learned that women were employed full-time tinting prints taken by professional photographers. As the writers described the addition of rose blush on the cheeks, the pale greens of studio ivy vining across elaborate trellises, and sky blue dresses, Kate imagined the black and white half-tone photographs in the magazines as being colored and liked what developed in her mind. If she bought a set of tints, could she teach herself how to do it? There was no time for that now. Maybe someday in the future.

This study of her craft buoyed her spirits a bit, but it was a lonely sort of existence except for the people who came for sittings. Fortunately their numbers had not diminished so maybe the Harold incident was safely past. One day while she was working in the dark room, there was a gentle knock on the studio door. Kate was surprised to find Bethany Trueblood. 'Good morning, Kate,' she said hesitantly. 'I hope I'm not bothering you.'

'My goodness, no, Bethany. Do come in. I'm sorry I'm looking so shabby.' She started to take off the large canvas apron that covered all but the sleeves and hem of her dress. 'It's just that it's a work day for me in the darkroom and I can't wear my nicer dresses.'

'I don't mind one bit. You should see what I wear around the chicken yard. Besides you weren't expecting me! I should apologize for coming without letting you know, but it's so hard when we don't have a telephone, you know.' It was the first time Kate had ever heard Bethany even hint about lacking a modern convenience, and she took some satisfaction in it because it seemed as if Bethany trusted her as never before.

'Come in! Come in!' Kate urged. 'I'll put the tea water on. I welcome an excuse to sit and chat over a cup of tea.' Kate led the way to the kitchen.

'You know, Kate, one reason I came by was to learn what you do in the darkroom. It all sounds so mysterious—like magic! Can I see it? Could you show me some of your tricks?'

'Why, of course, but they're not really tricks. It's all a matter of light and dark and chemicals—which I frankly don't understand too well myself. I just know how to make them work. Or, at least most of the time they work the way I want them to, but sometimes they don't and I can't always figure out where I went wrong. But Bethany, I thought Mr. Trueblood doesn't really approve of photographs—even though he was polite enough to listen when I went on a bit at your house.'

Bethany Trueblood blushed, discomfited by the truth. 'You're right, Kate. He doesn't. You know, some people think that the camera steals a person's soul. That's not his complaint, but he says there's no need for recording a person's image on paper.'

'Then, you mean, you have no pictures of your family and your children to pass on to your grandchildren?' Kate frowned. The possibility of it had never occurred to her before. It was hard to imagine anyone not wanting to save this kind of family history, now that the technology was available. 'After all, people have been painting portraits for hundreds of years. Doesn't he approve of them either?'

'Well, no. Quakers believe in simple living, you know, and these would be counted as frivolity, I think. My family, of course, never had any objection to pictures, and I have some of my parents and brothers and sisters stowed away in a trunk, but I haven't even shown them to the children.'

The women drank their tea and lapsed into silence, Kate trying to fathom this new idea, and Bethany swallowing to avoid tears. Kate began to wonder if this seemingly ideal love marriage had its problems. They spent the next hour talking about picture-making, but then Bethany hastily excused herself and said she must go. 'I'm glad for whatever time you can and want to spend with me. Do come again. I think we have much to talk about,' said Kate as she saw her to the door.

* * *

Kate walked down the block to the post office on the morning of Valentine's Day, as she did every morning about ten. That was when the postman, Raymond Spencer, finished pigeon-holing all the letters and catalogs and bills. Jake Whitely delivered mail to most folks in town, but Kate decided a post office box address would sound more professional for the studio—MacLean Studio, P. O. Box 55, Tingle Creek, Nebraska. It meant, of course, that on rare occasions, a blizzard or the ague kept her from postal contact with the world outside. Today, though, the sun shone brightly and last week's snow had become slushy on the boardwalks and the street. The trick was to go anywhere without being splashed by a passing buggy.

'Good morning, Mr. Spencer!' she said and smiled at the business men twiddling the tiny combination locks on the boxes.

'Morning, Miss Katie!' Through the barred window, Kate saw that Mr. Spencer wore a quizzical smile which caused his thick blond mustache to twitch. She felt, rather than saw, the other men turn toward her. She assumed her entrance had caught them in the aftermath of a joke not meant for a lady's ears. She merely smiled.

Standing behind Bill Sedlow, waiting to get to her box, she saw Mr. Thompson tweak Bill Sedlow's arm. As he turned, Mr. Thompson pointed inconspicuously behind him. 'Oh, Miss MacLean. I'm so sorry!' He hastily stepped aside. 'Thank you,' said Kate as she twisted a left and a right and a left, 8-9-2. Opening the box, she pulled out a photographic supplies catalog and a rather large, square envelope with a red heart in the return address corner, nothing more. Chancy McDonnell, who had just stepped in the door, roared, 'Why, Miss Kate, what have you got?' Kate blushed and tucked the envelope into the catalog. She hastily exited past the knowing looks of the men.

She frowned. Who might be sending her such a grand Valentine? Certainly not Angus, and she hadn't spoken to Harold Jones but once since the dance when she ordered a buggy for a Sunday afternoon visit to the Truebloods. He never said anything about the dance or the gossip or the possibility of another occasion—and his usual jovial tone was missing. Kate wondered if she should apologize to him for the incident, but she didn't think that was appropriate in the light of her innocence. In any case, it was certain he wouldn't be sending her a Valentine!

After climbing the stairs to the studio, she set the envelope on the table to be opened at noon. When finally she sat down to her dinner of beef stew, she pondered more about the sender. There was no clue in the handwriting on the front though she guessed it to be a man's.

Carefully she slit the envelope so as not to harm the card itself. She pulled out a very beautiful Valentine with a cupid and hearts and lace and a message reading simply: 'To my Valentine.' There was no signature. She turned it over and over and examined every detail for a hidden name, but could find none. She could think of no way to determine who her admirer might be—well, she didn't really think she could call him an admirer. Was someone playing a cruel joke on her? One of the regulars down at Jackson's Tap? Not likely. Was it related to the poem slipped under her door earlier? Could it have been Gyorgy? Like her suspicions about the poem, she dismissed this possibility though she wished it could have been so. She could do nothing put it away and wait for the sender to make his identity known.

One day in late April, after picking up her mail and taking a few minutes to deposit her money at the State Bank, she hurried back to the studio, shivering in the cold north wind. Winter had hung on and the trees had reluctantly bloomed just the week before. She glanced toward the park where the vulnerable blossoms blew about in a snow-swirl around and through the bandstand and under the park benches. Her spring coat, which had seemed appropriate to match the bright shafts of sunlight streaming in her window an hour earlier, now sifted the chill air like so much gauze.

At the top of the stairs, she traded the coat for the practical sweater Lizzie had knit for her and hugged herself to feel the warmth of the soft wool. In spite of the brightness of the day and the promise of pear and apple blossoms, she was dispirited. Life had become so routine that she wondered again, if this was all there was to life. No amount of pink and white blossoms flattened on her windows like sleet in November could shake her lethargy and the feeling of sameness.

She set a pan on the back of the range and opened the cupboard. Among the piles of crockery, she selected a soup dish from her mother's set and ladled chicken and carrots and turnips and potatoes with her metal one-cup measure. She placed the steaming plate on the table and mechanically reached into the silverware drawer.

Kate had no enthusiasm for eating and certainly not for this nameless concoction in her bowl. 'Maybe if I sit by the window, I'll see something interesting,' she thought and took her food to the small spindle-legged table she used for a prop.

The street was empty at noon, except for Mr. Simpson on his way home for dinner. The quiet was interrupted by the town whistle followed by chirrupy children's voices below her and out of her line of sight. Whoever they were, they seemed to be playing some game on the boardwalk alongside the meat market. It was curious because schoolchildren going home for dinner wouldn't reach the main part of town until a half hour later. She swallowed a mouthful of soup and strained to see the children below, avoiding a position too close to the window where someone might see her. Just then Harold Jones appeared, driving one of the livery stable wagons. She pulled back with a jerk, but relaxed when he reached the intersection and turned north out of sight.

She attended to buttering one of yesterday's leftover biscuits. Tomorrow she would be making fresh, light biscuits to eat. As she applied honey, a child darted away from the side of the building into her line of sight with another in pursuit. She was surprised to see they were Gypsy children. That's odd, she thought, when Bethany was at the studio a few days earlier, she hadn't mentioned their being in town. In fact, neither of them had mentioned the Gypsies. Now, the children ran quickly to the corner and crossed the street disappearing into the post office. Almost as quickly, they emerged holding the hands of a man. The two little boys danced and laughed, looking up mischievously as the man walked steadily across the street toward the meat market below her studio. It was Gyorgy!

Kate's mind raced. Was Gyorgy coming to the studio, at last, to see his pictures? She quickly pushed her chair back, picked up the remainder of the stale biscuits and the soup bowl with its last spoonful and dumped the remains in the garbage. She must be prepared in case Gyorgy came to the studio. But, oh! What if he came with the children? All the shopkeepers told about the petty pilfering Gypsy children were said to have done while their mothers 'shopped'. 'Beasts' was what Mr. Simpson called them. How could she watch them and talk to Gyorgy as she wanted to? Oh, my. Here she was echoing the townspeople's opinion of the Gypsies. She'd have to think about that.

She untied her apron and hung it on a nail in the kitchen. The knock should not have startled her, but it did. She took a deep breath and walked firmly to the door. She cautioned herself to be wary and lifted her chin to appear self-assured. Stepping aside, she opened the door. There stood Gyorgy, an imposing figure, but his impish grin and sparkling eyes made him seem more like a fun-loving schoolboy. She couldn't help but laugh. He released the hands of the two children and with a sweep of his right hand, he brought his stained leather hat from off his head to below his knees as his body bent in an ebullient bow. 'Miss Katie!' he exclaimed. 'How are you?'

Kate reddened. Was he making fun of her? Or, was he being funny for the children's amusement? She opened and closed her mouth twice before she could speak. 'Very well, thank you.' Her voice was pleasant but her gaze was on the children. Immediately Gyorgy understood her tentativeness.

'Go, boys: Sit on the bottom step until I come down.'

'But can't we see your pitchers?' the older boy protested.

'Of course, you will be the first to see them when I am finished with my business, but only if you go now and sit quietly. Do not move from there no matter what happens. Do you hear?'

'Not even if a wild dog comes after us?'

'Not even if a whole pack of dogs come. Now go!'

The little one took Kate's hand and looked up at her earnestly. 'Say, Miss, is it really true that you work magic with people's faces?' Kate smiled.

'The answer is no!' Gyorgy said loudly and reached out a hand as if to spank the nearest little boy. The two turned promptly toward the stairs but then turned to take one last curious look at this woman as if she might really be a magician in spite of what Gyorgy said.

Gyorgy laughed and suddenly Kate laughed, too. They were such beautiful children and obviously adored this man. 'Well, Miss MacLean, here I am at last to see what magic you've accomplished with this ugly face.'

'Oh, but—' Kate began, but decided it would be improper for her to say how handsome she really thought he was. 'Yes, well—Do have a seat in the studio—the throne, perhaps! I'll just get the pictures.' Gyorgy, smiling broadly so that his dark eyes sparkled in the half light of the hallway, made a slight bow and did as he was told.

Flustered by the unexpected visitors, Kate hurried into her rooms. She thought her interest in Gyorgy had waned, but the shivery feeling that enveloped her body worried her. She plumped down on the bed to clear her head. She mentally shook herself and then physically did so. How silly she was, she told herself. He came only for his pictures. She must get up, find the pictures, and be rid of him.

As she stood up, she checked her hair in the mirror and dabbed at a few stray eyebrow hairs. She had never liked the bushy brows she'd inherited from her father, but chastised herself for giving them a thought. After all, who would notice?

Finally, she opened the wardrobe and stretched to lift her linens from the overhead shelf. Then she brought down the brown paper wrapped bundle of Gyorgy's pictures. She gave fleeting thought to the fact that she would no longer be able to open them in the privacy of her room and gaze at his wonderful face whenever she felt like it. She knew that she could print more from the glass negatives at any time, but deep in her heart she knew she should not. No! It was time to be rid of them once and for all, but at the last minute she tucked one of them, the full length pose, back into her cupboard.

Gyorgy stood by the window looking across the park. Kate placed the package on the wicker table. She did not want to interrupt his thought, but she felt she must. Rather more loudly than necessary, she said, 'Here you are. I hope you like them.' She stepped back so he could take them to the diffused light of the north window. Instead, Gyorgy stood turning the package over and over as if trying to figure out how to open it.

Finally, he said, 'Why, thank you, Miss Katie. I'll have the children bring the kettles tomorrow. They're repaired good as new. You won't find a leak in any of them.'

Kate's right thumb massaged her left palm as she stood puzzled by Gyorgy's seeming disinterest in the pictures she'd worked so hard to perfect. The focus was sharp and it was just the right shade of light and dark to bring out the shine in his eyes and his hair and his shoes. 'Perhaps you'd better check to see if you are satisfied.'

He stared at the package. 'I'm sure they're just fine.' Gyorgy looked directly at Kate and smiled broadly, but seemed quite serious. 'I'm proud to have them, and I'm sure my new bride will be pleased also.'

Kate was startled. The announcement astonished her more than anything could have. She seemed to shrink away from his gaze though her feet remained unmoved. She blinked and the color of her eyes took on the intensity of a cold blue flame. They seemed to disappear as if behind a veil of delicate lace. She struggled to speak. 'Why—Mr. Gyorgy—I'm—I'm very happy for you. I hadn't heard of your marriage.'

'Well, I'm not married yet, but I will be when we reach Osawatomie. It is arranged that I will meet my bride there. Her clan will join ours for five days of feasting. You would enjoy a Roma wedding. There'll be music and dancing and every kind of special food, and then I'll be introduced to my wife.' Kate looked surprised. 'You see, we don't have choices about who we marry. We bow to the wisdom of our elders.'

Kate could not look at him. 'I'll look forward to getting the kettles tomorrow. I think you'd better go now, Mr. Gyorgy. May you and your wife be very happy.'

Gyorgy tilted her chin up with his free hand and smiled at her. 'You are a beautiful woman, Kate MacLean, and some man will be fortunate to make you his bride!' With that, he tucked the packet of pictures under his arm and opened the door. Kate stood where he had left her.

IV

In the next few weeks Kate applied herself to her work. As clients' faces began to emerge in the developing fluid, she thought about all those she had seen appear over the years as if by magic. Somehow, the glass plates of Gyorgy were blotted out in her reverie. She took this as a good sign, a sign that she was facing reality, a sign that life would go on in this little town of Tingle Creek much the same as it always had. She thought often about what might have happened if Benny Barlowe had been more attractive or the evening with Harold Jones had gone well or if Gyorgy had been a local farmer. She smiled at that idea, but quickly sobered and hung up the print she was working on.

Her future seemed clear. She would continue taking pictures of weddings and baby christenings and aging grandmas. She had balked at taking funeral pictures. She knew that in some foreign communities (was it the Bulgarians? she couldn't quite remember), pictures were taken of the recently deceased in all their funeral finery in their caskets, but she could not imagine taking such photographs. Somehow it seemed grotesque. No, she loved the joyousness of celebratory family occasions with pictures to record them.

Not too long after Gyorgy's visit, Kate was at work posing Mrs. Larimore when the telephone rang. Kate freed herself from the black cloth over her head and spoke to Mrs. Larimore. 'Will you excuse me while I answer the telephone?' Her client demurred, shifting slightly in the red velvet chair so Kate knew she would have to reposition her on returning to the task at hand.

There were times when she resented the intrusion of the telephone, but she could not deny its usefulness. She admitted to Angus and Lizzie that, with more families having telephones, the convenience of almost instant communication about matters both good and bad did outweigh the interruptions.

She picked up the receiver and stretched toward the mouthpiece. 'This is the MacLean Photography Studio.'

'Kate? This is Esther. Esther Fergus Allan, remember me? I'll bet you're surprised to hear from me, aren't you?'

'Why yes, yes I am. How are you?'

'Oh, we're all very well. And you?' Without waiting for an answer, she went on. 'It's been quite awhile since we've seen you, and I was just saying to Robert the other day, why don't we have Kate MacLean come out some Sunday for dinner. And Robert agreed it would be a good idea.' Esther called her husband Robert, but everyone else called him 'Bud'.

'How about it?' Esther urged. 'Can you come next Sunday? Some of the family are coming, and they would like to see you.' She bubbled as she had when they were in Normal School together.

'Why, yes, Esther, I'd be glad to come. But now, if you will excuse me, I have a customer waiting for me.' Esther apologized and said she was delighted she would come, and no, she mustn't keep her customer waiting. Finally, she hung up, and Kate when back to Mrs. Larimore's sitting.

On Sunday, Kate greeted Harold pleasantly and let him help her into the buggy. Kate had had few occasions to hire a buggy since her evening with Harold, but that was all right. Thank goodness, Harold now had a telephone so she could call to reserve Billie Jean. Harold was very cordial on the phone. 'I'm going to be going to the Allans,' she said. Harold assured her Billie Jean would be harnessed and waiting for her. Their business relationship would continue, but it would be no more than that, she thought ruefully.

On the way to Esther and Bud's place, Kate began thinking about her friendship with Esther. She didn't feel she knew Esther very well anymore even though they had gone to school together from childhood and had taken Normal Training together after high school.

The Ferguses and MacLeans had immigrated to Nebraska from the Orkney Islands about the same time which gave them a common tie, but a tenuous one, as the families lived too far apart to visit often. The families got together once every summer when Kate and Esther were growing up. These 'children of Orkney', as they called themselves, picnicked together on the grounds of the old stone mill. It was a beautiful site, far upstream from the Long's Creek School at a place where glacial boulders had settled during the ice age.

Food seemed to be the main item of business with each housewife trying to outdo the others. There were baskets of fried chicken and potato salad and beans, baked long hours in cookstove ovens, and sliced cucumbers and sweet white onions in clabbered milk and tomatoes from the garden and and fresh gooseberry pies made from the tiny wild gooseberries that grew in rough pasture thickets. Kate remembered all too well the pain of pricked fingers and the discouragement of tin pails that filled with the slowness of molasses.

These were pleasant remembrances as she drove along. She thought about how Esther and her sister Mattie, a year younger, and Kate and the other girls joined the boys playing hide-and-seek around the mill and the boulders and the nearby woods. One year Mattie was recovering from typhoid fever so she sat on one of the big horsehair blankets next to the rocking chair which had been brought along for her Grandmother Fergus.

Kate felt sorry for Mattie, so she came and sat squat-legged opposite her for a game of pease-porridge-hot. They continued quietly until something Grandmother Fergus said caught Kate's attention and she turned to listen.

'Oh, yes, they'd hardly been married two years.'

'Who, Grandma? Who?' Mattie tugged the hem of her grandmother's long brown dress.

'Why, Kate's great-grandmother and great-grandfather. You never knew them. This was back in Orkney,' Grandma Fergus repeated patiently. 'As I was saying, they hadn't been married but long enough to have little Edward. Well, the way Mary told it James and his brother took the boat across the bay to pick up a farmhand. Now Mary and James lived in a house up on a hill overlooking the passage. Anyway, about the time she expected them, Mary went out and saw the men coming across the bay in the boat so she went back in the house to put on the tea water.'

Kate started to interrupt. 'Hush, Kate. Listen to the story,' Kate's mother had cautioned.

'Well, after awhile when Mary was pretty sure the men would be walking up from the beach, she picked up little Edward and went to the door. She said the wind'd picked up to where she thought they'd be blown back inside, but the men were nowhere to be seen! It was hard to hold

Edward and her skirts in the wind and keep her balance as she walked a few yards down the slope to have a better look. There was no boat on the water—and no sign of the men. And nothing of them was ever found.'

'Oh, my! What happened?' Kate's voice was suddenly worried. She rose to her knees and looked imploringly in the old woman's face.

Stern as Grandmother Fergus usually was, she responded to Kate's distress by stroking her hair. 'I'm sorry, child. The wind must have blown the boat up on the shoals. Your great-grandfather James and his brother Joseph and the farmhand never came back.'

'Then how can I be here today?' Kate asked, incredulous.

'Well, you see, little Edward grew up and married and they came to Nebraska.'

Clopping along in the buggy now, Kate smiled to remember the story though it was always sad to think of her great grandmother all alone with little Edward.

When Kate halted the buggy in the Allan farmyard that day, she wasn't surprised to see Angus' buggy already parked under a large burr oak, shading the house on the south. She knew Lizzie had been best friends with Esther's youngest sister when they were in Normal School.

'Hello, Aunt Katie! Betcha can't find me!' cried a small voice with a muffled giggle. Kate looked up to where the old tree spread like a mantle over the gate to the yard, and in the foliage she could just see a pair of high-topped shoes dangling from one of the branches. She reached up but couldn't quite touch them. They disappeared into the foliage as she stretched. Just then Angus stepped from behind the tree and lifted her off the ground with an impetuous swoop.

'Hah, that's what you get for being so short!' He whirled her once and dropped her gently onto her feet. It had been a long time since they had been so playful together and it felt good. She had seen very little of this good-humored side of her brother in recent years.

'Come get me, Aunt Katie,' John cried, but Kate ignored him.

'Look, Kate, come on in the house. Esther's been anxious to see you. And Mary and her husband are here, too. By the way, do you remember Esther's older brother Henry? He was one of the big boys who teased us little kids when we had those summer picnics. Well, he's here with his boy Will. Henry's wife Harriet died a couple years ago. He's got a farm north and east of Tingle Creek.'

'Maybe I'll remember him when I see him.'

Angus put his arm around her shoulder as they walked up to the house. 'I think you've shrunk,' he laughed.

'I have not and you know it,' she argued. 'How's baby Jenny? Growing a lot, I'll bet.'

'You'll see how big she's getting. And smart, too. Like you!' They reached the house just as John caught up with them.

* * *

Sometime later, the telephone rang as Kate was posing the Pedersen children for a Christmas portrait. Mrs. Pedersen had said when they arrived looking resplendent in their best dresses and knickers that the picture was to be a surprise for Mr. Pedersen. Kate had just found the perfect pose when the telephone interrupted.

'Excuse me a minute. I'm sorry. Sometimes the telephone can be a real nuisance, can't it?' Kate said.

As she walked across the room, she saw Mrs. Pedersen put her forefinger to her lips and whisper, 'Shhh . . . Auntie Kate is going to talk on the phone now and you must be very quiet. Paul, no, you must be quiet. I'd better take Ida Jane. Sit still, Marie Elizabeth. Now mind. Auntie'll be back in just a minute.'

'This is the MacLean Studio,' Kate said into the phone very professionally. A look of thoughtful surprise crossed her face as she recognized Henry Fergus' voice asking how she was and if she remembered him. 'Why, I'm fine, and yes of course I do,' she said guardedly.

'Well, Miss Kate, I enjoyed seeing you at Esther and Bud's place, and I wondered if you were ever free of a Saturday evening. I thought maybe we could go to the dance at Almora this Saturday.'

'If you'll excuse me,' she said, 'I really haven't time to talk just now. I have some clients in the studio. Perhaps if you could call at a later time we could discuss this more.'

'Oh, I'm sorry to interrupt. May I call at 6 o'clock today?'

Kate agreed, but did not immediately turn back to the job at hand. Instead she stood with the receiver to her ear while pressing the cradle down with the other. Her mind turned to that dinner at Esther's, and she smiled, finally returning the receiver to its cradle.

'Now then, Paul, let's have Ida Jane back on your lap!' Her commanding voice sent the children scurrying to their former positions.

She moved quickly from the camera to the children to change the angle of Marie Elizabeth's chin and the position of Ida Jane's grip on the little rubber ball she held and to smooth back a lock of Paul's hair that lopped over one eyebrow. As she re-positioned them, her spirits were light and she fussed more than usual to make the picture as pleasing to her friends as she could.

'And now, Mrs. Pedersen, suppose you stand beside me, holding this rag doll. All right, children. Keep your eyes on dolly and don't move until I say so.' Kate pulled the darkslide away and returned it after what must have seemed an age to the children. 'Good for you!' she exclaimed. 'Just a couple more and then you may go.'

After Mrs. Pedersen and the children clattered down the stairs, Kate went to the kitchen to pour herself a cup of tea. She sat by the east window to watch the children from the south end of town trooping home from school along Third Street. Sometimes they pushed and jostled and teased, and they were usually noisy. She was watching the activity, but thinking about the phone call from Henry Fergus.

Yes, she did remember Henry Fergus from the time at Esther's. She noted that he teased Esther the way Angus used to tease her. When Henry looked at Kate with his liquid green eyes, she had the feeling he was sizing her up, but other than pleasantries, they had talked little. His attention to her during the dinner consisted of asking her which pie was hers and eating two pieces, one after the other, raving about the one while helping himself to the other.

She was amused. She had made two apple pies to take, assuming Angus would be there. Over the years, Kate had experimented with her apple pies. Angus and Lynus used to groan that, if she happened on a good combination, why didn't she just stick to it? Yesterday she added a half teaspoon of cardamom to the cinnamon and left out the nutmeg. It was an idea she'd gotten from Bethany Trueblood who'd gotten it from her Swedish grandmother. Everyone raved about the pies and wanted to know her secret.

Now she sipped her sweet, milky tea and rocked. Kate had not refused Henry Fergus's offer outright—mostly because of the Pedersen's being in the studio. Now, remembering the dance at Burton with Harold made her cringe. If she went with Henry Fergus, what might happen? Was she willing to risk it? Somehow it seemed like it would be more acceptable for a woman of her age to be seen with a widower a little older than with a shy single man a few years younger, as Harold was. She did like to dance, and maybe there would be no gossip this time.

She wondered whether Henry was a good dancer. If he were cloddish, she would be disappointed, but surely he would not be totally inept. Besides, there weren't many eligible men her age in the Tingle Creek area and not much to do of an evening, except for a band concert or a picnic at Connor's Grove in the summer. Church socials were nice but didn't allow much private conversation, and after all, at their age romance was not so much of a factor.

Kate refilled her tea cup and broke off a bit of biscuit. She frowned. Suppose something came of this interest in each other? There was the matter of his son, of course. She had only seen Will the one time and he had seemed nice enough, but would he like her? She realized she was getting ahead of herself, but still, there was much to consider.

Outside, the autumn dusk was closing in. Kate brought the rocker to a halt and put her tea cup down. What was she thinking of? Will, indeed! She might not even like this Henry if she had a chance to talk to him. Certainly, he was nice enough looking in spite of the bald spot which showed signs of enlarging. (How far would it engulf his thick, straight sandy hair? And did it matter?) His eyes twinkled when he laughed and deep crows' feet formed at the outer corners that gave him a decidedly elfish look. His body was hard and not too lean, but he had no paunch. She was surprised—and a little embarrassed—to realize she had paid so much attention to his looks! She stood up and turned on the light, determined to get back to her work and determined to give Mr. Fergus a chance.

He called promptly at six o'clock, exactly the time the MacLean Studio ad in the Tingle Creek Herald said she would close Monday through Friday. 'Hello. MacLean Studio,' Kate said.

'Miss Kate, this is Henry Fergus calling back. Are you free to talk?' This time he thought to ask and she was impressed.

'Yes, Mr. Fergus. Just fine.'

'Please, do call me Henry. Now, about the dance in Almora. I got to thinking after seeing you at Esther's. I watched you. Maybe you didn't know I did, but I did, and you seemed to enjoy the family a lot. I thought I'd like to get to know you better, but I'm kind of shy and so I've waited all this time. Esther keeps telling me to call, but, you know, Kate, it's been kind of hard since Harriet died, and all, to think about other women. Still, I said, Esther's right. So what I'm saying is I'd like to have you for a friend,'

Henry took an audible breath and paused. 'I thought maybe if we took it kind of easy and went to a few social gatherings together, we might get to know one another, and, well, would you like to go to the dance over at Almora Saturday night?'

Henry Fergus hesitated, but Kate did not say anything. He went on, his voice a little strained. 'I don't know. I'm not too much of a dancer and all. Before we were married, Harriet and I went once in awhile. She was much better than I am. Oh, I'm not too bad with a slow waltz but we could just talk if dancing doesn't work.'

Kate laughed. 'Now, Henry Fergus, before you go further, just let me say I don't mind if you don't dance those new-fangled dances. Actually, I'm not too much of a dancer myself,' she apologized.

'Will you come with me then? We could just have a nice time together. Besides it'll be my birthday and I think an evening with a pretty lady like you would make it very special.'

'You're very convincing, Henry Fergus. I would look forward to accompanying you.'

Henry Fergus sounded relieved as they settled the arrangements. 'I thank you, Miss Kate. I used to just call you Kate—would you mind if I called you that now?' Kate wanted to teasingly remind him that he already had, but she held her tongue.

'Yes, you may. Thank you, Henry Fergus. I'll be ready.'

* * *

That first evening she went with Henry to the dance at Almora, she felt more light-hearted and carefree—young even—than she had in a long time. Every time Henry made a misstep, he screwed his face up. She laughed out loud. This seemed to delight him and made him laugh as well. So absorbed was she in the enjoyment of Henry's amusements that she quite forgot the evening with Harold.

On the drive back to Tingle Creek that night, Kate remembered the roughness of Henry's hands and the gentle, but muscular feel of the boost he gave her into the buggy. Neither spoke as they rode along, as if listening to the gentle slap of the reins on the horse's flanks and the soft plopping of each hoof on the soft earth was enough. Suddenly Kate was aware that Henry had turned off the main road onto a side road with thick woods on either side.

'Where does this road go?' she challenged him.

'Past Charlie Hampton's place.'

She was caught off guard by the change of direction and drew her arms close across her chest, wondering what Henry might have in mind. She wanted to reach out and grab the reins to halt their forward progress, but she knew his more powerful arms could easily prevent her from doing so. She felt the buggy slow, and sensed rather than saw, his gradual pulling back on the reins.

'Whoa. Whoa there. Easy now,' Henry whispered and the horse stopped. 'I thought maybe we could talk better here than on Main Street in Tingle Creek. The fellows leaving Jackson's Tap would have something to say about us for sure.' Kate wondered if he, too, had heard the gossip about her and Harold Jones. Rather earnestly now, he added,'—And I do want to talk to you, Kate!'

'What did you have in mind, sir?' She emphasized the 'sir' as if challenging him because she didn't know whether to trust his intentions.

'Well, I was wondering how you liked growing up on the farm.'

The question startled her for its simplicity, but it seemed a fair enough question—even a useful one since living in town gave her a basis for comparison. 'Why, I quite enjoyed living on the farm. There was always lots of work to do, but the good clean air and the openness and the trees made me happy. There were the smells, of course . . .' Kate paused and Henry laughed. She added. 'But even the animal smells were tempered with the smell of new mown hay and flowers.' Henry smiled in encouragement.

They carried on a lively discussion, then, much as she might have had with Angus or Lynus or even her father. It all seemed quite natural, and Kate relaxed. Thinking about it later, she decided she'd never had a more interesting talk about—well, about life itself. Henry talked easily about Harriet as the occasion arose, but Kate sensed he still felt pain over her death. Even so, he seemed to accept her death as a fact of his life.

Then, without warning, Henry reached out and took Kate's hand in both his own. 'Kate, I like you. You're a fine person and a joy to be with. I never thought after Harriet took ill and died that I would ever find a woman that I'd want to be with, and I made up my mind that I would go on farming and taking care of Will by myself. But then Esther started to work on me.' Henry laughed. 'Yup. One day she mentioned how much she admired you when you went to Normal School together. Of course, I remember you from summer picnics, but you were just a child then.

'Anyway, Esther kept bringing up your name, so I guess I shouldn't have been surprised when she invited you and Angus and Lizzie to come to the picnic last summer, but I was. I mean, I was mainly surprised at how right Esther was about you—and she and I don't always agree, you know.'

Kate laughed remembering the good-natured arguing between Henry and Esther that July day. Henry went on. 'Esther must have been watching me carefully because ever after she's been reminding me about how smart you are to own your own business and how clever you are with a camera and how pleasant you always are, but it took me a long time to convince myself that maybe you might consider going out with a simple farmer like me.'

'Why, I—'

'Shhh. I'm not through and if I get interrupted, I might not be able to go on. Y'see, Kate, tonight I realized that I really could like another woman and maybe someday that woman might come to like me after she got to know me better—someone who liked me enough to want to get to know me. What do you think, Kate? Do you think you might be willing to at least try to get to know me better? Maybe you won't find me worth the time, but I sure wish you'd give it a try.'

'Well, Henry, I'm flattered that anyone would want me to try. After all, I'm—'

'You're what! You're the kind of lady who could make any man happy, Kate. I'm glad you waited—for my sake!'

'Why, Henry, that's the nicest thing! I believe I would like to get to know you better.'

'Good.'

'But we'd better be getting back to Tingle Creek now.' As Henry turned the horse around, Kate wondered if her life was about to turn around as well. She closed her eyes and in the quiet darkness, Gyorgy's handsome face popped into her consciousness. What a contrast these two men were, but she knew it was time to say goodbye to Gyorgy no matter how well she might come to know Henry.

* * *

Angus stopped in every week now to ask how their courtship was progressing. The truth was Henry and Kate could not see each other often.

There was his farm work and her business, and the distance between them hindered frequent visits. Kate put Angus off as best she could, but she knew he would keep asking until he got the answer he wanted. The truth was that, in her mind, she felt sure she would give Henry a positive answer, if and when he asked, but there was much to think about—like whether a marriage would work.

She made a special trip to see and talk with Bethany Trueblood, who was much less sanguine in her appraisal of the match. 'Kate,' she said, 'I'd suggest you reconsider. Have you thought—really thought—about what your independence has meant to you?' This was surprising coming from Bethany. 'After all, you're the best photographer for miles around. Aren't you letting down the very people who've come to depend on you to record their family history? Why, you'd be giving up your art! I know this must sound odd coming from someone who doesn't much believe in photographs, but it's a part of who you are—and that's important. Besides, how much do you know about Henry—really know about Henry?'

Bethany's caution caused Kate to ponder long and hard. 'You're right, of course, but you have a partner to go into old age with. I don't.' Bethany granted this was true. Kate, in thinking about the years ahead, however few they might be, yearned for a companion to share them with. 'I haven't found anyone that suits me perfectly,' she argued, 'but Henry is very agreeable to me—so far at least! Do you think anyone ever enters into a marriage agreement without some doubts?' There was much to be considered.

'At least,' urged Bethany, 'you ought to keep your photographic equipment, just in case. Of course, I suppose you could always go back to teaching though I got the impression you didn't like it very much.' Kate acknowledged that was true, but she could if she had to.

As she was leaving, Kate said almost tearfully, 'The hardest thing for me, though, is that if I marry Henry, we'll live so much farther from you, Bethany. I will miss seeing you and talking with you!'

Bethany reached out and hugged Kate. 'I'll miss you, too, but you will write to me and tell me how things are going. And I do wish you the very best, whatever your decision.' Kate knew she must leave; otherwise, she was afraid she would weaken in her resolve to marry Henry. She waved as she drove out of the drive, still wondering what was the best thing to do.

The next time Kate and Henry were together, they went to Esther and Bud's place for Sunday dinner, but excused themselves early. It was a cold

March day but bright and sunny and the smell of spring was in the air. Henry tucked Kate into the buggy, checking to see if her feet were warm enough with the extra carriage robe he brought along. He arranged the robe over her knees and up to her shoulders. Then he tickled her ears. The physical sensation spread throughout Kate's body and she blushed. 'Now, Henry Fergus, you know you oughtn't to do that!' He laughed delightedly and climbed in beside her, pulling a horse blanket over his own feet.

At the end of an extra long ride through the countryside, Henry stopped beside a thick grove of cedar trees. He put his arms around her and kissed her nose and her forehead. She couldn't help giggling. 'Now,' he said solemnly, 'I want to ask you something.' Kate sobered. He cleared his throat as if he were going to make a very solemn speech about something very monumental. She waited. Finally, he smiled and blurted out, 'Kate, will you marry me? I know I'm not much of a catch and all, but I'd be mighty proud to be your husband. What do you say?'

Kate looked at her feet and the warm tingling started all over again. 'Why yes, Mr. Fergus, I believe I will marry you!' Henry was jubilant and kissed her full on the lips. 'Ah—ah—but wait! There are things we need to talk about,' Kate declared.

'Kate, my love, they can wait, and I promise you we will talk about every thing you think we need to talk about, but not today! I must get you back to Tingle Creek, but some day I'll be taking you to my house instead—and then it will be our house!' Kate laughed, and they rode the rest of the way without talking, in the comfort of their new-found intimacy.

In the weeks that followed there was much to discuss, much that needed a mutual understanding. The disposition of the studio was paramount in Kate's mind. Henry advised her to advertise closing her studio a month ahead and simply close the door on the last day. 'You know it's not a question of money,' he said. 'I have plenty to take care of you.'

Henry went on. 'You could even have your business in the attic of our house, if you want.' It was these last words that rang in Kate's head now. It was nice to know she would not have to worry about money, but did she need to be taken care of? Hadn't she proved that she could take care of herself? She inwardly longed to continue the work she had grown to enjoy so much, but she knew she couldn't, no matter what Henry said. If she opened a studio in Henry's house, customers would have to travel to the farm and it simply wasn't practical. And besides, she was taking on a new job—that of a full-time farmer's wife and even a mother (though she had no idea how this was going to work out).

No, she could not deny the fact that she was faced with closing—and hopefully, selling her photography business. For several evenings after her last customers had clomped down the wooden stairs, Kate wandered aimlessly from room to room, thinking about the practical problems of leaving the business.

Standing in the darkroom, she surveyed the shelves of negatives taken over the years. There were the first pictures of the Bennetts' twin babies, the marriage pictures of Mrs. Bennett's nephew, the pictures of Milton Mason and his second bride whose dour expression remained no matter how hard Kate tried to improve on it. The rows of neatly filed negative plates reminded her that there was one print still tucked away on the shelf in her bedroom.

She left the darkroom and crossed over to Gyorgy's chair in the studio and sat down. A pain shot through her—a pain as real as a heart attack. Why had she agreed to marry Henry anyway? Was this what she really wanted to do? She almost wished she could get Gyorgy's blessing for the marriage. She stroked the red velvet on the arms of the chair and noticed that they were showing signs of wear. She really should reupholster it, But, why, if she was going to leave the studio?

The chair aside, how much of a risk would this venture be? One by one, she was reminded of all the risks she hadn't taken in her life. What if she had married Benny Barlowe when she was 19? What if she had left Tingle Creek when Mr. Langley in Fremont had invited her to go into business with him?

Bethany's caution caused Kate to ponder long and hard. Even now she was nervous at the thought of starting a new life—an uncertain life—as a wife. She had found Henry to be very agreeable—so far at least. But what if . . . ? There were so many unknowns.

Looked at this way, marrying Henry seemed like quite an adventure in itself. Her fingers traced the carving of the wooden leg where it met the red velvet on the arms. The scrolls of the carving felt so different from the rich cloth, yet together they created a beauty she'd never thought about before. She half smiled. What if she'd had a chance to marry Gyorgy? That would have been risk enough for a lifetime, she thought, and jumped out of the chair. She walked around the chair feeling the carved wooden berries and vines along the upper back of the chair. Of course! Why not! She would take the chair with her to Henry's place—even if she had to store it in the attic! It would remind her of where she'd been and the interface of that life with her new one.

Suddenly she remembered she must change her clothes quickly before Henry arrived to take her to Sunday dinner at Angus and Lizzie's place. If only she could have such delightful children as theirs! She knew it could never be. She would have to be content with Will.

On the drive to Angus' place, Henry said he wanted her to come see his house, but she said, 'No, not until we're married. What would people think about me being in your house when we're not married yet! No, I don't want anyone to say I'm not being proper.'

'Well, you know,' he said, 'you can do anything to the house you want to.' Kate thanked him, but she knew she probably wouldn't. Henry and Harriet had built the house, and it was really Harriet's, not hers.

Actually, she had been thinking a lot about the house. She did want to take some of her things. She'd be taking her dresser, of course, and Henry assured her she would have plenty of space in the chiffonier to hang her dresses. She had told Angus she'd be taking the organ, and he agreed she should. She would want her grandmother's rocker, too, and the secretary she had bought to keep track of her bills in the studio. When she mentioned these things to Henry, he readily agreed, saying there was room for them all.

Even so, she was curious as to what the house was really like. 'Henry, I know you called me on the phone once. Do you have a phone in the house?'

'Of course, Kate. I was one of the first to install one in our neighborhood. I think it's a necessity, don't you?'

'It certainly was for my business,' she said. That settled, her thoughts turned to the familiar road to Angus' place—to the place she had always thought of as 'home'. I've got to quit thinking that way, she said to herself, frowning. She reached over and patted Henry's hand. He turned to her with a broad grin, and she knew it was going to be all right.

At dinner, Henry cleared his throat as if he were ready to make an important speech. Everyone turned in his direction. He reddened and then smiled broadly. 'Kate and I are to be married! he declared, looking very pleased with himself. Angus and Lizzie were delighted. Their congratulations came with an almost audible sigh of relief. 'Why, Kate, that's the best news you could ever have brought us,' Lizzie said. 'Henry is such a fine man. You'll never be sorry.' Even the children clapped! It seemed to be the right decision, after all, Kate thought as she smiled at Henry.

* * *

'Kate! My goodness, what's this I hear . . .' Esther's voice squealed over the phone.

'Esther? Is this you, Esther? I can't understand you. We've got a bad connection. I'll hang up and have Jean Burchett reconnect us,' Kate replied, but didn't bother to hang up. She knew Jean would be listening. Jean said nothing, but there was a moment of dead silence and then Jean's voice came on. 'You may continue with your call to Miss MacLean now.'

'Kate? Is this better? I could hear you perfectly.' The shrill excitement had gone from Esther's voice which had dropped several tones and become more matter of fact.

'Yes, Esther. I can hear you very well now. What were you saying?'

'Well, Kate, I've just heard the news. Henry was here this morning. He didn't even have the sense to call me. That man! He thinks a long distance call can only be used for emergencies. Well, I'd say this was some kind of emergency!'

'Emergency, Esther? Whatever kind of emergency? What happened?' Kate teased.

'Oh, you know very well what I mean, Kate. Honest-to-goodness, you'd have thought Henry was 21 again! Those green eyes sparkled like—Oh, but Kate, I'm so happy for you. And I intend to take all the credit! I expect it'll be quite a change after all these years alone, but then you grew up on a farm so I'm sure you'll get along just fine. At least you'll have a son now, even if you can't have any of your own.' Esther paused. 'Well, what I mean to say is, you're not old—not really old, but then—well, I just assumed—I mean, at our age . . .'

Determined to continue with her little fun, Kate said, 'You assumed what, Esther?'

'Well, ah, ah, ah . . . that is . . .'

Amused, Kate said gently, 'It's all right, Esther. I've had my photography business which most women couldn't have, and indeed, it will be fine to become Will's mother though he hardly needs one!'

Red Geraniums

'I'm sorry. I didn't mean there was anything wrong with marrying so late. When will the wedding be?'

'Not until after harvest. There's too much to be done before then.'

'If there's anything I can help you with . . .'

'Thank you, no, Esther. It will be a simple ceremony. I'll contact you later.' Kate didn't want Jean repeating everything to the women of the Methodist Episcopal Ladies' Aid Society. 'I really must go now and finish Mr. Kline's pictures. He is coming by to pick them up this afternoon.'

'Oh, Kate, I'm so sorry I've kept you from your work, but I just had to tell you how happy I am for you and Henry. My, I was a good matchmaker, wasn't I? Bye.' Kate smiled. The idea of marrying would take some getting used to.

That evening there was a knock on the door as Kate was finishing her supper. She hurriedly stashed her dishes in the basin and went to the door. There stood Jean Burchett. 'Well, Jean! How nice to see you! Do come in.'

Jean stepped in but it was immediately obvious that she was not her usual gushing self. She walked into Kate's apartment and plopped down on the rocker, keeping her coat on. 'I don't know what to say, Kate. I thought you were my friend, but here I'm the last to know about your engagement to Henry Fergus. I'm glad, of course, but you could have told me!'

'Oh, Jean, I'm so sorry. I thought we ought to tell the family first. Would you like some tea?'

'No! I thought I was like family to you.'

'Yes, of course, Jean. Well, anyway, Henry and I won't be married until after harvest.'

Jean perked up. 'Oh, good. I'll have time to make myself a new dress for the wedding!'

Kate didn't know what to say but to tell her the truth. 'I'm sorry, Jean, we're just having a small wedding at Angus' place with only Angus and Lizzie and Esther and Bud there. Oh, and Henry's son Will and Angus' children. After all, we're older and don't need a fancy wedding.' Flustered, Kate repeated, 'I'm sorry. There probably won't even be anything in the paper. I hope you're not mad at me. I was hoping you'd feel happy for me.'

Jean got to her feet. 'Well, I do. Really. I just wish I was getting married, too.'

'Oh, Jean, you will! You will!' Kate emphasized the positive—though she wasn't so sure. 'Do you have to go now?'

Jean walked to the door. 'Yes, I've got things to do,' she said and went out the door. Kate locked it after her and leaned against it for a moment. She felt bad for Jean and sincerely hoped that, indeed, she would find someone to marry—soon.

Kate didn't have time to regret the rift in her relationship with Jean. There was much to be done in the next few months. First of all, she would need to advertise the studio equipment in several papers. She decided that she would keep the camera, in any case, and the glass negatives she had taken. They seemed like her property, but if somebody wanted another print, she could loan them the glass negative to have someone else make a print for them. The plates she would keep would include, of course, the plates of Gyorgy, but she was quite sure he would not come back for more prints.

Their wedding time was coming closer, but Henry was very busy with the harvest so they seldom saw each other. As the the day approached and no one had offered to buy the studio equipment, she was resigned to taking it to the farm though she was sure she would never use it again.

Angus and Henry moved most of her things to Henry's place a week before the wedding, but she insisted on keeping the studio intact until the very last minute. Three days before the wedding, there was a knock at the studio door. Kate left her job of organizing the photographic equipment to answer it. There was Mr. Berringer. Kate swallowed hard, determined to be civil. 'Good day, Mr. Berringer. I trust you are well.'

'Oh, yes, yes, indeed,' he replied. 'I've just heard that you are selling out. I'm surprised. I always thought your business was very good . . .'

'Yes, Mr. Berringer, my business has always been good, but I am marrying and leaving Tingle Creek, and it won't be convenient for me to continue the business. Now if you'll excuse me—'

'Oh, but Miss MacLean, I thought maybe we could do business. I want to take the business off your hands. I mean, you sell the business to me. The missus has been wanting me to quit the traveling that my job requires, and I can see how she needs some help with the children. Omaha's getting pretty big now, so if I had a photography studio there, I would be in town all the time. I think I'd be pretty good at it. What do you say?'

Kate was flabbergasted. She needed to sell the business, of course, but to Mr. Berringer? It appeared that she had no choice. She could keep the business and lose her investment, or sell to a man she didn't much trust and certainly didn't like. She needed to talk to someone about this offer.

But who? She knew what Henry's answer would be and she thought she knew Angus'. What would Bethany say?

No, it was her decision to make. She had advertised, after all, and her ad had not included caveats. Kate looked squarely at Mr. Berringer. 'You must understand. I am not selling my camera. If you are all right with that, then please allow me some time to think about this. Come back at 3 o'clock, if you're still interested.'

'Thank you, Miss Kate. I will be here.'

* * *

The day before the wedding, Kate stopped in at Mr. Sedlow's meat market. 'Good morning, Mr. Sedlow! I guess I won't be wanting any more dressed chickens. I'll have to do my own from now on.' She screwed up her face to show her distaste for the task.

'Oh, but Miss Katie, I hope you will stop in to see me from time to time when you're in town. It's been real nice to know you and real nice to do business with you,' Bill Sedlow replied. Kate reached out to shake his hand. He smiled and wiped his hands on his apron. 'I'm afraid my hands aren't shakeable at the moment.'

'Well, then,' she said, 'I'll consider that we've shaken! Thank you for all the help you've given me over the years in getting my business set up. And please remember me to Mrs. Sedlow.' Kate smiled broadly.

'Oh, Miss Katie, I understand you've sold the studio.'

'Yes. Yes, I have. Mr. Berringer from Omaha will be taking the equipment in a few days. It was a hard decision.'

'That means Tingle Creek won't have a photography studio anymore. That is not good news, but we certainly wish you well.'

Kate stood with her hand on the doorknob as if she were going to say something more, but then she turned and went out the door and up the stairs. Angus was coming to take her to his place to stay the night and she needed to finish packing.

The next day, her wedding day, she took pains to make herself look nice—for Henry, she told herself. After all, at her age, it would take some doing. She had dreamed of her wedding for a long time. She always thought she would wear an elegant gown of a delicate blue georgette or a sky blue moire. She knew her mother would have thought either of those too fancy, saying Kate would never find an occasion to wear such a dress again.

In the end Kate made herself a dress of a practical, pale lavender voile to wear with her treasured purple hat and a white cashmere shawl. As she looked into the small mirror in Netta's room where she had slept, she decided she had done all she could do to look special. Well, there was one curl that refused to be tamed. She dampened her fingers and pressed it in place.

When she heard Henry's voice downstairs, her heart leaped. This was really happening. To her. She blinked back tears of joy. 'Kate!' Angus' voice came up the stairwell. 'Kate! Are you going to be married or not!' he teased.

'I'm coming, I'm coming,' she answered. Halfway down the stairs, she looked out the west window, remembering how she had enjoyed sitting there, reading books and dreaming. Now she was fulfilling one of those dreams.

As Angus walked her into the parlor to take her place beside Henry, Kate noticed that Will was not there. This was no time to ask after him, however, and the ceremony began. She was sure her mother would have approved of the ritual followed by Rev. Wesley from the Methodist Episcopal Church. After they repeated their vows, Rev. Wesley intoned, 'I now pronounce you husband and wife, Mr. and Mrs. Fergus!' There were congratulations all around. The children had sat solemnly in their Sunday best but scampered off to play as soon as the ceremony was over. Angus hugged her tight and said, 'Congratulations, Mrs. Fergus! I know you'll be very happy.' Kate nodded, but too emotional to speak, she simply kissed his cheek.

Lizzie had cooked a special wedding dinner for everyone to enjoy. Kate was most grateful and complimented her cooking several times. It was a lovely occasion, but she couldn't help wondering what happened to Will. She assumed she would know soon enough.

After the wedding ceremony and dinner, Henry and Kate climbed into the buggy for the hour's drive to Henry's farm. Neither Henry nor Kate did much talking at first. Kate was caught up in remembering details about their wedding. Lizzie, wearing a new blue dress, looked very pretty with dark ringlets framing her face. Kate reminded herself that she must tell her so when she wrote to her.

Red Geraniums

Kate was startled when Henry pulled off on a side road. He leaned over and wrapped his arms around Kate and kissed her. Her hat tipped backwards and they both laughed, trying to retrieve it. 'Now, Kate,' Henry began seriously, 'there are some things I want to talk to you about before we get home.' Kate wondered why he waited until this moment to tell her whatever it was. She said nothing.

'Kate, you know my Will. He's a good boy. Harriet brought him up well. You'll grow to like him—and he can't help liking you. There's something more I must tell you about Will. See, he's Harriet's child, but not mine. Her first husband died when Will was only two. When I married Harriet, I adopted him as my son and he has been my son ever since. I wouldn't have expected you to know this, and I was sure it would make no difference to you, but to be honest, I didn't tell you before because I couldn't hazard your saying no. I have come to like you so much, I wouldn't want to lose you.'

'I'm glad you trusted who I am, Henry. No, I would never have let this relationship come between you and me. Will is very lucky to have you as his father. I hope he will be as lucky to have me as his—well, if not his real mother, at least a favorite aunt!'

Henry squeezed her tightly with tears in his eyes. They held each other without talking.

She had met Will, of course. The one or two times together were cordial, but then there had been no thought of a future familial relationship, and she didn't find much to say to him. She had been impressed that his hair was combed and his clothes were neat—as if his mother had supervised his dressing. The fact that Will was already as tall as she was somehow disconcerting. It made it hard to think of being a 'mother' to this almost full-grown child.

Now, Kate's mind raced. 'But, Henry, where was he today? I thought you'd be bringing him.'

Henry hung his head for a few seconds. 'At the last minute he decided to stay home. I told him I wanted him to come, but he said he'd find it boring just like he finds going to church boring. But don't worry. After he gets used to having you help him with his clothes and his meals, and after he sees how happy you've made me, he'll just naturally think of you as—well, at least a loving aunt. He will. I just know he will.' Kate frowned. She hoped Henry was right. His absence was not an auspicious beginning.

'And, Kate, there's another matter that you need to know about.' Kate shrank back a bit from his hold.

'What's that?'

'Don't worry. It's nothing big. I took on a young boy last year to help around the place. He's just 11 same as Will, but he's a real worker. His name is Hjelmer—some sort of Scandanavian name.

'His family in Keyapaha County are very poor immigrants and they farmed out several of their children to farmers like me. I learned about him from a neighbor who took one of his brothers. It means one more mouth for me to feed, but so far, he's been worth it and it's nice for Will to have a friend. I see to it that he goes to school and he's doing all right in school. Well, I guess that's about it.'

'You mean that's all, Henry?'

'Yes.'

'Well, for land's sakes, I thought you were going to tell me about some dire problem that you have.' Kate looked greatly relieved.

'I'm sorry, Kate. I didn't mean to worry you, but I hadn't talked to you about the boys and I thought I should.'

'It's all right, Henry. I'm sure we'll make the best of it though you realize I've never been a mother so I won't always know how to act. By the way, how do you spell Hjelmer?'

Henry smiled. 'It's got an "h" and a "j" in front of plain old Elmer.' Henry clucked to the horse, turning him toward the farm. 'Oh, and one more thing, Kate. What with 3 men living together, you might not find the house as neat and clean as you'd wish. We tried to gather it up a bit, but well—I hope you'll forgive us.'

Kate laughed. 'I expected that.' She had already figured she'd be spending the first few weeks scrubbing and tidying up.

* * *

'Well, there it is, Kate!' Henry swept his arm in the direction of a farmstead coming up on the left.

As they drove into the dooryard, Kate exclaimed, 'What a lovely house! What a lovely farm! I know I'm going to be quite happy here,' and squeezed Henry's hand. 'Oh, my, Henry, it's beautiful!'

'Well, barns are barns. I'm glad you like it,' he said and squeezed her hand.

As soon as the buggy turned in the driveway, the boys came to meet Henry and Kate. Will helped Kate out of the buggy. She smiled and said 'Thank you, Will!' Then she turned to the shy-looking, but rather tall boy with a shock of wheat-colored hair that threatened to cover his eyebrows. 'You must be Hjelmer,' she said and smiled.

'Yes, ma'am, I am,' he said shyly.

'Would you carry the basket in for me?' she asked. Hjelmer reached in and lifted out the rather substantial basket of food Lizzie had prepared for their supper. 'I'll bet you boys are hungry, too, aren't you? I can guarantee you plenty to eat from your new Aunt Lizzie. She thought of everything. Will, would you bring my valise in for me?'

'Now, then, I've never been here before so I'm counting on you to help me find things,' Kate said as Hjelmer held the kitchen door open for her. 'Oh, my, what a wonderful kitchen!'

Henry had been following along behind Kate and the boys. 'Welcome to our home, Kate,' Henry said jovially. 'It's been a long day. Kate, you must tired. Here let me take your shawl.'

Kate was used to hanging up her own shawl. 'My goodness, Henry, I certainly can hang up my own shawl!' she said, but let him take it anyway. She was determined to get off on the right foot. Soon the basket was unpacked and the table set. While they were eating, both boys were very quiet and did not speak until they were spoken to, but she realized they were kicking each other under the table.

The boys' reluctance to speak made it quite awkward though Henry tried his best to be jolly and pointed out that Kate had been a photographer and wasn't that impressive? The boys just nodded. Kate didn't know what to say to them to let them know she was interested in them. Finally, she said she would show them her camera sometime. 'Oh, we already saw it when Pa brought it home the other day,' Will said.

After supper, the boys and Henry went out to finish up the chores, leaving Kate alone in the kitchen, cleaning up the dishes and putting food away as best she could. It took a lot longer than her simple suppers in Tingle Creek. After she finished, she took the lamp and went into the parlor to sit and think. She knew this was to be 'her' house as well as Henry's, but tonight she felt like a stranger, not daring to venture farther on her own. It felt good to just sit quietly.

Soon the men came into the house and it seemed quite lively all of a sudden. 'Why are you sitting in Pa's chair?' Will asked rather sharply.

'Oh, my,' said Kate and got up hurriedly. 'I guess I didn't know any better,' she suggested.

Henry gently pressed her back into his rocker, saying, 'Now, now. I don't have to have a particular chair. You just be comfortable, Kate.'

'But you never let us sit there,' Will complained.

Henry looked at him rather crossly and said, 'Kate is different. Now you boys go wash up and then go on upstairs and start your homework.'

'I'm afraid I'm feeling rather tired, Henry,' said Kate.

'Of course, of course, let me show you to the bathing room and then I'll show you our bedroom.' Henry had said nothing about this so the small room off the kitchen was a happy surprise. No more bathing in the kitchen and having to worry about privacy! There was a tin tub and a small cupboard with a marble counter top with a china wash basin and pitcher. Harriet's washstand set was still there. It was beautiful, but Kate thought she'd want to use her own. She would have Henry take Harriet's set to the attic. There was even a commode. Even though she would seldom use the commode, she was delighted to have its convenience—if necessary.

In the bedroom with the door closed on this their wedding night, Kate was suddenly very shy and suspicious of every noise. She was conscious of the boys' room so close by, though it was in the opposite corner of the house from hers and Henry's. She wondered whether Will accepted his father sharing his bed—his and Harriet's bed—with her.

She suggested that Henry leave the room while she change into the pretty pink lawn nightgown she had saved all these many years in her hope chest. She climbed into bed covering most of her body with the hope chest quilt she had been using on her bed in the apartment. She knew what was supposed to happen on this special night, and all that, but it didn't make it any easier to think about going to bed with a man—an almost stranger—with the two boys just down the hall.

'Henry!' she called softly. 'Henry!' she repeated. Almost immediately he opened the door and came in. She had turned the lamp very low. Henry came and sat on her side of the bed and took her hand.

'Kate, you look beautiful! I don't know how to say it. I'm not good at such talk, but you do, you look like the prettiest rose ever!' Kate, realizing it was quite a speech for Henry, reached out to put her arms around him. It was a lovely feeling, and she was happy.

* * *

Kate awakened the morning after their wedding at her usual time, the time she usually needed to prepare her breakfast and to make sure the studio was ready for the day. It surprised her that she was alone in the bed. 'Oh, my,' she said out loud. She must have been more tired than she thought and quite forgot the hours farmers must keep. She hurried around to get breakfast ready for the men when they came in from their chores. She opened the door to listen to the farm sounds and to smell the farm smells. Ah, it seemed just right. She smiled, glad to be 'home'—though it didn't quite feel like that yet.

'What shall I put in your lunch?' she asked the boys.

Hjelmer frowned. 'Nuthin.'

'But you're going to need something to eat.'

'Yes,' said Will, 'but we've been fixing our own lunches and I reckon we still can.'

'Now that was sweet,' Kate thought when the boys had left for school on their horses and Henry went to the barn. After she cleared up the breakfast dishes, Kate wanted to assess what needed to be done. She'd had a glimpse of the house's layout the night before, but she was too tired then to take it all in. Her overall impression was that it was a nicer house in many ways than Angus's—much newer, for one thing.

There was a wonderful kitchen with floor-to-ceiling cupboards. She would need a stool to get to the top ones—or depend on someone else. One of the cupboards had a built-in flour bin with an attached flour sifter and below it drawers for storing flour and sugar. In the middle of the kitchen was a large sturdy table. 'Oh, this is perfect for kneading bread dough,' she thought to herself. Best of all, there was a fairly deep tin sink with a pump beside it so she wouldn't have to go outside to pump water at the well—or even to the back porch, as was the case at Angus's. The large wood range had a substantial reservoir on the side to keep water hot at all times. What a delight! She would soon need to start some bread to rise, but she figured they could get along one more day with what Lizzie sent.

She wandered out of the kitchen into the adjoining dining room. It was not so nice as Angus' but it would do very well. There was a large buffet on the west wall with glass in the upper doors and a large square oak table in the middle of the room. Henry insisted she bring her mother's transfer printed dishes and said they would find room for them. Now she wondered if that would mean putting Harriet's dishes in the attic.

The dining room table and chairs were fairly ordinary, but the hardwood floor was beautiful. She stood with arms akimbo wondering how hard it was going to be to keep polished. She turned to the wide, pocket doors leading into the parlor. It was similar, but nicer than the one at Angus's. There was no formal parlor such as Angus had. It was just as well since Angus' was seldom used.

The room was very comfortable with a large window looking out on the road. She smiled to herself that the window would help her keep track of the comings and goings of their neighbors. There was the big oak rocker and Henry and Angus had brought her grandmother's rocker and set it next to the other one. A couple of rather angular arm chairs faced the rockers. Her pump organ now sat next to the dining room wall. The secretary she had bought to do her business bookkeeping in the studio had been squeezed in between the stairwell and the pocket doors, but it appeared to fit well there. The Persian-looking rug in this room was well-worn and rather nondescript. It would do.

Kate recognized that Henry and Harriet had planned the house well though she was sure they didn't have a second wife in mind.

Kate glanced at the open stairwell and hesitated. It was an almost eerie feeling being alone in this house that was more Harriet's than hers. She felt like she was prying. At the foot of the stairs, she paused, wondering if it was all right for her to go up. Well, of course! What was she thinking, she admonished herself. She'd already slept upstairs! The remembrance was enough to make her march up the stairs with confidence.

She wanted to see the boys' room, but didn't feel right about entering. She hesitated and then cracked the door open just a bit. Oh, my! It was a mess. She shook her head and wondered if she dare say anything about it to Henry or the boys. As she was closing the door, she heard Henry call to her from the kitchen. 'I'm upstairs, Henry,' she replied as she stepped into their own room to make the bed.

His footsteps sounded on the wooden stairsteps, and then he came up behind her as she was straightening the quilt. He tapped her on the shoulder, and as she turned around, he put his arms around her and kissed her soundly. 'Oh, my, Henry! I'm not used to that!' she smiled and then kissed him.

'Well, Kate, how does it feel?'

'It's so quiet, Henry. I'm used to town noises. There I could look out the window and see lots of activity.'

'Oh, but have you looked out the window at the beautiful morning?' Henry asked. 'As to people noise, I guess I can't give you any people but me,' he grinned. 'Will I do?'

'Oh, yes, Henry, you will do very well. I'm sure I'll get used to the farm sounds again and then it won't seem so quiet. Have you come in for dinner already? I can hurry and put something together . . .'

'No, no,' Henry assured her. 'I was just checking on you. I'll be in about noon and then just the two of us can sit and talk.' He squeezed her hand and went back downstairs. She finished making the bed and then went to peek in the other rooms. Finally, she opened the door to what she assumed was the stairway to the attic.

The light was dim as she cautiously made her way up the steps. At the top, the stairs turned and she went up the last two. As her eyes became accustomed to the gloom, she gasped as she beheld her camera. Henry had already set it up for her in the center of the large attic. She wondered where he had put Gyorgy's chair, but just as quickly she dismissed the thought and turned and made her way back downstairs, vowing to wash the attic windows in the near future. She could see that her job was going to be full-time as a cook and housekeeper and laundress for this little family of four. It would take some doing but she was ready to make a go of it, to bring happiness and tranquility to her new home.

* * *

One night, after Henry deposited his work boots in the back porch entry way, he walked into the kitchen. Kate was still finishing her cleanup work. 'Well, Kate,' Henry whispered as he wrapped his arms around her waist while she was washed the dishes, 'how are things going for you—for us?' Kate laughed delightedly.

'Well, I'd say things have been going quite well—since we are one of Tingle Creek's "fine young couples", according to the Tingle Creek Herald that came today!' They both laughed. It seemed a bit disingenuous, they thought, to call them 'young' when they were in their forties already.

He blew on the damp curls at the nape of her neck. 'If that's so, we should be acting like it!'

She turned and put her soapy hands on his cheeks. He pulled away in feigned disgust. She laughed. 'Oh, Henry, you know what would make me happy?' Henry frowned. 'I'd like to get some starts of my mother's lilacs from Angus and plant them around the house. What do you think?'

Henry laughed. 'You had me worried because I thought you were happy! Of course, we'll dig them in the spring and plant them wherever you like. They would make the place look nice.' He kissed her forehead and went to his rocking chair to read the paper.

* * *

It had been several months since their marriage and Kate was glad she had made the decision to marry Henry. Not that those months had always been easy. She found Henry pretty fixed in his ways—and she guessed he found her so, too. In many ways, it was fun being married, having someone to love who loved in return. Well, maybe it wasn't real love yet, perhaps, but she hoped that their caring for each other would help gloss over some of her unease with having the boys around.

'Oh, Henry,' she said, standing in the doorway to the parlor, 'I hope it all works out. I wish I were more comfortable with Will and Hjelmer. Sometimes they seem to barely tolerate me.' Actually this was more true of Will than Hjelmer, but she didn't feel right about singling him out.

As time went on, their presence was more annoying to her than she had anticipated even though the boys were in school in the middle part of every day or out doing chores. Henry, of course, supervised their outside chores, but once in awhile one or the other would forget to clean the cream separator and she had to scold the delinquent one. Ordinarily, she took care of feeding the chickens and gathering eggs but a couple of times she asked one of them to do it and neither was happy to cooperate and did so only reluctantly.

She had been thinking about these things as she scrubbed the kettles that night. Now she said, 'What can I do to make them like me more? I shouldn't complain, I guess. Maybe they're just being normal boys and I don't know what that means.'

Henry looked serious. 'I suppose that's part of it. You didn't have the chance to be with them growing up, but you did teach boys this age in school.'

'That's true, but there they were bound to obey me or I'd tell their folks and that always settled them down. I don't know . . . I guess I just understand girls better. And, mind you, girls can be a problem, too. Oh,

Red Geraniums

Henry! Wouldn't it be nice to have a girl?' Henry agreed it would and went back to his paper.

Still, Kate fussed about the boys' behavior under her breath, not liking to bother Henry too much. At meals, Kate wasn't quite sure whether she should correct their manners or not. Licking fingers after eating juicy drumsticks was one thing, but licking a serving spoon was totally unacceptable in her mind. Once, she told Will that he shouldn't put his elbows on the table. He pouted and said, 'Well, Pa does that,' and indeed, there was Henry with one elbow on the table which he quickly removed. She clucked at him with a grin and a scowl and he smiled back.

Many of the problems occurred at night when the boys went to their room where they were supposed to be doing lessons. Kate and Henry sometimes heard them scuffling so Henry went to break up whatever fracas was taking place. She wondered how her mother and father had dealt with her brothers. Surely, they had been fractious. Maybe Pa had taken care of it down at the barn. She smiled remembering that, after all, they turned out to be fine upstanding citizens.

Now she wiped her hands, turned down the kitchen lamp, and went to sit in her grandmother's rocker opposite Henry. He put down the paper, an impish grin on his face. 'Kate, my dear, it's going to be all right. We're in this together.'

That assurance felt good, but she didn't tell him she still was uncomfortable making love to him with the boys so close by in their room. That subject could wait for another day.

* * *

'There have been hotter summers,' Kate thought to herself after she'd lived in the house several months, 'but I was young then.' Now she felt the weight of aging pulling her down. She looked at herself in the mirror above the dresser, glad that she couldn't see her plump breasts which these days rested on her pouchy stomach when she rocked. Her ankles swelled in the heat making her feet more than fill her proper oxfords.

As she turned her head this way and that in front of the mirror, she wondered why some women's wrinkles seemed to follow parallel patterns like furrowed fields and other's wrinkles were like braided streams criss-crossing each other at will. Men's wrinkles seemed much deeper furrowed, more rugged than women's.

She liked to take her bath after the children were safely in school and Henry off to the barn. Afterwards, she pulled on the lightest weight cotton print dress that she had. Then she giggled, suddenly remembering she'd forgotten to put on her long petticoat. She frowned, cocked her head to the side, and said outloud, 'I don't care if Henry doesn't like it. It's too hot.'

'Doesn't like what?' Henry's voice startled her, and then she spied him off to the side of the mirror.

'Nothing. What are you doing here?' she challenged.

Henry ignored it. 'No, you said I wouldn't like something so I think there is something,' he parried. 'Remember? We agreed to be open with each other.' His arm encircled her waist and she was afraid he'd feel the thinness of the dress with just her underwear underneath.

'Oh, Henry, we're too old for that,' she sputtered and twirled out of his grasp.

'Oh, no, we're not,' he laughed and followed her as she ran from the room. The breeze from the window on the stair landing caught her skirt as she flounced down the stairs. 'Aha! So that's it! And where were you going like that?' His voice scolded but his eyes twinkled.

'I was going to the kitchen to heat up that old cook stove and make a hot day even hotter.' She saw him wince. It was true that being out in the hot sun in the cornfield with any kind of a breeze was always cooler than being in the range-heated kitchen.

'All right, Kate, we'll buy that kerosene stove you've always wanted, but it won't bake bread so good.' Kate knew he was right, but she also knew that snow would be flying before he got around to doing anything about it. She'd learned that much in the three years they'd been married.

It wasn't that finances had been a problem between them—although Kate naturally deferred to Henry on most expenditures since he obviously had more money than she. When they married, they had agreed that all large expenses would be seriously considered by both and both would agree on the amount of the purchase before the money was spent.

Before they got married, she had said, 'Henry, I want to keep my bank account, even though there isn't a lot of money in it. I'll just change my name on the account to Kate Fergus.'

'Well, I guess that's all right,' Henry frowned. 'Though you don't have to. I've got plenty of money for both of us.' Somehow it just felt like something she needed to do for herself. When she sold the studio, it felt like a nest egg for future contingencies. After all, what if Henry should die? Besides, she only used her account for what she called 'little things' like a new pair of shoes and a 'nice' tablecloth.

Now she smiled at him and went to the kitchen to start the bread just as he went out the back door headed for the barn. 'Hmm,' she said to herself, 'I wonder why he came in the house in the first place.' She shrugged and set about measuring flour.

V

One day midmorning the telephone jangled, interrupting Kate's thoughts as she kneaded the day's loaves of bread. Her hands hung limp over the mound of dough as she listened for the two long rings and two short—their number. Flustered, she dusted her floury hands together to shake off the bits of dough clinging to her fingers. 'I'm coming. I'm coming,' she shouted at the box on the wall. Ineffectually wiping her hands on her apron, she climbed on the little stool Henry had made for her to reach the mouthpiece.

Lifting off the receiver, Kate said, 'Hello.'

The voice from the other end asked, 'Kate Fergus?' The voice was tentative, but she went on. 'Kate? How are you and the mister?' Without waiting for a reply, the caller pushed on. 'You remember how you really wanted that foundling baby?'

The caller had not identified herself, but Kate recognized Mrs. Simpson's voice. In fact, she remembered all too well. She hesitated and thought about hanging up, but she was curious. 'Yes,' she said quietly. 'Yes?'

'You'll have to speak up. I can hardly hear you.'

'Yes! I remember,' Kate said a bit more loudly than was required. 'Why?' she asked with a faint hint of bitterness. 'Do you have another foundling to give away?'

'No, no. I just thought I'd let you know that there's an Orphan Train coming through Tingle Creek. They're going to bring the children to the Methodist Episcopal Church. I'm going to go over. Now, don't get me wrong. Lord knows I don't want any more children. I'm just curious to see the little tykes. Aren't you? I mean, this is the first time an Orphan Train has come through here.'

Kate brightened. She was indeed interested. 'When does it come?'

Red Geraniums

'Next Saturday. It'll be the 10:45 morning train to Fremont. They'll leave again on the 2:10 train. Why don't you come? Bet there'll be a baby for you!'

'We'll see,' Kate said. 'We'll see.' She realized she was a bit curt so she added hastily, 'Thank you for calling to let me know.'

'Goodbye then,' said Mrs. Simpson and hung up. Kate looked at the receiver in her hand, frowning about the message that she had just heard. She finally returned the receiver to its forked cradle.

Stepping off the little stool and turning to the kitchen work table, her mind elsewhere, she seemed puzzled by the puffy lump of dough sitting amidst a skiff of flour. Her mind turned to the foundling. The newspaper had said he was adopted by a family over near Broken Bow. It had made her feel better to know that he would be taken care of. Touching the dough brought her back to herself, and her hands fell into their accustomed rhythm—push pull turn push pull turn—leaving her mind free to contemplate Mrs. Simpson's message about the Orphan Train.

Kate first heard about Orphan Trains several years ago from Flora Mayfield who graduated with her from Normal School in Almora. One day while Flora was sitting for her portrait in Kate's studio, she told about how she had gone down to the depot at Almora one time when an Orphan Train came in. She told how they lined up all the children on the platform from the youngest to the oldest. The lady that accompanied them held one baby and one of the older children held another.

Flora said the preacher with them told the crowd that these children needed homes. He said they came from New York City, and sometimes when they were orphaned, they had no choice but to live on the streets. That's why some of them are even skinnier than others,' he said. 'They need food, they need shelter, they need someone to love them. The good Lord didn't intend for these little ones to be victims of starvation and predators and disease,' Flora quoted him as saying. 'My, how I'd love to give one of them a home,' she went on, 'but the good Lord has already blessed me with six mouths to feed and I don't know how I'd manage even one more. But—poor things. Someone ought to take care of them.'

At the time, Kate busied herself with her camera, eyeing Flora through the lens, the black cloth over her head. 'I don't suppose they give children to single women, do they?' she asked, not daring to look directly at her friend and customer.

'Well, I don't know, Kate,' she said. 'Maybe you could ask. But how could you take care of a little one—with your business and all. I mean, children take a lot of time and you don't have a man. . .' Her voice trailed off.

'No, I suppose not,' Kate had replied, dispiritedly.

Today things were different. She was a married woman. She had Henry. Could she—could she and Henry, that is—take one of those babies for their own? What would Henry say?

Before they were married, Henry said she should consider Will her child, too, but so far it hadn't worked out that way. She and Will tolerated each other but they had not grown to like each other very much. She was sorry about that, but she didn't know what to do about it. It hadn't become a point of contention with Henry, but he made his disappointment clear. 'I don't understand, Kate,' he said. 'You're a wonderful woman, a motherly sort. I've seen you with Angus' boys and they love you dearly. Maybe if you'd just try harder to love Will, he would love you back.'

Kate had not answered. So far it hadn't happened. How could she tell him about her doubts? That she had seen Will sneaking off to the orchard when Henry asked him to help Hjelmer in the garden? She had spoken to Will about it in a kindly way, but he became surly. 'You're not my mother!' he snarled. And she couldn't tell this good man she married that she was quite sure Will had taken two dollars from her handbag when she had insisted he help her unload the buggy one day after a trip to town, now could she? How could she love someone she couldn't quite trust? Of course she couldn't tell Henry. It would hurt him too much—and what if he were to side with Will?

She plopped the neatly shaped loaves into the four waiting pans and brushed their tops with butter, the way Henry liked his bread. She put them in the proofing oven and set to scraping the work table surface, thinking about what a change a baby would make in their lives. Maybe, when it came right down to it, she really was too old to raise a baby, whether it was one of her own or an adopted orphan.

It had taken many months for her to recover in body and spirit from the child she and Henry had conceived but lost because of his too early birth. She had reached the age where it now would be impossible to bear one of her own. She didn't know but what God was trying to tell her something. She cleaned up the last of the flour crumbs from the table, quite determined to be at the church when those Orphan Train children arrived—if only, like Mrs. Simpson—out of curiosity.

She thought it wouldn't hurt to at least go into town and look at these poor children. Kate wanted Henry to go, too, but when she served his oatmeal and fried potatoes at breakfast on Thursday, she still had not mentioned it for fear he'd say she was foolish—or worse, that she was being disloyal to Will. Suddenly she blurted out, 'Henry, look!' and picking up the newspaper, she stabbed her finger at the newspaper advertisement. 'There's an Orphan Train coming. Coming right here to Tingle Creek. We could go have a look. Maybe it would be good for us to have a child of our own.'

'But, Kate, we have a child, my Will.'

Kate sighed. At the counter behind him, she poured his coffee and set it before him on the table. Then she very deliberately poured her own and sat down.

'But wouldn't it be nice to have girl, too?' she argued. 'A girl could help me around the house and knead the bread and such. Oh, I mean it would take a few years, but wouldn't a little girl be nice? I mean, we'd be doing the Lord's work to take her in and give her a good home and lots of love.' Kate wasn't given to religious arguments very much, but she thought it might reach Henry.

Henry got up out of his chair and came around the table. He put his arms around her and kissed her cheek. 'Kate, I love you, and I'm glad I found you after Harriet died. If you want a child, you should have one. You'd make a terrific mother. You can certainly go, but we have to be realistic. These children may have lice and may not even speak English!'

'Oh, Henry,' she cried and, standing up, kissed him on his rough cheek. 'Let's do go.'

'Well, now,' he said, drawing away, 'I don't know that I need to go. I've got hogs to do and corn coming on that I need to check. You know best when it comes to children. I trust your judgment and you certainly know how to sign the papers.'

Kate was disappointed that Henry didn't think choosing a child was as important as hogs and corn, but she wanted a child so much she said it would be all right if he didn't go. She left it at that, knowing full well that she would speak to him about it again the next day.

* * *

On Saturday morning as Miss Bowes finished her final exhortation to the folk gathered in the Methodist Episcopal Church, she raised her arms and the gathered sleeves of her flowered voile dress fell back against her ample shoulders as she tilted her head upward toward the heavens with her eyes closed. She stood motionless for some minutes.

Kate stared, her mind distracted from the children arrayed in front of the chaperone. Others also appeared transfixed in the multi-hued shafts of sun through the stained glass windows that bathed the pews and the curious. No one moved. A child's voice was heard, 'Mommy, can we go home now?' and then the mother's whispered, 'Shush, child!' Kate smiled. She looked around and saw two women tap their husbands on the shoulder, nodding toward the front of the room. Their men sat stolidly, apparently unmoved, but the women edged forward on their seats.

Miss Bowes continued to stand, as if in a trance, without a muscle moving. Finally, a young couple Kate recognized from Cedar Township stood up and made their way to the aisle. Almost at once another couple sidled out of their pew and strode toward the line of children. Falling in behind them, the Bartletts from Tingle Creek and another couple made their way to the altar rail. Everyone craned to see who was going forward.

Just as dramatically as she had assumed her beatific stance, Miss Bowes lowered her arms in a sweep to encompass the growing group of would-be parents. She smiled as each couple approached the altar rail. She shook their hands and said a few words to each of them. Then she spoke to the wider congregation. 'Praise God! Mr. and Mrs. Bill Everett have come to the altar to share in the Lord's work! Praise be to God!' Moving down the line, she acknowledged the Barletts' dedication to the Lord and the children. One by one the couples expressed their desire to take a child.

Kate frowned, counting. That would be four children, possibly five. She had assumed the youngest child, a babe in arms, would be the first to be chosen, but one after another, the couples pointed in the direction of other children. Maybe there was hope for her and Henry after all. She was relieved that he had decided to come with her to help make a decision. 'Henry,' she whispered, 'Henry, let's go up to the front before they're all gone!' Henry made no sign that he'd heard her.

Kate stood up and tugged at his rough, sun-browned hand just as two more couples left their seats to go forward. She felt a counterpull, but her sense of urgency impelled her to stand up, still grasping his hand with a determined grip. Excusing themselves to the couple between them and the aisle, she pulled even harder until Henry had no choice but to follow her. His face turned red, and he whispered hoarsely, 'Kate, what are you doing?' She had not made a major decision on her own since their marriage, but now she ignored his reluctance as she got to the aisle with him in tow.

They reached the altar rail just as Miss Bowes lifted the baby into the arms of the couple ahead of them. Kate's heart sank. She was too late. She would never have her baby. Tears rimmed her eyes and caught on her eye lashes. She blinked hard, but then as she looked up, she saw an extraordinary look of fright and sadness on the face of the biggest girl who had been holding the baby. The girl's large dark eyes were brimming with tears and her jaw muscles quivered as she watched the baby being cuddled in the newly-chosen mother's arms. She looked sadly surprised. Her head dropped to her chest and her shoulders shook with silent sobs.

Gazing intently at the girl, Kate pulled Henry so that they stood directly in front of this child. The girl was scrawny and not very tall with lifeless brown hair that strayed from the braids behind each ear. Her dress was made of flour sack cloth, with only a bow at the neck to brighten it. Her shoes were barely held together as they straddled a beat up valise.

She lifted her head to look at Kate momentarily just as Miss Bowes came to them. 'And what is your name?' Miss Bowes asked Kate. Kate did not hear her. She could not take her eyes off the girl who was so obviously bereft at giving up the baby she had been holding. Kate smiled gently at her. Something in Kate made her want to take the girl in her arms and comfort her, knowing she would be comforting herself at the same time.

Miss Bowes turned to Henry. 'What is your name, kind sir?' Henry shook Miss Bowes' hand and stammered, 'H-H-Henry Fergus.' Miss Bowes stepped to one side, out of Kate's direct line of sight and spoke to the crowd. 'Praise God for Mr. and Mrs. Fergus who love the Lord and want to share in His work of saving the children.' Then she turned to Kate. 'I believe you have a liking for Margaret . . . ?'

Kate echoed, 'Margaret! What a nice name!' Margaret looked as if she would cry. 'Well, Margaret, would you like to come home with me—with us?' Margaret just stared at Kate. She did not smile and her thin lips quivered.

'Margaret—? Mrs. Fergus—?' Miss Bowes started to speak, but stopped short as Margaret suddenly left her place at the altar rail to be swept up in Kate's outstretched arms, her tears wetting Kate's ear. She whispered fiercely, 'Yes!'

As they clung to each other, Kate turned to Henry apprehensively. It suddenly occurred to her that she had left Henry out of the decision-making. Over Margaret's shoulder she looked to his face for a sign. His face was flushed, and Kate's heart pounded. He put his hand on Margaret's shoulder and his eyes were solemn. 'Well then,' he said, 'welcome to our home.' Margaret turned, and he swept her up into his arms.

* * *

With Margaret between them in the buggy and her shabby valise stowed under the seat, Kate was happy. She hardly noticed that Margaret said very little on the ride to the farm. Of course, as Henry pointed out later, how could she have said anything with Kate bubbling over telling her about all the new places she was seeing!

Once at the farm, the boys came out to meet them. 'Will! Hjelmer! Meet your new sister, Margaret,' Kate announced. It was plain that having a new sister was a bit of a surprise for them, but Kate couldn't have told them ahead of time that they actually would be bringing home a new sibling. Hjelmer nodded shyly to Margaret and went to take care of the horse and buggy, but Will had a wary look as if he wasn't at all sure about this new development.

'Where did you come from?' he asked almost belligerently.

Margaret did not look at him, but said quietly, 'I came from New York City.' He just grunted and headed for the barn.

Inside the house, Kate took charge. 'Well, I'll just get some bread on the table for our dinner. We've got some leftover chicken and some pickles. Henry, could you show Margaret to her room? Then do you suppose you could set the table?' Kate said breathlessly. Oh, my, she thought, should she put Margaret alone on one side of the table and the boys on the other? Or, should she put Margaret and one boy on one side—and if so, which one? She finally decided to put Margaret alongside Hjelmer, but she couldn't have said why.

When all were seated at the table, Kate said, 'Margaret has come from the city, and so she probably doesn't know much about a farm. We'll all have to help her get acquainted.' The boys were rather stolid and barely glanced in Margaret's direction. Henry's voice was kindly as he helped

Margaret with her food. The boys bolted for the barn as soon as Henry dismissed them from the table.

Kate went with Margaret to her room. 'Well, let's see what you brought with you,' she smiled. Margaret hung her head as Kate opened the little wicker valise. 'I see you have another dress and some underwear. We'll have to get busy and sew you some things! Oh! What's this?' Kate picked up a little ikon of St. Mary. Kate had only seen pictures of ikons in books. 'Where would you like to put this?' Kate asked. Margaret just shrugged, but she stepped forward and took the ikon from Kate. She wrapped it in the petticoat and put it back in the valise. 'Shall we keep it in here?' Kate asked. Margaret barely nodded and turned away. 'I'll tell you what. I'll leave it in the case and put it in the attic and when you want it, you can go and get it. Will that be o.k.?' Kate asked, but there was no reaction from Margaret. Kate gave her one of Henry's old shirts to wear to bed and then tucked her in. 'Sleep well!' she said as she kissed Margaret's forehead and slipped out of the room.

'Oh, my,' said Kate to Henry that night after everyone was safely tucked into bed, 'There's so much to teach her—where do we start? It would be helpful if we knew more about her background. You remember Miss Bowes thought probably Margaret is about 10. Since she spent those years in the orphanage, I wonder how much she remembers about her parents and brothers and sisters in New York.'

'Well,' said Henry, 'remember she said Margaret's parents relinquished three of their girls and Margaret is the oldest of the three—and she was the last to leave the train. I can't imagine sending little children away.'

'I thought maybe the baby she was holding was her sister, but she wasn't. Margaret was just helping take care of him,' Kate said. 'That's not much to go on to figure out who she is and what's she's been through.' Kate paused and then went on. 'Even so I don't want to pry overmuch because Margaret needs to know we will respect her privacy. There might be some things about Margaret's past that the boys don't need to know at all.'

After Henry went to sleep, Kate kept thinking about Margaret when suddenly it occurred to her that they didn't knew very much about Hjelmer's early life either, and he never talked about his family. So here they were—a family with three growing children who were unrelated, with Kate and Henry as their stand-in mother and father. A strange little family with so many unknowns.

Even so, life settled down rather more easily after Margaret's arrival than Kate had any reason to hope for. Margaret obviously knew how to work around the house, but was totally ignorant of anything about raising a garden or taking care of chickens. Hjelmer and Will did most of the large animal chores, along with Henry, and they continued to do them.

One of the first days, Kate took Margaret out to the henhouse to hunt for the eggs. She showed her how to reach in under a hen if the hen was on the nest. As she left her to finish the job, she wasn't too surprised when Margaret came running to the house to say one of the hens had pecked her hand. 'Don't worry, you'll soon find out how to outsmart those women down there! You can wear a glove if you want to, but I'll bet you won't need it very long!'

'But Moth—' Margaret started and stopped, rubbing a red spot on the back of her hand. It wasn't the first time Margaret stumbled over what to call Kate.

'It's all right, Margaret. You can call me Auntie Kate if it's easier for you. I know you still have a real mother.'

Margaret seemed relieved. She went on. 'The thing is, I know I'm bigger than those hens, but it really hurts when they peck. See that big red mark.' Kate did indeed see it. She lifted Margaret's hand and kissed it and smiled. Margaret went back out to the hen house to finish the job.

At supper that night, Will couldn't help teasing Margaret. 'Sooo . . .' he began, 'that naughty old hen got the better of you, did she?' He laughed and pointed at Margaret who started to cry.

'Now, Will, that wasn't necessary,' Henry said. 'Margaret has lots to learn and we have to help her and . . .' Will stuck out his tongue at Margaret and laughed some more. Henry told him to leave the table. Kate was glad that he reprimanded Will. That kind of teasing needed to be nipped in the bud and she still wasn't comfortable doing it.

After supper, Kate sat down at the organ and started pumping the pedals. It had been a long time since she'd played anything, and she was surprised that it wasn't as easy to pump any more. Henry looked up from his rocking. 'Kate, I haven't heard you play in a long time! Angus will be happy that you're playing again.'

Margaret came over and leaned on the elaborate organ with its fretwork panels and turned walnut knobs. She watched Kate intently as she pulled and pushed the round knobs of the stops. Kate was enjoying hearing the music again and realized she missed it. Impulsively, she asked Margaret if she'd like to learn to play.

Margaret's eyes glowed. 'Oh, could I?'

'Of course,' Kate said and moved off the round stool with its red velveteen cover. 'You have to put your feet on the pedals. Sit forward a little further. Yes, like that. Now, move first one foot then the other and keep it going.'

Margaret's skinny legs could barely reach the pedals. 'Oh, that's hard!' she declared. She struggled but finally seemed to get the hang of it. 'Now what do I do?'

'Try out the keys. Do you hear what notes they make?' It crossed Kate's mind that maybe teaching Margaret to play the organ would be a way to help Margaret feel closer to her. Margaret pressed her fingers on a couple of keys, but her feet slipped off the pedals.

'Is this the way?' Margaret asked. 'What do I do first?'

Kate realized then that Margaret probably could not read music and she had never heard her sing. 'Well, we'll try it tomorrow afternoon after the dinner dishes are done, unless something comes up.' Making an absolute promise of time was hard when the farm and house work were somewhat unpredictable, but Kate hoped they could.

First of all, though, Kate needed to work with Margaret on her lessons so she could attend school. Kate went to meet Miss Reynolds, the teacher at the one-room school just beyond the orchard. 'Margaret said she's only had a smattering of school before and at the orphanage, so it may take her a little to catch up with her class.'

Miss Reynolds said, 'I think we can do it all right, but I'd suggest you work with her a couple of weeks and then we'll see where she fits into school.' Kate was glad she had kept all the books she used to teach from at country school. Margaret obviously had a basic knowledge of reading and math, but even so, Kate knew it wouldn't be easy. Even though she'd left teaching some years before, she was confident with the curriculum but it did take time away from the household chores which were many and ongoing.

Will and Hjelmer had already passed their eighth grade exams and had gone on to high school in Appleton. They had no time to help Margaret, and Kate seriously questioned what kind of help they would be anyway. Kate was determined to see it through.

After supper most nights Kate and Margaret sat at the dining room table by the light of the kerosene lamp. She seemed to catch on well, but she was near tears when she couldn't immediately solve a particularly knotty arithmetic problem with fractions. 'Oh, Auntie Kate, I don't think I'll ever understand!' she sighed. Still she was triumphant when she finished reading the whole of *Little Women*. Most of all she liked geography because she'd lived somewhere else.

* * *

Some time later Kate was removing the loaves of daily bread from the oven, when she heard the sound of an automobile. 'Oh, my,' Kate thought, 'I wonder who that could be!' Kate had heard automobiles go by before, but she was startled to realize that the roar of a motor car seemed to be coming into their farmyard. She cocked her head listening to the motor sputter to an even put-put-put. She hurriedly removed her apron and scurried out to see who might be coming to visit. They didn't know any people with a car, except Angus, but he wouldn't be coming midday on Thursday.

From her first sight of an automobile on Main Street of Tingle Creek, Kate thought it would be magical to ride in one—to feel the air moving the thin veil she would have wrapped around her hat and under her chin. She thought of the blur of trees she would experience as she passed by Maynard's Wood, like the blur of the countryside she had seen from a railroad car on her few trips to Almora. She thrilled to imagine moving so quickly she would arrive at Angus and Lizzie's farm almost before she started from home.

She dreamed of seeing places she had never seen before. It was not that she couldn't have experienced much of this by buying a train ticket to places she had never been before, but the train seemed so impersonal. In a car she could smell the plum thickets in the spring and even stop to pick them. Indeed, in a car she could stop anywhere she wanted to. She could surprise Bethany by driving into their yard one day. Still, the thought of actually owning a car never occurred to her on an earlier August day when the banker and his pretty wife chugged along Main Street past the livery stable, Halley's Department Store and her studio, waving to townspeople leading their every day lives.

Out in the driveway now, Kate stopped short. There was Henry—and only Henry—sitting in the front seat of a black touring car right in their driveway. He wore a broad but proud grin. 'Henry Fergus! Whatever are you doing in that automobile?' Her fists were jammed into her hips. 'Who loaned you that car and what do you intend to do with it? I thought you went to town to buy feed.' She shook her finger at him.

'Why, Kate,' he said above the rhythm of the motor, 'I came to take my favorite girl for a ride. Hop in! You'll love it.'

'Now, Henry,' said Kate becoming suddenly wary, 'you're not thinking of buying one of those things, are you? Because if you are, I want to remind you that we didn't get as much for our corn . . .' She wanted to add that they didn't get that kerosene stove either, but she didn't.

Without waiting for her to finish, Henry pulled on the big hand brake and stepped off the running board to come around to where she was standing with her arms folded across her chest. He grabbed her hand and pulled her over to the car while she sputtered. With a boost to her broad hips, he planted her on the front seat.

'There!' He said as his mustache twitched, and he clapped his hands as if dusting them off. Then, more spryly than Kate had seen him move in some time, he ran around the car and hopped into the driver's seat. 'Well, my pet, how do you like our new car?' Without waiting for her protest that she didn't have her hat on, he turned the car around and headed east down the road.

Kate sat quietly fearful, but inwardly excited. All she could think of at that moment was how Bethany Trueblood had said the automobile was surely the work of the devil. In the first place, Henry had said 'our new car' as if he had already purchased it. Was it to be the first of more purchases to be made without her consent? Still, it was a beautiful vehicle with its shiny black paint and thin gold stripes on the edges of the fenders. She wondered if the stripes cost more, but she couldn't ask over the noise of the motor.

'Henry, Henry!' she shouted. 'Henry, turn this car around. I have things to do at home,' she demanded. He laughed heartily. It was obvious he was having the time of his life and looked as if he never wanted to quit. 'Henry, I'm warning you,' Kate yelled reaching for his right arm. He shook her off, but slowed the car down and turned at the next intersection. He no longer laughed as he turned again at the next intersection and she could see that they were headed home.

That night, she was ready to talk about what she called 'Henry's foolishness'. As soon as she heard the children's bedroom doors close, she started in. 'Now, Henry, what is the price of that car?' She was careful not to say, 'How much did you pay for it?' She didn't want to admit that it was probably a done deal. 'Why didn't you ask me first?'

'Why, Kate, it only cost $550 for this model, the finest Ford ever built. It's a real bargain. The price came way down this year. Just think of the places we can go now, Kate, and just think of how fast we'll get there. And we have room for the whole family! Don't you think the full leather seats are beautiful? And it even has rain curtains! I didn't ask you first because I just knew you were going to like it, and I wanted to surprise you.'

It was obvious to Kate that Henry thought it was a wonderful idea and that his mind was made up, but she couldn't help add a final note to the discussion. 'Henry, have you told your horses yet?'

* * *

The first Saturday after Henry bought the car, he said to the boys and Margaret, 'If you finish you chores and your homework by midafternoon, we'll all go for a ride. What do you say?' There were smiles all around as they piled into the car and drove to Tingle Creek where the drug store had just put in a soda fountain. 'What do you think, Will? Should we have an ice cream soda?' Will grinned broadly as they stepped into the drug store. Margaret wasn't sure about the fizzy nature of this treat but finally decided it was something special.

On the way home, Will asked, 'Gee, Papa, that was really keen to ride in our car! When can I learn to drive it?'

'It'll be awhile,' Henry frowned, probably imagining what young people, especially boys, might want to do out driving in a car. When Will started to whine about having to wait, Henry said, 'You're just postponing your chances, Will.' There was no more argument.

Henry had found a way to squeeze the car into the implement shed where it would be out of the elements. Kate could see the back of its shiny black chassis from the kitchen door. Over the next several days its presence alternately annoyed her and tickled her. She wanted it but she didn't want it.

Then one day she said to Henry, 'If we're going to keep that thing, I'm going to learn to drive it. It has to be shared. And if we're going to use it, we might as well get rid of one of the horses, but I won't tell you which one. At least it'll be one less horse to feed.' Henry appeared a bit daunted by her determination but finally agreed she should learn. He didn't agree on selling the horse, however.

It didn't take Kate long to get the hang of driving. Cranking, though, was another matter. She either asked Henry or one of the boys to do it before she started out, but then she had to beg some man at the other end of her trip to crank it so she could drive home. She'd heard that even men sometimes get their elbows out of joint trying to crank a car. She wasn't going to take any chances. In any case, she was enjoying her new freedom and the looks of admiration she got from pedestrians.

She tried not to overuse the privilege. After all, it did cost more to operate a car than a horse, and gas wasn't readily available, though Henry did keep a spare can of gas down in the implement shed.

Riding along through the countryside, she had plenty of time to think and dream. Once, after leaving Angus' place to return to Henry's farm, she began musing about how long a period she'd thought of Angus's farm as 'home'. Even after moving to town, the farm seemed like 'home'. Her little apartment in town never quite had the same feel to it. It was cozy and she felt 'at home' in it, but she didn't think of it as 'home'—not like the place where she was born and spent her early years.

Moving to Henry's farm was different. She knew it wouldn't be 'home' at first, but she had assumed it would become 'home' in time. It was certainly a nicer house than the one on Angus' farm. The house was, after all, planned for Henry and Harriet, not Kate. She had hesitated to change the furnishings that Harriet had chosen—changes that might have made the place seem more like hers and Henry's. Oh, they were nice enough, but not to Kate's taste. She was glad she had brought her grandmother's platform rocker and the secretary she had bought for the studio and the organ. Henry always told Kate she could change anything about the house she wanted to, but she didn't feel right about changing something that was serviceable as it was. It could be that's the way women always felt when they moved into other women's houses.

Maybe that's why she found it so hard to think of Henry's farm as 'home'. But no, she suspected it was more than that. After all, it was Will's home, too, and he didn't seem to like her very much. She guessed she couldn't blame him. It would be hard for a child to lose his mother. Still, she felt like she was trying to fill a role for Will that she couldn't fill. She sighed, remembering the incident of the cup.

Will had teased Margaret and Hjelmer mercilessly one suppertime. It wasn't the first time he made fun of Margaret's coming on the Orphan Train and belittled Hjelmer's sometimes awkward handling of farm tools. Henry said, 'That's enough, Will! I won't have any more of that talk. Your mother didn't raise you to be unkind.' Will, embarrassed and angered, started to leave the table.

'Sit down!' Henry said between clenched teeth. Will reacted by picking up his coffee cup and slamming it down. The cup teetered on the edge of the table. Kate watched in horror as this piece of her mother's wedding china gradually, almost in slow motion, overbalanced and tumbled to the floor. The sound of its shattering in the sudden quiet was like the toll of the town clock in the middle of an icy winter night.

Tears appeared in Kate's eyes. Then she sensed, rather than saw, the swift motion of Henry's long arm as it swept out and grabbed Will's collar. More than once she had seen Will on edge, teetering like the cup, dangerously close to full-blown violence, but she had never seen Henry so angry as at this moment. His usually placid face was florid and the tiny trickles of blue veins that ran along his temples just beside his eyes stood out from the barely-wrinkled skin so that they looked like rivulets of purple ink.

No one spoke. Will's eyes seemed to bulge with the tightness of Henry's grip on his collar. His Adam's apple had a difficult time struggling through the noose of the collar but he seemed to make no effort to undo Henry's tight hold. Finally, Kate could stand it no longer.

'Henry!' she screamed. 'Henry Fergus, you let go of him—now. Let go of him, I say!' Kate tried to pull Henry away from Will. Finally, Henry let go and shoved Will back into his chair. Both were breathing heavily from the altercation. They ate nothing more. Kate and Hjelmer and Margaret dabbled at their food and then gave up also. Everyone left the table to do evening chores.

Margaret went to get the broom and the dustpan while Kate removed the dishes from the table. Margaret looked very concerned and asked, 'Are you all right, Auntie Kate? That was one of your special dishes, wasn't it?'

Kate nodded. 'Yes. Thank you, Margaret, but you go along upstairs and do your home work.' Upset as she was at the breaking of the cup, all Kate could think of as she swished the suds in the dishpan, was the crude display of Henry's anger provoked by Will. She had never experienced anything like this before and it shook her deeply.

Later that evening Henry marched Will in to apologize to Kate, and he himself apologized, but they all knew it would take awhile to heal the hurt from the outburst.

Thinking about this as she was driving along in the car that day after leaving Angus' place, she was deeply conflicted about this idea of home. Bad as her sessions with her mother and Lizzie sometimes were, they never involved physical violence. She frowned. 'Could this happen again? Maybe I should have given my relationship to Henry more time, especially where Will is concerned,' she thought as she arrived at Henry's farm. 'I wonder if this place will ever seem like home?'

* * *

The ice was melting into spring the fourth winter after Margaret had come to live with them. It was hard for Kate and Henry to believe she and the boys had become so grownup.

Earlier, on eighth grade graduation day, Margaret had been radiant in the pretty pink voile dress Kate made for her. Her dark brown hair was loosened and hung about her face in soft waves. She looked very pretty as she stood in front of the whole school and the parents and recited a poem. Henry said he couldn't have imagined having such a pretty child! Kate said she couldn't have imagined having such a smart child!

All three of the children were now going to high school in town. The boys would ride horses into town each day as usual, but Kate made arrangements for Margaret to stay in town with Mrs. Buchanan and work for her board and room during the school week. 'Can't I ride a horse into town, too?' Margaret asked. 'Like the boys? Why do I have to leave home?'

'Well, Margaret, you always said you wanted to finish high school, and it would be too hard on you riding a horse day after day. Boys are different,' Kate said. 'Besides, this way you'll be right in town in case of bad weather and you won't miss school. I expect you could even sing in the chorus that meets after school, and you'll be able to make friends with some of the other girls. Either Henry or I will drive you to town on Monday morning and pick you up Friday evening.'

Margaret was still apprehensive. 'But I'll miss you so much,' she said and added. 'Oh, I guess I can do it.'

'That's settled then,' said Kate. 'I don't need to tell you that you must keep up with your homework even when I'm not around to supervise. It'll be important if you want to go to college. We really hope you do.'

Kate had taken her to town the first week. Mrs. Buchanan welcomed her with a big smile which Kate was glad to see. When Kate turned to get into the car to go home, Margaret hugged her tight and said she'd miss her! Kate realized how much she'd miss Margaret, too.

* * *

When Christmas time came, Kate planned a lively celebration. 'Henry, why don't you and Hjelmer go down in the draw and cut us a cedar tree?' asked Kate at breakfast a day before Christmas Eve. 'And make it a nice big one. Oh, dear. I guess it can't be too big. We don't have space for a really big one.'

'Well, Kate, we'll do our best—like we always do,' Henry smiled as he tweaked her ear. 'C'mon, Hjelmer. You go get the sled and I'll get the horse.' Kate watched them stride off toward the barn. With the heavy new snow, their return with the tree strapped to the sled made a pretty picture—a Christmas picture—she thought. 'I wish I could photograph that,' she said out loud.

'Oh, Auntie Kate, shall we string pop corn for the tree?' Margaret asked that evening. She asked for it every Christmas after her first one—the first time she'd seen a decorated tree. Kate smiled and got out the old popper that sat atop the wood range. Soon the sound of popping filled the room with gentle bursts. Margaret smiled as she turned the handle on the lid which threatened to pop off.

'We won't butter the first batch so we can string them without getting our fingers greasy, but then I'll do another so we can have plenty to eat later this evening,' Kate said as she poured out the fluffy white kernels into the blue enamel bread bowl. 'You'd better get started stringing!' she admonished. Margaret's first Christmas with them, she had to learn how to avoid pricking her fingers with the needle. That was no longer a problem for her. Each year Will and Hjelmer joined in the stringing although they grumbled as if not wanting to admit that they, too, enjoyed it.

Although the family seldom went to church—it being too far away—Margaret said she'd like to go to the candlelight Christmas Eve service this year. 'I'd like to go,' said Will and then Hjelmer said, 'Me, too.'

Kate was surprised and pleased since, with Will going to college in the fall, he might not be home next Christmas. It was a cold night riding home in the car, but tucked under the same horsehair blankets they used in the buggy, every one was singing to celebrate the season.

At breakfast on Christmas morning, each of the family found a package wrapped in white tissue paper, a luxury Kate had found at Halley's Department Store. 'Oh, my!' said Margaret. 'Just the paper is special!' She was very careful not to tear it as she opened it. She was delighted to find a purse, crocheted and beaded with jet black beads. 'Oh, Auntie Kate!' she breathed. 'I have never seen anything so beautiful! Did you make it?' Kate smiled and nodded. Margaret came around the table to give her a hug.

The boys opened their packages of argyle socks that Kate had knit for them. They nodded politely and said, 'Thank you.' Henry also opened his gift very carefully so as not to tear the tissue paper. Inside was a woolly scarf that Kate had knit for him in a pale green that matched his eyes. At first, he looked a little teary, but then he said, 'I think we all have a lot to thank Kate for.' Then he sobered quickly and said, 'But I have nothing for you, my love!'

Kate smiled. 'You have all given me more than I could have hoped for by being such a wonderful family. I'm glad you like my little gifts.'

That night after they snuggled under the comforter, Kate said, 'You know, Henry, things are going so well, do you think we could take a few days and go to see Lina in Kansas? It's been years since I've seen her, and she's getting older, you know.' Indeed, Kate was quite young when Lina married John and moved to Kansas. She'd only been back to the home place once since then. How her mother must have missed her!

Henry was reluctant, as she knew he would be. 'Kate, it would take a bigger hunk of time than you imagine right now. You know I've got to get ready for planting as soon as the fields are dry enough.' Then he added that he'd think about it. 'Maybe when this snow melts.'

'I mean, I could go alone, but I do so want Lina and John to meet you and you to meet them. I don't ask for much, do I?'

He reached over to kiss her as he wrapped his arms around her. 'No, my sweet, you don't. Well, we'll see,' Kate laughed and tugged at his ears. 'That was a very special Christmas, Kate. Thank you for making it happen! I love you. I do love you very much.' Kate snuggled happily against his warm chest.

* * *

Three weeks later, Kate looked out the train window and was glad to see Will as he stood on the train station platform waiting for the train to stop. 'Thank you, Will, for coming to get us. You're right on time!' He seemed to look and act very grown up.

'You know I like an excuse to drive the car!' Will grinned. 'Anyway, I had a couple of errands in town so I did those first, and I was right here when the train pulled in.'

'Good timing! Now I'm anxious to get home!' Kate noted her use of the term 'home' and this time it felt right. 'First we have to pick up Margaret in Appleton,' Kate said as she climbed into the front seat of the car.

'Well, no, Auntie Kate,' said Will, 'you see, I saw Margaret at school on Friday and she said she'd like to come home after school. I argued, but she said she'd happily ride on the horse with me. Hjelmer brought her bag.'

Kate stared at Will and frowned. If they'd asked her ahead of time, she would have checked with Henry, of course, but she really didn't approve of this change in the plans. She'd made special arrangements with Mrs. Buchanan for Margaret to spend an extra night there. It was obvious there was nothing she could do now but chastise Margaret about it when they got home.

As she stepped out of the car at the farm, she spread her arms wide and whispered, 'My, the farm looks beautiful. I guess spring will come after all.' She turned to Will. 'Where's Hjelmer? Where's Margaret?'

'Oh, I guess they're just finishing up some chores,' said Will as he lifted their bags out of the car.

Margaret met them in the kitchen. She did not smile, and Kate noted that she was extra quiet. 'My goodness, Margaret!' Kate exclaimed. 'Don't you look grownup!' Margaret seemed almost shy. Finally, she asked Kate if she'd had a good time and then excused herself to do some homework. Kate looked at her quizzically but let her go. Henry came in and carried the bags upstairs.

Smiling to herself, Kate hummed a bit the next day as she wrung out the laundry. She was surprised how much the trip had added to the weekly laundry, but it had been a wonderful week and she was glad to do it. When Henry came in to wash up for dinner, she hugged him and said, 'Oh, Henry, you just don't know how good it made me feel to get away from home and visit Lina. It's been such a long time since we've seen each other. John seems so nice. Wouldn't it be interesting to own a greenhouse business like he does? But, of course, it would be a lot of work, too.'

Henry folded his arms around her. 'Kate, I hate to admit it, but it was good for me, too, and I do like your family!' It was good to hear. She felt she'd had to talk him into making the trip, but now everything seemed all right. The children seemed to have gotten along fine while they were gone and that made her feel at ease, too. There were no problems too big to solve, and all was right with her world.

* * *

Soon after they returned, planting season was upon them. It was a good thing that Will was still home to work with Henry and Hjelmer. Next year would be different. Will would be off to college. More than once, Henry encouraged him to take that step. 'You know, Will, I've said before that that year I had in college was worth it. I wanted to continue, but my father died, so I came home to run the farm. I don't want you to have to do that—unless you want to. I want you to have every opportunity to succeed at whatever you want to do, so I'll help you get through. What do you say?'

Will always grinned and said, 'I'll be glad to get out of here! Yes, yes, I'll try hard. I'd like to be a lawyer, or maybe a teacher.'

'Fair enough,' said Henry. 'You'd be a good teacher. Don't forget—you need to get your application in soon.'

Kate admitted that Will was looking more like a man than a boy and wanting to do more things on his own. These days he seemed to resent Henry and Kate's telling him what to do and when to do it. As Henry and Kate rocked in the evening, they talked about this, realizing that Will needed to be considered a grownup even though they were well aware of his shortcomings in this area. It would be hard to run the farm without him, but they still had Hjelmer. Henry lamented that it would be hard to see Will go, but guessed with Hjelmer's help they'd make it through another year. 'I may sell some cows, but soon I suppose Hjelmer'll want to be on his own, too.'

Kate nodded. 'At least we'll have Margaret for awhile longer.' Then she frowned. Margaret had been extra quiet since they returned home, but she didn't know why.

Some weeks later Margaret came into the kitchen with her head down, her arms hanging at her sides, her fingers nervously twitching. Kate went on kneading the bread, but observed her carefully. She noticed that Margaret's eyes were puffy as though she had been crying. 'Is something the matter—?' Kate began.

Margaret interrupted. 'Auntie Kate—' she began, her voice a thin whine much as it had been when she first came to them. It was the voice of a child's despair in those early days, and though Margaret's voice had modulated considerably over the years, Kate still heard it as an expression of inner pain. There had been nights when Margaret's nightmares had brought both Kate and Henry to her bedside to comfort her and assure her that she was safe and loved. They never knew what agonies she must have suffered in her short life. They never pried, and though they had given her many opportunities to talk about those other years, she seldom did.

Kate stopped her kneading. The bulges of dough oozed out from under her plump wrists as she paused. 'Auntie Kate, I—I—' Margaret began again. Kate looked at her quizzically. It had been apparent to her for some time now that this half grown young woman was troubled. Though Margaret's normal demeanor was generally serious, she often went about her work humming a soft and pleasant tune as she mopped and dusted and scrubbed the men's crusty socks on the washboard. She seldom complained.

'Go on, child. Is something bothering you?'

'Auntie Kate—' Suddenly she burst into tears and fled upstairs, her feet pounding on each step. Kate dusted the flour from her hands as best she could, finishing the job with the skirt of her apron and followed Margaret's long strides with her own short ones. She climbed the stairs breathlessly in time to hear the door to Margaret's room close with a bang.

'Margaret!' Kate's tone was more severe than she intended, but she was truly worried. She opened the door without knocking which she never would have done under ordinary circumstances. She closed it gently behind her with only a muffled click. Margaret lay crying into her apron and shaking the feather bed with her sobs.

Kate felt keenly her lack of experience at raising children, a far different experience than teaching them in a classroom she had found out. A warmth of caring spread over Kate, an alien feeling of motherhood she had never felt for Henry's son Will. She reached out to embrace the girl and realized that Margaret was now a grown woman and strong from the hard work of the farm.

'Margaret.' Kate's voice choked. 'Tell me what's wrong. I can't help you if I don't know what's wrong.'

'You can't help me! You're not my mother.' Margaret had reminded Kate of their unlikely relationship more than once. How Kate wished now she had asked Margaret to call her Ma instead of Auntie Kate. At the time it had seemed the right thing to do since Margaret, like many riders on the Orphan Trains, was not a true orphan.

'I can try, Margaret. I want to try. Of course, you wish your mother were here, but she can't be. I wish I could be a real mother to you, Margaret. You're a wonderful girl and a big help to Henry and me. I'm glad you came to live with us. You are like our own daughter and we care about you. I guess I've never said that before, have I? I hope you will trust me to help you. I love you!' she exclaimed.

Margaret pulled away from Kate's warm hands rubbing her back. She spoke into the pillow. 'No! You can't help me. I'd be better off dead.'

'Margaret! What are you saying? You have your whole life ahead of you. You must tell me what's bothering you so I can help.' Kate stretched further and gently stroked the cotton fabric stretched across Margaret's back as Margaret cradled her head with her arms.

'You wouldn't understand.' Momentarily she stopped her sobbing, her tone becoming accusatory. Then her body was convulsed again. Kate slipped off the bed onto the small, faded blue rag rug Margaret had braided from Henry's old overalls. She lay her head next to Margaret's, her hand patting Margaret's shoulder as she would have patted her in babyhood had she known Margaret then. They rocked gently as one.

The intensity of Margaret's sobbing finally subsided. Kate handed her a clean handkerchief from her own apron pocket, and Margaret sat up to blow her nose, now an ugly red. The impolite sounds of hard blowing were like a welcome rain after a thunderstorm. Kate stroked Margaret's long brown hair which had fallen loose from her heavy braids. Neither spoke. Kate could only wonder how and when the thunderstorm would pass.

* * *

A few days later, as Kate and Margaret prepared dinner, they were occupied in their own private worlds. Working alongside Margaret in the kitchen, Kate was tempted to ask important questions—to demand answers even. Still, she knew her prying might not fully satisfy her own curiosity and might possibly alienate Margaret who, after all, had lived with them such a short time.

Kate often imagined Margaret's childhood before the Orphan Train, but she had very little to base her assumptions on. Over time she had gleaned several clues, none of which seemed pertinent to the Margaret who stood beside her just now. She was not surprised that Margaret's father had difficulty finding work and was away long hours when he did find a job. She'd read the newspapers and knew about living conditions in New York City. She also gathered that Margaret's mother must have taken in boarders because Margaret talked about crowding all the children in two rooms so there'd be room for 'friends' in the other rooms upstairs.

Kate could imagine that sending Margaret and little Lillian and Marybelle to the orphanage did more than relieve the family of three mouths to feed. Her parents would know that, unlike their brothers, the girls would never bring home much pay and their jobs might have been ruinous. The two years the three girls spent in the orphanage probably meant they had a little more food than at home, but it couldn't have been easy. Riding the Orphan Train may have been adventurous in a way for these little girls, but it must have been heart-renching for Margaret when her sisters were taken from the train before they got to Nebraska. No wonder Margaret had looked so forlorn when the train came to Tingle Creek!

Now, Kate was slicing cabbage for slaw, and Margaret was mashing the potatoes. Breaking into Kate's dreamlike state, Margaret, in a small, frightened voice broke the silence. 'Auntie Kate, I'm—I'm going to have a baby!'

Kate's chopping knife hung in midair. She leaned against the kitchen work table and whispered, 'You're what? You're—what? Are you sure? Oh, Margaret! How can that be?' Kate could not keep the disbelief and disappointment out of her voice as she reeled from the news.

'It's been almost three months.'

'Oh, my goodness! Maybe something else is wrong. Maybe you should see the doctor.' At that, Margaret visibly cringed as if to deflect a blow to her body. 'Oh, Margaret!' Kate went on. 'You must be wrong! You must be,' she insisted, her voice fading. She frowned and then spoke rather sharply. 'How could you be having a baby? There's got to be a man involved!' Kate stared at Margaret rather overly long. 'When did it happen?' she demanded. 'Where did it happen? Who did it? Didn't you know this could happen? Did you want this to happen? How could you let this happen?' She realized now she should have been paying more attention to Margaret's private wash line. But what good would that have done? she scolded herself. 'We'll talk about this later. We've got to finish dinner. Oh, dear, here come Henry and Hjelmer already.'

Henry stopped to wash up at the kitchen sink. 'Smells good! he remarked and went on into the living room. Margaret, sniffling, said nothing as she moved between the kitchen and the dining room setting the table and pouring water into each of their glasses. Kate was having difficulty paying the necessary attention to carving the roast beef.

'Oh, dear!' she thought. 'So this is what was bothering her. But—it can't be true.' She frowned thinking there will be talk in the neighborhood, even if Margaret goes to a home for unwed girls in Omaha or Sioux City or Lincoln. Kate's instinct was to find a way to avoid all that. But how? 'A baby! What to do? What if Margaret wants to keep the baby? She'll have to drop out of school.' Kate's mind was awhirl. 'Who *is* the father? And when did it happen? Kansas! Oh, my. It could have been while we were in Kansas.' Kate's mind tested all the Whats and What Ifs that came to her.

Suddenly she snapped back to the present. 'Where's Will? The food's almost already and he isn't even in the house,' she said to no one in particular.

'He's coming. He had to return the tools to the implement shed,' Henry said from the living room where he sat in front of the big bay window to rest after his morning's work. Kate appeared in the doorway to the living room. She smiled at Henry, hoping a smile would straighten out the worry lines she knew must have formed across her forehead.

'Margaret and I made pie with some of the peaches we canned. Oh, here's Will now. We'll eat as soon as he washes up.' Kate and Margaret put the food on the table and they assembled to eat. Kate started passing the bowls of food. As they ate, the two women sat quietly absorbed in thought while Henry and Will and Hjelmer talked about plans for moving the pigs that afternoon.

After awhile, Will said, in a mocking tone of voice, 'Well, Margaret, ain't you the quiet one!' Margaret mostly looked at her plate, but Kate caught Margaret's sideways glance in Will's direction. What was in that look? Will's remark to Margaret was not particularly surprising since he had continued taking verbal jabs at both Margaret and Hjelmer. Henry repeated his reprimands from time to time, but it didn't stop. Kate had to assume Will made similar rude remarks when she and Henry weren't present. Henry excused him saying that Will was simply 'teasing' the other two, but it was obvious that Henry, too, was becoming more irritated with his remarks.

Now Kate interrupted tentatively, trying to diffuse the tension, 'How are your plans for college coming along, Will? Have you been accepted?' Kate knew Will loved to talk about himself.

'Well, I guess you know I got a scholarship,' he began. 'I ought to get first in my freshman class.'

Henry said, 'You can't count on that unless you really work hard. College isn't Appleton High School, after all. There's no room in college for laziness.'

'I'm not lazy. You know that,' Will retorted.

Kate stood up and started to clear the table. Margaret hastily joined her, and the men left the table soon after.

Kate's thoughts turned to Margaret's problem as she scraped the plates and stacked them by the sink. She was reminded of how painful it had been to be unmarried and childless. She still felt a certain 'emptiness of the womb' as she described it to herself. Now her patience and genuine feeling for Margaret's pain surprised her, and her heart ached for this child-woman. She wondered if it could have ached any more had Margaret indeed been born of her womb and lived with her for her full fifteen years. She had come to love Margaret more than she ever thought she could, but she still didn't know her very well. Still, Kate refused to intrude on the girl's right to privacy, the same right she claimed for herself.

Her thoughts turned to Henry as she swished the dishes in the sink. In general, her years of marriage to Henry had been good. He was as fine a man as she could have found to marry. But now she wondered about how he would react to finding out Margaret had been violated. She suspected he would be no different than any other man in that situation. Kate remembered how Herman Bradley had taken his rifle and headed for the Pervayiences' to 'git that Pervayience boy' because Ottie Pervayience had been fooling around with Herman's daughter. His wife had called the Pervayiences after Herman left so Ottie could get out of town. Not that Kate expected such a reaction from Henry, but she was sure he would be very angry, maybe the more so if Margaret could not or would not reveal the perpetrator. How then would he vent his anger? She couldn't be sure.

*   *   *

A day passed and then two, and nothing more was said. Kate very much wanted to talk about Margaret's early life. Down deep she felt that, if she could only get to know the little girl Margaret, she would be better able to counsel her and help her through this time of trial. She pictured the two of them—just the two of them—chatting while they baked bread or shelled peas or whipped egg whites for an angel food cake, yet none of these settings seemed right. Whenever it might take place, she wanted to have Margaret's undivided attention, not allowing her to drift away from the subject at hand.

Margaret was a rather sober child, not unlike Kate herself. Now that she was about to give birth to a child, talking to her about her early life took on a new importance. Kate knew Margaret must have had life experiences a child in most midwestern communities would never have had. She guessed that Margaret may have been chosen by the orphanage for the Orphan Train because she was older and could help with the little ones on the train, but she had no way of knowing if this was so.

One day while the men were in the field safely out of earshot, Kate said, 'Margaret, take off your apron'—as she was taking off her own—'and let's just sit and visit a bit.' Margaret looked startled, like a cornered animal. 'I've heated up that coffee left from breakfast,' Kate continued. Margaret slowly untied the unbleached muslin apron trimmed with bands of blue and hung it on the back of the kitchen door. Kate picked up her coffee cup and indicated Margaret should do so as well and they went into the parlor.

Margaret sat on the organ stool, looking rather uncomfortable with her hands twisting the hem of her skirt, her body twisting with the motion of the stool. She did not look at Kate. The physical distance between them was all too indicative of their emotional distance, Kate thought. She determined to be as gentle as possible, leaving behind the strict school marm persona.

'You know, Margaret,' she began, 'we've never really talked about your days in New York before you came here. Is there anything you'd like to tell me?' Instantly, she realized this sounded too vague and not at all sympathetic. 'Uh, let me start again. Do you remember when you first went to the orphanage?'

Margaret caught Kate's eye briefly. 'Yes.'

'But you weren't an orphan, were you?' Kate asked.

Margaret looked down at her restless hands. 'No. There were just too many of us, and there was another one coming,' she said. 'They kept my brothers—they had to go to work, but my next younger sisters and I weren't worth much. They said it would be best for us.' Margaret's eyes began to fill with tears. 'They kept my baby sister.'

The image of a large family in a tenement in New York City formed in Kate's mind, however inaccurate it may have been. She could imagine the feelings of a little eight-year-old girl as her father deposited her and her sisters at the orphanage. Kate started to reach out to pat Margaret's hands, but Margaret pulled back. Kate wondered if she'd asked too much. She tried to put herself in Margaret's place.

'Margaret, when you were at the orphanage, did they take you to church?'

Margaret looked up directly at Kate. A slight smile made its way across her face. 'Oh, yes!' she said. 'My folks weren't much of anything, but we kids had to go to the Catholic Church. I even had my first communion.' Remembering seemed to please her. 'The nuns gave me a nice, clean dress to wear. I felt like a princess.'

'I'm sure you looked like one, too!' Kate said. 'I don't know much about the Catholic Church, but there are lots of saints, aren't there?'

'Yes.'

'Did you have a favorite saint?'

Margaret's smiled slyly. 'Of course! Saint Margaret!' They both laughed.

It was good to laugh again and to hear Margaret's laugh. 'Well, we'd better finish in the kitchen,' Kate said, and they both jumped up. Kate followed Margaret to the kitchen.

Later in the afternoon when they were dressing the chickens for stew, Kate very quietly said, 'Margaret, how could this have happened? Did you want this to happen?'

Margaret dropped the knife she was using and glared at Kate, as if Kate were somehow responsible for the whole affair. 'No!' she mouthed in a low voice between clenched jaws. 'No. Never. Never. Never.'

'Margaret, I believe you. Can you tell me who is responsible?'

Margaret leaned on the edge of the table and hung her head. Very quietly, almost inaudibly, she said, 'No. I can't. Never. I'm so sorry. I never wanted to hurt you and Uncle Henry.' Her shoulders shook as tears formed.

'You haven't, Margaret,' Kate said and added, 'I'm so sorry this had to happen to such a wonderful person as you. We will always love you and care for you.' Kate patted her back as she might have a small child deciding to leave it at that for the time being.

Still, the weight of Margaret's problem sat on Kate's shoulders like a yoke. Her whole body shrank from the fearsomeness of the task before her. She shuddered to think about it. She was now sure Margaret would never voluntarily reveal her assailant. Kate didn't really want to know. There were, after all, two young men right in their own household capable of such, and she did not want to—indeed, could not bring herself to—suspect either of them.

* * *

Several days after Margaret's confession, as Henry and Kate did up the supper dishes while the young people were off to a church social, Henry began hesitantly, 'Kate, you've been awfully quiet the last few days—and I'm afraid your eyebrows are going to be permanently knit together.' He grinned his most impish grin. 'C'mon. What's troubling you? Life is too short to let something eat you up.' He leaned over and kissed her cheek. Kate looked at him in astonishment.

Henry had always been a steady and reassuring hand when Kate felt she could not deal with the work. He would come in from the fields, hot, dirty, and tired after a long day in the field, but after supper he would stand beside her, dishtowel in hand, to relieve her unspoken resentment. He seemed to sense when she missed her 'other life' as she called it. He seemed to know that her photography studio and its gentility were in sharp contrast to cooking for threshers and chasing hogs back into the pen after they rooted under the fence and picking and stemming endless pails of wild gooseberries.

On those nights, as Kate dropped into bed exhausted, he did not insist himself upon her but lay cradling her in his arms and blowing gently at the ringlets at the back of her neck. Such a good-humored man was more than Kate could have dreamed of marrying, and occasionally she wondered if Gyorgy would have been such a kind, cherishing husband.

Now she turned to reach the pans on the kitchen table and scowled. Was she so transparent that her life, her independence, had slipped completely away from her while she scraped the chicken roosts and weeded the carrots and stomped the hay on the wagon and accepted Henry's attentions as more than flattery? It was frightening to think about, and she did not at that moment know how to answer him. She looked directly at him and smiled, reaching up to daub soap suds on his ruddy cheeks. 'All right. I won't let anything eat me up!' she said and turned back to the dishes.

Henry accepted the smile and teasing, but Kate felt she was betraying his trust in keeping Margaret's situation from him. It would in time, of course, affect him directly, but she couldn't tell him until she'd had a chance to think through how to handle this awful business. She would have to remind herself to smile more when he was around and respond more enthusiastically in bed, but it would be hard.

That night Kate lay awake long after Henry's arms relaxed from around her waist and his breathing slipped into the quiet rhythm of exhaustion. She sometimes longed for her photography business, the continual meeting with customers who were more than satisfied and most complimentary of her work, and she longed for the quiet of her rooms at the end of a busy day. She thought about how she had passed the time of day with merchants up and down the block as she stopped in to buy supplies. She even missed the voice of Jean Burchett on the telephone. Jean, who she seldom saw any more, now seemed well entrenched in her old maidhood.

Kate wondered sometimes who was better off. She seldom saw folks from Tingle Creek, except for rare Saturday night forays to buy supplies not available in nearby Appleton. She missed seeing the Pedersens, the Methodist women from the Ladies' Aid, and Rev. and Mrs. Barton. She missed occasionally going to church at the Truebloods, but Henry had made it clear that he preferred she go with him and Will when they went to the tiny Methodist Episcopal Church out in the country on the other side of Appleton—though they didn't go often. She missed seeing Angus and Lizzie—though even when she was in town, she had seen them less and less often as they became more and more involved with their children who now numbered four with a fifth—and Angus declared, the last—on the way. She was painfully aware of how lonely her life had become though she had married a wonderful man and had three bright young people in her care.

Suddenly she came wide awake and sat up in bed. Yes, there was much in her previous life that she missed, but most of all, she realized how much she missed the companionship of Bethany Trueblood. With that revelation, she lay back against Henry, feeling his strength and his warmth, and fell asleep.

At breakfast the next morning, she announced, 'I'm going to Tingle Creek,' while she flipped pancakes for the assembled household. 'I want to visit Bethany Trueblood.' She kept her voice as even as possible while she bent over to stoke the coals under the cast iron griddle and stood up to serve another round of pancakes from the ironware platter in the warming oven.

Henry raised a quizzical eyebrow, but said simply, 'Well, Kate, I'd hoped we could move the chicken house today, and I'd need your help, but I guess it can wait until tomorrow if it doesn't rain. While you're in town, you might as well get me some nails and some screen wire for that back porch door. Might as well get groceries there, too. It'd save a trip to Appleton.'

'And what about a surprise for us children?' Will teased.

'I'm not a child,' Margaret declared, and Will looked at her strangely. Kate thought Margaret was sounding more like her old self. For a fleeting moment, as she looked at the girl, she wondered if the horror of the last couple of weeks had been real or only a bad dream. Hjelmer didn't look up from his pancakes.

'I'll take the buggy so, Hjelmer, I want you to hitch up Jessie just as soon as you're through eating. Margaret, I'll leave you to do the dishes and start up the bread. The beds can wait until that's done.'

As she hung up her apron, Henry touched her on the shoulder. Looking around, Kate saw the same quizzical expression on his face that she had seen often the last few days. Her heart sank. She had no wish to betray the trust of this good man but for now, it couldn't be helped. 'You can take the car,' he said.

'No, I think visiting Bethany is best done using horses,' she smiled. 'I'll pick up those things you wanted in town, and I'll be back soon,' she said lightly and gave Henry a big smile.

* * *

In the buggy on the way to Tingle Creek, Kate had time to think—away from the distractions of home. The quiet clip-clop of the horse's hooves was soothing, unlike the raucous belching of the motor car which scared ideas right out of one's head.

Away from the farm it was surprising how clearly she could think about Margaret's problem—which really belonged to all of them. She thought about the fact that Margaret was not just 'some young woman'. She was an integral part of Kate's and Henry's life now. Other young women might have sometimes become pregnant without benefit of wedlock, but not 'our Margaret'. Even without being 'flesh of their flesh', Kate saw the problem in a whole new light after only four years.

Henry had come to regard her as a daughter, and Kate treasured the time she and Margaret had together when she helped her with her school work or they worked together in the kitchen or doing the laundry or cleaning. She enjoyed passing on her housewife's skills to this bright, adaptable young woman. Looking back at her conversations with Margaret, Kate was disappointed with herself that it had never occurred to her to teach Margaret about life itself. In fact, she mused, she wouldn't have known how to begin.

She had wondered how much upbringing Margaret could have had—or would have had—in the large family she grew up in. She was young enough before she left them that probably nothing was said about giving birth—even though her mother experienced it frequently. Probably her mother had supposed motherhood to be a long way off in her daughter's future. Kate wished now that they'd had some meaningful conversations about what it means to be a desireable young woman, and how some men—even older boys—were not to be trusted.

As she drove along, enjoying a light breeze on her face and the sight of fields beginning to show green along with the smell of newly turned sod, all her troubles seemed less intractable. She tried to concentrate on the passing farmhouses and the occasional newborn calf in a barnyard, but her mind kept slipping back to Margaret.

Kate wanted to believe that Margaret confided in her because she trusted her, but she knew very well that Margaret had no one else to turn to—at least she would have been unlikely to turn to Mrs. Buchanan. Faced with the problem, Kate was outwardly calm and reassuring, making promises to Margaret about the future that she had no idea how or whether they might come about. Inside she was torn apart wondering again how it might have happened. In town, surely Mrs. Buchanan was keeping Margaret busy when she wasn't in school. She could not believe Mrs. Buchanan would have allowed for such a situation to occur. But that left the farm, their farm or some other as a possible place where it might have happened. When she asked Margaret, Margaret had simply said, 'I can't tell you,' and had run from the room.

Now Kate was hardly aware of the horse's gentle tug on the reins as she pondered all these things. How could she be expected to be wise in dealing with someone else's daughter who somehow had become involved with someone she had no desire to marry? Marry? Kate could not think of Margaret marrying. She was too young, yet Kate knew that forced marriage was one of the few options for young women in a compromised situation.

Last night, when Kate was darning Henry's socks, she agonized over this very problem. She assumed her own marriage was as good as many, but she also knew that her love was not unqualified. Maybe she could never have been an ideal love partner to any man—even Gyorgy—but in her mind she felt she could have—just not to Henry. At least that was the way she felt at this juncture in their marriage.

What other options did Margaret have? She could go to a lying-in home to have the baby and relinquish the baby to a childless couple for adoption—just as the foundling had been adopted. 'No!' Kate said outloud and her voice sounded even louder in the open air. There must be a better solution!

For a few selfish minutes Kate entertained the idea of claiming Margaret's child as her own. Hadn't she always wanted a baby? She knew that some part of her agreed to marry to Henry with the vague hope that she might, even at her age, have a child of her own. That hope had been tragically dashed when Henry's and her child was stillborn. This much she knew—she must have patience to wait for the right, the best, answer. She could only hope that Bethany would help her clarify what needed to be done to best protect Margaret. Yes, it would be good to talk all these things over with Bethany—well, at least most of them.

As she drove slowly in the spring air, Kate, her mind never let go of her problem. In the past she'd been impatient traveling the long ten miles to Tingle Creek, but not now. Being emotionally caught up in Margaret's case, it had been hard to think with any of the family around.

Now she weighed each option carefully. Kate really needed Henry's help with solving Margaret's problem, but she couldn't be sure how sympathetic he would be, and she needed him to be sympathetic. So far she hadn't felt comfortable with telling him. She knew only too well what disgrace a too-early pregnancy could bring to an unmarried woman and her whole family. Still it happened, and when it did, families were wont to devise ways to save their honor, either with or without saving the woman's honor. Family honor didn't figure in Margaret's case, as for as Kate was concerned, but she didn't know about Henry.

In the worst case, he might demand that Margaret tell them who did it. If he did, and she refused, she might run away, and Kate could not bear it if that happened. Or he might blame Margaret for this affair, and he might insist on throwing her out of the house. Kate knew that would be totally unfair and she could not risk that happening. Kate was sure that, if Henry chose this course of action, she herself would leave him to make a home for her and Margaret, but she really didn't want to leave this Henry she liked so much and who provided such good companionship. She looked forward to spending her old age with this man who loved her and wanted to care for her.

On the other hand, he might take umbrage at some man's compromising his daughter and force Margaret to tell them who the culprit was and then insist that Margaret marry him. Or, Henry might want to do something to harm the man. Henry seemed gentle enough, but there were cases where seemingly harmless people had turned on others rather violently. Kate didn't want to take a chance on such a possibility.

She reasoned that if she could find a place where Margaret could go to have the baby—where her identity could be masked and she would be well cared for—then, when she told Henry, he ought to listen more openly. It was important that she plan her strategy well to avoid the disaster that might follow a hasty decision. Still, she knew if she kept it from him much longer he might think she didn't trust him, and in turn he might come to distrust her.

She was greatly relieved when she saw the Trueblood's house in the distance.

* * *

Kate's stomach had quieted by the time she turned south toward the Trueblood farm. The familiar territory served to comfort her. Through the windbreak, she could just see their house not more than a hundred yards down the road. Kate sighed, feeling that she had gained a little more wisdom about how to handle her choices than when she climbed in the buggy that morning. At least she felt she could talk them over with Bethany more logically without the enormous emotional upheaval that had clouded her days.

Turning into the driveway, she saw that the lilacs showed signs of budding. Their sweet perfume haunted her memory. No matter how she disagreeable she felt her mother was, the memory of her lilacs always softened her assessment. As she drove toward the house, Calvin saw her and came running up the drive from the barn. He beamed as he took the reins from her. 'What a happy surprise, Mrs. Fergus! I'm glad I'm home from college so I could see you! You're looking well. Farm life must be good for you!'

Kate gave Calvin her hand as she stepped out of the buggy. 'My goodness, Calvin. I think you must have grown six inches since you went off to college. What are they feeding you there?'

Kate put her hands on his shoulders to study his smile—the smile of a full-grown man framed by a young man's beard—hardly the boy she had known at the drug store. That seemed like a long time ago. 'Well, ma'am, I really haven't growed any taller, but Ma says she's had to let out the waist of my pants some. How long can you stay? Shall I unhitch the horse?'

'Not "growed", Calvin, "grown"!' Kate laughed. Calvin laughed, too. In any case, it was easy to lapse into hometown language once away from college.

'I'm afraid I'll not be staying as long as I'd like,' Kate went on, 'even though it's been too long since I've seen you and your mother. I wish I could stay long enough to hear all about your studies, but I told Henry I'd be home by midafternoon, and I've got things to buy in town and some business to talk about with your mother. Is she home? I know she's terribly busy what with spring planting and all. Be honest with me now. Will I disturb her very much?'

'Oh, my, no, ma'am. She'll be very glad to see you. She often says how she misses you. In any case, she can iron or peel potatoes while you talk so she won't miss a minute of work. I'm afraid I have to be excused to see to some repairs for the plow handle.'

Kate walked to the front door of the Trueblood house to see if Bethany's tulips were showing through the thatch of leaves in the flower bed. What a lovely time of year. Too bad to waste even a minute of it worrying, but stepping onto the porch, she was brought back full force to thinking about

Margaret. She knocked on the screen door which banged rather more loudly than she had planned as it gave under her knuckles.

Behind the screen, the inside door opened. 'My goodness, Kate MacLean! Oh, I mean Fergus. What a happy surprise. Come in. Come in. We haven't seen you for ever so long. Did you see Calvin out there? I know he'd want to see you. What a wonderful thing you did for him. Here, let me take your shawl.' Kate stepped into the coolness of the largely-unused parlor. 'Come, come, Kate, we'll sit in the kitchen where it's warm.'

'It's nice to be here again, Bethany. I've missed you so much and I hate it that I've come to talk about a prob—' She looked beyond her hostess just then and saw Gyorgy standing by the kitchen door to the outside.

'How de do, Miss Katie?' Gyorgy smiled and bowed slightly. 'Oh, I guess that's not right anymore, is it? Mrs. Trueblood told me you married a farmer.'

Sobered by the unexpected encounter, Kate concentrated on breathing deeply and evenly. 'Yes. I married a good man. Henry Fergus of up near Appleton. Do you know of him?'

'I'm afraid not.'

'It's nice to see you again,' Kate began, uncertain about what to say. 'How is your wife?'

Gyorgy's face clouded and pain etched the edges of his mouth as the arc of his smile disappeared. She was surprised to see signs of aging in his handsome face. 'Unfortunately, my Rosita—she died when our second baby was born.'

'Oh, I'm so sorry,' Kate whispered and the consternation on her face expressed genuine concern. She struggled for something more to say but drowned in the swirl of mixed feelings that surged through her.

Bethany broke in, as if sensing Kate's discomfort. 'Gyorgy said it happened when they were traveling through Mississippi. The clan midwife was sick with flu and couldn't help her and no doctor would come from town. The women managed to save the baby though. He's a beautiful child. You'd want to take a picture of him if you could just see him.'

Kate's head shook from side to side. 'Oh, I'm so sorry. I'm so sorry.' The injustice of the death moved her deeply. She swallowed and asked, 'Will your family be staying at Tingle Creek very long?'

'No, I just came to tell Mrs. Trueblood that we will be leaving very early in the morning. It was nice to see you again, Miss Katie.' Gyorgy managed a grim smile. He added, 'I hope that you are very happy.'

Red Geraniums

At that, Kate looked directly at Gyorgy. 'Thank you. I am happy.' She knew it was not the whole truth, but she could not discount Henry's goodness to her. 'May your travels go well.'

Gyorgy bowed deeply to Bethany Trueblood and thanked her for the use of the land by the creek. Then, saying no more, he slipped out the door.

'I'm sorry for the delay in our visit, Kate, but of course, you needed to know about Gyorgy's wife. It was a sad, sad case, but in a Gypsy caravan, his little children will never want for loving. Life on the road must be very hard indeed, but he says they wouldn't have it any other way. Now, Kate. You haven't been here for ages, and we have much to talk about.

Sad as she was for Gyorgy, Kate's mind did not linger on his plight. She turned to Bethany. 'Oh, yes, Bethany. I've missed talking with you. You know, I really don't have anyone nearby that I know well enough to share a lot of my interests with. It's rather lonely.' Kate's face clouded and then brightened. 'Tell me about your family. How glad I was to see Calvin all grown up!'

'He is, Kate, and we have much to thank you for. Studying at the college has broadened him both mentally and physically. You remember how skinny he always was. As for the other two—they're doing well. Naomi's teachers often praise her work. And Benjamin is doing well though I'm afraid he has a tendency to play rather more than he should, but still he works hard around the farm and is very willing to do anything for us. Calvin is insisting that they must go to college, too, and he says he'll earn enough to help them. What a good boy he is. Naomi says she wants to go to the University, not just Normal School. I mean—I mean there's nothing wrong with Normal School—'

'It's quite all right, Bethany. If I could've gone to the University, I would have, but with my father gone, there was no money for me, and Angus had to drop out of the Agricultural College before he finished. Besides, I couldn't leave mother with all the housework to do for the boys.'

As Kate talked, Bethany picked up the steaming teakettle and poured the water over the fresh mint leaves she'd picked that morning from the south side of the house next to the stone foundation—the first of the season. 'There that ought to set about five minutes. Don't you just love the fresh spring smell on those leaves?' Kate smiled her agreement. They sat across the kitchen table from each other, as they used to do.

'I mustn't keep you from your work, Bethany . . .'

'No. No. Some things are more important than work. Tell me about your life, Kate. You're looking a little peaked. Have you been ill?'

'Oh, no, I'm fine, but—' It took her some time to gather the words in her heart to make sense for her friend. 'I've wanted to come for ever so long, but what with one thing or another, I couldn't make it. Now I need your advice. I need your level head to think through my problem with me—and even to tell me what to do.'

Bethany frowned slightly. 'But Kate, you're so much smarter than I am. How could I help? I'll do whatever I can, of course, but I'm not very smart.'

Kate sipped the hot mint tea, the steam clouding her blue eyes. 'Just seeing you again gives me hope!' she said as the first tears appeared. For a moment she felt like the five-year-old Kate who ran to Lina for comfort when Angus teased her. The problem was less clear all of a sudden. She scowled. Why did this problem bother her so much? Was it the fact that she was lonely and feeling overwhelmed at being a wife and mother? Or feeling confined by the marriage, invisible on the farm, incapable of handling situations she was unprepared for? Perhaps seeing Gyorgy again simply confused her. She shook her head to clear it. No, she couldn't blame Gyorgy. The problem was her own. She blinked, but tears appeared and coursed down her cheeks. Bethany squeezed her hand gently, pulling her back to reality.

'Is it so bad then?'

Kate shook her head, but sipped her tea and said nothing for a long moment. Finally, she cleared her throat. 'Bethany,' she began, 'do you remember our daughter Margaret?'

'Why, yes, but I haven't seen her for a while now. She must be quite grown up.'

'Yes. That's the problem, Bethany. She—she's going to have a baby.' Saying the words out loud both horrified and relieved Kate, but she quickly covered her mouth like a child who says a naughty word and immediately wishes she could take it back.

Bethany drew back as if she had been struck. There was a long pause. 'Yes, Kate, you do have a problem.'

An hour and a half later, Bethany walked with Kate to the buggy. Kate felt at peace with the world at that moment. Bethany's promise of help had been just what she needed. 'Let me give you a hand,' Calvin appeared as she started to put her right foot on the buggy step. She felt

Red Geraniums

his strong arms almost lift her into the carriage. 'Well, Calvin, I expect the next time I see you you'll be well established in doctoring the sick animals around here.'

'Goodness, Mrs. Fergus! I hope you don't wait that long.'

'No, Calvin, she's not going to wait that long—are you, Kate?'

'No, I hope not, but I suppose the distance between here and home won't become miraculously shorter just because I want it to be! I do miss seeing your family.'

'And we all miss you. Please remember me to Mr. Fergus,' Calvin said as he handed her the reins.

'Thank you for taking time to talk to me, Bethany.' Bethany nodded her head slightly, but merely smiled. Kate flicked the reins gently and the buggy slowly rolled out of the driveway. She waved her handkerchief and then wiped her eyes with it.

* * *

With a last wave to Bethany, Kate clucked to the horse as she drove out of the Trueblood's driveway and turned south toward town to pick up Henry's supplies. Once she left town and headed north to their farm, she sighed deeply, already immersed in recalling her visit with Bethany. She smiled broadly to realize that it was the first genuinely good mood she'd had for some time. Oh, she'd smiled at Henry occasionally to keep from appearing distraught, but those were teacher smiles meant to hide true feelings. They disappeared as quickly as the necessity for them abated. And she'd smiled at Margaret from time to time, thinking a pleasant smile might slice through the cloud of gloom that enveloped the child and might give her hope that she, too, would smile again some day.

Kate was relaxed on the return trip in a way she could not have been that morning. She thought again how beautiful the day was with the trees clothed in the tentative spring green that so enchanted her each year after a long winter. Her smile was different now. It reflected the warmth of the friendship she enjoyed with this kind and gentle and strong woman. Kate's creativity and business sense seemed brash in comparison to Bethany's calm, giving, understanding nature.

While Kate rather envied Bethany her quiet dignity and the simplicity of the Quaker life she had chosen to share with Abraham, she knew that she could never have traded places with Bethany. She had come to appreciate that Bethany's personality and life complemented her own.

With Bethany, she always felt free to think for herself—to think differently than others if that was the way she saw things. There was an intellectual sharing that she had sought but never quite achieved in her association with the Pedersens—especially with Mrs. Pedersen who could never shake her primary role as mother. It was the close woman-sharing-with-woman that she had hoped to find with Jean Burchett, but Jean proved to be too shallow to do much serious thinking at all.

Perhaps most valued was the freedom from conformity that she experienced at the Truebloods. The Tingle Creek community had little use for the likes of the Truebloods who lived by their Quaker principles, different as they were from the community norm. No one could have understood their giving a safe place to a band of Gypsies—if they had known, but the Truebloods' Christian principles were more important to them than community approval. With Bethany, Kate felt free to be the non-conformist she'd always been in her own way.

The horse whinnied as a bird swooped low in front of it. The reins hung loose in Kate's hands. The horse knew the way home, freeing Kate's mind to review her conversation with Bethany after Gyorgy left. For a flicker of a second, her heart wanted to dwell on Gyorgy, but she wanted even more to reaffirm Bethany's promise of help. Telling Margaret's story had been a struggle—her words so infused with her turmoil and heartache. Even more difficult, Kate had sensed that, as she talked, Bethany initially shrank from the facts, but Kate persisted. Finally, she concluded, 'Oh, Bethany, I'm so inadequate as a mother. Being a teacher is one thing, but feeling personally responsible for Margaret and Will and Hjelmer is quite another. Maybe I'm just too old to be a mother.'

Bethany did not answer immediately. Kate wiped her eyes and dabbed at her nose. After some time Bethany leaned forward, patting Kate's arm. Her voice was quiet, but laced with deep emotion. 'Kate—I know it doesn't help for me to say that you're not the first mother to have such a problem. Certainly not all of them were bad mothers. And it can't possibly be because of your age because after all, these children could have been your own. You know every mother fears for the safety of her daughter.' Bethany swallowed hard and paused. 'I pray that my Naomi never has to face such a terrible thing. Margaret is fortunate to have such a caring mother. That's what families are all about—to help each other in times of trouble, but I'm sorry that you—or anyone—has to be confronted with such difficult problems. Does Henry know?'

'No. I've been afraid to tell him. That's why I had to talk to you first. I couldn't ask just anyone because I don't know who to trust. I'm realistic enough to know that whatever happens people will talk and come to their own conclusions about why Margaret would go away for several months—no matter what we tell them. I'm convinced she's not at fault—unless being an attractive girl is a fault—but you know that people will always say it's the girl's fault.' Kate paused, glad that Bethany let her tell her story without interruption.

'Margaret's not dumb. I'm sure she's heard the talk about other girls. She hasn't said anything, but I'm sure it must scare her to think of having to face that kind of talk. Now mind you, I can take the neighborhood gossip—and I think Henry can if I'm careful explaining the situation to him, but—Oh, Bethany, I don't want her to be hurt. I just want her to be taken care of and be able to live a normal life. I'm sorry to worry you about it, but you are the only friend I can trust to judge fairly.'

'It's all right. It's all right. Your secret is safe with me. But let's think what we can do.' Bethany's use of 'we' was reassuring.

Kate studied the mint leaves at the bottom of the tea cup. 'I think the best thing is for her to go away until the baby is born and then give it up for adoption, but I don't know how to arrange for such things. I don't mean that you should know about such things, but Quakers seem so deeply committed to helping others I thought you might know somebody who would know.'

'It's true, of course. We are committed to helping the least of our brothers—and sisters. We take God's command very seriously. Let me think.' Bethany rose and opened the pie cupboard. She returned with a plate of doughnuts which she set in front of Kate. 'I'm afraid they're yesterday's, but I think we need something to eat just now.' Kate chose one of the generous doughnuts rolled in sugar, and both women lapsed into silence as they drank the hot mint tea and bit into the sweet pastries.

'Ah!' Bethany suddenly brightened. 'I've just thought of an old friend from Colony—you know, not far from South Sioux City. She's a Quaker woman, a grandmotherly sort who I believe would give Margaret a place to stay until her lying-in time—if she's well herself. Her name's Hattie Pennington, and she's a good solid woman who's very spare in her speaking and insistent on good behavior, but very loving. In her younger years she used to be well-known in the community as a nurse and midwife though I'm sure she didn't have any formal training. Just good common sense, I guess, and a pretty thorough knowledge of home-grown medicines and such.'

'Is she married? I mean, would her husband object?'

'Who? Jeremiah? Oh, no, he's a jolly, forgiving sort. He wouldn't preach at her at all and they'd both treat her like kinfolk. Margaret could work for them while she waits. If you want me to, I could write to Hattie. It'll take a few days, of course. I'll have her write directly to you.'

'Would you? Oh, Bethany, thank you. You can tell them that we'll pay all Margaret's expenses—and she is a good worker.' Kate's face showed her relief, but then clouded again. 'But what about the baby? Margaret's very worried that the baby might not find a home and have to live in an orphanage. What will we do with the baby?'

'Now, Kate, that's several months ahead. We can wait a bit on that. The Lord will provide an answer. You'll see.'

Kate pondered this conversation over and over as she drove along. Up ahead she saw their neighbor's buggy coming toward her. She slowed the buggy now as they came alongside. 'How do you do, today, neighbor?' she called. The children waved and their mother smiled broadly at Kate as she assured them she was fine and drove on. Kate reflected that, on her way to Bethany's, she would have dreaded meeting this neighbor or any neighbor, but now she felt warm toward her as she drove on home. Suddenly she thought about seeing Gyorgy at Bethany's and was startled to realize she had not given him another thought until this very minute. She was chagrined that this was so, but glad that it was so.

VI

The day after her visit with Bethany, Kate watched Henry puttering around the house yard in the evening, picking up sticks and pulling weeds that had grown too big. From the kitchen window he looked older, his shoulders a bit hunched and he seemed to favor his left knee as he bent down. He was a good man and didn't deserve having to deal with this difficult situation. She reminded herself that, after all, he hadn't been anxious to take a child from the Orphan Train in the first place. He had thought Will would be child enough for them, but it hadn't turned out that way.

Kate had just finished cleaning up the kitchen when the back door opened and in walked Henry. 'Will and Hjelmer went over to Dorseys to see the new horse Bill Dorsey bought up in Norfolk,' he said.

'Oh? Well, since Margaret's in town tonight, I guess we have the place to ourselves,' Kate began, trying to choose her words carefully. 'Tell you what, I've been needing to talk to you, so why don't we sit down for awhile.'

'Well, let me wash up first,' said Henry as he winked at Kate and smiled broadly. Kate ignored his gesture. She knew telling Henry about Margaret's dilemma would be one of the most difficult things she'd ever done in her life. It was almost as if she herself were the one who was experiencing an untimely pregnancy. She was glad for this chance to talk in a quiet, calm, collected manner.

Henry washed his hands in the basin under the hand pump by the kitchen sink and wiped his hands as Kate hung up her apron, the pink one Margaret made for her in domestic science class from a flour sack. Henry teasingly put his hand on Kate's shoulder as they walked into the living room. Kate paid no attention and sat herself down in her grandmother's rocker, picking up her knitting needles from the basket beside the chair.

Henry leaned back in his rocker and folded his hands across his belly. He cocked his head and looked at her expectantly. 'Well?' he asked with a twinkle in his eye.

Frowning, Kate concentrated on the stitch she'd just dropped. Finally she caught the stitch and put the knitting down. She looked up at Henry, but then quickly looked at her hands in her lap. 'Henry . . .' she said, her hands twitching restlessly. 'Henry, you know Margaret is becoming a woman. I mean, she's only 15, but, well, she's . . .' She glanced up at him and down again. 'Well, she's . . . she's . . .' It was hard for her to say the words. Henry waited as she nervously interlaced her fingers and looked down at them. 'This is not easy to say, Henry, but . . . well . . . well, Margaret's . . .' Her voice dropped to a whisper, 'Margaret's expecting a baby.'

'What!' Henry exploded as he rocked his chair forward with a start. 'What did you just say? Did you say what I think you said?' he demanded, his face an angry red.

Kate thought he might be apoplectic. 'Oh, Henry, are you all right?' she gasped and went over to him.

He pushed her away. His face was grim. 'Did you say what I think you said?' he demanded again.

Kate edged her way back to her rocker. She whispered, 'Yes, Henry.' He turned away from her.

'How can that be? Is that what it means to send her to school in town! I thought we could trust her! She was supposed to have work to do.'

'Now, wait, Henry. Calm down. She does have work to do. We can trust her. Margaret didn't ask for this to happen. Somebody took advantage of her. She won't tell me who did it or where it happened or even when—except it's been three months now.'

Henry leaned toward her. 'Now wait a minute, Kate. This isn't something to joke about. Tell me the truth, Kate!'

'I did, Henry.'

'If what you say is true, whoever did this to our girl is going to pay for it!' he jabbed his right fist into his left palm and leapt to his feet, his face contorted. He grabbed Kate by the shoulders. 'Kate, you've got to make her tell us who it was, so I can take care of him.'

Kate grabbed his hands. Her heart pounded but her voice was calm and commanding. 'No, Henry. Margaret was afraid you would do something to him so she said she'd never tell. She said it would be her shame alone.'

Henry withdrew his hands and dropped back into his chair. He pulled his kerchief from his pocket and wiped his face. 'I'm sorry, Henry, for her and for us. We've got some mighty serious thinking to do. That's why I went to talk to Bethany Trueblood.'

'Bethany Trueblood! Why did you bring her into this? Now people in Tingle Creek will know.'

'No, Henry, she's a very wise and kind person. She would never tell anyone. I asked her what we could do to protect Margaret from local talk and what to do about the baby. She suggested sending Margaret to her friend Hattie Pennington who lives near Colony. She said Mrs. Pennington had a large family and did a lot of nursing in her younger years and she will understand. Hopefully, Margaret can stay with her until the baby is born. In fact, Margaret can work for them on the farm while she's waiting.'

'And then what?' Henry demanded, and then repeated it more vehemently, 'And then what?'

'We don't know yet. Bethany is writing to Mrs. Pennington. She's asking her to write directly to us. If that doesn't work out, I'm sure Bethany will help us find a good solution. Of course, Margaret could go to a lying-in hospital, but then everybody would know. And Margaret had enough of orphanages that she doesn't want her baby to go to one of those.' Kate's words rushed out and she wished she could assure Henry more, but at this point, she could not.

When Will and Hjelmer came in, Kate and Henry were quietly sitting and rocking. The boys said, 'G'night,' as they tromped up the stairs. Kate whispered, 'G'night.'

That night in bed, Kate worried out loud to Henry. 'Maybe you're right that we need to find the man who did this, but only if Margaret will agree to marry him. Otherwise, our searching would only call attention to Margaret's condition.'

Henry lay in bed staring at the ceiling. He sighed 'I guess you're right.'

'And what if we found who was at fault and Margaret refused to marry him? And what if he claimed he didn't do it and would refuse to marry her? Right now Margaret says she'll never marry him,' Kate added and went on.

'I wouldn't want to, either. Still it seems like, no matter what, Margaret will have to give up the baby. We can only hope that Mrs. Buchanan will let her stay there when she comes back to school. We don't have to tell

Mrs. Buchanan why Margaret is going. We'll just tell Mrs. Buchanan that Mrs. Pennington needed some help for awhile and asked if Margaret could come. She doesn't need to know just why.' Kate continued, 'Oh, my. I never dreamed when we took an older child that this would be the result. It's embarrassing and scary. Like we haven't done right by her.' She paused, then slowly added, 'And maybe we haven't.'

'Now, Kate, you know that isn't true. We've done all we could in the time we've had with her. After all, we don't know what her parents taught her, if anything. You'd better get some sleep. We'll think better in daylight,' Henry said and patted her arm. 'We'll talk about it tomorrow.' Kate turned her head away from him, but she knew she would not go to sleep, at least not for awhile.

* * *

Life resumed its normal pace after the initial shock of Margaret's confiding her predicament. Hjelmer and Will didn't indicate they detected anything amiss. Still, the uncertainty of it all never left Kate's consciousness.

She watched Margaret very closely as they worked side by side in the kitchen boning chickens and peeling potatoes. Once in awhile Kate broke into their chitchat about making doughnuts or the possibility of rain to ask Margaret about her life before she came to Tingle Creek. 'Did your mother teach you how to dress chickens?' she asked.

Margaret nibbled on a piece of raw potato and said she hadn't, probably because she was too young to handle sharp knives. 'Once in awhile I would have to pluck a chicken, but mostly we couldn't afford them.' What was unsaid in the conversation, Kate could only guess at.

'I'm going to miss you, Margaret, when you go to Mrs. Pennington's,' Kate remarked one day. 'You're such a big help to me. But the time will go fast, I expect.' Margaret gave a muffled reply.

Kate assumed she would be leaving soon even though she hadn't heard from Hattie Pennington yet. She still had questions that only Margaret could answer. She wished she could find a way to ask Margaret about Henry's growing suspicions that Hjelmer was the father of Margaret's baby, but she couldn't bring herself to ask because she didn't want to believe that either of their boys—well, young men—would have done such a thing.

One night while they were doing dishes, Kate ventured a hesitant question, 'Margaret, do you want lots of children?'

'Oh, my, no!' Margaret answered, shaking her head. 'Not like my parents had. Never!'

'Would you like to keep this baby?' Kate asked with especial gentleness, being careful not to look directly at the girl. Margaret stood, a dripping plate in one hand, the dishrag in the other, staring out the window above the sink. A tear started an uncertain course down her cheek, and she attacked the plate vigorously, turning it round and round, but she did not answer.

Kate could understand why Margaret would be reluctant to give up this baby or any baby. Kate winced at the thought and her face clouded. She whispered, 'I wish my baby hadn't died.'

Margaret looked stricken. 'I'm sorry, Margaret, I didn't mean to . . .'

'I never knew you had a baby,' Margaret cried. 'When was that?' Seeing Kate's tightly drawn lips, she patted Kate's shoulder and said ever so softly, 'I'm sorry. I'm so sorry. I didn't know.'

'It's all right, Margaret. The baby was born dead, and I couldn't have another.' Kate left the kitchen abruptly, leaving Margaret to finish the dishes alone. Kate chided herself for bringing up the subject of her lost baby. Her situation and Margaret's were so different. But were they? No mother wants to give up her baby whether to adoption or premature death. She sat in her rocker trying to think through the implications of both outcomes. She shook her head, knowing neither was acceptable. She wondered how Margaret would choose.

She shook herself and got up. Going back to the kitchen, she said calmly, 'Let me finish, Margaret. You go on upstairs and get your homework done.' Margaret wiped her hands, gave Kate a quick hug and a gentle smile, and said, 'It will be a good tomorrow,' as she left the kitchen.

* * *

Every day Kate watched for the mail carrier to come by in his wagon, and she often met him at the mailbox. 'Good morning, Joe!' she called as gaily as she had before she was expecting an important letter.

'Why, good morning, Miss Katie!' Joe called out. 'Mighty fine weather we're having, don't you think?'

'Yes, it is, Joe. Yes, it is.'

'Are you looking for something special? I expect you're looking for letters from Will now that he's off working at the college farm this summer. You've been out to meet me most every day lately. You know how young people are once they get away from home—'specially boys, don't you think?'

'Well, yes, I do, and I hope we get a letter from him soon, but I expect he's doing just fine. I'm always wishing for a letter from my sister Lina down in Kansas, too. And I'd hoped the Sears Roebuck catalog would be here by now, but I guess I'll have to wait awhile longer. I'm needing to order some things.'

'Nope, no catalogs. Mail gets awful heavy when they come out. Well, let's see here. There's a couple of letters for you. Can't complain about that now, can you?'

'Not at all, Joe. Thanks.' Kate tried to stay calm until Joe was out of sight, but then she anxiously leafed through the mail as she walked back to the house. Each day she had hoped for a letter from Hattie Pennington. At last it was there! She stopped. There it was with a return address of: Pennington, RFD, Colony, Nebraska.' Her smile changed to a frown. She wanted to open it, but she didn't want to. She knew that this letter might change everything for Margaret—or nothing.

Coming in the kitchen door, she bypassed the dough rising in the bread pans, waiting for its final proofing, and went directly to her rocker. She inserted her index finger under the flap of the envelope and tore it open, leaving a ragged edge, a detail she would never have allowed under normal cirumstances. She carefully unfolded the sheets of writing paper. Mrs. Pennington's hand was plain, but readable.

Dear Mrs. Fergus,

>*I have had a letter from my dear friend, Bethany Trueblood. She spoke of your girl's unfortunate circumstance and asked if we might be able to help her out. From her description of the child, I believe she must be very pleasant and responsible. How sad that this has happened to her. Mr. Pennington and I would be very glad to have her come to us to stay for whatever time is needed. I could certainly use her help and I believe she will take the situation seriously. Please let me know how soon she will arrive. We can meet her at the station in Belleville. Just let us know her arrival time.*

Red Geraniums

Now, my dear Mrs. Fergus, I know you must be very upset. Please be assured we will do all we can to help Margaret through this situation and, with the help of the Lord, we can decide later what would be the best outcome for all involved.

With kind regards,
Hattie Pennington

Kate reread the letter several times and then got up to stash it in the secretary. She hurried to the kitchen to catch the bread almost oozing over the edge of the pans. She dumped each loaf onto the floured bread board and kneaded it well. She sighed, knowing today's bread would not be her usual fine product but with Hattie Pennington's letter now in hand life felt good again. Even so, an uncertainty still lingered in the pit of her stomach. She lay a clean dish towel over the loaves and dusted her hands together, as if ridding herself of her previous uncertainties.

* * *

By now, the mail carrier could trace a series of letters from the farm to Colony and back, though he never commented on their existence. Each one was necessary to clarify what Margaret needed to bring, which day the Penningtons could best meet her, which train she would take, how payment would be made for Margaret's care, and so on.

One evening, thinking of how Margaret would travel, Kate said to Henry, 'Would it be all right if Margaret took your leather valise?'

'Oh, my goodness, I don't know why not—it's not going to get any younger by sitting in the attic,' said Henry.

'I'll just go get it,' said Kate and headed up the stairs. She carried a lantern up with her but it was still very dim light. It seemed a bit spooky. Looking around, she found the little wicker suitcase that had come with Margaret on the Orphan Train. It was shabby and very small, but it had sentimental value for Kate, marking the day Kate chose Margaret from the little group of forlorn-looking children at the Methodist Episcopal Church.

Kate carried it and Henry's valise to Margaret's room. She wanted to see the contents of Margaret's wicker case once more, to be reminded of the waif she was so taken with. Margaret's simple cotton dress and mended underwear and coat were still there, but there was no ikon of Saint Mary. She rummaged among the contents again but it simply wasn't there. The ikon had been a curiosity to Kate. She had wondered if maybe the ikon had been a special blessing that someone had given her on leaving New York.

She remembered it being no more than 6" tall, carved out of a reddish-colored wood and painted in somber browns and reds and greens with a gilt halo that had tarnished and faded. But it wasn't there! She hadn't seen it anywhere in Margaret's room. Curious as she was, Kate knew she could not ask her about its disappearance, though it was tempting. What had Margaret done with it? Surely she had not thrown it away. There was nothing to do but close the suitcase and return it to the attic. Kate decided to let it be for now. After the baby was born and Margaret was back home, she'd ask her about it. The ikon was just one more piece of the puzzle she didn't have an answer for.

She put the wicker suitcase back in the attic and brought Henry's into their bedroom where she closed the door, and fell in a heap on the bed. She realized the strain of the last months had taken their toll. Sometimes it was all too much. She had been unable to talk about how bereft she felt when she lost her baby even with Henry. She had wanted him to take her in his arms and comfort her, and he had not done so. She must make sure that she would be available for Margaret to talk to whenever she was ready. She gathered herself together and headed downstairs.

The next few days Kate puttered around trying to think of everything that must be done in preparation for Margaret's leaving. She felt there were important things to say to her before she gave birth. She could easily tell this girl-woman how important it was that she eat properly and rest often, but talking to her about the actual birth and its aftermath was much harder. Kate felt frustrated because Margaret was at school in Appleton that last week before she was to leave so she wasn't around when Kate thought of things to say and do. She hoped she wouldn't forget them.

It was reassuring that Margaret and the baby would be well cared for because the baby would be born in the Pennington home. Nevertheless, Kate worried because sometimes mothers—and babies—die unexpectedly—during the birthing process. She knew she would not rest well until she'd received confirmation from Hattie that all had gone well. But then . . . Oh, my, what will become of the baby? She simply had to put the possible outcomes aside and trust the good Lord would take care of the child—though she wasn't quite sure that she could leave it to Him.

* * *

One night as they sat rocking after the chores were done, Kate interrupted Henry's newspaper reading. 'Do you think Margaret'll be all right? I mean, she's so young to have a baby.'

'Why, Kate, you know very well that girls younger than she is have babies all the time and everything is fine.'

Kate frowned. 'I know, but I still worry about her and the baby. And you know what gets me, Henry? How Margaret could allow herself to be deceived by whoever did this?'

Henry put down his newspaper and sat thoughtfully for a minute before answering. 'Well, Kate, I don't know how to say this but I've been thinking.' His rocker slowed and then stopped. 'How we can be sure it was just the boy that was at fault?'

'What!' Kate was flabbergasted. 'How dare you say that, Henry Fergus! No nice girl *ever* asks for it. No no no. Margaret would never have encouraged this.'

'Now—now, wait a minute, Kate. We're talking about a very pretty, very charming young woman . . .' Henry raised his hands as if to fend off her expected protest. 'We have to admit that, yes, she is a woman and yes, she's got feelings of her own.'

'Are you saying you don't believe her?' Kate's voice dropped to a hoarse whisper. 'I asked her if she loves him, and she said she never did and never will. I believe her. Margaret is too shy to carry on like some of those girls do. I don't know how you can even suggest such a thing.'

'Well now, Kate, weren't you ever tempted when you were that age? Didn't you ever think what it would be like to be really close—I mean really close—to a boyfriend when you thought you were in love?'

Kate started to say something, but then thought better of it. She remembered that sometimes when Benny Barlowe put his arms around her and kissed her goodnight, she had felt really loved and wanted more of it, but she knew she would never take a chance on getting pregnant. She grimaced, thinking about the night when Benny's hand wandered to the buttons of her shirtwaist. She pulled away quickly and ran in the house. She flushed now to think of it, but she could never tell Henry about this.

'Maybe I was,' Kate admitted finally, 'but nevertheless, Henry, I wouldn't and didn't. Besides when I was boarding in town, Mrs. Greene wouldn't let any of her girls stay out past 9 o'clock. I know there's lots more temptations now than when I was growing up. Anyway, Margaret's like me—too timid to be daring.' Kate paused.

'Poor Margaret. First her parents rejected her—and she couldn't have gotten much love in the orphanage—and she only had us for such a short time before she went to school in town. I feel like I could have—should have done so much more for her.' Kate sighed.

'Kate, you've been a good mother to her. Nobody's perfect, you know.'

Kate smiled faintly at the compliment and lapsed into thought. Henry picked up the newspaper. Finally she said, 'Come on. Let's go to bed.' She finished winding up her knitting yarn and put out her hand for him to pull her up out of the rocking chair. He put his arms around her and kissed her. 'I only hope,' she whispered, 'that Margaret can find a nice man to marry—like you.'

When the day for departure came, Will was nowhere to be seen. Henry tucked his valise and Kate's hat box and a lunch basket into the car beside Margaret in the back seat. Hjelmer was clearly tongue-tied trying to say good-bye. Seeing his discomfiture, Kate explained, 'Margaret is going to Colony to help the Pennington family. She'll be back in a few months.' Hjelmer gave Margaret a shy smile, but asked no questions. Margaret waved to him as they drove away.

Approaching the train station in Tingle Creek, Kate wondered if Margaret was thinking about the last time she rode on a train, the Orphan Train. She turned around and patted Margaret's hand. 'The train'll be coming most any time,' she said. 'Oh, I hear it now! Hurry, Henry, we mustn't be late.'

'Now, now, Kate, we're just fine,' said Henry as he bumped across the tracks to the C&NW station. 'I think the town fathers ought to fix these tracks!' he declared, just as he did every time they crossed the tracks. 'Well, here we are.'

'Oh, Auntie Kate, I don't want to go! I don't want to leave home! I don't want to have a baby!' Margaret's words tumbled out with her tears as she hung back in the car. Henry opened the door for her and put his hand out to help her down. He put his arm around her shoulders and gave her a squeeze.

'Never you mind, Margaret. You're going to be all right—and everything's going to be all right,' he said and patted her cheek. 'Now, then, I'll help you find the train car you're to ride in.' The two of them strode along the platform together with Kate trailing behind. She was glad to see Henry and Margaret solving a problem together, but the butterflies in her stomach told her there was much to be sorted out yet.

In bed that night she couldn't sleep thinking about Margaret. Before they left for the station, Margaret had hugged Kate's bulk and sobbed into her shoulder, the tall girl and the small woman. 'Oh, Auntie Kate, I feel so ashamed. I've disgraced you and Uncle Henry. I can't ever go to school again and—and what will I do with my life?'

'Of course you can go back to school,' Kate had assured her. 'Just like I told you—while you're at the Penningtons, you'll have to study on your own, but I know you can keep up. You're a smart girl. Now Margaret, I have to ask one thing before you go. You've never told us who did it and we haven't insisted that you tell, but whoever it was, would you consider marrying him? If you did, you know, then you could keep the child.'

Margaret pulled away from Kate, her face dark with anger. 'Never!' she said in a low agonized voice. 'Never.'

Kate, stared at her, startled by her vehemence. That Margaret could be so strong and forceful and sure of herself left Kate wide-eyed in surprise. 'Then, of course,' she said, 'we would never think of asking you to do so.'

Kate and Henry stood on the platform and waved until they could no longer see her at the train window. Kate was quiet on the drive back to the farm. Margaret was gone now, but still the question nagged. Who did it? Perhaps in time the truth would come out. But did she really want to know? Whoever it was, if Kate did learn the truth about him, she knew she would lose every shred of respect she might have for him, and that might make a further problem if Margaret should decide to marry him.

*   *   *

Sometime later as Kate was walking back to the house from the mailbox, she leafed through the letters as she went. Along with a postcard from Lynus' new wife, Anne, a check from the creamery, and the county paper, she found the postmark she'd been hoping for: Colony, Nebraska. Margaret's large rounding letters addressed the letter to 'Mr. and Mrs. Henry Fergus'. Somehow that seemed to emphasize the distance between them even though she knew it would not have been appropriate for her to address it to 'Auntie Kate and Uncle Henry'.

'Let's see,' Kate said to herself as she walked, 'Margaret left on ... That makes it about two months since she took the train from Tingle Creek.' Except for a letter from Hattie Pennington at the end of the first week, they had heard nothing from or about Margaret even though Kate wrote faithfully twice a week.

Sometimes she sat at the secretary to write her a letter wondering what to say. She couldn't think of much to tell Margaret, so she might prattle on about the bantam hen that she'd discovered setting on eggs behind the old plow in the implement shed and reported on Will's liking his work and the Ladies' Aid inviting her to talk to their group about taking photographs. She always added that Henry and Hjelmer and Will were just fine.

Once Kate decided to tell Margaret about the secretary itself. Even though it had belonged to Kate's mother, her mother had never used it for letter-writing. She had bought it for its glassed-in book shelves above, its pigeonholed storage space, and the wide drawers below. After her death, nobody wanted the secretary, everyone deeming it too ugly to put anywhere in their houses. 'Now I'm glad to have it,' she said. She ended her letter saying that maybe the secretary would go to Margaret when she was older and settled down.

Fondness for Margaret welled up in Kate from time to time, along with a certain anxiety that Margaret might already have found the Penningtons more likeable as parents. Why else wouldn't she have written earlier? Henry told her she was silly for worrying. She tried to stop, but it was hard. Now at last there was a letter, but her anxiety mounted as she waited for Henry to come in from the field so he could read the letter first and soften the pain if necessary. She didn't understand why she was so fearful that Margaret's closeness to her—which had intensified with the revelation of her pregnancy—might have diminished. It wasn't logical, but then emotions seldom were.

She had been thankful that the plan to go to the Pennington's had met with Margaret's approval though she supposed Margaret had little idea of just what lay ahead of her. She had been thankful, too, that while Henry was upset that someone had compromised Margaret in this way, he did not demand that she reveal the perpetrator.

At night as they lay in bed, they sometimes speculated about the boys who could have done it. Kate said, 'Hjelmer is just too shy to do something like this.' She could easily dismiss him as a possibility.

'Jed Weatherwill's the type,' Henry said, cataloging the boys in the neighborhood, 'but Margaret's hardly had contact with him. I know you say Hjelmer couldn't have done it, but I think he could have, so I give up. I just don't know who it could have been,' he concluded.

Kate had no greater wisdom, except for the one boy neither of them ever mentioned. She held her peace until she thought she would burst from withholding consideration of him as the culprit. This possibility gnawed at her until one evening as she and Henry sat rocking after a hard day's work, she quietly whispered, 'You haven't mentioned Will as a possibility.'

The suggestion hung in the air for a second, and then Henry exploded, 'How dare you suggest such a thing! How dare you!' Henry was out of his chair in a bound and lifted her out of her chair. Grabbing her shoulders, he shook her until she cowered from him. Ducking her head, she expected him to strike her at any moment.

'Will would never even think of doing such a thing to Margaret—let alone actually doing it! Never! I demand that you never think such a thing again.' He shoved Kate back into her chair. Kate hugged her arms across her chest and stared at the carpet. Tears rolled slowly down her reddened cheeks, but she made no attempt to wipe them away. Her world had suddenly crumbled, and she didn't know how she could or would find her balance again. She was clearly frightened. Only when Henry confronted Will about the broken cup had she ever had reason to question his generally mild-mannered behavior.

Now Henry stomped out of the house into the dark of the summer night. Kate felt she dared not move. What had happened to her Henry? She could understand his being protective of his boy, but the fact was that Will very well could have been the doer of what she perceived to be an evil deed. Didn't the facts demand that they consider all possible suspects? Had Henry no feelings for Margaret? Was she wrong to have brought up the possibility? Kate rubbed her bruised arms and finally wiped her tears, afraid that something drastic in their relationship had changed forever. Slowly she padded upstairs to bed.

The next day after Henry's outburst, they went about their chores without their usual banter. Hjelmer looked from one to the other at the table, but said nothing. The hurt that Kate felt from Henry's outburst still smarted and her shoulders were sore where he had grabbed her. She rubbed them from time to time, remembering. She grudgingly accepted his apology for shoving her, but she couldn't forget. Over the next few weeks they had gradually recovered at least an outward appearance of a normal routine.

Kate now deposited the letter from Margaret on the counter unopened afraid to learn its contents. Braising the roast and new potatoes and onions and parsnips from the root cellar in the cast iron dutch oven, she stopped briefly to eye the letter as if she might divine its contents by some special power such as she'd read Gypsy fortune-tellers have.

While the stew simmered, she mixed a large bowl of biscuit dough and kneaded it gently before rolling it out on the floured cutting board. She cut two-inch rounds with her mother's biscuit cutter, one of the treasured items she'd inherited. She preferred large biscuits for eating out of hand with butter and honey from the neighbors' hives, but the smaller ones fit the stewpot better. Exactly eight biscuits rimmed the dutch oven. She rolled the remaining dough into two rounds, each a half-inch thick, and placed each of them in the bottom of a pie tin to make peach shortcake—a favorite of Henry's. Some people preferred their shortcake biscuits with sugar in them, but not Kate. It would have been nicer to have fresh peaches, but these canned ones were a good substitute.

'Is dinner ready?' Henry's voice startled her, so deep in thought was she.

She flinched. 'Oh! You frightened me!' She watched him take off his outside boots.

'I didn't mean to,' Henry apologized and slipped up behind her, putting his arms around her waist and blowing on the tight curls about her neck escaping from the graying bun at the back of her head, as he always delighted in doing.

Kate did not smile and there was an edge in her voice. 'Now, Henry—' she remonstrated, 'we're not young anymore.' There was no doubt that their life together had been more pleasant and their love-making more playful after Will had left for college and Margaret had gone to the Penningtons, but these days it was non-existent after the confrontation with Henry about Will. She wanted to believe that 'the problem'—as she had come to call it—had disappeared, but she knew it hadn't. It hung like a filmy, grey veil over their relationship.

Her eye spotted the letter. 'Henry, there's a letter from Margaret. There—by the bread box.' She wriggled out of his bear hug to reach the long cream-colored envelope she'd given Margaret to use. 'Would you open it and read it and tell me everything's all right?'

Henry laughed. 'What're you afraid of, Kate—that the baby's already born and nobody told you about it? Everything's all right and you know it.' He stuck his stubby forefinger under the edge of the flap.

'Henry, wait!' Kate stayed his hand. 'Here comes Hjelmer. We'll have to wait until after dinner.'

Kate watched Henry's eyes narrow as a frown spread across his wrinkled forehead. 'You're right, Kate. Hjelmer doesn't need to know.' He put the letter in the pocket of his overalls to read later.

* * *

After dinner Kate cleared up the dishes while Henry went to lie on the couch and Hjelmer went back to the barn. 'I must be getting old, Kate,' Henry called out to her in the kitchen. 'I used to be able to work from dawn until dark without hardly stopping to eat, but I can't take it any more. Well, my own father was dead by the time he was my age so I guess I shouldn't be too surprised. Sure do appreciate my nap.'

Through the doorway, Kate saw him ease himself onto the couch and pull a knitted coverlet over himself. She knew that he was slowing down, but it was hard to think of him being that old. After all, he was still doing heavy farm work. She remembered her own father at 49 had seemed very old.

'Well, open Margaret's letter and read it before you go to sleep. You can tell me what it says after your nap,' Kate called from the kitchen.

A bit later, Henry called from his rocker, 'Kate! Come sit down and listen.' Kate couldn't tell from his voice whether the news was good or bad. She just knew she would have to hear what Margaret had to say, no matter how good or bad it was. She wiped her hands on the towel by the kitchen pump and unrolled her sleeves as she walked over to her rocking chair. She put her head back, scrunched her shoulders and took a deep breath. Then she looked at her shoes and thought briefly that she should polish them sometime. There never seemed to be enough energy for such trivial things.

She wished she didn't dread bad news so much. Henry seemed to take good or bad news with great equanimity. Surely he knew that children sometimes turned away from their parents, but if he did, the possibility of it apparently hadn't occurred to him, or if it had, it didn't frighten him, as it did her. Wouldn't he be as hurt as she if Margaret rejected them? If she were to choose not to return to them? Kate could think of no other reason why she hadn't written.

Maybe it was because Henry had a son of his own that Margaret's problem didn't seem to worry him, but Margaret was the only child Kate had, really. For a fleeting second, she wondered what might have happened if she'd been able to adopt the little foundling boy as she so foolishly wanted to do. She sighed at the thought. She was glad he'd been adopted by a nice family, but that seemed like a long time ago. Now it was all so overwhelming, Margaret's being pregnant and their not knowing the father of her baby, and all. Finally, she said, 'Go ahead, Henry. What does she say?'

Margaret's letter rested lightly in his rough hands. Kate felt his eyes scrutinizing her as she rocked. Rocking and reading a book or the county paper had become a comfortable way to pass the evenings, but rocking midday seemed downright sinful. Nevertheless, today it seemed the right thing to do before she began her afternoon chores. 'Well, Kate, I don't understand what you are so worried about. Anyway, here's what Margaret says.' Henry held the paper at arms' length and then pulled his magnifying glasses out of his overalls pocket.

Dear Auntie Kate and Uncle Henry,

How are you both? Thank you for your letters. I've been meaning to write, but I've been afraid that you're glad I'm gone. I couldn't bear it if you were. Being here has made me glad I live with you.

Kate's frown turned to a smile. 'Go on. Go on.'

The Penningtons are very nice and helpful, too, but they're very strict and it's hard to please them.

'Oh, I hope she doesn't disappoint them.'
'Now, Kate, just be quiet and listen.'

They don't make me work too hard now that I'm getting closer to my time, but there's always something to be done. Except for going to Quaker Meeting with them (they don't even have a preacher!) I don't see many people or go anywhere. Nobody much comes here except family and they're all right.

Mrs. Pennington is teaching me to tat. Leastways I'm trying, but I don't think I'll ever make lace fit to look at. I love the pretty lace you made for my pillow case at home and wish I could do as well. At night I study my school books like you told me to.

'Thank goodness for that.'
'Stop interrupting, Kate. Let's read it all the way through.'

Mr. Pennington helps some but he doesn't know algebra and Latin. Mrs. P. says she didn't go beyond third grade.

The baby kicks and moves around a lot. I talk to him when I'm alone. I think the baby must be a boy. I don't know why. I wonder what color his hair will be and who he'll take after. What if he has a sharp nose like my mother's? I wouldn't like that. I wonder who will take him. Do you think it will be somebody kind and good? I wouldn't want him to go to somebody who would be mean to him.

Sometimes I think I'd like to keep him. I know that would be hard, but when I feel his heart beat, he seems so much a part of me. Do I have to give him up? Mrs. P. says I must, but maybe I could get a job sewing for people in Lincoln and I could take care of him while I sew. I'm good at sewing, don't you think? I could learn more if I lived close to you, but I know it would be too hard for you to bear my shame. No. I won't keep him (but I want to).

This much I can promise you. I will never, never let this happen again. I will kill myself first. I wish I were home. Sometimes I wonder whether my real mother would have cared as much as you do. I like getting your letters telling about the farm. Please write soon. Give my greetings to the boys.

Love, from your Margaret

Kate smiled. 'See, Henry, she does love us after all.'

* * *

Two days after Margaret's letter arrived, as Kate sat down to write to her, she studied the crackled varnish of the writing desk and traced its gouges with her fingers. As her hands moved about restlessly, she tried to think of cheery news to write to her child. Immediately she reminded herself that the term 'child' no longer applied. She would have to get used to the fact that Margaret's pregnancy and the rite of childbirth about to take place fully qualified her to be called a woman. Oh! But for all intents and purposes she would fall back into the role of a school girl when she returned. Only she and Henry and Margaret would know that she had matured in a way that left her in the limbo between childhood and womanhood.

Kate picked up the pen and twirled it in her fingers. She'd already written to Margaret about the calf born too late in the season to survive, despite Henry's and Hjelmer's best efforts. The thought of Hjelmer brought a frown to her face. For some years now, Hjelmer had been a part of Henry's family, joining in family conversations in his quiet way and often going to family reunions and picnics with them. He shared in the planning for planting and harvesting, for breeding and birthing, and all manner of farm chores. He seemed to respect Henry as a father-substitute for his own father. It was a mostly congenial—even a fond—relationship between the old farmer and his farmhand, so a recent incident at the table had truly surprised Kate.

Henry had no more than sat down in his usual place at the head of the table than he began criticizing Hjelmer. Kate could hardly remember what started it. She just remembered Henry saying, 'Hjelmer, for goodness sakes, didn't you wash your hands? I've told you and Mrs. Fergus has told you over and over that you can't come to the table until your hands are clean—and that means under your fingernails, too!'

Hjelmer ducked his head to the side and scowled, slowly hauling himself off the chair. In passing, he excused himself to Kate and went to the sink. Kate could hear him pumping water into the basin and then the soft swish swish of the small scrub brush they kept there for the purpose. Neither she nor Henry said anything while he was gone. When Hjelmer returned he thrust his solid Norwegian hands in front of Henry's nose. His tone was sarcastic. 'There! Is that good enough?'

Henry reddened and shoved Hjelmer's hands away and shouted. 'Don't put your hands over my food. Sit down and eat.'

Hjelmer did not return to his place at the table. His liquid blue eyes all but disappeared into narrow slits and his lower jaw jutted out pulling his thin lips even thinner. His chest heaved and Kate could see he was breathing heavily. Without a word, he turned and walked out the back door, slamming it as he went.

'Hjelmer—!' Kate half rose from her chair, but a sideways glance at Henry caused her to sit down again. 'Henry, what's—?'

'It's none of your concern, Kate. Let him go!'

Kate blinked. She sensed there was more going on here than simple hand-washing. 'But, Henry, wha—?'

'That's enough, Kate.' They fell silent for the rest of the meal. Kate hardly raised her eyes from her plate. By suppertime that day, an uneasy, but civil, atmosphere had been restored.

That evening as she and Henry rocked and watched the sun set over the fields across the road, Kate began, 'Now, Henry . . .' but Henry refused to talk about it. She tried again, 'Look here, Henry, we've . . .'

'I said that's enough, Kate. Don't ever speak to me about this again.' Kate wondered whether Henry was going to send Hjelmer away, or whether he was ashamed of his treatment of Hjelmer. She hoped it was the latter.

Since that day, Hjelmer had not seemed comfortable in their presence and talked even less than before. In fact, now that she thought about it, when Hjelmer did speak, he spoke only to her at the table, not Henry. For some time even before the incident, Hjelmer had excused himself from joining them for church on the few Sundays they went, and Henry had not insisted. In spite of this, he still did whatever they asked of him, but took no interest in the farm plans as he had before. He became rather more dour than pleasant and almost lethargic.

Thinking about it now as she tried to write to Margaret, her letter paper lay as blank as her understanding of Henry and Hjelmer's differences. There was no escaping that something was wrong. Kate tried to clear away the veil that hid the truth, but she could not. She felt sure that if it had something to do with the farm operation Henry would have shared it with her. She was afraid that Henry still thought Hjelmer was responsible for Margaret's predicament. In any case, it was not something she wanted to write to Margaret about.

The thought of dissension in the family troubled her. It occurred to her that her life as a single woman photographer had been relatively free of such worries except for the occasional differences with Angus and Lizzie and, earlier, her mother, but these had consumed very little of her time and thought.

While she had been lonely much of the time in town, she'd had constant contact with a variety of people through her business, and she had rarely been concerned about other people's problems. Now, as she sat mulling over the last few months, she wondered if she might have been better off to have declined Henry's offer of marriage in the first place.

Still, marriage afforded her many advantages. She enjoyed the family outings and the company of Henry on quiet evenings after a hard day's work. They had talked at length about the family and the community and news in the county paper or just sat rocking waiting for a summer breeze to come through the open windows. True, these pleasant evenings had taken on an edge in the last few months, but she was confident they would return.

It occurred to her that one of the biggest advantages to her present situation was the availability of money. She'd never had much money to work with in earlier years. Her teaching job paid very little and would not have been enough to buy the photography studio if she hadn't saved money by living at home. She was proud that her photography business had been successful. It grew every year as her work became known and allowed a small savings account for the day when she could no longer work—a savings account to keep her out of the poor house, she used to say to Jean Burchett.

Her marriage to Henry, whose farm was one of the largest and best in the township, had given her a kind of freedom that she had not experienced before. She really didn't know how much money Henry had. He never talked about it, but whenever she asked for money for the house or a new dress for Margaret, he paused only slightly before giving her whatever she wanted. Still, the thought of having to ask for money for any reason was not easy to adjust to.

When they were planning their marriage, Henry had said very firmly that she would never have to work again. Even with this assurance, she knew that with her camera set up in the attic, if the necessity ever arose, she could pick up her business again—and she might have been tempted to do so simply because she loved the work. Once, at the dinner table she'd said, 'Henry, if I started up my photography business again, we'd have enough money to put a flush toilet in the house.'

'Why, Kate,' he said obviously surprised, 'if you want a flush toilet, then you shall have it. You don't have to work for that. You go talk to Judd Rexroth the next time you're in town and decide what you want and we'll put one in the bathing room.'

Kate had smiled and thanked Henry, but she was chagrined. She knew that he would never understand her need to have money of her own, money under her command, so to speak, money to spend any way she wanted to. But it was more than the money of her own that she missed; it was also the contacts with the people she photographed and the business people she dealt with. She wondered if Henry or any farmer could understand the loneliness that farm life breeds for a farm wife. That was one reason she so desperately wanted to take a child from the Orphan Train. And now this.

Kate had not written a word yet when the teakettle whistled, and at the same moment, the telephone rang. She scurried to the kitchen to set the teakettle to the back of the range as the phone rang twice more. She raised the receiver and shouted toward the mouthpiece above her head on the wall. 'Hello!'

'Missus Fergus? This is Owen Bauer at the Western Union office. Do you remember me? I was in the Lotts Creek School for 3rd and 4th grade when you taught there.'

'Yes, I remember you. You were a very active little boy.' Actually, she wanted to call him a 'scamp' or 'rascal' which would have been truer, but she thought that he must have outgrown it to have such a responsible position now.

Owen Bauer laughed. 'That's a nice way of putting it! Well, anyway, I have a wire here for you. Shall I read it over the phone, or do you want to come for it?' Kate hesitated. She knew that reading it over the party line was a risk since she wasn't sure who sent it and what it might say. Still, a telegram must be an important message, and she had no plans to go to Tingle Creek in the near future.

'Yes, Owen, please read it.'

'Here it is, Ma'am. "All work finished. Home in two weeks. M." That's it. Did you get it all, Missus Fergus? I'll repeat it if you like.'

'No thank you, Owen. That will be enough, thank you. Goodbye.'

Kate sat on the kitchen stool, suddenly exhausted as if she herself had just given birth. Then a smile broke across her dimpled face. 'My, my,' she said out loud, 'won't Henry be surprised! I'm a grandma!' Forgetting the blank sheet of paper on the secretary, she checked the roast and potatoes for dinner.

She was busying herself with the finishing touches on dinner when the men came in with Henry in the lead and Hjelmer a sullen two paces behind. 'When we sit down,' she said, 'I have some good news.' As they passed the platter of roast beef, roasted potatoes, green beans and onions, she reported her conversation with Owen Bauer. 'Isn't that good news? Margaret will be here soon.'

There was no response from either man until finally Henry spoke in a flat voice. 'That's good, Kate. It'll be nice to have Margaret home.' He looked at Hjelmer and the look gave his words a defiant tone. Hjelmer said nothing. Kate's joy vanished.

In bed that night, Kate finally confronted Henry about his bullying Hjelmer. 'Henry, I don't understand why you've been so hard on Hjelmer. He's been such a good worker. You've said so yourself. He's been like another son. But something's obviously wrong. Did he do something terribly bad—or didn't he do something he should've?'

'No. There's nothing wrong.'

'But there is, Henry. I can feel it. Women know about such things. Tell me what it is.' Henry didn't answer. Finally she put her worst fears into words. 'Henry, have you accused Hjelmer of fathering Margaret's baby?'

'Well, he did, didn't he?'

Kate gasped. 'Why, Henry, how can you say that. We don't know that. There are any number of young men who might have been responsible.'

'Oh, go to sleep.' This was a side of Henry she'd never seen before, and she didn't like it very much.

Ignoring his deprecating tone, Kate sat up in bed. 'I can't go to sleep, Henry. This is an injustice. How would you like it if someone accused you of doing something bad that you didn't do?'

'I wouldn't do anything bad like he did.'

'But if you did . . .'

'I wouldn't. Now go to sleep.'

'I can't. You're not being fair, and I don't like it. I don't believe he did anything bad. Besides, now Hjelmer knows why Margaret went to the Penningtons. Oh, Henry, how could you!'

Without saying more, she swung her feet off the bed and pulled on some stockings, twisting their tops with her index finger and tucking the knots into the top of the stockings to hold them up. She groped for the knitted blanket she kept on the chair. Bundling herself up, she crept down the stairs in the darkness tempered by the full moon. She crossed to the rocking chair by the window and sat pondering the future of her little family, the family so strangely put together and seemingly so compatible until Margaret's unfortunate pregnancy. It was a long night until sleep finally forced her back to bed.

* * *

Kate's excitement over Margaret's impending arrival was tempered by the everydayness of their lives. One day at dinner she stopped mid-bite, then put her fork back on her plate as Henry went on and on about Louie DeVoort's new method of planting corn. 'Louie's got some pamphlets from the college and thinks I ought to read them,' he said. 'I told him I'd let him try it out first and when we see how much corn he gets, then I'll try it.' Henry went on, but Kate wasn't listening. Hjelmer stared dully at his plate.

It wasn't what Henry was saying that captured her attention but a sudden awareness of the way he always twirled his fork and made emphatic stabbing motions in her direction as he talked. It was a curious gesture, she thought. In fact, Henry had several odd quirks. They didn't exactly bother her, but she had begun to reassess her life with Henry as he railed on about Louie's farming methods. She realized she really didn't care about the farming part of their life. She would have to give it more thought.

After dinner, Henry and Hjelmer went down to the barn as usual. Kate cleared away the dishes and carried them to the sink. Out the kitchen window, she watched Henry's back receding down the well-worn path. Yes, they were getting old. Henry was hunched in the shoulders and Kate's knees always hurt just before a rain. She reckoned the dishes could wait. She pulled off her apron and went up stairs.

At the top, puffing a little, she grasped the knob of the attic door and tugged. The door always stuck in the summer—extra humidity, she figured. As it finally gave way and Kate ascended the steep stairs, she was enveloped in a whiff of musty air. The smell brought back the hours she retreated to the attic when she was a little girl to play with her dolls, but mostly to avoid her brothers.

The light from the window at the head of the stairs was dim with the cobwebs that had accumulated, but with the light sifting in from the other dormers, it was enough to see her camera on its tripod, shrouded in the black hood she'd used. She winced. It was like seeing an old friend she'd neglected.

Sally Salisbury Stoddard

When she and Henry were courting, he suggested she could carry on with her photography business. She had agreed to marry him knowing full well it wasn't likely to happen. Indeed, the peaches were ready the week after the wedding, and when they were canned, there were the pears to be canned and apples to be dried and a dozen chickens to kill and clean and put up in jars for the winter. Now as she passed the camera, she swiped at the dust that gave the black hood a gray sheen, but it merely made her sneeze.

Under the eaves, she came to her small chest of drawers. She opened the bottom drawer, hoping mice hadn't gnawed a hole in the wood. Seeing no evidence of damage, she reached under a layer of lawn and pongee dresses, unworn because they were too nice to wear on the farm, and pulled out a large flat package wrapped in brown paper.

Sitting on the floor, she carefully unknotted the twine that held it, wrapping the twine neatly around her hand so it wouldn't get tangled. Opening the heavy paper she gently turned over copies of special photographs she had taken—Duncan Anders' family, the Olsen baby, Jedidiah Lewis III and so on. She smiled, remembering the various sittings and the various people. Each one had presented a different challenge. She'd kept copies of only the best of her work.

On the bottom of the pile she found the picture of Gyorgy which she had promised herself not to keep, but did anyway. Suddenly the world of Henry fell away from her consciousness. The world of the stabbing fork and the boring farm stories and the disappointment of the idle camera—and Margaret and Hjelmer and Will. All of them fell away as she stared at the swarthy handsomeness of Gyorgy.

She looked into his flinty black eyes and ran her hand gently over the thickness of his black brows and down his broad nose. She could almost feel the texture of his hand-woven shirt and the rough wool of his jacket. Finally, she looked at his full, dark beard and his well-trimmed mustache. Even in sepia she could remember the flecks of red in it. The unsmiling Gyorgy in the picture did not do justice to the Gyorgy who smiled so easily, showing his even, white teeth.

She wondered what it would be like to kiss such a handsome bearded man. Immediately she felt her breasts swell and her nipples become hard under her tight bodice. A warmth crept over her entire body and she felt a deep longing for something more—an unnameable desire. She felt her cheeks burn. She wanted to hold the moment forever. It's true, she told herself, she wanted to love and be loved in return. She knew it couldn't be Gyorgy, but Henry's flaws were becoming all too apparent.

She heard the back screen door slam. Startled, she quickly picked herself up off the floor. She hastily rewrapped the pictures and slipped them into the drawer again. Brushing off her skirt and apron, she slipped down the attic stairs to see what Henry wanted.

VII

The date was set for Margaret's return, and Kate was anxiously looking forward to it. It would indeed be a glad day. There would be so much to talk about, so much to learn about her life with the Penningtons, and the ordeal of her baby's birth. As curious as Kate was about all these things, she was determined to hold back on asking her direct questions. Margaret would need time to adjust to the Fergus routine again—this time without Will.

As the train pulled in, Kate was anxiously watching each car as it slowed to a halt. Finally she spied Margaret, suitcase in hand, ready to step off the train. Kate threw her arms wide and enveloped Margaret. 'My but it's good to see you, home at last.' Kate looked her up and down and smiled at what she saw. 'You look well,' she said and hugged her again.

'Oh, Auntie Kate, it's so good to be home!' declared Margaret and kissed Kate on the cheek. Kate put her hand to her cheek to preserve that tender gesture.

As soon as they were in the car, Margaret handed Kate a sealed letter from Hattie Pennington. Kate tucked it in her handbag to read later. For now, she was just glad Margaret was home safe and sound. It was a large undertaking she had just been through, and Kate knew it couldn't have been easy.

Margaret seemed to melt back into old family routines quite easily. Hjelmer seemed genuinely glad to have her back and teased her gently about missing school and leaving him to take care of gathering the eggs. She smiled at these gentle forays at familiarity and said she would be glad to see the old biddies again. Kate noted this genial interaction. If Hjelmer had been at fault, surely Margaret would not have been as relaxed with him as she obviously was.

Supper was a lively affair—except for Henry who couldn't seem to smile at anything. Kate saw Margaret look at him with a quizzical expression, but she didn't say anything. It was obvious nothing was going to spoil her joy at being home again.

That night after everyone had gone to bed, Kate sat at the secretary and opened the envelope. She perused it quickly. It outlined only a few facts—including the brief statement turning the baby over to the Baby Fold in Norfolk, but none of this informed Kate about how Margaret had lived through the time with the Penningtons or the birth or giving up the baby. Kate sighed. She knew she would have to wait until Margaret felt safe enough to talk about it.

Kate hastily pulled out a sheet of paper and wrote a quick note to Hattie telling her of Margaret's safe arrival and thanking her profusely for taking such good care of Margaret. Then, she added: 'We are indebted to you for caring. May God bless you.' She folded the paper and slipped it into an envelope which she addressed and sealed. She would have to wait to buy a stamp from the mailman when he came in the morning. At least now she could sleep.

For a while after Margaret returned, Kate felt as if her load had lightened and her heart had sprouted wings. Henry now seemed genuinely glad to have Margaret join them at the table. He smiled gently as he patted her shoulder and said, 'Well, well, Margaret, we're going to have to make up for all the slacking off you've done!' Margaret responded with a shy smile and a serious promise that she would.

Kate was happy that Margaret's absence had indeed seemed to make Henry's heart grow fonder, but she also suspected that Henry's solicitousness had something to do with his persistent belief that Hjelmer was the father of the baby. Since nothing in Hjelmer's or Margaret's demeanor had ever suggested a doubt as to Hjelmer's innocence, Kate watched the two of them even more closely now for any sign that he had been the perpetrator. She detected nothing and lapsed into a kind of euphoria that lifted her heart. Did it really seem that Henry was less accusing in his attitude toward Hjelmer? Time would tell.

As the days went by, Kate waited as patiently as she could before broaching the subject of the birth with Margaret. Finally, after Margaret had been home two weeks, they began to talk one afternoon after dinner dishes were done and they were alone.

Margaret cried as she talked. 'Those women who were helping were kind and nice and I pushed and pushed as hard as I could. Oh, Auntie Kate, it was so painful! And then those women wouldn't even let me see my baby! They said it would be best if I didn't. But, Auntie Kate, I wanted so much to see him. Wasn't he mine?'

'Of course, Margaret,' Kate said as she stroked Margaret's hair. 'Of course, you wanted to, but it would have been even harder for you to give him up if you had seen him, don't you think? What did they tell you about him?'

'Only that he was a beautiful baby—really perfect, they said. I suppose that meant he had all his toes. Oh, Auntie Kate, somebody is getting a special child. I only hope they will appreciate him and be good to him.'

'We will have to have faith that that's the case, Margaret, and certainly someone who wants to adopt a baby would care a lot,' Kate said as she patted Margaret's cheek and kissed her lightly on the forehead. 'You know now, Margaret, how hard it must have been for your mother to let you and your sisters go. And you know how lucky I am to have had the good sense to choose you as my child.' Tears glistened on Margaret's face.

'I don't think I could have gotten through this trouble if it hadn't been for my ikon,' she said.

Kate couldn't help looking surprised. 'Did you take it with you?' she asked.

'Yes, I remembered it at the last minute. When my mother gave it to me, she told me that, if I ever got into a tough situation, I should ask Mary to help me and I did and she did!'

Kate gathered her in her arms again and, in tears, whispered, 'I'm so glad. Your mother is a wise woman.'

Margaret worked happily alongside Kate during the day, and in the evenings, she retreated to her room to study so she would be ready to return to school in a couple of weeks.

* * *

One evening, Kate bustled about the kitchen, hurrying to finish the icing for the applesauce cake she had baked that morning for Hjelmer's birthday. She'd never baked one for him before. It hadn't seemed appropriate, or needed, for a hired boy. Her family had never done such for hired men, but now she felt sorry for him mostly because Henry had become so demanding—and so accusing at the same time.

The men were due in from the field almost any minute and she especially wanted to surprise Hjelmer. Just her remembering the date would surprise him, she was sure, but to have someone actually act on that remembering would please him very much, though in his shy way he would probably say, 'It ain't important.'

Earlier in the day, she had sent Margaret upstairs to see to the darning that had accumulated over the last month, telling her only that she felt like baking a cake and wouldn't need her help. The cake was now done waiting for some fancy, boiled icing. To test the hot syrup to see if it had come to the soft ball stage, she dropped some off her stirring spoon into a bit of cold water in a shallow dish, the way her mother had taught her. Gathering the sticky sample into a ball with her fingers, she plopped it into her mouth and smiled, remembering how she had begged her mother to let her eat the test balls. Pronouncing it ready, she gradually poured the boiling liquid with her left hand while folding it in the beaten egg whites with her right hand. All the while she was saying a little prayer, urging the good Lord to let it be just right for spreading without going to sugar crystals.

She frowned as she beat the icing, peering into its silky froth until she knew it had reached perfection. Quickly, but gently, she spread the fluffy sweet concoction on the bottom layer of the cake. Then she carefully lowered the top layer in place making sure it did not hang over anywhere. Just as carefully she spread icing to completely cover any hint of the dark spicy cake underneath. Standing back, knife in hand, she tipped her head to the side and turned the cake to check from every angle. With a flip of the wrist, she created a series of twirls around the top edge and smiled. With her hands on her hips, she surveyed her creation and her gratification seemed equal to that of God's when He surveyed His creation and declared that it was good.

She couldn't dwell on her accomplishment very long. She needed to hide the cake in the pantry until time to surprise Hjelmer. Perhaps she could carefully place it down in the large Dutch oven on the shelf and cover it, but she worried that there might not be enough clearance and she might smear the icing in the process. She would have to fit it in the corner behind the jars of tomatoes and hope no one would see it there.

She was mashing the potatoes as she heard voices approaching the back door, deep male voices that sounded on the edge of anger, as if coming to the end of an argument that was unresolvable.

At the table, Kate carried on a bright, cheerful conversation, mostly a monologue. She saw Henry scowl at his plate and Hjelmer seemed to shy away from Henry's end of the table. Margaret answered her questions about the darning in a polite, but distracted manner. The talk was more strained than had been the case before Margaret left, but today Kate didn't worry about it. She was almost giddy with the delight of anticipation.

The only reason she had thought of the birthday cake was that, once last summer when she and Hjelmer were cleaning the hen house, she had asked him what he remembered about his family. 'My folks was poor, really poor, ma'am.'

'Well, but didn't you have some good times—some nice Christmases and birthdays?'

'No, Miz Fergus. We never had nothing like that. We didn't always have a place to live, let alone food to eat. Potatoes. That was about it. Until Mr. Fergus took me on, I hardly had three meals a day. We lost the farm when I was about five, and there was three babies besides me by that time. In some ways it was a little better after Pa left because Ma took in washings, but there were too many kids to feed. It ain't easy t' take care of four children when there ain't no man around. I was just 8 when Pa left home.'

'It's hard to believe, Hjelmer, but you always tell me the truth so I believe you. Didn't you ever feel sad not to have a birthday cake?'

'Well, maam, I did. I mean other kids in school used to talk about having parties, but they never paid no 'tention to me anyway, 'cept to make fun of me and my little sisters—our clothes, ya know. Ma couldn't help it. She didn't have money for such things.'

Hjelmer had never spoken of these things before, and Kate was buoyed by his trust in her, but sad for his meager childhood. She determined that he would not go further in his life without someone celebrating his existence.

As they ate dinner that day, she told them that she had made a special dessert so they should save some room. 'Margaret, you clear the table, and I'll get the dessert. Bring in the small plates and a cake knife.' She knew Margaret would be curious but she would never question what Kate did. In the kitchen Kate pulled out the used and reused birthday candles from the back of the top drawer and stuck them on the cake. There weren't enough anymore for an eighteen-year-old, but what few there were would have to do. Touching a bit of wadded up newspaper to the fire in the cookstove, she lit the candles.

With a sparkle in her eyes, Kate marched triumphantly into the dining room. All jaws dropped at the sight of the cloud-like cake with its tiny flames streaming in the breeze Kate created as she moved. A glance at Henry showed him to be at once curious and furious. 'It's too bad Will isn't here with us, isn't it?' she remarked. She placed the cake in front of Hjelmer. 'He always enjoyed birthdays, didn't he, Henry?' Kate glanced around. Margaret, who had been smiling, looked down at her plate. Henry said nothing.

Kate told Hjelmer to blow out his candles. He was speechless. 'You'll have to blow them out before they burn down to the cake!' she declared. He ducked his head and gulped.

'Is this for me?' Hjelmer whispered.

Margaret's smile returned. 'Yes, Hjelmer, you should blow out your candles.'

Looking at Margaret and then at Kate, Hjelmer managed a shy smile, took a deep breath, and blew out the tiny flames. The sudden warmth of Margaret's and Hjelmer's reactions caused tears to come to Kate's eyes. She cut the cake, giving Hjelmer an extra large piece. As she handed Henry his piece, he grumbled, 'I don't want any. Could I see you in the kitchen, Kate?'

'After we've eaten our cake, Henry. We are celebrating Hjelmer's birthday just now and that should not be interrupted.' She seldom defied him, but it was her party and she was determined that Hjelmer should get his due. 'Now then, can we all sing "Happy Birthday" to Hjelmer?' Only she and Margaret sang.

That night when Kate and Henry were preparing for bed, Henry grabbed her by the shoulder and said, 'Kate, whatever in the world are you doing? Now that boy will think he's got it coming to him.' Kate squirmed away from him and continued undressing.

'Kate, I forbid you to ever do such a thing again for that worthless boy.'

Kate felt as if Henry had as good as slapped her face. Very quietly she said, 'Henry Fergus, I will do as I see fit. You told me this is my home and I will do as I see fit in my home.'

Henry fumed and sputtered until he dropped into bed and started to snore. Kate lay wide awake, realizing how exhausting it was to argue. Finally sleep overtook her.

* * *

Looking back on it now, Kate remembered that the Sunday morning after Hjelmer's birthday dawned as beautiful a September morn as Kate could have dreamed of. She had awakened smiling in anticipation of a Fergus family reunion down at the old stone mill. Kate always considered a family reunion to be a special time—even if it was Henry's family, and not her own (although she assumed Angus and Lizzie would be there). Having Margaret home made the day even more special.

There was much ado about what to take and whether her contribution would be good enough. She baked a couple of apple pies and some scones. Scones were 'holy' food to folks from the Orkneys so she was taking a chance in even trying. She fussed about it, 'Oh, Margaret, I don't know why mine are never as good as my mother's. I've always used her recipe.'

Margaret laughed. 'I think they're wonderful,' she said, her mouth full of a big sample bite. Kate decided they would have to do. She hoped Margaret would make them for her future family. She winced at the thought that Margaret's family had already started and Margaret would not be able—ever—to see her first born grow up.

Kate planned to mix up some cole slaw to take, so she had to hurry to grate the cabbage and carrots after breakfast dishes were washed up. Margaret packed the picnic baskets with extra bottles of sweet pickles and some cheese to go with the pies. Hjelmer carried the baskets to the car. 'I've left some food for you on the kitchen table, Hjelmer,' said Kate as she climbed into the car.

Kate knew Henry wasn't happy leaving Hjelmer in charge of the farm for even part of a day. 'I don't know why you're so fussed about leaving Hjelmer. He's taken care of things before and everything's been just fine. So why would that be different now?' she demanded to know. He just grumbled and went to change his clothes. She knew he was still upset about the birthday cake, but he'd settled down some. He even ate a piece of the birthday cake after she finally persuaded him it would be all right.

The grounds of the old stone mill were very pleasant, even in the heat of summer. The towering oak and elm trees gave shade under which to spread blankets to sit on. Someone brought planks and some sawhorses for a table to put the food on, and there was a great plenty of it. It was good to see Henry's sister Esther again, but their reunions would never be the same without Grandma Fergus who had died the previous spring. Angus and Lizzie and their family arrived with their boys eager to wade in the creek with their cousins. Little Netta hung back shyly hanging onto Lizzie's skirt. Kate rang her old teacher's bell to call folks to eat. A couple of people remembered when she rang it for real to call the children into the school building.

'What do you hear from Will?' asked Esther.

'Well, not much, but he seems to be getting along just fine. He's started his classes now so I expect we'll hear even less of him,' said Henry as he picked up a chicken leg from the platter. 'I don't suppose he'll be home now until Thanksgiving.' He wandered off to sit with the men who were talking hogs and baseball.

'We're glad you're back, Margaret,' said Esther. 'How was it in Colony? I've heard there are a lot of very pious people over there.'

Margaret thanked her politely, and said she didn't have time to find out much about the community, being out on the farm and all. Then she had managed to pry Jenny away from Lizzie and was dancing with her in her arms with Netta hanging onto her skirt. Kate and Esther and the other women chattered about the price of eggs and the newest feed sack patterns—in between coralling the children and reminding the older ones to keep the younger ones away from the ruins of the stone mill. Once the sun began its ride toward the horizon, the families gathered up their children and their baskets and said goodbye, each declaring the need to get together more often. The family parties departed, one by one, going their several directions.

On the way home, Kate smiled at Henry and said, 'Wasn't that a fun time? It's always good to see each other again, isn't it?' Henry just grunted He had seemed more relaxed than she'd seen him for awhile now, and he appeared to be having a good time discussing the prospects for the crops with Angus. Kate had overheard them talking about whether it would pay to buy one of the new gasoline tractors like Louie DeVoort bought.

It was nice to see Margaret talking to her cousins—and smiling, but even more so that her aunts and uncles seemed genuinely glad to see her. On the way home, Kate said, 'I must say, Margaret, several of the women remarked about how pretty you've become—and I had to agree!'

Margaret smiled at that and said that couldn't be, but Kate knew she was happy to hear it. Kate was thinking as they rode along about the many ways Margaret had changed over the years. They approached home just as the sun reached the peak of the barn.

All of a sudden, Henry leaned forward over the steering wheel. 'What the—! What's going on here! I knew I shouldn't have—My God, Kate! What has he done?'

Henry's language startled Kate out of her reverie. She leaned forward. 'What's the matter, Henry, I don't see anything—'

'My God, Kate! The whole place is ruined! Dammit! You'd have to be blind not to see that.'

Kate tried to appeal to Henry's better self. 'Now, Henry—'

'Don't "Now Henry" me, Kate. It's your fault. You talked me into leaving that no-good boy in charge.' Henry turned the car into the driveway, and Kate realized that something had happened though it wasn't clear just what it was because the lowering sun was in her eyes.

'Well, we'll just have to ask Hjelmer about it,' Kate said in an even tone though her heart was beginning to beat hard. 'I'm sure he has an explanation.'

'There's nothing to explain. He's ruined Margaret and he's ruined me. That's the explanation.' Hjelmer came running from the direction of the barn, clearly agitated. Henry steered directly toward him. Kate was sure he was going to hit Hjelmer—and maybe even kill him. He was that angry. She reached for the steering wheel with all her might to turn the car at the last minute. Henry grabbed her arm. 'What are you doing, woman?'

Margaret screamed from the back seat, 'Papa, Papa, no!' Henry slammed on the brakes. He jumped out of the car and grabbed Hjelmer by the collar with his twisted fist. Kate feared that he would let go and smash the boy's face with his other hand which was a menacing, squared fist. Henry's voice, angry and accusatory like his face, came as near to screeching as its deep bass tones could inflect. 'Whathappenedhereboy? Whatchabeendoing anyway—sleeping under the haystack? What happened? How could you let this happen?'

'No! No, Henry, no!' screamed Kate, climbing down from the car. 'Let him go!'

'Dammit, you get back there and shut up. I'll take care of him,' Henry snarled.

Kate and Margaret stood rooted to the spot where they scrambled from the car. Behind the men, Kate could see the open hen house door and the chickens scattered everywhere, scratching in the dirt as if nothing had happened. She couldn't see the pig pen in the shadow of the barn. She saw that the barn door was ajar and there were dark, wheel tracks and footprints gouging deep holes in the soft earth of the barnyard that appeared to have been caused by a dancing horde of giants. She reeled at the sight.

'All right, you lowdown . . .' Henry's words were swallowed as he sneered through gritted teeth. 'What happened?' Henry lowered his voice to a growl and his chin jutted forward to reveal thick blue veins embossed on his neck. 'We leave you in charge and you sell us out. That's enough. You're through here! Kate,' he said, without turning to look at her, 'I told you this boy wasn't man enough to take charge of things. He tried to ruin us and I don't know but he's done it.'

Margaret stepped closed to Kate, taking her arm, forming a feeble phalanx against the onslaught.

'Who's been here, boy? Why didn't you stop them? Where were you?'

Hjelmer jerked his head back away from Henry's face which only tightened Henry's grip on his collar. His face turned a deep red and he gasped, 'I . . . I . . .' His voice gurgled with Henry's tightening fingers. Suddenly Henry let go of Hjelmer, lurched forward, and slapped him hard across his face.

Kate threw up her hands as if she had been struck. She launched herself the few feet between her and the men. Henry pushed her back and she fell to the ground. Margaret ran to help her. Kate's blue eyes were blazing as she picked herself up and stepped in front of Henry. 'Kate, you stay out of this!' demanded Henry, thrusting his arm out to keep her back. Breathing heavily now, Henry moved forward as Hjelmer moved back out of his reach.

Kate grabbed Henry's sleeve. 'Henry! Henry! Stop. I will not have this.'

'Kate, I told you to stay out of this.' Henry swung his arm forward to free himself from her grasp.

'I will not! I will not stay out of this!'

'I will not put up with this lazy, insolent, no-good. We're through talking. Talking didn't get us nowhere.'

Stepping up to Hjelmer then, Kate started to speak but Henry grabbed her and cut her off.

'I forbid you to speak to that boy.'

Kate freed herself and whirled on him. 'You listen to me, Henry Fergus. You don't forbid me to do anything!'

Henry started to push her aside but Margaret stepped in, screaming, 'Papa, no! Don't!'

She caught the force of Henry's arm in her chest knocking the wind out of her and she staggered backwards. Realizing what he'd done, Henry took a step back. 'It don't change anything. Boy! I put you in charge for one day and what have you done?' Henry's fists remained doubled up ready to strike again and his breathing was labored. His voice waned. 'I can't trust nobody no more,' he groaned.

Kate put her hand on Hjelmer's arm and pleaded desperately, 'Hjelmer, Hjelmer, tell me what happened! Who's been here? What'd they do?'

Hjelmer had the wary look of a trapped animal. He held his hand to his cheek which was fiery red from Henry's blow. He glanced at Kate and shifted his body away from Henry. 'Go on, Hjelmer. Tell me what happened,' Kate quietly urged.

'Gypsies,' he whispered, his voice still strangled from Henry's grip. 'I—I—didn't know what to do. There were too many of them.'

Kate blanched and stepped back. 'Gypsies?' she echoed. Could it be? She knew enough about Gypsies from her reading and from Bethany to know that Gypsies would only have committed such a blatant robbery if they were desperate for food. She hadn't thought about Gypsies for quite awhile now, except for seeing Gyorgy's picture. She blushed at the thought and her stomach reeled. Surely it could not have been Gyorgy's clan. Or could it?

She turned to Henry. 'Well, Henry, if it was Gypsies then that solves it. It wasn't Hjelmer's fault!'

'That solves nothing,' he snapped, but he seemed to wilt. 'Get busy and get this place cleared up!' Kate and Margaret moved toward the chicken house. 'No, dammit, not you women! You get up to the house! Hjelmer's got to do it.' Hjelmer glowered at Henry, but turned toward the barnyard.

'Henry, do you think we should call the sheriff?' Kate asked hesitantly.

'Call that old sot? What good would that do? Besides, those Gypsies would be clear into the next county before you could find that sheriff on a Sunday night.'

As the two men walked to the barn, Henry was a step behind, shouting at Hjelmer, 'What'd they take? What'd they take?' Kate could not hear Hjelmer's answer, if indeed he did answer.

She and Margaret carried the picnic basket and blankets to the house. While they were cleaning up the dishes, Margaret said very quietly, 'Auntie Kate, what did Papa mean that Hjelmer ruined me? Does he think Hjelmer was the father of the baby?'

Kate felt apologetic and hardly knew what to say. Finally, she stuttered, 'Well, Margaret, I'm afraid that's just what he meant.'

Margaret looked stricken, her face drained of color. 'Oh, no,' she whispered. 'Oh, no!' she repeated and ran from the room, her feet pounding on the stairs. Kate, weary and afraid, heard a door slam. She did not have the strength to call her back or go after her. Her world had come to a crashing halt and she could not think straight. The only thing that made sense was putting the little piece of her world that was the kitchen back in some semblance of order.

Henry came in as Kate was finishing up in the kitchen. His shoulders sagged and he looked haggard. She said nothing about the condition of the barnyard. It would be better to let it rest overnight, but she did confront him about his saying that Hjelmer had ruined Margaret. 'Henry, Margaret wanted to know if you thought Hjelmer caused her pregnancy, and I had to tell her you did. She was extremely upset and ran upstairs. I'll go up and talk to her but I don't know what I'll say.'

Henry groaned. 'Well, Kate, you just tell her we know better. She's just covering up for him.'

'No, Henry, I won't tell her that. We don't know better. She wouldn't cover up for him. Why would she? If that were the case, I think she would have found some way to stay in Colony, or something like that.'

Henry sank into his chair and covered his face with his hands. Finally, he muttered, 'I'm sorry for hitting you and Margaret.' Kate merely grunted and started up the stairs with the lamp. She knocked gently on Margaret's door. 'Margaret, can I come in?' She heard a muffled voice and tried the knob. The door was locked. She sighed deeply as tears rolled down her cheeks. 'I'm sorry, Margaret. I'm so sorry.' She sighed to herself, 'Oh, my lord, what have we done?' and made her way to bed, dabbing at her wet cheeks. She lay awake for a long time waiting for Hjelmer's footsteps on the stairs, but there were none.

* * *

The next two days were tense. Henry had called the Sheriff the day after the theft. He came out and looked over the damage. 'Well, Henry, I've only been called for two or three cases like this. Dunno what we can do. We've got no clues. It seems if someone wants to steal from a farmer it's not too hard to do. I expect that hired boy of yours is right—Gypsies, and we know they're long gone for wherever they're going. I'm sorry, Henry. Well, I guess I'll be on my way.' The two men shook hands and then shook their heads with a 'what's the world coming to' look. Kate and Henry watched him go. Kate was relieved that Henry hadn't tried to implicate Hjelmer.

The damage done had been less than Henry feared that Sunday night. There were three baby pigs missing and who knows how many chickens and how much chicken feed. There wouldn't be many eggs for awhile until they could build up the flock again. It was a substantial loss but not as big a one as a fire or tornado would have been. Thank goodness, their horses weren't worth stealing, especially by Gypsies who knew their horses.

Kate knew that it would take some time to recoup the money lost, but it could be done. They were not yet too old to do so, but she also knew the loss of Henry's trust in his family and the world in general would take longer and might never be salvaged. This saddened Kate who knew that a man of his age would find it hard to rebuild even if he could find the gumption—which she questioned at the moment. She worried more about what was happening to Hjelmer. Even though he was young, his future was in jeopardy just as much as Henry's.

Nevertheless, as hard as Henry had been on Hjelmer over this, Hjelmer set about to gather up the few straggling chickens that had escaped capture earlier. He fixed the pig pen and rounded up the remaining hogs, but he could not immediately erase the telltale footprints that would remain until the next hard rain. He did all this without complaint, but it was obvious that he was both grieving and seething down deep.

Henry rarely spoke to Hjelmer at meals and when he did, he growled at him. 'You're going to have to pay for the chickens and pigs and all those tools the Gypsies took. You won't get any pay till that's taken care of, mind you,' Henry said at dinner one noon. Kate knew that taking the loss out of Hjelmer's meager wages would take forever so he might as well be an indentured servant. Kate watched Hjelmer turn a livid red and leave the table, stomping out the back door. 'You come back here!' Henry yelled, but he didn't go after him, and Hjelmer didn't return. He took to sleeping in the barn at night.

Later that day Hjelmer saw Kate surveying the scene. 'Miz Fergus, I don't think I'm guilty here. If I pay for the damages, I'd be admitting I'm guilty—and I'm not! The same thing would have happened if Mr. Fergus had been home.'

'Well, that's right, Hjelmer. I've tried talking to Henry about it, but I'll try again. Don't you worry.'

'I can't help but worry, maam. He thinks I—I—well, he thinks I did something to Margaret. Honest, ma'am, I swear I didn't do nothin' to Margaret. She knows I didn't. I don't know who did, but it wasn't me.' Hjelmer was almost in tears. 'What can I do to make him see that?'

'Right now, I expect there's nothing you can say or do. I don't know why Margaret doesn't tell us. It's not right, but I'll work on her and Henry. You've done all we've asked of you. Give me some time to see how I can help resolve this,' Kate touched his sleeve and really wanted to give him a hug but she knew it would embarrass him.

'Thank you, ma'am. I'll try to be patient.'

Nothing was resolved a week later. Henry really needed Hjelmer to fix things up and help him with the farm chores, but they worked without speaking to each other except for a few grunts and a few essential words, and it seemed as if they might break out in a fist fight at any time. Meals were quiet affairs with an occasional request for someone to pass the potatoes. After a meal, each of them returned to usual routines.

Kate and Margaret were preparing for Margaret's return to school at the end of the month. Mrs. Buchanan said she'd be happy to have Margaret board with her again and work to pay for it as she had before. Kate had hoped she and Margaret could spend these days talking about Margaret's time away from home and her future. Even now, all Kate knew about Margaret's living with the Penningtons and giving birth were snippets of information here and there. The flare-up between Henry and Hjelmer had profoundly affected her and Margaret, too. She wanted to come right out and ask Margaret why she hadn't told Henry that Hjelmer didn't do it, but it always seemed like there would be a better time, a more appropriate time.

Kate suggested that Margaret take over the bread making for the few days left before she went back to school. It might be more satisfying than darning socks and ironing. There weren't many chickens to feed, nor eggs to gather. The physical labor of kneading the dough might give her a chance to work out her grief over the baby.

The next morning early, standing at the kitchen table, Margaret didn't say much. She seemed to know just what to do and measured ingredients as she had been taught. With Margaret making bread, Kate went to work on other parts of their dinner. She sighed. It would be so good to have a couple of old hens to stew up for chicken and biscuits, but now the old hens were gone. Instead she opened a jar of home-canned beef and set about preparing the other ingredients.

After Margaret covered the buttered tops of the bread loaves with a clean feedsack-towel and set the bread in the warming oven to rise, Kate asked Margaret to go upstairs and fold the sheets while dinner was cooking. 'All right,' said Margaret as she washed her hands in the basin and wiped them. She turned toward the stairs.

Suddenly the back porch screen door banged loudly. Like a menacing grizzly bear, Henry stomped into the kitchen, glowering, his rough hands clenched as if ready to fight. 'Where's Hjelmer?' he demanded. 'Where is that no-good leech of a hired boy!'

Margaret gasped and ran up the stairs. Kate was taken aback by Henry's ferocity. She wasn't sure she could mollify him. 'Goodness, Henry, you mustn't get so upset. I don't know where he is. Have you looked in the barn?'

'The barn! Of course, I have. I've looked everywhere—in the barn, in the hen house, in the corn crib, the implement shed. Where haven't I looked? Where? Where? Everywhere but the cistern.'

'Calm down, Henry. You know he wouldn't have gone far.'

'He's supposed to be helping me with the cows.' His face got even redder. 'I'll kill that sneak the next time he slips out on me like this.'

'Now, now, Henry. You know he's always been there when you needed him. He's a good boy. He must have some good reason for being wherever he is. Did you check the cellar?'

'The cellar! Why would he be there? Oh, all right, I'll go look, but Lord knows why he'd go down there.' Kate watched him as he went outside. The cellar door was open and Henry, still muttering, clumped down the stairs into the dim light which the open door and the one small window afforded.

Kate was relieved to have him out of the kitchen and turned back to her beef stew makings. She'd hardly recollected where she left off when Henry came stomping back into the kitchen. 'He's not there,' he screamed at her. After Henry's behavior on Sunday, Kate worried about how violent he might become and edged toward the dining room door.

'M-m-maybe he went into town,' Kate suggested, turning her head away from an expected blow. This was not the Henry she thought she loved. She didn't know this Henry. She realized she could no longer anticipate his actions, and she feared what he might do to Margaret.

'He knew we had work to do. Good boy! My eye! If he's such a good boy, why isn't he here when he's supposed to be,' he stormed. 'Where's that girl!' he demanded. 'If Hjelmer isn't going to do his work, she'll have to do it.'

'No, Henry! She can't! She's just—' Kate's heart was pounding under her apron. 'She's too weak yet. Besides, I need her in the house.' Kate's eyes shifted from the floor to the door and back. She was afraid of what he might do to Margaret if she couldn't handle the job to suit him. Margaret had never worked with the cows before, not even to milk them.

'Now, Henry, dinner'll be ready in five minutes. Why don't you go sit down and cool off. We'll all feel better when we've eaten. Maybe when Hjelmer gets hungry enough . . .'

'Oh, yeah, he always manages to show up to eat,' Henry said. Henry's chest was heaving with his heavy breathing. She was afraid he would he would have an apoplectic attack.

'Are you all right, Henry? You seem to be short of breath. Anyway, go call Margaret for dinner. She's upstairs, folding the washing, I expect.'

Hjelmer didn't show up for dinner. 'We'll just go ahead and eat,' said Kate. None of the three ate much, and they ate in silence, pushing food around their plates. When Henry stood up and headed for the kitchen, Kate pleaded with him. Putting her hand on his arm, she said quietly, 'You go, Henry. Do your cows. I'll send Margaret out to find Hjelmer. I'm not sure Hjelmer likes us very well just now.' She wanted to add that she didn't like Henry very well now, either, but she held her tongue.

'If it hadn't been for that scoundrel of a boy . . . I should never have given him any responsibility, that's what. I should never . . .'

'Stop it, Henry. Just stop it,' Kate said, 'What would you have done differently if you'd been here? Huh? Nothing. That's what. You couldn't have done any more than Hjelmer did. Now just go to the barn. I'll send Margaret out to find him and I'll talk to him. You just leave Hjelmer to me.'

'You! You're such a pansy, you won't give him what he deserves.'

'Just go, Henry. Go now,' Kate begged. Henry's face reddened and he clenched his fists as though he wanted to hit somebody. Instead he turned and stomped out the door.

Kate shivered. Suddenly she was aware of Margaret watching her from the kitchen doorway. She put her arms around Kate's heaving shoulders. They stood like that until Kate whispered, 'I'll be all right. We'll be all right.'

Margaret handed Kate a handkerchief, and Kate realized that she was crying. 'I guess I'm just not used to having so many problems all at once. And I guess Henry isn't either.' She knew she was excusing him to reassure Margaret, but she herself was not reassured.

'Was what Hjelmer did all that bad?' asked Margaret.

'Well, he shouldn't have gone off when Henry needs him—and Hjelmer knew he needed him today. Margaret, you'll have to go look for Hjelmer. Can you do that? I would but I'm too slow and I think I need to be here in case Henry comes back. When you find Hjelmer, tell him I want to talk to him. Don't say Henry wants to see him. Even so, he may not want to come to the house so tell him I'll meet him wherever he wants me to.'

'Where do you think he went?' Margaret asked.

'I don't know. I'm sure he won't be in the barn. I suppose he could have cut across the corn field and headed for town, but somehow I don't think so. He might have gone to the woods down by the creek, or to the orchard. In any case, I'm sure he would answer if he hears your voice. You go put on that pair of overalls I gave you for gardening. I'll make some sandwiches for him. He'll be hungry. Oh, Margaret, it's not right that you should have to do this, but I don't know what else to do.'

Margaret turned to go upstairs as Kate began to slice the bread thicker than usual. She put extra butter on each piece. She sliced some leftover roast beef and spread some horseradish over it. Then she wrapped the sandwiches and an apple in a piece of newspaper and tied it with a string.

Margaret came back into the kitchen wearing the baggy overalls and hugged Kate again. 'I'll just go now,' she said. If I don't find him by suppertime, I'll come back.'

'Margaret? Be careful. Be very careful. I couldn't stand it if something happened to you.'

Margaret smiled and then her face became serious. 'I will be careful, Auntie Kate, but you be careful, too.'

* * *

Kate watched through the north window as Margaret swung out along the driveway where it curved behind the implement shed. She tried to concentrate on cleaning up the kitchen. Margaret's loaves of bread were baked and looked beautiful—County Fair blue ribbon quality, Kate thought to herself. Maybe next year Margaret could bake some for the fair and they could all go and have a good time. She shook her head. Certainly they needed a good time right now. Gradually she cleared up the dishes and cleaned the stove and swept the floor. It was good to have work to do to keep her mind off the task she'd assigned to Margaret, but it wasn't enough to keep her mind off Henry and Hjelmer.

Gardening! Maybe weeding in the hot sun would help her put things in perspective. That's what she would do: go out to the garden and pull weeds. She put on her sun bonnet and found her old gloves and went to the back porch where she gathered the tools, a hoe and a rake. In the plot to the northwest of the house, the sun was warm in midafternoon, but Kate concentrated on the weeds in the rows of turnips. She always thought a well-weeded garden would grow better, but she'd never really liked working outside. She turned to the tomato plants, picking a few large ones and set them in the grass ready to go inside when she did.

She looked up just in time to see Henry striding toward her as fast as he could. His face was livid as he came straight toward her. 'You!' he screamed at her and she grabbed the rake gripping it with both hands, tine side up. 'You! You! You told him where the rifle was hidden! He's taken it and he's gone and God only knows where he is or what he's gonna do with it.'

Kate was aghast. It didn't sound like Henry would listen to her no matter what. He was shaking his fist in her face. Putting the rake head in front of her face she said, 'Henry! Henry! Wait a minute! I didn't know you even had a rifle. How could I tell Hjelmer something I didn't know?' Kate was at a loss as to how to straighten things out. She put her hand out to calm him down, but he shoved her hand away.

'You! . . . You! . . .'

Kate's voice was shrill. 'I don't know about any rifle. Maybe Hjelmer took it, maybe he didn't. Maybe the Gypsies took it! They could have, you know.'

At that, Henry reeled backwards and then caught himself. His shoulders drooped. It was obvious he'd forgotten about the Gypsies. Finally, he slunk away toward the barn, muttering, 'When that boy gets back here, we'll find out the straight of it, by God!' Kate leaned on the rake and tried to still the palpitations in her stomach. It was a close call and she didn't know what to make of it.

She headed back toward the house, the only safe haven she could think of at that minute. Her steps were halting and she squinted with concentration trying to make sense of her life so suddenly topsy turvy. She looked over her shoulder to make sure Henry wasn't coming back.

It must have been over an hour since she started weeding. Just then she thought she saw some movement between the implement shed and the corn crib. Could it be Hjelmer? No. It was Margaret! As she came nearer, Kate saw that Margaret's hair was in disarray and her face florid—from crying or from running Kate could not guess from a distance. Her pace slowed as she came nearer as if her feet would carry her no further. Kate hurried to meet her.

Kate was aghast when Margaret arrived in the shade of the implement shed. She caught her in a tight embrace, both of them too breathless to speak. It was obvious that Margaret was highly distraught. Kate did not press the girl but began to gently move her toward the house. Kate chastised herself for sending the girl on this mission, the outcome of which she still could not guess.

Once inside the house, Kate helped Margaret to sit on the kitchen stool. Then she wrung out a towel in cool water and patted Margaret's face which was scratched, perhaps from the trees in the orchard. Kate filled the dipper with cool water from the pail and handed it to her. Margaret took a few sips and handed the dipper back to Kate.

She still had not spoken. It was as if she'd seen a ghost and could not speak. Suddenly she screeched—a piercing, deathly screech that distorted her face and jaws and it kept coming from somewhere in the depths of her.

Kate held her tight. 'It's all right, it's all right,' Kate whispered, knowing that nothing was all right.

'Oh, Ma!' Margaret cried out. 'Oh, Ma!' She covered her face with her hands, muffling her voice. 'Oh, Ma!' The agony in her voice was soul-piercing.

'What is it, girl? What is it?' A terrible fear gripped Kate but she waited. She wanted to ask, 'Did you find him?' but she didn't want to hurry her in the state she was in. Instead she continued to wrap her arms around Margaret and hold her tight. With Margaret apparently unable to talk, she could not imagine anything but bad news. 'Oh, Margaret, I should never have asked you to go. I'm so sorry. You poor dear.'

Margaret pulled away then. 'No, no, Auntie Kate. I needed to go.' Then so quietly Kate had to lean close to hear, Margaret said simply, 'He's dead, Ma! In the orchard. He's dead. Hanging in a pear tree.' Margaret seemed shriveled in the bulky overalls. 'I couldn't do anything for him. Oh, Ma, what shall we do? I'm so scared. He looked awful. Ma! I killed him!'

'Killed him!' Kate was struck dumb. She had imagined a strong and belligerent young man lashing back at Henry—and even herself—but never this. 'What do you mean *you* killed him? *We* failed him, Margaret—Henry and I. If anybody killed him, it was us.' Her voice dropped to a whisper. 'He was such a good boy.'

'No, Ma,' Margaret said softly, 'you didn't kill him. I did.'

Kate seemed not to hear her. Her eyes glazed over and she buried her face in her apron. Her mind could barely comprehend that Hjelmer was gone. Hjelmer couldn't be gone. 'Oh, Margaret, you shouldn't have had to see him there. I should have gone myself. Oh, what have I done? Please forgive me for sending you.'

'Oh, Ma, I wouldn't want you to see him,' Margaret breathing a bit easier. 'It was right that I should go, Ma. I saw worse in New York.' The two women rocked back and forth as they hugged each other.

The slamming of the screen door startled them, and Henry stomped in. 'Well!' he demanded. 'Well! So Margaret is back. Where is he? Couldn't find him, hmmm? I thought as much. No good as he was.'

Kate stepped toward him keeping Margaret behind her. She touched him on his arm. He drew back as if she'd hit him. 'Henry! Stop!' she said rather more loudly than necessary. 'The boy is dead—dead, Henry, dead—hanging in the orchard. Margaret found him. Henry, he's gone and we did it to him.'

Henry's eyes bulged and his ample cheeks sagged. His voice croaked. 'Did—did you say he's dead? What do you mean he's dead?' His voice trailed away as he appeared to lose his balance. He clutched at the bib of his overalls as he reached for the countertop. 'Kate. Don't scare me like that. You can't joke about something like this. Tell me the truth! Don't say stupid things like that.'

'Listen carefully, Henry. I *am* telling you the truth, Henry,' Kate said gently.

'My God! Oh, my God!' Henry gasped. He went suddenly pale.

The two women took him by his elbows and guided him to his rocker. His feet were reluctant to move. 'Henry! Henry! Calm down. Are you all right? We need to talk about this. We need to take care of—of Hjelmer.'

Her voice was suddenly choked with fear, but not for what Henry might do to Margaret or her. She patted his cheek and felt of his forehead. It was clammy. 'Margaret, go get some smelling salts. They're in the upper cupboard to the right of the sink. On the bottom shelf near the spices.' Then she knelt by Henry's rocker, taking his hand in hers. 'Henry, we'll have to call someone to come and get Hjelmer's body. Did he have some family we should notify? We'll have to have a funeral.'

Henry did not respond. Slowly his chin fell on his chest and lolled to the side. 'Henry! Henry!' Kate patted his cheeks, but there was no response. 'Henry! It's going to be all right,' she breathed. 'We'll take care of everything!'

'Margaret!' she called with some urgency. 'Did you—' Margaret arrived just then with the smelling salts. As Kate opened the bottle, she told Margaret to call Dr. Bellman to come right away. Then she waved the spirits under Henry's nose. There was no change. His nose didn't even twitch. She'd never had an occasion to use them before so she wasn't sure she was using them correctly, but she seemed to remember her mother saying they ought not be used too much.

Fear rose in her as she watched Henry's face become blotchy. 'Henry! Henry!' she called loudly as if greater decibels would call him back from wherever he seemed to be. She gently slapped his face to rouse him. 'Henry! Henry!' She put her ear to his chest but wasn't sure what she was supposed to hear so she wasn't surprised when she heard nothing.

Tears came, but she felt she must keep trying to rouse him. 'Oh, Henry! Henry, speak to me!' Her voice was scolding and harsh, angry even. She heard Margaret talking on the phone. Kate was so grateful for having a telephone and so glad Dr. Bellman had a car, unlike those country doctors still using a horse and buggy.

Margaret returned and patted him on his face. 'Uncle Henry, the doctor is on his way. Auntie Kate. Ma! You come sit in your rocker. You need some rest, too. I'll keep trying to rouse Uncle Henry until the Doctor gets here.' Kate did as she was told, but when she closed her eyes all she could see in her mind's eye was Hjelmer hanging in a pear tree.

She tried to get up. 'Margaret! We've got to find someone to get Hjelmer down! The sun's too hot.'

Margaret turned from trying to rouse Henry. 'Auntie Kate, the doctor will be here in a few minutes. He'll see to Hjelmer after he takes care of Uncle Henry. You just sit back down and rock. You must!' Kate blinked through her tears. Margaret was right. In front of the large front window, two women kept a silent vigil, waiting for the sound of a motor car.

* * *

Two weeks later the house was quiet. Too quiet. The family and well-wishers were gone. Will returned to college shortly after Henry's interment. He had insisted on driving the car back to school, saying, 'After all, it's mine.' Kate suggested that he drop Margaret at Mrs. Buchanan's house where she was to stay full time just now. He said it wouldn't be convenient and drove off without saying goodbye.

After he left, Kate was still fussed when Margaret came in the kitchen. She told Margaret about Will's refusal to take her to Mrs. Buchanan's. Margaret turned pale but quickly suggested that the Hendersons could take her into town when they took the cream to the creamery. 'Oh, of course,' Kate said. I hadn't thought about them.'

Earlier that morning, Kate had heard the Henderson boys when they came to do the chores Will hired them to do, but they had finished and left. Kate's mind turned to straightening up the kitchen. Margaret looked relieved. 'I'll go up there now and see if it's o.k. with them, Auntie Kate. But are you sure you'll be all right if I leave?'

'Yes, yes. You go now. Good girl,' Kate said absently as she put away the dishes from their breakfast.

Two days later, Margaret was ready when Mr. Henderson drove in the dooryard. Kate was relieved that Margaret was in good hands. It would be healing for her to be away from the awful events that had happened. 'I'll write to you,' Kate vowed and hugged her tight. Margaret whispered, 'I love you, Auntie Kate,' and ran to the Henderson's wagon.

Kate watched the cream cans bounce in the wagon until the dust from the wheels blotted them out. Now she was alone, truly alone, and at loose ends. She leaned forward over the kitchen sink and looked out the north window. What was this? Was she seeing right? Was it Margaret or just a ghost of Margaret running in the baggy overalls toward the house from the implement shed? Was she going mad? She blinked furiously. The illusion was so real she had to shake her head to clear the image from her mind, but it did not disappear completely. Tears welled up in her eyes, reminding her of the despair that haunted her days now.

She wandered from room to room. Finally, she sat in her grandmother's rocker, stroking its wooden arms with their rounded hand rests worn from years of just such stroking. As she rocked, she glanced around the room at the organ and the secretary—her contributions to the household. They reminded her of pleasanter times, but sad ones, too, when she had sat at the secretary writing cheerful letters to Margaret while her heart worried about what Margaret's future would be.

Now she had her own future to worry about. Several people, including Angus, asked her to come stay with them after the funeral, but she refused them all. She couldn't envision what was to become of her. She longed to be back in the little apartment next to the studio where she could be alone, quite alone without the memories that swirled around her now. She needed time to pull herself together before she tried to be part of anyone's family again. She knew that the process would be hard, too hard just now, but whatever it turned out to be, she hoped she and Margaret could be together eventually.

Slowly she stood up from the rocking chair, a bit unsteady in the knees. She climbed the stairs to the second floor and then pulled open the door to the attic. The musty smell was familiar. It smelled of home. She climbed the attic stairs. Each step seemed to be higher than it used to be, and she was winded by the time she reached the last two risers. She paused to catch her breath.

Even though it was a brilliant late September morning outside, inside the attic everything appeared to be in a spring fog, partly because she never had gotten around to washing the attic windows as she had promised herself. In the gloom, it took a few minutes to orient herself. She lifted off the cover of her camera and pulled the dark slide out to make sure that it still worked. She looked around and was reassured that her small chest of drawers still stood under the south window, but she merely noted its existence and not its import as the keeper of Gyorgy's picture. The old dining room chairs still occupied their berth under the eaves to the west. Harriet's chest stood amidst odds and ends of trunks and boxes. She had reminded Will that it was there but he seemed to take no interest in it.

As she scanned the attic now, in the northwest corner, she saw an unfamiliar object covered with an old quilt. She scowled, wondering what that could be and why she hadn't seen it earlier. Her memory must be growing dim. She stared, her face screwed into a frown, until her curiosity got the better of her. Swishing between the boxes and trunks, Kate's black dress gathered swatches of dust as she worked her way to the corner which had very little light even at this hour of the morning.

She pulled off the dusty tattered quilt and stared. It was Gyorgy's chair—the red velvet throne! She had quite forgotten it. She struggled to drag it through the tumble of storage items. Amazing, she thought as she stationed the chair next to her camera. She remembered insisting that it be brought to Henry's house, but then she quite forgot about it in the ensuing months and years.

She stroked the lines of the carved wood back rail and the gold fringe edging the red velvet arms. Tentatively, she eased herself onto the seat as if fearing it would not hold her. Her eyes teared up remembering the happy years in the studio, and she winced. This chair and her camera were like old friends coming out of the fog of the past. Theirs was an absence of her own doing. She sneezed and rubbed her nose as the tears ran freely. She pulled a handkerchief from the sleeve of her dress and wondered how long she would be expected to wear this ghastly dress.

Sitting in the gloom, her mind could not let go of the recurring nightmare of the last two weeks which gave her no peace and no avenue of escape. What happened? Oh, dear God! What had happened to their little family? She reached out to hold onto one of the camera's tripod legs and leaned against its solidity. She didn't want to remember, but she couldn't forget.

That day—that terrible day—was etched in her mind. She relived it every day now, over and over, beginning with the seeming eternity it took Doctor Bellman to arrive. Margaret, bless her, had taken charge. It was a big responsibility for one so young. She met the doctor at the back door and quietly explained to him that they had tried smelling salts on Uncle Henry as she was leading him to where Henry's form was slumped in his chair. She stood by as the doctor checked Henry's heart and his pulse and lifted his eyelids.

Dr. Bellman frowned and draped his stethoscope around his neck as he knelt next to Kate's rocker. 'As I'm sure you surmised, Mrs. Fergus, Henry is, indeed, gone.' He looked down and paused. 'Bless his soul. It was very likely a heart attack. At least he didn't suffer long,' Dr. Bellman had concluded. Margaret put her arms around Kate as Kate's breath became halting and the buttons on her shirtwaist heaved with her every breath. The doctor held Kate's wrist to check her pulse. 'Are you all right, Mrs. Fergus?'

Kate had fought to stay alert although every part of her wanted to blot out the events of the day. Surely this was all a bad dream. 'I'm all right,' she whispered, but she knew she wasn't and would never be again.

'I will call Mr. Wilson, if you would like me to,' said the doctor gently.

'That would be helpful,' said Kate, her voice muffled in her handkerchief. 'The telephone is in the kitchen.'

'There is another matter, Dr. Bellman,' Margaret whispered. 'There is another body to be taken care of.'

'Another body! What do you mean?' the doctor looked up from his kneeling beside Kate. 'How could there be—'

'Our hired boy,' said Margaret. 'Hjelmer—Hjelmer has killed himself using a rope. In the orchard. He was missing.' Margaret shuddered, and Kate grasped her hand in both of hers. Margaret looked haunted by a ghost as she whispered in a wavering voice, 'I found him. Could that have caused Mr. Fergus' heart failure?'

'Oh, my, you poor dear,' the doctor said as he stood and put his hands on her shoulders.

'Do you think Hjelmer's—Hjelmer's dying could have caused Henry's heart attack?' Kate asked the doctor echoing Margaret's question.

'Yes, I'm afraid so,' the doctor replied. 'Such devastating news sometimes does cause a stroke or a heart attack. I'd best find out a little more about how Hjelmer died. Tell me, girl, just what you know.' Margaret answered carefully as best she could. Kate sat in a numbed state not wanting to hear, but forcing herself to listen. 'Well, then, Mrs. Fergus, I must tell the undertaker. Could some of your neighbors help bring in Hjelmer's body?'

Kate was startled. Did she really want the neighbors to know what had happened? She shook her head as if to clear it of the unfortunate facts of Hjelmer's suicide and Henry's death. 'Yes,' she said softly, 'the Hendersons've got two big boys, but they don't have a telephone.'

'Margaret,' Dr. Bellman said calmly, 'would you go over and ask if the Mr. and one of the boys could meet me by the implement shed?'

'You can take one of the horses, Margaret,' Kate said, knowing that Margaret could ride bareback and be over and back in a hurry—if Mr. Henderson wasn't out in the field.

When the doctor and Margaret were gone, Kate was left with Henry's body slumped in his chair. She knelt on the floor, stroking his rough hands. 'Oh, Henry,' she pleaded. 'How could you leave me? We could have lived through this! I tried to tell you he was a good boy. He wasn't responsible for Margaret's baby. Oh, Henry, what shall I do now without you?'

Slowly, her mind had turned to the reality of what must be done next. She got up and went to the buffet in the dining room. She lifted out two white damask tablecloths Harriet had left neatly folded in the drawer and gently covered Henry's body. She looked for a long minute at the agony etched in his face and then covered that, too. She wondered briefly if she should have laid his body out as they had done for her father. She seemed to recall that people weren't doing that so much anymore. 'Forgive me, Henry,' she whispered, 'if that's what you would have wanted. Mr. Wilson will take good care of you.'

She needed to start writing an obituary. No, she'd better send a telegram to Will. She went to the kitchen and lifted the receiver on the phone to call Owen Bauer at the Western Union office, but then she put it back. She'd do that in the morning.

Looking out the north window, she saw Margaret returning with the neighbor and one of his sons. The doctor emerged from the barn carrying an old horse blanket and some rope. She saw Margaret walking with the doctor toward the orchard. The doctor put his arm around Margaret's shoulder. Kate guessed how it would be.

About then Mr. Wilson and a helper arrived in his new motor hearse painted a shiny black. Kate never liked Mr. Wilson much, but she was relieved to see him. She thought about meeting him in the yard, but she wasn't sure her legs would carry her that far. He knocked and walked in the front door—which almost no one used—and immediately saw Henry. 'Dear Mrs. Fergus, it is so hard when these things happen,' he said and patted her on the shoulder.

She drew back from his touch, but spoke evenly, 'Mr. Wilson, I am so glad you've come to take charge of Henry's—Henry's—umm, body. This is such a shock, I don't know what to do.'

Mr. Wilson was very reassuring, saying, 'You just let me take care of things. I'll do whatever's needed.' He took his helper aside and asked him to bring in the frame. Kate swallowed hard to choke back tears. She decided she could not watch and went to the kitchen. She dipped some cold, fresh water from the pail and drank it slowly. Her head was awhirl thinking about all that had happened and was happening.

Out the window she saw the doctor and the other men carrying the horse blanket bundle toward the hearse. Hjelmer's feet dangled from the end. Margaret came into the house then. Her face was streaked with tears. 'Margaret, you must sit down.'

'Yes, Auntie Kate, we both need to. The doctor wouldn't let me go all the way to see Hjelmer's body.' Kate was relieved to hear that. 'I'll put on some water for tea,' said Margaret. 'Let's just sit here in the kitchen.' They held hands in the dwindling light, each lost in her own thoughts.

Finally Margaret broke the silence gently, her voice cracked with emotion. 'Auntie Kate, I know I'm responsible for Hjelmer's death—and now Uncle Henry's. But what can I do? I should have been the one to die!' Her tears gushed forth. 'I don't want to live knowing it was my fault. I am guilty. I will always be guilty.' Kate came around and held her convulsing shoulders tight, but Margaret brushed her away.

'No, Auntie Kate, I have to say this! Please hear me. I should have told Uncle Henry that Hjelmer didn't make me pregnant, but if I told him that much, I was afraid—afraid he would have made me say who did it and I couldn't—and I wouldn't—and I won't. Oh, it's too awful to talk about, and Hjelmer and Uncle Henry's dying is too horrible.' She shook her head, 'No, no, no. Oh, Ma! Oh, Auntie Kate! What should I have done? I love you all so much—and now they're gone. I didn't know this would happen.' She put her head on the table and sobbed.

Kate patted her, crying quiet tears of despair for herself and quiet tears of hope for Margaret. 'Of course, you didn't know. I understand. In life we are sometimes called on to compromise our principles to save a loved one. But you must realize you were not responsible for Henry's and Hjelmer's quarrel—for whatever Henry believed.'

Just then, Mr. Wilson stepped into the kitchen. 'I believe we have everything taken care of, Mrs. Fergus. You can let us know where and when the services will be held.'

Kate stood up, dabbing at her tears. 'Thank you, Mr. Wilson. I'm not thinking very well today. Tomorrow we will let you know.' Mr. Wilson nodded and went out the door. She heard the hearse making frightful noises as he cranked it and started up the gravel driveway. Then all was quiet.

The two women looked at each other without speaking, the pain and sorrow apparent on both their faces. 'I'd better go gather the eggs,' said Margaret.

'Yes,' said Kate, 'the rest can wait until morning.' In the parlor, she found the linen tablecloths neatly folded over the back of Henry's chair.

As soon as word had gotten out about the unfortunate deaths, neighbors and church people began coming by with food, as was customary—though Kate and Margaret didn't feel much like eating. It was hard to accept even the most heartfelt condolences because each one reminded them of the tragic circumstances that occasioned their good will.

'Oh, Auntie Kate, I know these people mean well, but I don't know what to say to them. I feel like a liar, but I never lied to anybody. They don't know about my baby and they don't know that Hjelmer died because of me,' said Margaret when they were alone once again.

'Dear dear Margaret, I will say it again. Please know the truth. Hjelmer did not die because of you. The reasons for this tragedy are many and complicated and not your responsibility. I will repeat this again and again. I love you, child, and you will go on to have a good life as long as you study hard and work hard. Now let's eat something and be ready for whatever comes next.'

'But what will you do, Auntie Kate?'

'Never you mind, I will be all right.'

The visitors did help take their minds off the awfulness of those days. Esther and Lizzie came and took charge in the kitchen while Bud and Angus worked in the farmyard. On the day of Henry's funeral, it had been good to have so many family and friends to share their sorrow, and it had been good to have Will home again.

Now here in the attic, thinking about all these things, she shook her head. Will. There was something troubling about their relationship. But then, there always had been, and Henry's sudden death would surely estrange him even more. She shook her head remembering his insistence on having a service for Henry—and Henry alone—with the preacher from the Appleton Methodist Episcopal Church conducting the service. It seemed mean-spirited, but Will had his wish. Kate had hardly had time to talk to him, but he said he couldn't stay long enough for Hjelmer's funeral.

Fortunately for Kate, Bethany came as soon as she heard the awful news. Her visit was a life-saver. For one thing, Bethany helped her put together a simple service for Hjelmer to be held at home several days after Hjelmer was buried in the pauper's section of the Appleton Cemetery. The day of Hjelmer's burial, Kate and Margaret had stood by the grave until the sun dropped to the horizon. How sad, Kate thought. How very sad.

She agonized now as tears came freely and she relived the past couple of weeks. Angus had insisted that she must come live with them but she wouldn't promise anything. She had learned from Will that the lawyer reaffirmed that the farm was his, but she didn't know what he would do with it. She doubted that his plans would include her but legally she had no right to expect that they would. Still, it made her sad that she and Will had so little to bring them together—farm or no farm. Fortunately, she had the little nest egg from her photography business but she couldn't guess how long it would last.

Now, looking down at the blackness of her mourning dress, she thought how appropriate it was since she had lost Henry and Hjelmer—and apparently, Will. Still, just thinking about a time in the future when it would be appropriate to return to her flowered cotton dresses made her smile a little. She longed for their familiarity and their prettiness. Yes! she thought, I haven't forgotten how to smile!

Suddenly an image of red geraniums and their bright cheery blossoms came into her mind. Of course! One of the first things she would do in the spring would be to plant red geraniums on Henry's and Hjelmer's graves. They would be so pretty. Then she must set some out in the Gypsy Cemetery, and under the brightest of them, she would bury Gyorgy's picture.

She stood up then and looked through her camera lens. It occurred to her that the upside down image was like her present life, all topsy turvy. 'What shall I do now?' she whispered in that cavernous silence. She only knew that whatever her future might be, her camera would be part of it.